My Friend Greg

Joaquim Procopio

Dedication

I dedicate this book to my parents.

May God have them.

Acknowledgment

This book was made possible through the extraordinary work and patience of George Williams, Adam Jamal, Lisa Brandon, April Brown, Walter Brown, Paul Hendricks (Harper Book Writers, Ontario, CA, US), who have shown me (for the first time) the pleasure of working with a dedicate, competent and amiable team!

Contents

Synopsis

This is a love story between two scientists: a terrestrial man and an extraterrestrial woman with much superior intelligence.

A Brazilian scientist and medical doctor called Jota is recruited by a group of human-like extraterrestrials (ETs) for a mission at an underground extraterrestrial base in Brazil, which is disguised as a farm.

While interacting with this group, Jota is submitted to some proofs and tests and, finally, is informed that they are extraterrestrials and have chosen him to help them in a mission. Jota then begins to be part of the group's routine in the farm. During this process, Jota becomes directly under the mentorship of Antonina who is an ET scientist belonging to the group. Soon, Jota falls in love with Antonina and, thereafter, begins his strange adventure.

Antonina, despite being an ET, is extremely beautiful and captivating. As Jota's love for Antonina deepens he discovers he is being conditioned by her into a strange form of love. Actually, Jota gets gradually dominated by Antonina, due to her much greater intelligence.

But, strangely, this domination occurs not by means of force or power. Rather, it occurs through the action of a sort of love. And it is this strange form of love that is the theme of the present story.

PART 1

Chapter 1

How I Met Greg

The facts that I report here markedly changed my life. I report them with no expectation that someone believes they actually took place. I just want to register what happened to me so that, in the future, someone can talk about my narrative without fear of ridicule. I must confess that I kept a diary as soon as these strange facts began. The present story derives from excerpts of that diary.

The year was 2019, and I was at a camping field in the countryside of São Paulo State, Brazil. The region was known to have very clear skies, free of light pollution. The annual meeting of The Amateur Astronomer's Club was held every year in this place and lasted 3 complete days. During this period, we observed the night sky and, during the diurnal period, we had conferences and workshops. Also, during the day hours some club members pointed their telescopes to the Sun, using special filters.

Having a meager bank account, I had at my disposal only a modest telescope that I had made myself some years before. The night was a bit cold; it was the beginning of July, winter in Brazil. A light wind blew from the south, bringing with it the delicious scent of a nearby forest. The night was just beginning but it was already dark enough to allow the more brilliant stars to shine. The Moon, in a very fine crescent, was dipping towards the western horizon.

My Friend Greg

To astronomers the Moon is a selfish celestial body. When it is present in the sky, the observation of more tenuous celestial objects, the so-called deep sky objects, becomes severely compromised. For this reason, the meetings of our Club were always held in periods "without Moon". Therefore, the annual meetings could not have fixed dates. They had to comply with the lunar calendar.

Everything pointed to this night being a good one. Many members of the Club had already set up their telescopes and, not far away, one could glimpse their tents, trailers and motorhomes. Absolutely forbidden were any types of light, flashlight, car headlights and bonfires. Only flashlights with red filters were allowed, a light type that does not glare the vision.

To astronomers, be they professionals or amateurs, extraneous light is a nightmare. High-volume music was absolutely out of the question. Our meeting was neither musical nor festive. Amateur astronomers are nerds by definition. The idea of our meeting was to observe the sky, exchange ideas, meet people and, most of all, meditate.

My initial plan was to take advantage of the winter nights to observe the area surrounding the constellations of Crux, Centaurus, Scorpius, and Sagittarius. My first target was to be my favorite, the globular cluster Omega Centauri. This is a compact star cluster containing roughly 10 million stars, concentrated into a spherical volume of "only" 150 light-years across. At a distance of 15 thousand light-years from Earth, these 10 million stars look, to the naked eye, like a small and inconspicuous luminous smear.

This particular cluster has always fascinated me since my adolescence when I first got hooked on Astronomy. I imagined how it would be to live on a planet revolving around some star in this cluster. Would the sky be so clogged with stars as to give way to an eternal day? Another fascinating detail in Omega Centauri was the fact that I was looking at its stars the way they were, not now, but 15 thousand years from now. In other words, a Time Machine free and without any danger.

My second target was the star known as Alpha Centauri, a very luminous star, the fourth most brilliant star in the sky. To the naked eye, Alpha Centauri appears as a single star. But, at the telescope, a beginner observer gets a surprise. Now, the observer sees double: two near identical stars almost "glued" to each other. This view goes against common sense since the observer finds it difficult to understand how the stars can get so close without colliding.

In fact, these two stars form a pair of stars that, roughly, resemble our Sun. They constitute what is called a binary star system in which the stars revolve around each other in an orbit that lasts 79 years. And they are not so "glued" together. The distance between them varies from 11 to 35 times the distance of the Sun from Earth. However, this pair is not alone.

At some distance, and gravitationally locked to the pair, there is a small star that revolves around the pair. This is the famous Proxima

Centauri, our closest star neighbor, at a distance of 4.3 light-years, a mere 46 trillion kilometers from us.

Despite having observed these two celestial objects hundreds of times, in Astronomy, there are no identical nights. Altitude, air pollution, transparency and thermal stability of the air, air temperature, and psychic factors make each night a new experience. The scent of the night, of the vegetation, of the instruments, the sensation of cold, and the majestic and silent presence of half the Universe transport a sensible observer to other realms.

I had just pointed my telescope to my target #1, the Omega Centauri star cluster, when a young man, relatively short, with a stout complexion, about 30, contacted me. He wore very dark sunglasses and had blond, almost white hair. He asked me if I knew how to find the South Celestial Pole. He had a not well-defined accent and did not seem to be a native Brazilian. However, despite the accent, he spoke perfect Brazilian Portuguese. He told me his telescope was nearby. I agreed to help him and followed him to his telescope, a beautiful 16-inch Celestron instrument.

Something in the guy's demeanor caught my attention: the way he walked. He seemed to tread carefully as if avoiding too vigorous steps. My general impression was that he was avoiding detaching from the ground. Two other traits were apparent in a more detailed observation: a higher than normal respiratory rate for a resting person as if he was physically tired and the use of sunglasses, even at night.

Arriving at the site of his telescope I checked his instrument, a nice one, almost professional. In the meantime, the night had darkened considerably, and the stars were plainly visible. I noticed that the guy's sunglasses were of the adaptive type and, now, despite being a bit clearer, they were still decidedly dark. The large and powerful telescope, being an older model, was not computerized.

More recent telescopes have software that "seeks" the objects in the sky and follows them against Earth's rotation. In order that my "friend's" telescope could find and follow a given celestial object it was necessary to orient its axis parallel to the Earth's axis of rotation. And, for that, the telescope axis should point to the South Celestial Pole. In this particular point of the sky, a star does not appear to move as the Earth rotates.

As opposite to the North Celestial Pole, easily located close to the famous star Polaris, the South Celestial Pole lacks an easy reference point and that was the reason the guy sought my help. In general, once the telescope axis points to the Celestial Pole, a motor moves the telescope, instructing it to follow a given celestial object. The need for such a follower motor hinges on the fact that our planet rotates in relation to the stars.

By just looking at a starry sky one does not perceive this movement. But as viewed through a telescope, a star, planet, or the Moon moves, continually, across the field of vision. Without a motorized telescope the observer needs to be continually "hunting" down a star in order to keep it inside the field of vision. In no time, I could adjust "my friend's" telescope to the Celestial South Pole. He told me his name was Greg. And I got very anxious to observe through Greg's beautiful 16-inch telescope.

One reason for my interest in Greg's telescope was that my target #1, the Omega Centauri cluster, as seen through my telescope, looked just like a circular whitish spot, more intense at the center and petering out towards the border.

However, individual stars were not easily distinguished. My telescope, a backyard done type, which I had assembled myself, had a mirror of only 8 inches across and not a good one at that. I knew that Omega Centauri needed at least a 10-inch mirror to fully show its "face" or, rather, its stars. I also knew that having a 16-inch mirror and a Celestron brand on it, Greg's telescope would provide me with a truly remarkable visual experience. For that, however, I needed to strengthen a bit more my relation with Greg.

Carefully, I suggested if he intended to observe the Omega Centauri cluster this night. To my surprise, Greg said he didn't know what would be the "Omega Centauri" star cluster. Well, someone who owns a Celestron Smith-Cassegrain16-inch, 10-thousand-dollar telescope and ignores Omega Centauri struck me as a suspect. However, I already had got into a point of non-return. Therefore, I explained to Greg what Omega Centauri was. Showing it to Greg in the sky, he immediately commented:

"Oh, this one? We know it quite well and even employ this cluster as a navigation reference. But we call it by another name!"

Centering Omega Centauri in my telescopic field of view, with 150 X power, I was immediately awed. My view was phenomenal and unforgettable. Thousands of stars filled the telescopic field.

At this time, the planets Jupiter and Saturn were well visible in the sky with Jupiter displaying a glorious shine that night. I noticed that Greg looked repeatedly at the direction of these planets. Finally, he asked me:

"What names do you people give to these two brilliant stars?"

"They are the planets Jupiter and Saturn", I answered. Greg looked surprised and said:

"I knew those planets well but was surprised that they were so brightly visible from here". Soon, however, he found out that he had talked a little bit too much. He tried to justify his ignorance of the sky, but it didn't work. Greg was not good at deception. For me, this was a trait of honesty.

This combination of facts occurring so close together made me disoriented. The meeting with Greg, knowing that he had so nice a telescope, but at the same time did not know the name of Omega Centauri nor could he identify two brilliant planets. And, on top of this, I had the thrill of seeing, for the first time, the stars of Omega Centauri.

Evidently, I took advantage of Greg's presence and his telescope in order to explore other celestial targets. My humble telescope was left abandoned. My next object was an open star cluster just beside the constellation Crux. This cluster was known by the popular name of Jewel Box. And, through Greg's telescope, a Jewel Box it was, indeed. Stars of many colors filled the telescope field.

At the same time I moved on with my observation schedule, and as the night advanced, my curiosity about Greg increased exponentially. Continuing our conversation, I asked Greg where he came from. He said he was born in a Chinese city called Harbin but added to having Russian ancestors. His full name was Gregory Melnikoff. He explained that his Russian nickname was Grischa but was called Greg in Brazil.

When asked about his family and some other life details, Greg began to either contradict himself or downright change the subject. I began to speculate if our meeting was not some setup to rob me or something on this line. At the same time that I was gaining evidence that I would not get more information regarding his private life I began to suspect that he knew more about me than would be expected from our short interaction. But, whatever malevolent plans Greg might have against me he, clearly, was poorly prepared.

Chapter 2
Greg's "Family"

While Greg and I were talking and observing the sky, there arrived three more people: two guys and a girl. Greg immediately introduced them to me: Marco, Frederico and Antonina.

"We are together," Greg told me. I noticed that all were wearing dark glasses of the adaptive type like the one Greg wore. Since the night was advanced, I could, now, clearly see their eyes behind the less darkened lenses of their glasses.

"Come round to have a coffee in our trailer," Marco said to me. I promptly accepted the invitation since I was sleepy and hungry. About 400 feet away was their "trailer", in fact, a full sized motorhome. Marco and Frederico had the same body type as Greg: about 30, relatively short, about 5 feet 5 inches, blonde hair, almost white. And all they strongly built. They wore shorts, and their legs were disproportionally strong.

Antonina was a beautiful young woman with blond hair, almost white, and about 2 inches shorter than the guys. She wore a provocative short and her legs were well shaped but a bit too muscular. Her figure, as well as the way she moved, gave me the impression of a mixture of ballerina and Olympic gymnast.

She appeared to be very light and trying all the time to avoid detaching from the ground. On our way towards their motorhome, I confirmed my impression that all of them had the same curious way of walking, as if they were lighter than their figures suggested. They moved as if being afraid of leaving the ground. I forced my mind to remember where I had seen this walking: The astronauts walking on the moon.

We all entered the motorhome. There was a central space containing a table and chairs. On the sides, there were electrical appliances. In another part, and solidly fixed to the walls, were about 6 sleeping berths.

We had a very nice and freshly prepared coffee, along with home-made bread and carrot cake prepared by Antonina. Every one of them spoke with an accent that seemed clearly to me as Russian. And they all had the same increased respiratory rate.

Curiously, Greg and his friends did not seem interested in the night sky, celestial objects, and the like. They seemed to have more interest in me, as I could infer from the many questions of diverse nature with which they bombarded me. Greg, by his turn, apparently lost his desire to use his powerful telescope.

Occasionally and inadvertently, they gave some hints that they knew things about me. Like Greg, they did not seem to master the art of deception.

The astronomer's club meeting was scheduled to last 3 days and 3 nights, and so was my stay. Greg and his friends told me they were also staying for the duration of the meeting. The next day, in the diurnal period, we would have conferences and workshops.

Many club members were to show their telescopes to the participants. Some telescopes were very sophisticated and interesting. During the diurnal period, we would also be treated to a small shop selling astronomical products at bargain prices.

Chapter 3
Greg's Farm

On the second day of the Astronomy meeting, Greg invited me to visit his "family's" farm. We would still have another day of astronomical activities in the meeting. I accepted Greg's invitation and, following the closure of the meeting, we left the camping site. I followed Greg's motorhome, driving my car. The farm was not very far, some 20 km away.

After about 20 minutes of driving we arrived at an extended Eucalyptus trees forest. Soon, we stopped at a wooden rural gate called *Porteira* in Brazil. Besides the *Porteira*, a written sign said: Entry forbidden. Private property *(Proibida a entrada. Propriedade particular)*. I, soon, noticed that the Eucalyptus forest was very extensive. Passing this entry, we continued through a well-conserved dirty road for about 1,200 meters.

Then, the motorhome left the road and stopped. Greg, who was riding in my car, oriented me to park beside the motorhome. I found it strange to stop there since I didn't see anything that looked like a house.

But then, I perceived that something big was there. Interspersed, inconspicuously, among the Eucalyptus forest was an immense geodesic dome covered with a plastic tarpaulin with a camouflaged color, with tones of green, black, and gray. We all got out of our vehicles, and as we walked towards the dome, its enormous size became apparent.

Joaquim

We all met at the dome entrance, a rectangular opening of about 3 x 3 meters. This was, in fact, a short corridor. I was invited to enter and followed the group into the dome. The dome interior was larger than I could infer by looking from the outside. Something like 30 meters in diameter by 15 meters in height.

The plastic tarpaulin covering the dome was translucent but cut most part of the solar radiation, filling the dome interior with a greenish and diffuse light. The inside temperature was agreeable, actually cooler than the outside, despite the winter sun being intense. Oriented radially across the floor, there were six ship containers.

Greg explained that each container was a complete individual apartment, containing a bed, closets, a table, and a complete bathroom. I was honored to know that I would have a container all by myself during my stay. This container, reserved for me, made me conjecture that the group might be expecting me. They took me for a brief tour around the dome interior.

In the center, there was a common area and a large table with many chairs. Sofas were scattered away from the table. A complete kitchen was at a side of the central area. Many low closets were arranged across the room. The floor was bare concrete, smooth sanded and with a very solid look. On top of the containers, there were many items in apparent disorder. Water and electrical connections were all apparent but very well designed having the look of high technology.

Chapter 4

My Quarters

Greg took me to my container so that I could store my things and take a much-needed bath. He explained that they lived ecologically without interfering with nature and using all possible natural resources. He entered my container with me in order to explain the general functioning of the facilities. There was a single bed firmly attached to the wall, as is usual in boats and prisons. Despite being minimalist, the bed was very comfortable and already made, with clean bed linen.

A bookshelf full of books took a great part of the wall opposite the bed. In a corner on the floor, there was a big pile of books in a disordered state. Sure enough, they had no time to arrange everything. Fixed to the wall opposite the bed, there was a heat radiator of the type used in cold climates. However, in the wall adjacent to the bed there were square devices that appeared to be aluminum blocks.

"Those are *Peltier elements*," remarked Greg, noting my attention to those structures.

"We use them to cool down," he said. I knew well these cooling elements. They are even used in some silent refrigerators. They have no moving parts and use an electrical current to create a temperature difference across the device. One side gets very cold, whereas the opposite side warms up. I also observed, above the cooling devices, slits from which a light incoming air flow could be detected. At the end of the container, facing away from the central "plaza" of the dome, there was the bathroom behind an interior divisor wall with a door.

The bathroom contained a walk-in shower closed by a glass box, a sink, and a toilet. The toilet was not of the usual type. It consisted of a cylindrical and movable recipient having, at its top, an open seat and a sophisticated hermetic lid. All parts were solid, high-tech plastic. The recipient, as Greg explained to me, was removed every day and changed for a clean one. The excrements were used as a natural fertilizer.

"Do not throw water inside: just clean the seat with a wet cloth. The toilet will be replaced by a clean one every day", said Greg.

The shower was not the electric type. It had cold and hot water and a mixer so that the water temperature could be controlled. Greg then left me alone and said that after I was ready, we were going to walk outside and then have lunch. I relaxed and took a good shower.

When I left my container, the group was already seated at the table, waiting for me with cold juices, coffee, and mineral water. Greg said that the lunch would be served soon after we got back from the walk.

Chapter 5

Walk Around The Farm

When we left the dome for the walk, I observed that all of them wore sunglasses that now, in broad daylight, were a lot darker than when I was introduced to them at night in the camping. In fact, the glasses were so dark that I could not see their eyes. In observing my curious look, Marco explained that they do not stand the day's clarity, having lived previously in dark regions.

"By the other hand," explained Marco, "our eyes are very sensitive to low light. For example, we can see stars up to magnitude 8, whereas the normal limit is magnitude 6."

"This means our eyes are 6 times more light-sensitive and, apart from stars, we have an excellent general night vision". I didn't quite understand what Greg meant by "we" and "normal" but decided not to push the matter further.

We had only a brief walk just close to the dome. Greg told me that the farm had 500 hectares (1250 acres) in area. I didn't see anything special except the immense Eucalyptus forest of the *Citriodora* species. Greg explained that they lived of what they produced.

In a small lake, he said, they raise fish of many species that they consume. Also, Greg told me, they maintain a chicken coop from which they get meat and eggs. Vegetables are produced in a few vegetable gardens scattered about the property.

Greg told me that they were self-sufficient of sorts and lived ecologically, causing a minimal impact on nature. They were not completely self-sufficient, since they used most of their electrical energy from the public grid. Their water supply, though, comes from local wells.

Most food products come from the farm itself. Sugar, flour, olive oil, toilet paper, etc., comes from the local market. Heating, both for water and cooking, employed local wood-burning high-tech ovens. The big and sophisticated ovens are high-performance ones and do not generate smoke, as Greg stated.

Besides producing their own food, the group developed a wood processing plant that makes "intelligent wood", according to Greg's definition. This is a commercial plant where the Eucalyptus trees furnish the raw wood, which is further processed in the plant.

A by-product of the fallen or dead Eucalyptus trees, which were plentiful, is firewood employed to feed the ovens. Greg told me that the farm was part of a program of carbon credits, and this gave important discounts on some of the taxes. The carbon credits, he said, are given to large green areas and conscious use of wood.

As Greg explained to me, the production of intelligent wood consists of compressing the Eucalyptus boles in a microwave oven of sorts.

In this oven, the boles are heated, softened by the heat, and pressed until a square and high-density wood piece results. Later on, the wood piece gets dried and receives a special treatment with preserving resins. The final result is a beam or column that is perfectly square and smooth has high mechanical strength, and is resistant to rotting. These structural elements can be made in different widths and lengths and are ready to be used in civil construction. Greg told me that the entire world is desperately seeking construction materials with a low carbon footprint.

"Would you mind telling me what a carbon footprint actually is?" I asked Greg with some impertinence in my voice.

"Calm down, Jota," he answered with a sincere smile. (I should have mentioned before that my "official" name in the group was Jota).

"The carbon footprint is a numerical index that defines the carbon dioxide (CO_2) quantity generated in the production of a given item," said Greg.

Greg went on: "Reinforced concrete, as well as steel, has a very high carbon footprint since, in their production, great quantities of carbon dioxide are thrown into the atmosphere." Greg explained that there is an important trend in using wood as structural elements, even in high-rise buildings.

After our walk in the neighborhood of the dome, we came inside and got prepared for lunch. The lunch was very nice indeed, and after it, we had a few desserts, coffee, and homemade liquors prepared on the farm from native fruits, as Antonina explained to me.

We spent a very agreeable afternoon relaxing and talking about many subjects. I found out that they loved playing chess, given the many chess boards and different sets of chess pieces, many of them made from exquisite materials and wonderfully crafted. I also spotted, casually strewn across the room, chess books and manuals, many written in English, others in Russian, and still others in a mysterious language.

Chapter 6

Discoveries in the Night

At 8 PM, a nice dinner was served, and after that, we had desserts, coffee, and homemade liquors, as in the lunch. I asked Greg about our astronomical observations (with his big telescope), since the sky was glorious, no clouds, no Moon.

"The telescope is yours and is ready to use in our small observatory!" he said, smiling and looking at the others.

This confirmed my suspicion that Greg did not have any special interest in Astronomy. And that the presence of the "family" in the Astronomer's Meeting might have been a head-hunter's expedition. I immediately became conscious of not having any "special talent". My theory was that, since they hadn't found what they were looking for they "took" me just to have some fun. I was wrong.

We exited the dome into the night, and Greg directed me through a short trail up to a clean region where there was a concrete platform. Planted, majestically, upon this platform and covered with a tarpaulin was "my" dear telescope, the 16-inch Celestron.

It was already connected to an electrical outlet and ready for hunting whatever celestial body. I asked Greg if I could use the telescope before we retired.

Joaquim

"Use it at your will; we close the dome at 12," he answered. It was still 9:30 PM, and Greg seemed to be curious about my plans. Encouraged, I asked him if he used to photograph with the telescope. Greg said that he photographed the night sky regularly but didn't use the telescope for this. Rather, he used a camera. "Will be right back; wait here," he said.

Soon after, he came back bringing a camera whose type or brand I had never seen, nor did its lens look familiar to me. I took the camera in my hands and examined it carefully. Immediately, I felt like I was holding an extraneous, alien piece of technology. The camera was very light despite being solidly built. The general look, the strange inscriptions, the buttons, and the surface feel all talked alien to me. I was mesmerized, but Greg interrupted my reverie.

"I use it to photograph the stars", he said. "Easier than the telescope, and you can couple it piggyback onto the telescope".

In this procedure, which I knew well, the camera "straddles" the telescope and sees what the telescope sees. But, before hooking the camera to the telescope Greg asked me to turn off my flashlight and suggested that I did a test, shooting "things" on the ground.

"What things on the ground?" I asked since I couldn't even see my own hand.

"Point the camera to the ground and press the shutter," he said. Still confused, I asked for the camera flash.

"No flash, no necessary," Greg remarked, laughing.

Hesitantly, I left the concrete platform and moved towards the grassy ground, covered with dry leaves and dead sticks, as I could feel beneath my shoes since viewing was impossible. I pointed the camera downwards and pressed the shutter. Then, I changed position and shot again. It was then that Greg advised me to turn on the back screen.

"You don't want to shoot blindly," he said, again laughing. Greg pressed a button, and what I saw on the camera screen left me open-mouthed. The dry leaves and dead sticks were there all right but with a brightness and definition unimaginable.

Gradually, I perceived that things were moving among the grass.

"Increase the zoom", shouted Greg, "let me show you".

He moved a small lever, and I was seeing hundreds of small creatures crawling randomly. There were small and winged insects, larvae, tiny bugs, and small ants. A somewhat frenetic activity. Changing the camera position, the scene repeated.

Whatever spot I pointed to revealed the same activity. Increasing the zoom, the small larvae got enormous. However, I could not steady the camera on my hands. Greg suggested that I shot many pictures to be seen later at home. I did this by pointing the camera to various places and shooting with varying degrees of zoom. I was delighted.

"Let's now shoot the stars," said Greg. I then hooked the camera onto a riding position to the telescope, screwing it onto a special pod.

"Now, I want to see how your camera performs under the stars and what it makes of the Omega Centauri," I said provocatively to Greg, pointing to that cluster containing 10 million stars.

I centered the camera on Omega Centauri and shot. Then, increased the zoom and shot again. Finally, at maximal zoom, I gave a last shot.

"Let's now examine our harvest," I said. Greg gave a brief laugh. The photo without zoom showed a very definite circular smear, stronger in the center and decreasing intensity towards the borders.

With intermediary zoom, the smear was larger, and a granulating appearance began to show up. With full zoom, the image was awesome. I saw hundreds and hundreds of stars of different colors: blue, white, yellow, and red.

"Point the camera at the Milky Way and shoot," said Greg. I shot without even looking at the screen. The playback showed an irregular white band having interspersed dark regions. Insecure, I asked Greg if the photo was OK.

He laughed and said: "Gradually, increase the zoom in the photo". The smooth white band got granular and then, with a larger zoom, transformed into a carpet of stars. I was flabbergasted. Since it was getting late we went back to the dome, where the group was waiting for us.

I told Greg, after we had coffee and liquor, that I would like to see the first photos, those of the ground, with the leaves and small creatures. I got hold of the camera and, comfortably seated on the sofa, began to playback the pictures taken previously. In one of the ground shots, I zoomed into a leaf that was still green. At increasing zoom levels, the *stomata* began to appear, those respiratory openings that looked like two beans mirroring each other.

Further increasing the zoom, the leaf began to show its cells. Greg only observed my doings and laughed. He appeared to be having a lot of fun by observing me. The others approached, curious to understand the reason for such an enjoyment.

I asked Greg how I could transfer the pictures to my cell phone, and he said this was not possible.

"But, wait," he said. He went to his container and returned a few minutes later with a stack of sheets the approximate size of an A4 standard paper.

I took one sheet carefully, in my hands. It had a completely different feel and seemed to be very thin and fragile, resembling a Bible sheet. The sheet had the feel and look of a metallic foil, but it also felt like plastic. Despite looking fragile, it revealed as being very strong. He then suggested that I fold the sheet and press the fold. And I did as request.

Then, he asked me to unfold the sheet. To my surprise, it left no vestige of the previous folding, no creases, looking like a perfectly virgin sheet. Following these initial performances and looking at the others, Greg asked me to tear the sheet apart. Despite my efforts, it didn't bulge. Then, I perceived the group laughing openly and clapping their hands. I began feeling like a clown, but strangely, I liked it.

I was so distracted with my involuntary and funny performance that I hadn't even looked at the photos. It was then that I saw what was impressed upon the sheets. It was one of the shots I took off the ground at a distance of about 1 meter. The photograph looked like a work of art, a masterpiece.

The colors were vivid at the extreme despite being natural. The image definition was awesome. Every detail appeared with a clarity and sharpness incredible. I took a powerful lens from my trousers pocket (Yes, I'm a nerd) and examined the picture carefully while I felt the group's eyes scrutinizing me also carefully.

The picture, as printed on the "paper," was way clearer and sharper than what I'd seen in the camera's back screen. There were about 10 different types of small creatures, some looking like miniature armadillos, others like wormlike, miniature beetles, and microscopic ants. Many were definitely dead and in various stages of decomposition.

The general impression was of a hyper-realistic canvas of some medieval painter. The same general impression I had in examining the shot of Omega Centauri, now comfortably seated and using my pocket lens. Yes, the stars were there, an infinite number of them: white, blue, yellow, and red. I knew the red stars were very old, the grand-grand-mothers of the Universe.

"And, now, I invite you to a brief chess match," shouted Greg to me while looking at the group. Without fully comprehending the irony behind the "brief" chess match, I answered that it was already 11 and, perhaps, it would be better to leave the match for the next day.

"No problem," said Greg, "if it becomes too late, we photograph the chess board and continue the match tomorrow". I considered Greg's argument to be quite reasonable, and we began the match. The group seated around the players, each one holding a beer can. Someone turned on a low music.

We began the match; I had the whites and moved my pawn two squares ahead. I sensed that the group was talking in a low voice as if they were betting.

Marco said something like "five moves"; Antonina said "eight moves" and so on. Well, indeed, in 8 moves, my king was definitely lost. Checkmate. Match duration: 10 minutes flat.

Chapter 7

The Book of Time

After my humiliating defeat in chess, I asked for leave to retire. I took another bath and prepared to lie down and try my luck in the dreams. However, I couldn't relax in order to sleep. The facts of the last days and, especially of today, filled my mind with doubts and theories about who could be these persons and what they want of me.

In order to relax and wait for the god Morpheus to take care of me, I began to take general look at the many books on the shelves. Most of them were scientific books in English and Russian. A few were fiction. Many of the books, however, were written in a language whose origin I could not grasp. Still, others looked like manuals.

One of these on the pile scattered on the floor caught my attention. Its general format was unusual. Its spine had something inscribed in a completely unknown language. The pages did not seem glued or stitched onto the spine. They simply attached there with ample margin for turning. The sheets were very thin and metallic in texture, not much different from the sheets in the photos Greg had given me. Despite looking fragile, they felt to be quite strong. I didn't try to tear them, of course, but by pulling them, their strength became apparent.

I also noticed that the material had a memory of sorts since after folding the sheets they returned to normal without showing any creases left. In that respect, they also resembled the sheets with my pictures, Greg had shown me before. The pages were full of small holes grouped into small blocks. The holes, however, did not cross the sheet to the other side; actually, they were more like depressions. Each block of holes had the approximate size of a letter font 15 and had between 10 and 50 "big" holes and hundreds of smaller holes. The difference between each block was the arrangement of both big and small holes.

A second book having the same layout of very thin metallic sheets but larger in width and height, something like 60 x 60 cm and having the general format of an album, caught my attention. The sheets were perforated close to the left margin, being held together by a wire spiral like a flight manual of sorts. The whole arrangement had a high-tech appearance, down to the smallest details.

On the first pages of the album appeared the same sequence of blocks of holes. After about 20 "written" pages, possibly an introduction, there appeared a page with small pictures of 12 cities, arranged in 4 lines, having 3 cities on each line. I could identify New York City, London, and Paris on the first line. There were Moscow, Cairo and Berlin on the 2nd line. On the 3rd line, Mexico City, Buenos Ayres, and Santiago of Chile. And, finally, Jerusalem, São Paulo City, and Istanbul were on the 4th line.

On the following sheet was an aerial photo of New York City 50 x 50 cm, taking most of the page area. On the back of this sheet, there was another photo of NYC, almost identical to the first. This pattern went on for 100 sheets or leaves, front and back, or 200 pages. Burning with curiosity, I jumped to the group of São Paulo City photos.

As I expected, the 1st page showed a photo of São Paulo, also 50 x 50 cm and relatively recent. Consulting the Google Maps, I could confirm that all photos covered a square 10 x 10 km and, therefore, had an approximate scale of 1/20,000. A typical block in São Paulo City, having 100 x 100 meters, would appear as a square 5 x 5 mm in the photos. The second photo of São Paulo, on the back of the first one, seemed, to me, identical to the first. I got hold of my lens to better examine the photos. Immediately, I perceived that they had a very high resolution.

As seen with the lens, more details became apparent without any image degradation or pixilation. I had in my backpack an eyepiece from my telescope that gave more power than the single lens I was using. Viewed with the telescope eyepiece, the photo delivered even more details. I could see small rectangles in the streets, most certainly cars. Bigger and longer rectangles were, certainly, buses. From what I knew from the city, the first photo of São Paulo was dated about 2 years from the present. In any part of the photo, I could see, with my eyepiece, infinity of details and even smaller dots, probably people.

As I was handling the first page of photos I, inadvertently, moved my finger onto the page. Immediately, the photo seemed to slip across the page. I thought I had somehow damaged the picture. I tried to repeat the "accident" now more carefully.

No question it was possible to drag the photograph across the page by just moving the finger onto it. This was, actually, no novelty for me. Clearly, the page and its impressed photograph were not static fixtures. I had, before me, a smart page, and the similarity with my smartphone was all evident. Now, encouraged by my "discovery," I began to drag the picture sideways and discovered that more and more parts of the city became visible. Taking the finger from the photo it moved rapidly back to the initial frame.

Up to this point, nothing different from Google Maps! I was so stupefied with this discovery that I decided to calm down and relax. *Maybe it was just a dream, and soon this would get back to normal*, I thought. Since the room was too brightly illuminated for relaxing, I turned off the main lamp and let only the weaker bed lamp on. In this semi-darkness, I lay down in the bed, closed my eyes, and began to relax.

But, I couldn't relax. Some part of my brain told me to make another check and bury this "hallucination forever." Another part, the curious one, said I had to explore more. Since both parts of my mind required repeating the page-dragging maneuver, I sat up in the bed and "attacked" the page. *Now, I am fully awake*, I thought and, then, tried to drag the photo. My initial suspicion materialized. I had hallucinated! I couldn't drag the photo anymore. The photo was now only a stupid, inert image anchored to the page. I tried different ways of dragging.

Using different fingers might work. Nothing I did could

"reanimate" the photo! That gave me some relief. The good news: I am sane. The bad news: too bad it wasn't real. But then, I remembered I was a scientist. In order to reproduce an experiment, one needs to work in exactly the same conditions! *What got different?* I thought. The illumination, of course! I had turned off the main lamp. OK, let's go to the initial conditions. I turned on the main lamp and "attacked" the page again. Moving the finger against the photo it, now, obeyed my finger and moved! It was the light! Of course, a smart page needs a minimum of energy, and light is energy.

My next move in exploring the photo of São Paulo was instinctive and the result of the thousand times I examined photos and maps on the smartphone. Placing two fingers on the photo, I separated them. The photo expanded. Not holding my curiosity, I went to a region where I had seen what appeared to be cars. Expanding the region with my fingers, I saw that I could repeat the zooming many times, exactly like I did on the smartphone. But there was a difference here! No matter how much I zoomed in, the image remained with the same definition. It didn't degrade or pixilated. I could zoom in to the point of seeing cars and people sharply.

No more need for my lens! That, I couldn't do with my smartphone. Suddenly, I felt powerful! Then, I remembered there were 200 photos of São Paulo. Why so many? From what I knew of the city, the second photo looked to be 10 years older than the first. Without concern for the details, I went to the 3rd photo and a difference of 10 yrs from the second was clear. While doing this reconnaissance, I examined the book as a whole. Since the leaves were very thin, even thinner than those of a Bible, I figured that there were about 100 leaves per millimeter.

The entire book seemed to be about 4 cm thick. A rough calculation told me the book should have about 4 thousand leaves and 8 thousand pages and, consequently, 8 thousand photographs. I was, then, taken by a great anxiety and began turning rapidly the pages. The photos of São Paulo covered 10 x 10 km, and each photo covered exactly the same region.

Counting the pages and adding 10 years per page, I got to the 1960s and found my grandmother's house. Indeed, there it was; colorful, super sharp. There were the cars in the backyard, a car in the ramp. I could even distinguish the cars' makes. In the year 1950, I could find my other grandmother's house, which was 3 blocks away. In the early 1920s neither house was visible, only empty lots.

Doing such an exercise was easy since the photos were precisely located on the pages. Going to the 1910s there were only a few sparse houses in our neighborhood. In any part of the city, whatever the date was, it was possible to zoom in and see persons individually. With further zooming in, the facial features could be distinguished if the person was looking upward or lying down. The makes of the cars were plainly distinguished.

I had retired to my container at 11:30 PM, and it was already 3:00 AM. However, I couldn't put down the book of the cities. I thought: *why*

*photograph the cities so monotonously every10 years and so
meticulously?* Then, it occurred to me that, in reality, this book might be
a collage or selection of a much more extensive collection of pictures of
the Earth covering, possibly, the entire planet during a long period of time.
How long?

Reasoning for São Paulo with 200 photos 10 years apart, that gave
a 2 thousand years' record. Extremely curious I jumped the pages, 100 at
a time. Indeed, as I could verify, around the year 1600, that some
constructions were already visible in Sao Paulo City. In 1500, there were
only the forests and some clean areas with Indian villages. This pattern of
forested Indian villages appearing and disappearing followed until the
beginning of the photos.

I then jumped to Paris. Its group of photos had 300 leaves, totaling
600 photos. If the interval between photos were 10 years, like São Paulo,
then the block of Paris would cover 6 thousand years. In fact, the interval
was 10 years, as I could check by looking at the car models and other time
markings. And, even as back as 6 thousand years ago, there were signs of
human occupation.

My next block was Cairo. And, yes, in the most recent photo was
the Giza plateau with the pyramids, the Sphinx, and the city of Cairo. The
block of Cairo contained 400 leaves with 800 photos. Turning the pages,
I found that the photos were more centered on the Giza plateau, despite
Cairo appearing to the East. In the Cairo block, the photos were sparser in

time. From the car models and other hints, a difference of 50 years was a reasonable guess. In the third photo, motorcars were not visible anymore.

A rough calculation seemed to suggest that the first photos were taken 40 thousand years in the past! From some pages down in the time, the pyramids were not visible anymore. But on the Giza plateau, in the region occupied by the pyramids, it was possible to distinguish, clearly, a city. People and animals were visible and a network of channels ran across the city.

These channels appeared to be very deeply cut and many types of boats were visible navigating them. They also appeared to emerge from the Nile. In the earlier photos, I saw many silver-plated and shiny discs between 30 and 50 meters.

They appeared to be casual objects like the planes we see over our modern cities in Google Earth photos. It would be necessary for many days to just take a superficial look at this marvelous book. To describe here everything I saw in these few hours with the book, many and many pages would be necessary, along with a huge dose of patience from the reader. Just to give a finishing touch, let me add that, in the photos of New York City, between the years 700 and 1000, there appeared large boats in what are the present Hudson and East rivers.

Some of those boats did not carry sails or masts despite leaving a clear and strong wake behind. And, going back to the pyramids, from what I saw in the photos, their construction did not follow what is the present consensus. All these findings would certainly give rise to many polemics, in which I would hate to get involved. At last, I went to bed and was able to get a few hours of sleep. I woke at 10 with Greg knocking at my door and calling me to breakfast.

Chapter 8

Playing Chess with Antonina

After breakfast, I spent the whole morning walking close to the dome and resting in my container. At 12 we had a very nice lunch. After we had relaxed and had coffee, the group went to work in different parts of the farm. Antonina, however, stayed in the dome, clearing the table. Before I went back to my container to get some sleep, Antonina called me and invited me to a chess match. In a corner, there was a table whose top was a nice chessboard. The pieces, beautifully crafted from a material looking like glass, were already in their positions. I sat facing Antonina, and, as the room was a bit dark, she removed her sunglasses.

Then, I could observe her features more closely. She was, indeed, too beautiful, more to the side of gorgeous, having well-defined feminine traits. However, she had a firm and austere look. She exhaled a sort of security and self-determination. From her eyes I could see a sort of shine which, to my perception, seemed to extrude intelligence. I felt, clearly, that I was way lower than her on the intelligence scale.

These traits robbed her of some femininity but what was left exerted, in me, a mixture of feelings which, at that moment, I couldn't define. To be so close and right in front of such a woman was an entirely new experience for me. Not counting the fact that we were, now, antagonists! Sure, in the medical course, I had a "platonic love" for a female teacher.

Joaquim

I had got the white pieces and Antonina told me to begin. I moved the king's pawn 2 squares forward. Antonina seemed undaunted, her eyes fixed on the board. This, allowed me to better scrutinize her features. Her beauty perturbed me. Her face looked like that of some Greek goddess. However, and almost imperceptibly, her features changed to that of a fragile and tormented woman who was feigning a secure air.

Then, her look changed to that of a suffering woman. These many impressions alternate, but all induced in me a desire to have her as a woman. Breaking my contemplative mood, Antonina sighed and moved her black pawn symmetrically to mine. Ten minutes had passed between my move and hers. A bit lost between my thoughts on Antonina and the match, I moved, this time the Queen's pawn, pairing it with the King's pawn.

Antonina looked firmly at me and said, with a bit of contempt: "Jota, do you want me to teach you to play chess?"

"Really? I would love!" I said in a somewhat sarcastic tone. My sarcasm went directly to the target. Antonina began a fierce and merciless attack upon my pathetic army. It was carnage. In no time, I leaned down my King, exhausted and humiliated.

Antonina perceived my reactions and gave me a benevolent smile. "Don't be upset, Jota.

Tomorrow we will wash your car!" she said. With that, Antonina went silently to her container, and I went to mine. As soon as I had "recovered," I went out for a walk, carrying "my" super camera that Greg, generously, had lent me. I hadn't, as yet, used Greg's camera in daylight. Distancing from the dome but keeping it in sight, I took some photos of the dome itself. Then, I approached the border of the Eucalyptus forest. Soon, the delicious scent of citric fruits filled my nose. I remembered that the name *Eucalyptus citriodora* is quite appropriate for these trees. A short distance away, a toc-toc sound caught my attention.

As I approached the sound origin, I could see that a woodpecker was working to make a hole in a tree trunk by earnestly pecking at it. I began photographing the bird. After some 10 shots in different angles, distances, and degrees of zoom, I got one picture that seemed, to me, the "perfect" one. The photo had an impressive degree of definition: the head plume, the marvelous color of the plumage and larger feathers, the position of its little legs and talons grabbing the trunk.

Everything contributed to a surreal scene. I reckoned that 90% of the picture credits were due to the camera itself, but I gave a little help. I was so distracted with the scenery, my pictures and the little bird that I did not perceive Antonina right at my side.

"Let me see the pictures," she asked me without even justifying her intrusion. I showed her my preferred photo of the woodpecker. She took the camera in her hands, examined repeatedly the screen and then became pensive, looking at the ground in a sort of reverie.

Then, she stared at me with a smile and said: "How beautiful he is!

You made him so beautiful!" Saying this, she continued to look at my eyes. Seeing that I had blushed, she laughed adorably. The day was rapidly getting to its final hours and the low position of the Sun in the west created vast contrasts in luminosity.

Antonina took off her sunglasses. Her eyes were light green, large and adorable. However, I perceived they were wet. She rapidly brushed off the remains of a tear. I then asked, pointing to her eyes, if she was sad for some reason. She answered, taking the camera and showing me the screen with the photo of the woodpecker: "It is just that he is so cute!"

"Yes," I said, "he is pure and innocent, and that is why he is so cute". As the reader will be aware shortly, Antonina and her friends weren't used to the beauty of nature, the Sun, the forest, the animals, the natural heat, and the water flowing in the rivers.

Antonina, pointing to the camera and the woodpecker picture, asked me: "Can you make me beautiful too?"

I answered that she was already beautiful but I would try. I asked her to sit on a flat stone. "Now, look at the horizon," I said. It was darker now, and some clarity emanated diffusely from the west, where the Sun had already set. Antonina was facing as opposed to the sunset and the light coming from that direction illuminated the contours of his face, producing an aura effect. For me, it looked surreal and mystical.

I began shooting, changing my position around her and trying different distances and zoom levels. Then, I asked her to face the sunset.

But I did not photograph her front-wise. Instead, I searched for angles in which the light touched her features, sidewise. In all angles and light incidences, Antonina revealed to be glorious, to my mind, a goddess. I didn't play with the camera controls since I didn't know their workings. That was, actually, a blessing.

"I have only the light and her," I thought. *"Photographing is painting with light"* came to my mind.

Antonina was serene and carrying a profoundly meditative countenance. Finally, I suspected that she was getting tired. I seated at her side on the large flat stone and we began reviewing the pictures. She had taken possession of the camera and we both looked at the back screen while she moved from picture to picture. Having finished the sequence of pictures, Antonina placed the camera carefully on the ground and looked vacantly at the forest. Then, she put her head on my shoulder and began weeping quietly. But, soon, she started sobbing.

I asked her what the matter was and she said: "I didn't know I was like that."

Fearing I had ruined her self-esteem with my poor pictures, I said: "Never mind, with this poor light, the photos never get satisfactory."

"No, no! I never knew I was so beautiful!" she said, wiping her tears and smiling at me. And what a smile it was! I had to restrain myself from hugging and kissing her. That would have been a mistake, as I later found out. The dinner, this evening, was very calm. We talked about many subjects. I had the impression that the male part of the group had, now, a slightly different interaction with me.

They seemed a bit insecure about what to say or ask, and they looked repeatedly at Antonina before and after changing words with me. After the dinner, coffee and liquors, Antonina brought a pile of those metallic sheets with the photos of the afternoon. I noticed that Marco was impressed with the photos, Greg a bit less and Frederico's comments were dry and educated.

The next day was warm and sunny. After breakfast with the whole group, Antonina came to me:

"Now, we are going to wash your car, like I promised you, remember, Jota?!"

"Who are the -we-?" I asked.

"You and me, of course! Didn't I promise?" she said, laughing.

Washing my car, I understood, was a compensatory treat for my humiliating defeat in the chess match.

Antonina was out of herself. She was humming some strange songs and was super active. I began to suspect that such things as going out in the sun, playing with water and breathing the warm and pure air of a sunny morning were new to her. She went to her container and came out wearing a polo shirt, no bra, and a minuscule short and sneakers with no socks.

Her legs were very strong but extremely sensual despite a

delineated musculature. As I mentioned before and, now, with the smaller shorts, she looked even more like an Olympic gymnast. As I also said, her treading was peculiar and more so due to her summary clothes. Somewhat, she permanently avoided leaving the ground. With no bra, her breasts were plainly delineated beneath the polo. And, they looked adorable.

My car was not far from a garden hose. A bucket containing water with detergent and 2 cleaning sponges was already beside the car. I then remembered that maybe it would be a good idea to run the motor for a few minutes in order to charge the battery. Then, I tried to start the car. Dead battery! Antonina shouted to Greg who was in the vicinity. He went to the dome and came out carrying a device that looked like a small brick, which reminded me of those first cell phones. Two wires ended by claws emerged from the device.

A regulation button and an LED panel completed the device. Greg asked me about my car's battery voltage and set the gadget to 12 volts. I opened the hood and Greg connected the device's terminals to the poles of the battery. Then, he asked me to crank the engine. Instantly, the engine started. I closed the hood with the device still attached to the battery, as suggested by Greg, and let the motor running a few seconds and, then, turned off the engine. According to Greg the car's battery would be continuously being charged by the device until it was full. Greg would remove the charger after we washed the car.

Antonina was full of energy, running and singing and throwing water onto the car like a child. She was, in fact, playing with water. She took out her sneakers. After wetting the car completely, we began sponging it with detergent. Each one of us tackled one side of the car. After the sponging session she began to wash out the foam, throwing water from the hose.

On an impulse, she said to me: "Now, I'm going to wash you!" and turned the hose over me. I was wearing shorts and was shirtless, and my "losses" were small. My hair, however, got soaked with water. Seeing me like a wet dog, she said: "Poor creature, I'm going to dry you right now!"

She took a towel and rubbed my hair vigorously with it. Then, she rubbed my shoulders and neck gently. She, then, embraced me tightly, pressing her breasts against my chest, and kissed me on the forehead, apologizing in the meantime. I got out of action, petrified, not knowing what to do. *When you don't know what to do, do nothing*, my primeval instinct told me. As I would later learn, my behavior was correct and that was the right move. Or " un-move" if you will.

Still full of the entire world's energy, she said to me: "Now, I'm going to teach you how to jump! You like jumping, Jota?"

Saying this and without waiting for my answer, she brought the stool closer to my car, threw to the ground a few things that were on the top, and said to me: "We are going to do a little training, Jota. Jump onto the stool, please!"

The height was about 50 cm and I, easily, jumped, landing a bit awkwardly on the stool top. "Now, it's my turn!" she shouted, laughing loudly, acting like a playful child.

And she jumped graciously onto the stool top. "Let's increase the height!" she shouted again, "and now, I go first."

At first, I didn't understand what that would be since there wasn't anything higher to be jumped to. Then, Antonina approached my car's door and stood facing it. Looking sidewise at me and smiling, she crouched and jumped, landing gently onto the car's roof, not in the middle but just above the door, where the roof was firmer.

Still looking at me she, then, gave a backward somersault, landing with both feet on the ground and not oscillating the least bit. Greg had seen all this performance without our perceiving it. He called Antonina to the dome entrance and the two talked briefly. By the gestures and high voice tones, I inferred that Greg was scolding her.

It was the lunch hour, and we had a nice meal of chicken, fish, eggs, vegetables, and a delicious salad. Everything was simple and bordering on minimalism. Antonina seemed a bit too concerned about me: if I was eating correctly, the right foods, if I wanted something else, if I was enjoying the lunch. The guys said nothing in this respect and just looked briefly at Antonina.

Clearly, there was an order in the group, a hierarchy of sorts. Things were being planned. What things I had no idea. The general talk was ecology, warming of the planet, and correlate subjects. It became clear to me that all were well-informed about world problems, famine, misery, and wars. *Maybe a bit too informed*, I thought. Their main concern, however, was global warming, the greenhouse effect, atmospheric oxygen, ocean level elevation, melting of the glaciers, all related subjects. No, they did not seem concerned with sea turtles, whales, dolphins, and other animals on the verge of extinction.

After lunch, I remembered that my car was still hooked to Greg's battery charger. I asked him if we could disconnect everything and that I would try starting the car without the charger. Then, arriving at the car and opening the hood it occurred to me that the charger itself was not hooked to any electrical outlet. I called Greg's attention to this. He said that the gadget was self-sufficient and had an internal battery.

"It's a battery of the same type used in "your camera," he said smiling, "but a more powerful one. It uses radioactive graphite included inside a block of artificial diamond".

"Radioactive graphite produces beta rays, which are electrons. The electrons, hitting certain materials, generate electron holes, which generate an electrical current that continually charges a super capacitor. This system can function for thousands of years without any maintenance," he concluded, looking at my dropped jaw.

On the afternoon of this same day, after we had tea with cakes, Marco asked a few questions about me in the presence of the entire group. However, I perceived that the questioning was just a formality since they seemed to know my curriculum. I said I was a bachelor, was 45, and was a retired medical doctor. I lived with an older brother, also a bachelor that took care of my finances since I was sloppy in what concerned money.

This seemed to satisfy them, at least for the time being. I also did some questioning of a general type, about them. It was then that it occurred to me to ask them what their interest in Astronomy was since they were camped at the Astronomy Meeting. Greg, promptly, answered that he was the "astronomer" and the others went there just to accompany him, relax and know different people. Antonina was silent.

When I asked about their mother country, they answered, without great conviction that they originated from many regions of Siberian Russia, and thus, their accent. When asked the reason for their coming to Brazil, they gave disparate but educated answers. I perceived that they were not being sincere and also were not prepared to lie or deceive.

And, most curiously, they did not seem willing to give me the impression they were being sincere. They seemed to be following some protocol dictated by a superior. However, my general impression was that they were of a good nature and had a high level of naivety. This last trait attracted me since I consider myself to be naive.

Sometime later in the day, Marco asked me to help him get a few things from the basement. Up to now I had no idea they had a basement down the dome. As we moved, Marco explained to me that there were, actually, 2 domes, one inside the other. I hadn't perceived this since, looking from the outside, I saw only the external dome and, from the inside, saw only the internal one. Across the gap between the 2 domes, we came to a hatch on the floor. Marco opened it and I saw a ladder directed downwards.

We went down the ladder, which was very well built, with a safety enclosure. The basement was large, approximately circular, and extended beyond what I imagined to be the dome border. A vast stock of food was kept there; many large freezers and refrigerators were aligned close to the walls. Shelves containing jars with conserved products and cans of food also lined the walls. In another part of the extensive circular wall, I saw what appeared to be a sort of furnace. It was working and let out a roar. From this roaring and hot contraption emerged, vertically, a duct that pierced the concrete slab that formed the roof of the basement and, certainly, the floor of the dome.

What impressed me most, however, was the structural design of this whole region. Immediately, it became clear to me that the floor and the roof of the basement formed, in reality, a unique structure. The floor and roof were united together by thick steel bars that formed 45-degree angles with the surfaces. I was, actually, inside a unique structural frame, where the roof and floor linked together by the steel rods formed a unique structure, certainly a very strong; the so called *space-truss*. Every detail perspired of an advanced civil engineering.

Another aspect also became clear to me. Why link the floor and roof with diagonal bars? If the basement floor were just supported by the ground below, a few columns from floor to roof would support the dome floor above us. The space truss design, however, clearly indicated to me the existence of a compartment below the basement. In other words, the basement floor would be the roof of something below.

Telling Marco of my "theory," he confirmed, "Yes, there is "the bunker" below us." He promised me a visit to the bunker. We were still in the basement since Marco was apparently having some fun watching my mesmerized looks at every detail. Leading me closer to the furnace, Marco explained that some part of the farm's electrical power came from the public grid, but they also generated electricity for "heavier" projects.

What would be those "heavier" projects? Marco didn't tell me. The big furnace produced hot water for the dome services and also generated electricity by means of a vapor driven turbine and a generator. A part of the heat generated by the furnace was also used to produce electricity directly from heat by the so-called *effect Seebeck*. The electricity coming from the public grid was used only for the general maintenance of the dome. Marco also told me that they stored electricity in a sort of battery, not a conventional one.

Electricity was stored in immense flywheels turning at thousands of RPMs. Those big flywheels were located behind the circular wall of the basement. It became clear to me that, beyond that wall, there might be much more than I could possibly imagine.

Chapter 9

The Bunker

After we took to the dome the items from the basement, Marco and I had a brief coffee and he led me to visit the bunker, as he had promised. We went down to the basement and, close to the circular wall, Marco opened another hatch on the floor. From it descended a ladder that ended on the floor below. Still on the ladder, I could sense a big drop in the temperature and the humming of workstations and big computers. Stepping onto the floor I saw an immense circular hall with an area close to that of the basement above.

However, the distance from roof to floor was larger. Whereas the basement had a height of 2.5 meters, here in the bunker, the height exceeded 4 meters. Behind a large console was seated Frederico, who was expecting us and greeted me amiably. It went to Fred the task of giving me a brief tour of the facilities.

He said this was the Center of Operations of the company. Here, he said, "are performed the accounting operations of our wood industry."

"The orders from many states in Brazil are processed here. Even, orders from abroad" he said, proudly. From the way Fred talked and from the constant exchange of eye contact with Marco I perceived I was getting "processed" information.

What surprised me, again, was that Fred was not trying to appear sincere. I felt that I was being somewhat tested. For my part, I pretended to be earnestly interested in learning about the details of the information center. It was evident to me that an extremely sophisticated computational system had been installed here. Many machines were new to me, with strange designs and strange sounds and, also, strange writings. A powerful communication system seemed to be connected with the workstations and individual computers.

All this electronic sophistication seemed to me as exaggerated for a "wood processing company". I put my questions to Fred.

"Yes, we communicate with national, international, and supra-terrestrial centers," he said. Then, he looked at Marco as if apologizing for something. Marco said nothing.

Still later, during this same day, Greg, Antonina and I toured another part of the farm. We came to a pond hidden in the middle of the Eucalyptus forest. Also, partially hidden, there appeared another dome, smaller than ours. There, we were met by 6 youths between the ages of 20 and about 25 years.

They were friendly and joyful. It was clear they were expecting the visit of a strange: me. There were three guys and three girls. Two of the guys had the same body type as my friends: short, stout, very clear hair and visibly strong legs since they wore shorts. They also wore very dark glasses. The other guy was tall, lean, and dark-haired. Of the girls, two were short and muscular, especially in the legs, as I could verify since all were wearing shorts. Their hairs were also very clear, like the guys'. They also wore very dark glasses. The third girl was taller, lean, dark-haired, and wore clear glasses with correcting lenses. Type 1 guys and girls had that peculiar way of moving, like my friends.

We entered the dome, whose internal disposition was different from our home dome. Instead of containers, this dome was divided into many rooms arranged radially. In the center there was a communal hall with a big table, sofas, lawn chairs, etc. We were served juices, coffee, mineral water, and cakes. The youths talked all the time among themselves. They looked joyful and were continually making jokes and funny gestures to each other and laughing all the time.

No question they were having a good time. The "strangers" did not talk Portuguese and seemed to be recent "acquisitions" of the farm. They seemed to be enjoying, extremely, their new surroundings and their new friends. The tall guy and the tall girl were clearly Brazilians from the North. The talking between the strangers and Brazilians was performed through gestures, mannerisms, funny sounds, and endless loud laughing.

One of the 2 stranger girls, Isobel was her name, impressed me strongly. She was extremely pretty, her body was that of a gymnast, and she exuded sensuality. She breathed rapidly as if she was tired and moved with an incredible lightness. I could sense that she and Antonina were not on the best terms as she looked sideways at Antonina.

However, what impressed me more were her eyes, when she

removed her glasses. It is true; they were magnificent, of a pale green. But, also, they were cold, calculating, penetrating. And she looked at me as if I were a curiosity or like I was some sort of prey. The combination of her heavy breathing, light movements, and penetrating gaze gave her the general impression of a beast poised to attack. Despite my fear, she brought to my mind very improper thoughts.

Chapter 10
Carbon Dioxide Sequestering

As we got back to our dome, we had some tea and, afterward, Marco explained to me the importance of intelligent wood in construction and its benefits as compared to reinforced concrete. He told me that wood has a negative carbon footprint when used in edification and, this, can generate carbon credits. Reinforced concrete, on the other hand, has a positive carbon footprint since its use generates a lot of carbon dioxide, both in cement and steel production.

Marco told me of the general trend in civil engineering in increasing the use of wood. "Assuming that a treated wood, of high quality, survives 100 years as part of a house, we grant that the carbon contained in this wood will not return to the atmosphere during all this period".

"So, extending this reasoning worldwide, it turns out that the use of wood in buildings corresponds to carbon sequestering from the atmosphere lasting about 100 years. But, in order to complete this cycle, for each cut tree one or more must be planted."

Then, Marco went on to tell me that oil is a fossil fuel since it is derived from the decomposition of pre-historic animals, plants and algae during millions of years.

"During this long process, the fossils are isolated from the atmosphere, beneath great layers of clay and rock. As such, the oil we use to produce fuels today derives from a huge amount of carbon dioxide that had been taken from the atmosphere millions of years ago. When we burn these fuels today, we release back this carbon dioxide content to the atmosphere. And this is not a good idea."

"On the other hand the great forests like the African forests or the Amazon Forest and others do not remove CO_2 from the atmosphere when analyzed across a period of thousands of years. What happens is that when the trees die, they decompose and release the carbon dioxide back to the atmosphere."

I asked Marco: "What, then, is the importance of preserving the forests?" Marco smiled and answered that my question was a complex one.

He told me that forests are very important to the planet for many reasons. First, the forests are essential for the maintenance of the ecosystems be they vegetal or animal. Secondly, the forests and sea algae are necessary for oxygen production. The forests also regulate the climate, the atmospheric humidity, and the rains. And the forests are very important to maintain...the forests.

"For example", said Marco, "in the case of the Amazon Forest, the organic layer of the soil is quite thin and a little disruption in the tree's density leads rapidly to desertification. In a few years without the trees, the region transforms into a desert."

Chapter 11

Yuri

The next day, soon after breakfast, I was told that another member of the family would arrive. His name was Yuri. Greg told me that Yuri was their leader in this particular family. And he was, too, their doctor. We went to the outside to meet Yuri. And arrive he did, driving and old Fiat, very dirty, old tires. Yuri was about 45, short like the other males, with blond hair. What most impressed me, at first sight, was his physical constitution. If the other guys were of strong constitution Yuri was an athlete.

He was very muscular with a firm treading, like that of a martial arts master. His features were very pleasing. Like the others, he wore dark glasses. Yuri had been informed of my presence and said aloud, pointing to me: "This all means that you have found a doctor and, now, I will have competition."

And he laughed loudly while shaking hands with me and almost breaking my hand bones. His voice was loud with a strong Russian accent. We all went inside and sat at the table while Yuri went to his container to wash and leave his things. He soon returned to the table, where we had coffee, orange juice, and water. Then, Yuri suggested that we went for a walk since he needed to stretch his legs.

While we walked Yuri asked what my specialty was in Medicine.

I said that my specialty was lack of specialty and that, after having initially worked in hospitals, I went to the University to pursue a scientific career. That information appeared to spark his curiosity, since he asked me which area of science I was in. I said my area was biophysics with an emphasis on membranes and bioelectricity.

As Yuri questioned me he made it clear to the group that his conversation with me should be shared with all as if he was using me as a sort of lecture for the others.

"What do you think is better for a patient suffering from terminal cardiac failure: heart transplantation or an artificial heart?" he asked me while looking at the others.

At this moment I felt that he really was the group leader since there was a distinct change in the group's "climate" after his arrival. He asked the same question in relation to kidney terminal failure. I answered, shyly, that this was a controversial subject and all depended on the availability of organ donors and that artificial organs were, still, at a very crude stage in our Medicine. Yuri seemed to like my answer and said, with some pomp, to all hear:

"The traditional Medicine on Earth cures very few diseases. Most diseases are treated or controlled but not cured. The cure is a reversion of the disease to the sane condition. Take arterial hypertension as an example. In most cases, the Earth's medicine doesn't even know its cause, much less the cure. However, if the patient takes the appropriate drugs, he or she can lead a normal life." And, he continued, now, looking more attentively at the group.

"But there is a Medicine that cures. We will talk more about this," he concluded, looking, firmly, at my eyes.

The group said nothing and nodded. I noted that, like the others, Yuri's dark glasses were adaptive and he displayed, also, a higher respiratory rate. Before we had left for the walk, still seated at the table I measured Yuri's respiratory rate at about 30/min. During our walk, he asked me, looking at the others: "Jota, what did you conclude regarding my respiratory rate?"

I got a lot embarrassed and flushed but answered that I had found it a bit elevated. And that the others also had higher respiratory rates.

"That's what happens when you have low oxygen in the air," Yuri remarked, looking at the others.

Chapter 12
The Cave

The following morning, we had breakfast, now, with Yuri. We had, besides the traditional coffee with milk, also fruit juices, fresh fruits, scrambled eggs and some bread. *Some improvement of the breakfast after Yuri's arrival,* I thought. After that, Yuri told me that they would take me to "the cave."

Before we left the dome for the cave, Yuri told me we would need to use helmets inside the cave due to falling stones from the cave's roof. Also, we put on special coats since the cave's temperature was a bit low. The helmets were not of the type used by the workers in construction.

They were of the motorcyclists' type. Yuri explained that the falling stones might fall diagonally sometimes, that being the reason for the lateral protection in the helmets. My helmet was, however, bulkier than the others. Marco explained to me that the helmets contained illumination devices, radio communicators, GPS and cameras.

We all proceeded to the cave, with the exception of Frederico, who could not leave the bunker. We walked for about 40 minutes on a well-kept trail. Finally, we got to the base of an elevation about 20 meters high, with a rocky texture. On one side of the elevation and hidden beneath some foliage there appeared a steel gate that seemed to be strong and heavy. The gate ran laterally onto two rails, one above and the other below. Marco switched his remote control and the gate began to open slowly. We all entered and the gate closed behind us. The cave had lights. The floor was concrete, very strong both in appearance, and it sloped down with about 8 degrees' decline.

The cave was 5 meters wide by about 4 meters in height. Those dimensions changed a bit as we moved since it was a natural formation. Indeed, as Marco had informed me, the rocky roof was reinforced by iron bars that held a mesh. On the floor, there were many loose rocks that the group members kicked aside. We began the descent. My helmet hummed weakly, and I asked Yuri if that was normal. He said it was normal since it had built-in navigation devices and communication gear. We were all silent and continued the descent, calmly.

After some 15 minutes' walk I thought we had traversed about 300 meters. The temperature had fallen to about 10 degrees Celsius, as I could sense in my hands since we didn't wear gloves. We, finally, arrived at a large natural hall. Our walk, up to now, was only through the access to this hall. Marco told me this was a natural structure in which they did only a few reinforcements and also made a concrete floor, like in the corridor we came from. The floor was smooth and level.

And, it seemed to be very resistant to my testing kicks. I couldn't initially grasp the actual dimensions of this hall since there were no visual cues. Only after we began to walk through it, I began to perceive its huge size. According to Marco, the hall was roughly circular having a mean diameter of 100 meters and 15 meters high, at the domed center. The lighting was low, coming from some lamps in the lateral walls. The walls weren't empty, though. Huge blocks covered by tarpaulin occupied almost the entire portion of the external border. They were stacks of intelligent wood.

Marco lifted one of the tarpaulins. Inside, there was a pile of wooden columns stacked to allow a forklift to move them. Marco invited me to examine one of the wooden columns. It was very smooth with perfectly plane surfaces. It had a perfectly rectangular cross-section. In this block the pieces had 20 x 20 cm in cross section and 3 meters long. In another covered pile, there were the beams, which had a cross-section of 20 x 40 cm and a length of 4 meters.

It was then that Antonina, silent up to this moment, explained to me that all wood pieces were maturing, "just getting old", as she put it. I was informed that one of the purposes of this huge deposit was sequestering atmospheric carbon by keeping the wood there for long periods of time. This argument, however, didn't convince me entirely.

"Of course, we can't modify the atmospheric carbon at this scale." Marco said.

"Our plan is to propagate the idea to other centers in order to expand the process globally. Exceptionally, we sell this wood to select contractors": Marco concluded.

Chapter 13

Intelligent Wood

The following day, after breakfast, we went for a visit to the plant where the beams and columns were produced. In a clearing within the Eucalyptus forest, I saw the long-shaped ovens, 10 of them. As Marco was explaining to me, the Eucalyptus boles, after being cut from the trees and their barks removed, were stored here. Many piles of trunks covered by tarpaulins lay on paved platforms.

The production of "intelligent wood" consisted, initially, of heating the trunks inside a microwave oven of sorts. Upon our arrival, one of the trunks was being processed in this way. After the initial heating, some water was introduced and the wood, hot and wet, gradually softened. This takes many minutes. The compression process, then, begins slowly. After about 50 minutes, the compression stops, but the heating continues. I was, then, shown another oven where this step had finished and the wood piece had been removed from the oven.

What I saw was a perfectly rectangular wood piece, still hot and fuming. The pieces were now stored inside a heated deposit at a temperature of 45 degrees C, where they would get dry. After some days, the pieces, now quite dry, get a resin bath where the wood interstices are completely permeated with resin. This also takes many days.

"After that, the wood gets eternized" said Marco. "They can, now, last for centuries!"

Hearing this, I asked Marco if this statement was not an exaggeration. "The wood, depending on its type and the environment where it will stay, can last indefinitely or rot in a few months," he said.

"The wooden pillars that support Venetian buildings are, for centuries, immersed under sea water. Tree trunks that ended up on the bottom of some of the Great Lakes in the United States are still intact and ready to be used. The wooden bridge in the Great Salt Lake in Utah, despite its age has yet no signs of decay. Some woods in some environs can even get more resistant with the passing of time. On the other hand, what favors wood decay is the alternating of wet and dry," he concluded.

And Marco went on: "The wooden columns of Japanese temples are centuries old. In tropical countries, there is some prejudice against using wood for construction. But, in cold climates like Europe and Nordic countries, parts of the United States and other countries, wood constructions are, in most cases, the rule. The roofs and steeples of the grand cathedrals, more than 500 years old, are supported by heavy wooden trusses, still original. The recent fire in Notre Dame Cathedral revealed, to an astonished world that, under the architectonic mantle, there was a wooden skeleton."

Chapter 14

High-Performance Bamboo

The following day, after breakfast, Greg informed me that we would visit the bamboo plantation. After a 30 min walk through trails along the dense Eucalyptus forest, we came to a large bamboo forest. Marco told me those bamboos were of the species *Dendrocalamus giganteus*. This species grows very fast, up to about 1 meter a day, and attains big dimensions.

"Bamboo is from the *Graminea* family and one of the plants with the fastest growth rate," Marco told me.

"As we do with the Eucalyptus, we sell our processed bamboo under the name of High-Performance Bamboo."

And, Greg added: "And performance it does have!"

The bamboo forest seemed impenetrable to my eyes. However, soon, Marco embarked through a half-hidden and clean trail and we all followed him in Indian file. The bamboo forest seemed endless but, at last, we came upon a great glade where another geodesic dome elevated majestically. It was covered with the same camouflaged tarpaulin.

This dome was even bigger than the one we were living in. We were met by 4 guys and 4 girls. In this group, the guys were all Brazilians, of a varied body type and all from the north. The girls, however, were all "strangers", short, pretty, and of a muscular constitution.

They were all very festive and receptive and, certainly, were expecting our arrival. The girls, however, did not talk to us nor to the guys, and only among themselves, in low voices and in a very strange language. They certainly were new arrivers. We were promptly invited to enter the dome, where they served us water, coffee, fruit juices, and cakes. Erico, who appeared to lead the group, soon perceived that I was a "visitor" and offered to brief me on their work.

"Our work is similar to the Eucalyptus team and we also process the bamboo. The bamboo is placed in ovens under high temperatures and humidity. They are thus softened. Differently of the Eucalyptus processing, the bamboo is cut into strips that are glued together and then pressed and transformed into pieces of square or rectangular section, for columns and beams," Erico concluded.

"And why use bamboo if you have Eucalyptus?" I asked. Erico, who later told me that he was a Forestry Engineer, explained that the bamboo pieces are complementary to those made from Eucalyptus.

"The difference is that the bamboo pieces carry a high-performance label."

"And what this high performance thing would mean?" I asked, giving a friendly laugh complemented by a 2 hand gesture.

Erico was clearly expecting my question since he certainly had given this same tour many times.

Joaquim

"Well," he said, looking at the group, "whereas Eucalyptus is used in the place of concrete, bamboo replaces steel," he concluded, checking once more his "audience," i.e., me.

Chapter 15

The Ceremony of "The Waters"

The next day, we had breakfast as usual, and we were all still seated at the table when Yuri announced that we would discuss something important following lunch. Since all of them were busy, I went out to take some pictures of some places a bit farther from the dome. Then, there came lunch, and after that, we had a nice dessert, coffee, and homemade liquor. Yuri asked that we remain in our seats since we were going to have a "big talk". We were all seated: Yuri, Greg, Marco, Frederico, Antonina, and I.

Then, two "stranger" women, which I had never seen, brought to the table six big bottles containing water and six pots containing a brown powder. Each of the big bottles and the pots had a name printed on it. My name was on one bottle and one pot. These items, with the corresponding names, were placed right in front of each of us.

Everyone had a formal and serious countenance. I began to feel uneasy, and a chilling sensation crept down my spine. *Had I messed up and this would be my trial?* I thought, perspiring. Yuri, seeing my perturbed features, said there was nothing wrong with me. All laughed and tranquilized me. Antonina was at my side and looked, assuringly, at me. Yuri began explaining that the bottle with water and the pot with the powder having my name were my water and my ashes respectively.

My ashes? I thought. *Had I died, and nobody told me?* The same held for the others. The water volume in each bottle was not the same for each of us but the changes were not appreciable. Yuri's bottle, however, had less water. He explained that the water and ashes were obtained from our excrements: the urine and feces we produced in these last days. The water was obtained by distillation, and the residue was incinerated, forming the ashes. Yuri added that the water was extremely pure. Then, the two stranger women placed a very clean glass and a clean spoon in front of each one of us.

The glasses also had our names. Yuri then asked that we fill our glasses with our own water and then drink it. Everyone did that. My water was delicious! Again, Yuri asked that we fill our glasses with water. This time, we were to take our ashes with a spoon and mix them with our own water. We were to mix the contents and wait for 5 minutes.

After this period, my powder went to the bottom at the same time that some insoluble salts remained in the water. After this, Yuri asked us to drink just one or two gulps of the supernatant water. My water was a bit salty and had a light odor of ammonia.

Then, the two "assistants" collected our soiled glasses and spoons and wiped the table with clean clothes. A set of clean glasses, with our names printed, were placed in front of us, and an empty big bottle was placed at the center of the table. Yury said that we were to fill our glasses with our water. After we had done that, Yury said we should empty our glasses into the empty big bottle at the table center.

After we did this, the assistants, using a long and very clean glass rod, mixed the water in the big communal bottle. And the assistants then, calmly, filled our glasses with the water from the communal bottle. All were silent and looking down at the table.

Yuri, then, stood up and asked us all to stand, pushing back our chairs. Then, Yuri said, "Let us all drink our waters". Saying this he took his glass and drank the water on it. And we all did the same with our glasses.

The group, then, formed a line facing me, with Greg closest to me and Yuri and Antonina at the end. Then, each one silently embraced me and kissed my forehead. Antonina was the last one.

After this, Yuri went to my side and, facing the others, said to me, holding my hand. "Now, we are almost brothers". I was weeping. Everyone clapped hands at me. Beer, coffee, and cakes were brought to the table by the assistants.

After this, we dispersed, and I went to my container, exhausted. Lying down in my bed, I imagined what would be necessary for me to become their "brother. *"Some blood ceremony? Some 3 days fasting? No, it was worse!*

Chapter 16

The Proof

The following day, during the breakfast, Yuri seemed more formal than his customary mood. He announced that today I would provide them with proof of confidence, proof that I trusted them. After some preparations, we left the dome and, this time, Frederico joined us. All were strangely silent. After some walking, we passed the great rocky elevation where was the cave entry.

But we would not enter the cave and, for some reason, I felt some relief. Contouring the big rocky formation that formed the external walls of the cave, we arrived at an extensive marsh. Walking along the dry border of the marsh, I was faced with a small forest of native trees; very big ones with many hanging vines. About 100 meters down the trail, I heard the sound of running water. Soon, we got to an interesting place. Leaving the marsh, a brook fanned across a bed of flat stones. Following with the eyes the flow of water I perceived that the stream ended abruptly.

Greg, holding my arm, firmly, asked me to be careful since the stream fell down into a waterfall. In front of us, there appeared a sudden interruption of the ground as if the ground suddenly ceased to exist. It was a deep cliff. We approached, slowly, to its border and halted about 2 feet from the cliff's border. Then, I could see that the stream fell abruptly into an abyss surrounded by an immense forest of giant trees. The roar of falling water, the partial darkness provided by the extensive foliage, and the giant hanging vines created an atmosphere of doom. Greg, still holding my arm firmly and with his other hand clinging to a thick vine, asked me to look down the cliff.

As I looked down, I felt immediately dizzy. A wave of nausea crept over my body. The view was apocalyptic. The sudden transition from the stone border into the void was shocking. I could see, well down the cliff, a bed of rocks on the bottom. At least 45 meters separated us from the rock bed below. I hadn't yet recovered from my awe when Yuri approached me with a solemn expression.

"You trust us?" he asked.

"I do", I answered with a dry mouth and a tightened throat.

"You completely trust us?" he asked again.

"Yes, I do trust you completely," I answered, shaking.

"Then, jump down and prove that you trust us," he said firmly. Greg was still holding my arm firmly. Then, he let go of my arm, looked firmly at my eyes, and nodded.

Then, I jumped.

Time came to a standstill. I felt like my whole life was parading across my mind. I was a baby in my mother's lap, then I was lying down on an operating table and, then, I was at my father's funeral.

Soon, there appeared a white angel and he held me, gently, in his arms. A great peace invaded me. *This is what it is like dying!* I thought.

When I opened my eyes I saw Greg at my side, hugging me. It was, then, that I perceived to be on a net of very thin and flexible threads, almost invisible even by looking at a close range.

"Now, we go down," he said, directing me to a 5-meter rope leading to the bottom. We descended the rope onto a bed of rocks surrounding a big natural pool, where the waterfall fell with a deafening roar, creating a mist. Then, I heard cries and hands clapping above and saw that Marco, Yuri, Frederico, and Antonina were on the net, preparing to descend the rope.

Soon, we were reunited beside the immense waterfall. The roar made it difficult for us to understand each other. Then, Yuri embraced me and kissed my forehead. The others did the same, in sequence.

After this, Yuri announced: "Now, Jota, you are our brother!"

"Our brother, our brother!" all repeated. I looked up at the cliff. Nausea invaded my body again, but I wasn't shaking anymore. As soon as we moved from the roar of the falling water, Yuri placed his hand on my shoulder and said, to all hear: "Jota, you, of three things, is one: mad, naive, or too brave."

"The three," I said, sobbing.

Chapter 17

Yuri's Revelations

Some days after the "ceremony of the waters" and my "jump of trust," Yuri assembled us soon after we had coffee and lunch was cleared from the table. He brought a stack of printed sheets. Everyone had a formal and serious demeanor.

"Finally, Jota," he said, looking at me, "we have all information concerning you. We have sequenced your genome from your epithelial cells shed in your feces and urine".

"You have not the bad gene sequence we know as EVL that characterizes the wrong behavior of humans, the criminal mind/personality. Also, from the analysis of your brain, done by the helmet you wore during our cave exploration, we have all its functional morphology".

"We have known for a long time that there is a correlation between brain morphology and certain behavioral aspects. This only came to be established here at the beginning of the present century. But, we needed to know how much you trusted us, your degree of madness and naivety. And you passed with flying colors in all items".

"And, we did not meet casually, Jota. You, as well as many other "candidates" were being monitored by our organization since a long time ago. Actually, since you were 12, we know all about you, well, almost all.

All about your academic career, all your publications and your non-publications, those rejected. And these last were many, as you well know!"

"You had many ideas, most of which you could not transform into publications. You are a sloppy manager of your time and your scientific data. You have no method; you begin too many projects but do not lead them to publishable results. Don't worry. This is a normal aspect of science. But, unfortunately, to succeed nowadays, you can't be normal. Your interest in Astronomy caught our attention, as well as the books you have read in the past and the books you read now. And, you have read a lot, I can assure you."

"A facet we considered most positive in your scientific career was your little concern with professional ascension. This told us that you were not seeking power or academic status. This trait of your personality, strange as it may seem to you, is very valuable to us. In due time, we will explain this to you."

"And, before you ask me what our interest in you is, I will answer."

"In fact, for a long time, we have been analyzing many people like you from all countries. And we have received, in our organization, hundreds of persons with your approximate profile. It is a continuous process. We are not looking for geniuses or Nobel Prize winners or scientists with a thousand publications. We are not seeking scientific knowledge or prowess. Knowledge comes to us in large quantities and superb quality and innovation; continuously, from our scientists and from many sources located in unimaginably distant places".

"As to your intelligence, we also evaluated it. Do not get upset, Jota. Your IQ is only a bit above the average of humans. It is 110, which is not bad for humans; you can still write and read and you can understand what we are saying to you. And, that, is a great deal, believe me," and, saying this, Yuri gave a good laugh and patted my back.

"But wait, how could you people measure my IQ?" I said, trying to remain calm.

"You were tested, Jota, and well tested at that," Yuri answered, smiling and looking at the others. "The helmet you used in the cave did that test for us."

"But, how can an electronic device measure such a complex thing as intelligence?"

"The helmet you used is not simply a magnetic resonance device as you know it," Yuri answered.

"In the IQ test the device has done an analysis of the synaptic firing patterns in different regions of your brain, in correlation with what you were seeing around you. This determined how your brain reacted to thousands of visual cues, patterns, terrains, sounds, and smells. In summary, how your brain interacts with the world. That's intelligence, Jota. But this is just one of the forms of intelligence, the one related to the brain's processing power. There are many other types of intelligence, as you well know, which we may discuss another time."

"OK," I said, showing some irritation. "So, in accordance with your helmet gadget what would be the intelligence of you people?" Yuri smiled, looked to the others, thought, and said:

"Jota, in due time, you will be told of our IQs, as measured by our device. Be patient, and let me conclude my report on you. However, this data on your intelligence refers, essentially, to the general processing power of your brain, as I was trying to explain to you. In more specific aspects of intelligence, we found that your abstract and mathematical intelligence are average. Your spatial intelligence is below average. However, by human standards, your power of observation is exceptional. You seem to analyze everything you see. And, this is valuable for us."

"But then, what would be important for you? And what do you need me for?" I asked.

Yuri looked at the group with a serious countenance: "As of now, we have no definite plans for you. We still need to know you more. What matters, at this moment, is that you trust us and enjoy our company. And that we like your presence here and, most importantly, that we can trust you. Gradually, you will be given certain tasks; each time more difficult ones, and then, you will be one of our team."

This information, coming from Yuri, made sense to me. I could find some meaning in his words and felt that I could help them with ideas. What wasn't still clear to me was what would be my gain in interacting with them. But, this, I would soon know.

"As a matter of fact," Yuri went on, "we also have the data from your origin, your family tree. Our files carry all birth certificates, deaths, and marriages from all notary offices and parishes in the world. And, this, spans a few centuries. As such, it was pretty easy for us to obtain information concerning your ancestors. We did your family tree up to 14 generations in the past. We could go to more generations, of course. And we haven't identified negative hits in our scanning. Certainly, we found some bohemian types which, for us, is a very positive mark," concluded Yuri, laughing and looking at everyone.

"So you have my pedigree?" I asked, jokingly. I felt an immediate exchange of glances among the group. Yuri smiled briefly; Frederico was covering his face with his hands, and Greg and Marco looked down at the table. Then, everyone looked, fixedly, at Antonina.

Yuri slapped the table and said to me: "You got exactly to the point, Jota!" and he laughed loudly.

"And here is your family tree," said Yuri recovering to a serious countenance and handing me a sheet.

Printed upon the metallic sheet 50 x 50 cm across, I observed a series of concentric rings with a single circle at the center. In the spaces between each increasing ring there were people's names. My name occupied the central circle. The whole diagram was intersected by a vertical line crossing the entire diagram but sparing the central circle. In the first ring was my father's name to the left and my mother's on the right.

The second ring was divided into 4 sectors, 2 sectors on each side of the vertical line. My grandparents from the father's side occupied the 2 sectors at left. From my mother's side the 2 sectors at right. The third ring had 8 sectors with the names of my grandparents. This ring disposition went all the way down to 14 generations. The print got progressively smaller as the generations went back in time. There were blank spaces and, in some, interrogation marks.

After some rings, I couldn't read the names; so small was the print. Yuri assured me that the names were there all right, down to the 14th generation. He said I would need a microscope to read all the names, but surely, they were all there!

Chapter 18

Yuri Talks about World Problems

During another formal meeting, where all members were present, Yuri told me that their aim was to transform Earth into a better planet. It seemed that Yuri was using me as a pretext to brief everybody on various subjects.

"As I told you, we have a huge amount of information on the most diverse aspects of life on Earth. And we increase, daily, our trove. We pursue concerns loved by everyone and so beaten down to the point of a commonplace. We want a better planet for our children, save the whales, save the forests, no global warming, no greenhouse effect, no oceans rise, no hunger, and other propositions embraced by everyone."

Yuri explained that any one of these proposals gets the support of disparate groups of society, even across totalitarian regimes.

"In this way, we find no opposition and our actions are met with sympathy despite a lack of enthusiasm. Among the many concerns we raise, one of the forest's destruction is used as a pretext by the richest countries to incriminate developing countries. And we know those same rich countries are the first to destroy their forests. Another aberration are the thousands of NGOs who view themselves as protectors of the forests, the Indians, and the poor. The reality is that those NGOs are only protecting their own interests. As you well know, Jota, certain NGOs in

Brazil pretend they protect the Indians when, in reality, they want the Indians to remain, eternally, Indians. They say the Indians need to be protected so that they can pursue their traditions and not be contaminated by the bad manners of the whites. They don't want to know what the Indians really want or need. And we know well that the Indians, surely, want to maintain their traditions. But they also want to have money, TVs, cars, and cell phones, and they don't even care about the "bad" customs of the whites. We have, for a long time, been following the human race's evolution. When I say a long time, I mean thousands of years."

"We know that you are curious, Jota, that you have examined our books, left there on purpose. You know now that we are an organization possessing an insanely huge amount of information by human standards. In that album with the cities' pictures, we have put a small sample of an enormous collection of images. Your planet, the Earth, has been visited and studied for thousands of years in the past by different civilizations that maintain contact with us."

Chapter 19

The Planet Landa

During one of our after lunch meetings, Yuri became very formal. The group became silent, certainly aware of the comings. Yuri began addressing me:

"Jota, now the time has come that you should know where we come from. Our race originated in Earth some 300 thousand years ago, at about the same period as the actual humans. We found fossils and inscriptions telling us this. There are, however, some other theories. A lineage of our ancestors was taken by a very advanced race, to a planet beyond the orbit of Pluto, at an average distance of 10 billion km from the Sun. We call our planet by the name Landa. Landa is very cold, due to its immense distance from the Sun. Despite the surface temperature in Landa may get to -100 degrees Celsius the planet's interior is composed by magma, i.e. molten rocks in semi-fluid state and at an average temperature of 1000 degrees Celsius, ranging from 700 to 1400."

"We don't know, exactly, what maintains this temperature for millennia after millennia. Like the Earth's magma, part of the energy comes from radioactive processes based on nuclear fission. But, differently from Earth's magma, in Landa there are, probably, remains of a fusion mechanism at the central region of the planet. One theory, well accepted by most scientists in Landa, is that the planet is a white-dwarf star fossil that incorporated a huge number of asteroids from the Oort

Cloud. This last is a vast belt of asteroids and comets. This mass of fallen asteroids formed the rocky crust of Landa, where we inhabit. This rocky crust is what you, on Earth, call tectonic plates. However, differently from Earth's plates, in Landa these tectonic plates, despite also floating over the magma, do not move and collide like those on Earth. The plates are extremely stable". And Yuri went on:

"Landa is much bigger than Earth and is similar in size to Uranus, having a surface area of 8 billion square km. Landa's atmosphere is also very peculiar: Nitrogen, Oxygen, CO_2 and water constitute the atmosphere in different physical states: gas, liquid, solid. Oxygen and Nitrogen have a proportion 50/48, different from Earth where $O_2/N_2 = 21/79$. CO_2, at 2% is much more abundant than in Earth's atmosphere"

"Our life would be impossible in Landa were not for some factors that contribute favorably. Firstly, the rocky mantle of Landa has huge holes that expose the magma below. They are known as *magma wells*. These wells are very stable; they last for centuries, unchanged. They have different diameters, from 50 to 100 meters, some even more. Their depths also vary, depending on the crust thickness. There is great number of these wells and they contribute, appreciably, to the warming of the atmosphere. Thanks to the magma wells the atmospheric temperature is high enough to allow Oxygen, Nitrogen and CO_2 to remain gaseous. And, this is the gaseous mixture we breathe. In Landa, the concentration of atmospheric CO_2 is much greater than in Earth's. This contributes to increasing the temperature by retaining a larger proportion of infra-red radiation through a greenhouse effect of large proportion. This greenhouse effect traps heat from the Sun, and despite the much smaller sun energy coming to the planet, this heat is well retained."

"Another aspect of Landa's geology that contributes for a temperature increase is the planet's surface color. The surface ice and snow are mixed with a very dark pigment derived from the soil below. This makes the Landa surface very dark, helping it to absorb the weak radiation coming from the Sun. A curious combination of a naturally dark surface and low solar illumination makes Landa poorly visible from Earth, that being one of the reasons Landa has not yet been "discovered" by Earth astronomers".

"But does not Landa perturb the orbit of Pluto?" I asked Yuri.

And doing this I took a chance to show them I knew something: "Look," I continued, "Neptune was discovered not because it was first seen but because astronomers were looking for it. A mysterious planet was perturbing Uranus' orbit. The astronomers Urbain LeVerrier and John Couch Adams, working independently (actually competing), predicted where this mystery planet should be sought in the sky. And Johann Galle, in 1846 could detect the mystery planet at less than 1 degree from the location predicted by LeVerrier and Adams."

"Yes, you are right, Jota," said Yuri. "Landa could well perturb Pluto's orbit and probably does perturb in some extent. We can explain why some discoveries do occur, but why they don't occur is out of our reach!" he concluded, laughing and looking at his "audience".

"However, one of the most important factors that make Landa habitable is that it is gravitationally locked with the Sun, presenting, always, the same face to our star," said Yuri

"Is this similar to what happens between the Moon and the Earth?" I questioned, just to show that I knew something.

Yuri ignored my comment and went on:

"Due to this gravitational lock with the Sun, about half the surface of Landa, or 4 billion square kilometers, gets permanently illuminated by the Sun. We inhabit this face directed to the Sun and, actually, only a small portion of it, a region where the Sun is always high in the sky and, thus, receives more heat and stays warmer. Despite solar radiation being weak due to the enormous distance from the Sun, the Sun's rays striking continuously, in an eternal day, contribute to maintaining a gaseous atmosphere on this side of the planet."

"The habitable area is about 200 million square km. However, the area we effectively inhabit is smaller, about 50 million square km, where the Sun stays very high in the sky. Around the magma wells, an interesting phenomenon occurs," continued Yuri.

"The ice and snow forming thick layers in the surface, creates huge avalanches near the border of the magma wells. As soon as this ice and snow encounter the super-hot magma it transforms instantly into water vapor that is violently ejected upwards, forming gigantic geysers. The water vapor, along with superheated water is thrown violently upwards to the sky and freezes, almost immediately, into snowflakes. Due to this phenomenon there is an almost permanent snowfall in Landa. As soon as the snow accumulates again around the wells' borders new avalanches occur and the process repeats indefinitely."

"Also, since the thickness of the rocky crust is not uniform, there are deep depressions where the rock gets closer to the magma below. In these depressions the temperature is high enough to maintain water in liquid state. Here, immense lakes form, having a thick layer of ice on their surface. In this lakes live many species of aquatic animals, some of them unknown to us."

Yuri finished his "lecture" explaining to me that, in Landa, gravity is twice that on Earth's. "That explains our peculiar mode of locomotion. Here, on Earth, we feel 2 times lighter," he said, laughing. Everyone clapped hands. Later on, I met Greg casually and asked him:

"Why is Yuri taking so much trouble to explain all this to me?"

"He is not explaining just for you, Jota. He explains to us all. Many things he told you were new for many of us. Not much for me since I am a navigator. But the medical ones were new to me! And, then, we will take our turn to teach the others".

Chapter 20

Procyon

In another "lecture" Yuri explained to the group that the great advance they had in communicating with other civilizations was the development of quantum computation many years in the past.

"Soon after our quantum computers became operational we began to receive some strange messages. They came from a location in the sky corresponding to the star the Earth astronomers know as Procyon. This beautiful and brilliant star is 11.5 light years away, both from Earth or Landa. The star Procyon is, in reality, a binary system consisting of the stars Procyon A and Procyon B. Procyon A is the main star, being more luminous and bigger than Procyon B. Procyon A is 7 times more luminous and 2 times bigger than the Sun. Procyon B, on the other hand, is 100 times smaller than the Sun and orbits Procyon A with a period of 49 yrs."

"One of our antennas began receiving a sort of binary signal that did not seem to be random. We found that these signals were being generated by electrons changing their spins, from UP to DOWN and vice-versa. From the way such signals arrived we believed that an answer was expected. We could decode the first sequence of signals. The emitter civilization was expecting an immediate answer, possibly, to calculate the signals' speed. We answered the request by emitting our signals according to their suggested coding. In a few seconds we received their answer to our signals. This indicated that the signal transmission was almost instantaneous. The civilization emitting the signals told us that they were located in a system of 3 planets orbiting a binary star system that corresponded to the position of the star Procyon."

"But how could you communicate with them since no signal can travel faster than light? A two-way communication would take 23 years," I said.

"Calm down, Jota, if you let me continue, very soon you will have the answer" Yuri said, smiling and checking the others' reactions.

"The signals' transmission is based upon a phenomenon that we have known since a long time ago and the Earth's physicists also known as "*quantum entanglement.*"

Very briefly, it works like this: it is possible to entangle 2 identical subatomic particles in such a way that if one of the particles changes its state, its pair changes its state instantly, without them "physically" interacting and despite they may be very distant to one another. And, I mean very distant. This will become clear with our case. Our scientists used electrons since electrons have spins either UP or DOWN which can translate into ON or OFF, 0 or 1 and, thus, this works like a binary code. As an example to illustrate this, suppose Peter and Mary live in different countries. Suppose, also, that Peter's electron is UP and Mary's electron is DOWN. Suppose, also, that they are entangled. Each time Peter moves his electron from UP to DOWN, Mary's electron will move from DOWN to UP. Peter and Mary are, now, communicating. Now, suppose Peter lives on Landa and Mary in the planets of Procyon. Each time Peter moves his electron, Mary's electron will move instantly. The Procyon civilization found that we had electrons entangled with some of their electrons. By trial and error, they began moving their electrons causing the electrons in our receivers in Landa to move in a complementary fashion. They were so smart that they could transform these electronic motions in signals that travelled instantly between Landa and Procyon. Gradually, we, in Landa, learned their electronic language and, then, their language proper."

"This, took many years but we, finally, began communicating with them. From this time on, our progress took a sharp turn. We began to receive a rush of information telling us how to improve our computers and receiving antennas in order to establish an operational and efficient line of communication. After this our scientific and technological advance was phenomenal. There came, in huge quantities, information in science, equipment projects, medical procedures, treatment and definitive cure for many diseases and a plethora of many other subjects. As a consequence, much of the knowledge we had accumulated from many and many years became obsolete. From this moment on we began to call this civilization by the name Procyans."

"However, from some period onward," Yuri continued, we were informed that the origin of the signals was the "second planet" and then, the flow of information began to arrive in an automatic fashion as if the source were a broadcasting station. They did not reckon our messages, did not answer any more our questions and did not ask for information regarding our planet. And it was, then, that the amount of information arriving to Landa became so large that our scientists and engineers could not process everything. The subjects were physics, mathematics, biology, geography, History of the Universe, cosmology, medicine, spirituality. Projects of equipments abounded; how to manage certain diseases; many manuals of a varied sort. We felt as if an encyclopedia had been opened and broadcasted into the space."

"What intrigued us still more was that the broadcasting from Procyon 2 let it clear that much information did not come directly from Procyon 2 itself. Rather, they had been retransmitted from other sources. We, then, began to rapidly organize our scientific, engineering, and technical medical institutions in order to process this huge inflow of information. At the same time our teams of specialists began expanding in the areas which had been receiving information from Procyon. In other areas, such as basic research we began decommissioning our laboratories in large scale. This was a very depressing situation since we have brilliant scientists whose minds do not possess practical attributes; instead, they were quite introspective. These scientists found themselves at a loss. We had to expand a new service of collecting, processing, organizing and distributing information. Much information arriving from Procyon was useful and lead to important venues. However, a lot of others were impractical, futile and downright nonsense."

"Can you exemplify some nonsense you have received?" I asked.

"Sure," said Yuri reading from a sheet: "how to rise walking fish, how to change flowers' colors, how to prevent birds from singing, how to make tortoises walk faster, do you want more, Jota?"

Feeling myself like an idiot, I looked down at the table and remained silent.

"Many important research facilities were transformed into mechanical and electronic shops. Brilliant scientists were relocated to desk functions."

"One thing that we did not understand: despite we were receiving thousands of plans for apparatuses, blueprints and a lot of imagery, there never came to us images of the Procyon 2 people, their cities, their facilities."

"Much information coming from Procyon 2 answered questions we had been pursuing for decades, such as how to extract energy from the vacuum, how to extract energy from nuclear fusion and others."

"What were the main advances you obtained from the information arriving from Procyon 2?" I asked Yuri with a questioning look to the others.

"Well, the information coming from Procyon 2 shook, in a positive sense, almost everything we knew. I will give an example," said Yuri, "in the medical area, in which information coming from Procyon 2 has upended our approach to spinal cord damage."

"As is well known, traumatic injury to the spinal cord is usually irreversible. Once an interruption occurs in the communication between the spinal cord nervous fibers, recovery is a remote possibility since the *proximal* (connected to brain) and *distal* (connected to members) segments cannot communicate any more with each other. It would be necessary to identify and to reconnect each one of thousands of individual proximal fibers to their distal pairs. In what concerns peripheral nerves this is often possible, since most fibers in a small nerve have approximate the same function and target tissue. Even so, since fibers with different informational traffic share the same nerve this reunion is usually complicated."

"Well, the solution for this problem has been sent to us from Procyon 2, despite we not knowing if this was a retransmission from yet another civilization."

Chapter 21

Spinal Cord Reconnection

Yuri went on: "The procedure is very complex to be explained thoroughly here. So, I will make a really crude simplification. Making an analogy with a camera sensor is useful. In order that a camera can translate an image from the real world, its sensor needs to have a minimum of pixels, where each pixel registers a tiny piece of the real image. The more pixels a sensor has, the sharper an image will be. Everyone who followed the evolution of digital photography remembers that the first camera sensors had few pixels and very crude images."

"In the same way that a photographic sensor can discriminate between small regions of the image, the electrical sensors developed in Procyon 2 can discriminate electrical active regions in a nerve or in spinal cord. And they do that with a high level of discrimination. Attaching such a sensor to the cut spinal cord of an experimental animal it was possible to detect signals coming from the stimulation of the motor cortex. In other words, if the animal decided to move its tail the sensor detected corresponding signals. The same thing happened connecting the sensor to the distal segment of the cut spinal cord. Pricking the tail, the sensor detected some signal. Animals, however have a problem: they don't talk."

"On the other hand, humans do talk. In Landa, we began a reverse engineering project of sorts, using the "recipe" sent to us from Procyon 2. We began using both Landian and Earthians that had suffered spinal cord trauma (yes, there are many of you people living on Landa, and more on that latter). We only employed those volunteers who had a complete transcordal lesion. We operated them and inserted, across the lesion, a wafer like implant consisting of 2 sensors of high definition."

"Now, consider a transcordal cut: one portion of the cord remains connected to the central nervous system (CNS). The other side of the cut remains connected to the periphery; for example, the members and all other regions of the body. The problem for the patient is that those two sides of the cut do not communicate any more. The cord segment connected to the CNS is called the *proximal segment* whereas the segment connected with the rest of the body is the *distal segment.* "

"Now, if you examine the segments, each one has a face in the cut region. So the face of the proximal segment looks directly to the face of the distal segment. Unfortunately, as I said, they cannot communicate anymore since they have, irremediably, been separated by the injury. Now, the Procyan "recipe", told us to glue, to each face, an implantable sensor. Then we have a *proximal sensor* and a *distal sensor*. These 2 sensors are physically connected forming a wafer like implant. What are the properties of this implant? First, each small group of neural fibers is glued and connected electrically to a given pixel in the proximal sensor. The same happens to the fibers of the distal segment: they are glued to a given pixel in the distal sensor."

"OK, Jota, I know what you are thinking about this "gluing"

process. Yes, that was a most complex procedure that took us some years of experimenting, even having the recipe from Procyon."

"The pixels on each of the sensors of the implant can be accessed remotely in such a way that each time an electrical nervous signal hits a given pixel the computers identify that pixel, in what sensor (proximal or distal). How this is done I can't tell you. Also, the computers can electrically connect any pixel on the proximal sensor to any pixel of the distal sensor. One more terminology and we are ready for the experiment: a nervous signal (which is an electrical wave called *action potential*) travels from the CNS to the periphery we say it is an *efferent signal*. When the signal travels from the periphery to the CNS it is called an *afferent signal*. Essentially, for our description purpose, efferent signals carry actions, say contract a muscle. On the other hand, afferent signals carry information, say a pinprick sensation. For this reason, most efferent signals are *motor* signals and most afferent signals are *sensory* signals."

"Also, Jota, before you interrupt me, let me tell you that there are many other signals, such as those involved with proprioception, that I cannot explain to you how they were handled in the procedure."

"Now, each pixel has a numerical code, like the lines and columns in an Excel spreadsheet. Each pixel has a code of 2 numbers, line and column. In the same way, the computers in Landa can identify a pixel by 2 numbers."

"Fast forward to action," said Yuri. "The patient, a tetraplegic (or quadriplegic), having the electronic wafer implanted in his or her ruptured spinal cord (this operation is done some months before), lies down comfortably. Let's use the index finger as an example. The doctor asks the patient to move the index finger. The patient can't move it (remember he is a tetra) but a pixel in his proximal sensor "blips." Say, it is the pixel (740,360). Now, the computers begin applying sequential pulses to the pixels on the distal sensor. Suddenly, the patient's finger contracts and the pixel (235,427) "blips." What happens next is fantastic! The computers connect the pixel (740,360) on the proximal sensor to the pixel (235,427) on the distal sensor. The patient is asked to move the indicator finger and ... the finger moves."

"Then we go to the sensory part. The same patient receives a pinprick on the index finger. Of course he feels nothing since his spinal cord has been cut. But, the computers get a blip in pixel (840,578) of the distal sensor. Now the computers begin firing pulses to the proximal sensor until the patient feels a pinprick in his finger. Say, this happened when the pixel (627, 1240) was stimulated. The computer now connects pixels (840, 578) on the distal sensor with pixels (627, 1240) on the proximal sensor. Again, the patient's finger is pinpricked and the patient ... shouts."

"However, this is super simplification of the entire procedure" said Yuri. "Each step required a long and persistent work. For example, just to glue the sensors to the cut cord segments took more than one-year continuous research with animals. Another simplification I did here was regarding proprioception which requires different neural sensors and, also, temperature. All this details had to be worked slowly and continuously. Another question was the implant itself. It turns out, I was later informed, that it is sort of biodegradable. But how the neural connections remain? Well, here entered molecular biology, stem cells, etc. At long term, it seems the nervous fibers could grow in such a way the implant wasn't necessary anymore."

"And what were the practical results?" I asked.

"Using this procedure, which requires many years for each patient we, in Landa, managed to reestablish movement and sensibility for many tens of paraplegics and tetraplegics. And many of these patients came from the Earth," Yuri concluded looking, firmly, into my eyes.

"Yes, "tetras" and "paras" from Earth came to Landa to be rehabilitated and are here, on Earth again, walking."

"What?" I said; "are you telling me that tetraplegics and paraplegics from my planet went to Landa and came back walking and live here?"

"Yes, this is exactly what I'm saying!"; he answered looking at everyone.

"But why nobody here knows about that?" I said, elevating my voice.

"Who said to you that nobody knows?" Yuri answered calmly and smiling.

Then, I remained silent, perceiving I had crossed some line and Yuri said, looking first at me and then to the others:

"Remember, Jota, that we are brothers. You have trusted us and we trust you". And, I nodded. Not having recovered entirely from the information overflow I had received, I asked Yuri if the scientific knowledge from Earth had in some way contributed to Landa.

"Yes, we have incorporated to our culture many things from Earth."

"The problem is that science on Earth is still in its infancy. The scientific method, the knowledge-based in evidence and not in beliefs is quite recent on Earth," he concluded.

"I don't agree; the scientific method is here from a long time!" I said, irritated.

"Calm down, Jota, let me finish my reasoning," Yuri said, smiling benevolently at me and at the others. "Look this way: the discovery of bacteria on Earth, in 1676, has less than 400 yrs, subatomic and quantum physics have less than 150 yrs. Antibiotics were discovered only in 1928 by Alexander Fleming, who discovered penicillin. One hundred and twenty years ago man didn't fly. General anesthesia was only discovered in 1846 by William Morton. I could give you more examples," he concluded.

Chapter 22

The Landians and the Brain

Some days later, after lunch, as usual, Yuri began talking about intelligence, brain development and related subjects, making some comparisons between Earthians and Landians. I believe this chapter is one of the most important to make the reader understand the gradual, dangerous and tragic circumstances in which I, Antonina and others became victims.

"According to the information coming from Procyon 2 we concluded that they, or their sources in the Universe, possess a deep understanding of the brain. A question which always has baffled us is this: it is generally established, in Earth, that the intelligence of the humans is the most developed among animal species. Let's compare man and cat. We know well that the cat, thanks to its olfaction, vision and vibrissae can see, sense and smell things we can't and can tackle situations that humans can't. Also, cats can explore the surroundings in ways humans cannot. Survival instinct appears also to be more developed in cats than man. But, the cat has its limitations. They haven't a superior language. Also, cats are here since millennia and, despite this, actual cats are not "better" as compared with the cats of Old Egypt. What we conclude from this?" asked Yuri to the audience.

I raised my hand and, since the others remained silent, I said:

"This might be due to the fact that their intelligence is stereotyped."

Yuri smiled and, without taking notice of my comment, continued:

"Let's take the gorilla. They have a somewhat more developed language, establish better defined relations between them and have a more complex social system than cats. And, having well developed hands, they are able to utilize crude tools such as a heavy stick with which they can break a coconut, for example. But, despite being here for millennia, they cannot use the same stick they break the coconuts with, as a weapon to crack an enemy's skull. So, they lack the insight to make the transition from tool to weapon. They use, since millennia, the same tactics to hunt, to make primitive shelters, to fight between them. Present gorillas do not show any technological improvement as compared to their ancient ancestors. And, they cannot make fire. The question of making fire goes far deeper that it appears. Making fire requires understanding what fire is. All animals know that fire is something that can burn them but that's it. And, fire to us Landians and to Earthians has no mystery. But, since no animal has dominated fire this means that Earthians and Landians have mental resources that no animal has," concluded Yuri.

"But maybe animals do not use fire since they eat food raw and, maybe they are minimalists," I suggested. This time the group began laughing loudly and Yuri clapped hands. "OK, Jota, this time you did it!"

"Then, in terms of certain abilities and intellectual development we can identify the aspects in which humans are "better" than animals," Yuri went on. "I mean, we can comprehend how do function intelligences inferior to ours by observing what those intelligences cannot perform and ours can. Now, for the point I want to arrive at: how would an intelligence "superior" to ours function? What those superior beings would be able to think, calculate, plan, and comprehend and that we can't? What kind of "fire "would they master that we wouldn't? This is a question that we discuss repeatedly in Landa and never arrive at a conclusion."

Then, one more time, I raised my hand and having Yuri nod and the group acquiesced, I went on:

"In my opinion, this is an absolute limitation. Let's consider a dog and his owner. From the dog's perspective his owner is a superior being. This doesn't deal with the dog's conveniences of having food or shelter. There are many evidences that dogs are absolutely faithful to their owners, irrespective of benefits. The dog, despite not entirely comprehending his owner, is aware of his immense intellectual superiority and obeys him without any questioning. From the dog's perspective his owner is a being infinitely powerful, wise, and generous. Therefore, from the dog's point of view, the owner is his master, his protector, his benefactor, his god."

At this moment I perceived certain restlessness in the group as if I were saying some unsettling information. As if I had touched a key point, a nerve. I felt I had been decommissioned as the court jester.

They looked to Yuri and to Antonina as if expecting some action from him. But, Yuri only raised his hand to others and nodded at me giving leave to continue. And, I went on:

"The dog, being in his master's presence feels complete, secure, protected. And, to finally address Yuri's question, I would say that if such superior beings were to come to Earth and they proved to be benevolent we would, spontaneously, be submissive to them. And, they would dominate us not by means of force or power. They would dominate us just because we would consider them to be our gods. They would dominate us by means of love."

All were silent and looked furtively at Yuri as if expecting some response from him. Yuri remained silent and looked down at the table. Then, he stood and said: "I think we all need a strong coffee!" and went to the kitchen to ask the assistants for it.

After coffee and juices we relaxed, each went to their container for some minutes. Then, we met again at the table. Yuri continued:

"Some experts in Landa say there is no answer to the question we are now discussing since we can't define what intelligence really is. One aspect that, clearly, distinguishes animals from humans, and by humans I include Earthians and Landians, is that animals do not increase their abilities with the passing of time. Bees build their hives the same way now as they did millions of years ago. The beavers build their dams the same way they did eons ago. I could give plenty of examples. All this leads us to conclude that the animal intelligence is stereotyped, as if programs are inserted in their brains. But Earthians and Landians evolve technologically and at a rate increasing rapidly. This is one of the biggest mysteries."

Chapter 23

Planetary Organization of Procyon

Yuri told us that, among the huge flow of information coming from the 2nd Procyon's planet, some messages began arriving saying: "Why you don't answer?"

Our answer: "To whom should we answer?"

Their response: "We are from the 3rd planet (of Procyon) and we are humans."

We asked: "And the others, who are they?"

The answer came a few days later: "The others are those from the 2nd planet, the executors of ideas, the creators and transmitters of knowledge. They are not humans and have no emotions."

"These messages made us very concerned," said Yuri. "What was the point of such broadcasting of knowledge? Particularly concerning was the information that "they are not humans and have no emotions.""

According to what Yuri explained us, on another day, the Landians' powerful telescopes could identify 3 planets around the binary Procyon A and B system. Yuri explained that Astronomy in Landa is very advanced as compared to Earth's. They have telescopes aboard mother-ships circling Landa (more about that later) and also on the dark side of Landa (more about the dark side later).

"The planetary system of Procyon needs some explanation," said Yuri:

"Remember that there are 2 stars, Procyon A and Procyon B. Procyon B is so small that it behaves like a planet in what concerns its orbit. The first orbit, closest to Procyon A (the gigantic main star), is that of the 1st Planet. The second orbit is that of the star Procyon B. The 3rd orbit is that of the 2nd Planet and the 4th orbit is that of the 3rd Planet. In this way, the 1st Planet orbits between Procyon A and Procyon B. The 1st Planet is at a very primitive life stage, being very hot, covered by immense forests, lakes, marshes, oceans. The beings there are very primitive (as informed from 2nd planet). In the 2nd Planet are those mysterious beings that are broadcasting information."

"But, it's about the 3rd Planet that we began getting informed more lately. The beings on the 3rd Planet," continued Yuri, "fall into 4 categories: the thinkers, the care-takers, the interlocutors and the spirits. The thinkers are a most curious type. They have the emotional development of children, while their brains are super developed, bordering geniuses. They cry, sleep and ask questions all the time. They can't take care of themselves and require the care-takers for that. Those are called "the mothers," most being women. The thinkers spend their time reading, studying and meditating/thinking. And, they do this when they are not sleeping or crying. They have a prodigious memory. Their brains do not mature with age and they remain naive. They are always open to new ideas and have no preconceived ideas. This complex social structure is maintained, logistically, by the 2nd Planet."

According to Yuri, naivety is one of the great virtues of a scientist.

"Also, in the 3rd Planet are the interlocutors or interpreters that are in permanent communication with the thinkers. The interlocutors receive, annotate and analyze questions and crude ideas from the thinkers. They also interchange ideas with the thinkers and try to answer their many questions. When ideas are "good" and questions "relevant" they send them to the 2nd Planet to be "processed."

"Can you give some examples?"

"Thinker question: "Does a photon travel with the light velocity?" one of the interlocutors has a good knowledge of Physics.

Interlocutor's answer: "yes."

Thinker question: "Then, for a photon, there is no time passage?"

Interlocutor's answer: "The time does not pass."

Thinker question: "Then, can a photon be in all places of the Universe at a given instant?"

Interlocutor's answer: "I don't know."

"When the answers are not given to the thinkers they get upset and, supposedly, stop thinking. Many of these questions are trivial and are promptly answered by the interlocutors. But, many are quite interesting and are sent to 2nd Planet to be processed."

"The idea we have from the 2nd Planet is that they work along different fronts. They serve as repository of information arriving from other civilizations and from the 3rd planet and from their own scientists. That knowledge suffers some form of classification and is used to their scientific advancement and to be broadcasted. But this is only a supposition."

"From our base, here on Earth, we have no direct access to the messages coming from the Procyon system. We receive part of them from Landa. We were told that in the 3rd Planet there inhabit what they call Spirits. It happens that about 12 years or so, from the moment we have established contact with Procyon's 2nd and 3rd Planets, a new form of message began arriving at Landa. We were informed that, from then on, the messages were using a conventional system, where radio waves were being carried by powerful lasers; in this way the messages were taking 12 years to travel from Procyon to Landa. They were not instantaneous any more. And they could carry a lot more of information. It was through these messages that we came to know about the Spirits on the 3rd Planet. Yuri explained that the Spirits are real beings but they lack a physical body. The Spirits live in special containers which are, in reality, waveguides. They receive energy from the Universe. But, not only energy. They exchange information with many sources in the Universe. Some of the interlocutors understand the Spirit's messages. However, the Spirits do not take messages from the interlocutors."

Yuri told us that the Landians presence in Earth has a twofold agenda.

"We came to Earth more than a hundred years ago, initially to explore the planet. From then on we began sending Landians here in a continuous program. There are, at present, about 5 million Landians here. They are divided into cells or kibbutzes. Each cell has a general program of activities such as ecology and has a specific program. The cells contain both Landians and Earthians as a general rule. Our cell here, in this farm, is not a typical one. It carries few people. Our cell is, essentially, a hub from where we distribute Landians arriving to Earth. It is an entry point for Landians. But, many Earthians travel to Landa, some exiting from our hub, as I will explain you later", said Yuri. "The specialty of our cell, here in the farm, is wood processing as you have seen". And Yuri looked at me.

"Our aim is to inhabit Earth in a large scale. However, we will not do this through force. We will just intensify, gradually, the coming of more of our brothers to here, as soon as the Earth has better living conditions for us: cooler and more oxygen."

I asked Yuri if they do not fear being exposed. "This is the least of our concerns," he answered. "One of the theories more discredited in Earth deals with UFOs and ETs."

"If you show the government agencies a reasonable proof of a being or craft of extraterrestrial origin they annotate everything carefully; say they will contact you. They never do that. If your proof is considered very good they say that they must retain the proof, they photograph the items and give you a receipt. And they take all items. You will never hear more of them, neither the materials you left with them. And, about the receipt? It got lost, unfortunately."

"Now, if your material and photographic evidence is excellent, unquestionable, they retain all evidences and disappear with you. On top of this we have teams of disinformation which fill the Internet with fake apparitions, captured ETs, 4th kind contacts, etc."

One afternoon Yuri began explaining to the group how Landians on Earth are organized. As usual, I was used as recipient pretext for those lectures.

"As I said, the Landians on Earth number about 5 million and organize in kibbutzes, a system employed since a long time, mainly in Israel. Each kibbutz has between 500 and 1000 members and they are specialized: technological, agricultural, factory, medical, and others. This kibbutz' organization has some similarities with the colonies in Landa, as we shall see. All kibbutzes generate profit, which reverts to the kibbutz itself. Our kibbutzes, here on Earth, have a rigorous organization, almost military, in what concerns discipline. The general rule is work and obedience. There is a hierarchy which is absolutely respected."

"Is this farm also a kibbutz of sorts?" I asked Yuri. "No, we are not a kibbutz. As I said, we are mainly a hub for reception of arriving Landians and an operations center/base, together with a commercial enterprise. But, despite not being a kibbutz we have, here, a military discipline and a hierarchy, however you don't notice, Jota!"

Chapter 24

Antonina and Me

In parallel to my "rites of passage" and Yuri's revelations, my relationship with Antonina was getting more intense and bilateral. An evidence of this was revealed to me when I asked Yuri if I could walk on the farm without the others' supervision. The reason was that I was curious to explore the many places and photograph them with the incredible Greg's camera, which I already felt as being mine. Yuri said that he, himself, had nothing against my solicitation but who should decide being not him.

"Ask Antonina, Jota. She is supervising you from now on," he said. I, then, asked Antonina, telling her about what Yuri had informed me. And, her answer was:

"After you have passed the tests, you may be seen as our brother and have a free transit on the farm's surface." What she meant by "farm's surface" was not all that clear to me, however.

"But remember that there are lines, and you should not cross them," she added smiling and messing with my hair. Since I had a chess match, a photo session and a car washing with Antonina, we were together during some periods almost every day. We walked together and talked about many subjects.

Much of those subjects were novelties to Antonina, like street crime in Brazil, life in the big cities, money issues, banks, payments, etc. She was extremely curious and revealed to have an almost childlike naivety on such subjects. From my part I was also curious to know about life in Landa, her planet. And, she delighted telling me stories from Landa, and seeing my surprised looks. And, I had an enormous desire to understand this woman: what did she like? If she loved someone and if she was capable of loving.

After some time in our walks, Antonina began holding my hand and pulling me to this or that location she wanted to show me. Some different stone, a small stream, a bird's nest, an ant hill, whatever. And, then, we began holding hands all the time in our walks. Initially, I thought *that this would signal to the others that I was, in effect, her property.* But, as it happens, I was wrong. I loved to stay in Antonina's company and I began to feel I was getting in love with her. But, I was cautious. My previous experiences with adorable women had told me to stay "defensive". According to my theory, these "fantastic" women chose their men, and it was just futile to make any advances.

And, importantly, it was always Antonina who invited me to the walks. To be exact, she did not quite *invite* me. She simply *told* me we would walk, we would have breakfast, we would play chess, and so on and on.

Joaquim

One day, Antonina said that I didn't need to lock the door of my container at night. She said the dome was absolutely safe, and if some emergency occurred it would be easier for the people to arouse me with the door unlocked. Of course, I took that it was forbidden to lock doors as of some internal rule.

I don't know if it was a coincidence but a few days after I began keeping my door unlocked, I woke with Antonina seated on my bedside and caressing my hair and my face. I looked at her, and she was smiling adorably. I then closed my eyes and smiled.

"Do you like it?" she asked me.

"Yes, I do like it..." but my throat tightened before I could say "very much". She sensed my emotion and then smiled, recomposed, and said:

"Jota, breakfast is ready, and today we will have a looong walk! I'm waiting for you at the table. Hurry up!" From that day on, every morning, Antonina would wake me exactly the same way. No progression, however, occurred in her caresses or her loving words, at least for some weeks.

In this respect, it must be said that I never, and I mean never, took the initiative of touching Antonina as a retribution for her caresses on me. I always remained passive, just showing I loved it. And, loving it, I was! I yearned for Antonina's caresses all night long! However, the reason for my passivity will become clear only later in my narrative. And, it also will become clear that I was right!

Parallel to that, a series of imperceptible things began to call my attention. The group seemed to be distancing from me, and there were no more communal breakfasts when the entire group was seated together. I got the impression that I was, now, some sort of Antonina's "property," and the others respected that.

To complicate a bit more my already confused feelings about Antonina and the group, I noticed that I was going through some mental changes. Surely, they were very subtle. Essentially, I was getting increasingly afraid of losing Antonina's affection, whatever it was. Well, at this point nothing different from what a man feels when he loves a woman.

But, this time, it was different from all the amorous situations I had been through.

At the same time, I desired Antonina as a woman, another part of me, and this part was strange to me, needed just to be at her side, to hold her hand, to be caressed by her, to be talked to by her. This new need transited, in my mind, in parallel to my "normal" desire for her.

Also, in addition to that strange need, the presence of Antonina gave me an intense feeling of power and security. In her presence, I felt I was complete. My conflicts disappeared completely while my whole being felt it had a well-defined and only task: stay with Antonina. Curiously, those feelings did not compete with each other. Actually, they seemed to be complementary.

From my perspective, Antonina radiated a huge mental power, precision and certainty in her movements, gestures, actions and words. And, I simply absorbed this and felt completely invulnerable while at her company. This feeling was not, however, totally strange to me. I forced my memory to remember where this feeling came from. Finally, I perceived that when I was a little child, the presence of my mother gave me peace, security, completeness and power. Being on my mother's lap, I felt powerful, inexpugnable and complete. This passed but I could still remember that feeling.

One day, it occurred to me to ask Antonina how she wrote. She said they did not quite write things and all communication was done by talking or through many devices.

"But I know how to write in your language, Jota!" she remarked. I asked her to write something for me and gave her a pencil and a sheet of paper. She then wrote: `"Jota, I like you so much!"`

Exactly, as it is written here: font Courier New, size 18. The precision of the writing was incredible, as if done by a printer. I was absolutely awed and, seeing my surprise, she asked: "Is it wrong, Jota?"

"No, Antonina, it isn't wrong. It's just "too correct."

I then explained to her that we didn't write this way unless on a computer or typewriter.

"What is a typewriter?" she asked, and I promised I would show her one if I found one, of course. For a few minutes after this I began to think she was a robot. But, no! She wept, she laughed, her body was perfect, her mouth sensual, perfect teeth. And Antonina had a scent, a marvelous, delicious scent, the scent of a female. No way could she be a robot!

One day, I was walking alone, since Antonina had some tasks with the group and I crossed with Frederico. I have already mentioned that Fred was a bit cool with me, bordering on arrogance or contempt. But, seeing me alone, Fred was friendly and asked me if I was enjoying the walk and if I needed anything in informatics, his area. I answered that I was OK and used my cell phone to communicate daily with my brother and my friends.

It was then that he looked at my eyes and then at the ground and said: "Watch out for her!"

I did not ask him with whom I had to watch for and why. Then, I thanked him for his advice, and we parted. But, during my walk, Fred's message continued to resonate in my mind. After some thought, I suspected that he might just be jealous of my walkings with Antonina. Maybe he was in love with her and was finding some way to separate us. Otherwise, I couldn't imagine how Antonina could harm me. Of course, I could suffer from loving her. Actually, I was already suffering! Only much later I could understand that Fred's advice concerned Antonina all right. But, for reasons I could never imagine.

Chapter 25
Antonina's Gifts

On a certain morning, a few days after my brief encounter with Fred, Antonina and I were walking through the farm, both of us competing for the use of Greg's camera. Antonina had got hooked on photography, and I was at fault for that. The day was gorgeous, a bit cold and a light breeze blew from the south. The air was extremely clear. She wore her customary dark glasses and shorts, sneakers with socks and a small shirt.

Antonina knew all the places on the farm and had a "list" of places that she either liked or felt might impress me. She knew all of the numerous trails crossing the farm in all sorts of ways. This morning, as we walked, she was holding my hand firmly and either pulling me forward, backward or towards her in accordance with her ever-changing interests. Indeed, so strongly she held my hand that a vague and fleeting impression came to my mind that she might be restraining me.

But, since she let go of my hand from time to time, this impression vanished. But, only to come back some moments later when I thought *that maybe, just maybe, she was conditioning me to be restrained, not now, of course, but at some time in the future.* Also, it came to me a feeling that I was part of some sort of process since I could vaguely discern some method in the dealings of the group with me. Suddenly, I was taken out of my reverie as Antonina let go of my hand, looked into my eyes and embraced me affectionately.

"Are you OK, Jota?" she said with an adorable smile. Those dark thoughts evanesced, immediately, from my mind.

We went through a trail as yet unknown to me and crossed a stream while drinking, from it, cool and delicious water. There was a plenitude of different birds around and Antonina and I fought all the time for the possession of Greg's camera. She pushed and pulled me all the time, messed with my hair and poked me in the back.

After a further walk we came to a place where stood a flat stone having the right height to be seated on. We took a seat on it, and Antonina told me that this was one of her preferred places. She said she used to sit on that stone in order to meditate. We remained silent, I waiting for Antonina to say something. Finally, she said that she would give me a present and opened her backpack, taking from it a small bag made of a fabric that resembled silk. Antonina placed the bag onto the stone between us. As she opened the bag I could see other bags inside, made of a different material.

"Take one of these, Jota and open it carefully," she said. The small bag I took in my hands had a cord closing it. Loosening the thread, I removed, carefully, a stone having the shape of an octahedron, which is a solid having 8 equal faces and one of the 5 solids of Plato. The stone I was holding in my hands was the size of a small plum, was translucent and had a clear pinky tonality. It was an uncut stone. Antonina asked me what would be that stone. Trying to buy some time to think, I asked her where she had obtained the stone. "I found this stone in Ganymede along our travel to Earth, "she answered.

"Well, Ganymede, one of the Galilean Jupiter's moons, I know well. I even used to observe it at the telescope, along with its sister moons, Io, Europa and Callisto, all named after gods or goddesses. Galileo first saw them in 1610" I said, still avoiding to name the stone.

"OK, Jota thanks for the astronomical lecture, but what stone is it after all? If you don't name it correctly, I'll put it back in the bag," she said with a menacing smile. I had to think rapidly. I knew that the basic structure of diamonds is the octahedron and this is the reason for their extreme hardness.

"Well, if this were a pink diamond, you would not be giving it to me," I said, smiling at her. "You got it, Jota. It is a pink diamond, and I'm giving it to you!" she said, messing with my hair.

"But wait, there are others" she said, letting me see the bag contents.

I replaced the diamond into its bag and deposited the bag, carefully, onto the flat stone, praying a big bird would not take it for food. Then, Antonina handed me another small bag. Inside, there was a larger stone. It was slightly elongated, had 6 irregular facets and would fit tightly inside a Cebion tube. Like the diamond, it was an uncut stone.

"Emerald?" I asked; "Also, from Ganymede?"

"No, this Emerald came from Africa; I exchanged it with a Masai warrior in Kenya," she said.

"And what you gave in exchange?" I asked. "Oh, yes, I remember now. I gave him my iPhone".

"Those natives are each time more demanding. Some time ago, you could get that same stone in exchange for a cheap vanity mirror!"

The third stone was inside a bigger bag and was irregular, as I felt holding the bag. "Now, open this one," she said. I opened the bag, and what I saw were two quite different stones "glued" together. However, the one that immediately caught my attention was that translucent stone, blood-red, but lighter than blood. It had the shape of a hexagonal prism, quite regular. Like the others, this one was uncut, the ridges being somewhat badly defined. It was about 4 cm high by 3 cm wide. Its red color was vibrant.

"It can't be a ruby!" I said. "It is a ruby and is yours," she said.

"And where did you find this one?" I asked.

"This one came from Tanzania, Africa," she said.

"And that other one glued to the ruby, what is it?" I asked.

"The other is the most valuable of these; it is a tanzanite. But do not separate them since they lose their value."

"And how much did they cost you?"

"This, here, was very expensive indeed. It cost me the life of a loved one," she answered, lowering her eyes.

Chapter 26

Scorpion Hunting

One evening, after dinner, Antonina informs me: "Tonight we are going to hunt." As I mentioned, Antonina never asked me if I would like this or that activity. She always *informed* me what I would do, together with her. And I loved it for two reasons: First, because it was Antonina, and second because I hate to chose.

"And, who are going to hunt?" I asked.

"You and me, of course. Why the question?"

"And what are we going to hunt?"

"Scorpions," she said. Antonina, then, explained that the living scorpions are taken to Landa to be extracted from their venom.

"From their venom are isolated many substances useful in Medicine." Antonina went on to explain that, from Earth's venomous animals, can be extracted numerous substances of medical importance.

"For example, in some spiders' venom there is a substance that produces an erection in men," she said, giving me a malicious smile.

"This effect was found, accidentally, in some men who were bitten by those spiders and experienced a persistent and painful erection. These substances are called *erectins* and were initially candidates for drugs helping in erectile dysfunction. However, with the discovery of the sildenafil and tadalafil that you people know, generically, as "Viagras," the erectins fell into oblivion. However, there are many groups, both here and in Landa, studying their properties", she concluded.

Despite I knew all that, I feigned surprise. However, she didn't buy my surprised look and "attacked" me with playful and painful pokes. "You made me waste my knowledge on you; what a shame!" and, with that uttering, she messed my hair.

After this initial waste of time, according to Antonina, she asked me to put on some boots high up to my knee. How did they know my size? I couldn't guess. My boots were made of the same material as hers: the same camouflaged fabric used in the dome's tarpaulin. She had, in her backpack, in addition to the regular items, an empty bag and some flashlights. She explained to me that two of them were ultraviolet (UV) light. Also, I was going to wear a headlight.

"In due time, you'll see what the UV light serves for," she said, "And bring your pink diamond."

Thus equipped, we left the dome into the dark night. Antonina explained that there was a local they had prepared to create a nice hiding place for scorpions. Despite a very dark night, Antonina navigated across trails and thick bushes as if she was in daylight. Her light was off, and I followed in her heels, my headlight illuminating her feet. The night was warm, and the Eucalyptus' scent pervaded the air. After we walked across a few different trails for half an hour, we arrived at a small clearing. A pile of old boards, loose stones and some garbage were strewn across the place.

"Now, take care, Jota. There may be snakes around here!"

Using a long piece of wood, Antonina lifted one large board, throwing it aside.

"Shine your UV light over there," she said, indicating the space below the board. As soon as I illuminated the place there appeared 20 "luminous" scorpions.

Antonina began, calmly, collecting them with a long metallic arm having a claw at its end. The claw could be closed by a mechanism from the handle. Then, she threw them, one or two at a time, into a large bag that was hanging from a branch. Having depleted the site of all scorpions, Antonina lifted a big rotten board, and another group of scorpions lit up. We repeated the procedure two more times until the bag was so heavy that its supporting branch was at the point of breaking. She closed the bag's mouth with a cord and grabbed the sac from its bottom, using both arms and placing it on the ground.

We were to carry the bag among the two of us, suspending it across a heavy and strong stick. I asked Antonina if the scorpions might not bite through the bag's fabric and she said this was impossible as she would me explain later. Before our trip back to the dome, we sat on a flat stone.

Antonina took from her backpack a big thermos and two cups and said I should drink coffee to give me energy and to stand the decreasing temperature. It was a delicious and strong coffee laced with cognac. Then, Antonina told me to hold my pink diamond in my open hand and asked me: "Jota, what do diamonds and scorpions have in common?"

"Sorry, I don't quite get your point," I answered, trying to avoid another embarrassment.

"OK, throw your UV light upon the diamond," she said. As I did it the stone lighted with a strong and beautiful green light.

"This is what diamonds and scorpions have in common: they both are fluorescent."

Our trip back to the dome was not easy for me. In addition to our backpacks we had now the task of carrying, between us, about 30 kilograms' worth of scorpions. The stick with the bag hanging to its middle was supported on our shoulders. The first 10 minutes went OK. Then, my shoulder began to hurt terribly. Changing my shoulder alleviated briefly, but then my legs began to complain.

There was no escape. I had to ask Antonina for a rest. That humiliating situation occurred two times, and we, finally, got to the dome. I asked Antonina if I could retire and take some pain reliever for my shoulders. I took a hot bath, and having put on only my pajama trousers, lay down in my bed, reading and waiting for the pain to go away. Half an hour later, I heard a knock at my door and, in opening it, I saw Antonina smiling at me. She wore a long and beautiful robe and, clearly, had taken a bath since her hair was wet and from her emanated a delicious scent of bathing soaps, shampoos and other bath things. She was barefoot and was carrying a box of medical emergency type.

"Can I come in?" she asked. I nodded, smiling, and she came in, closing the door behind her.

"How's your shoulder?" she asked, taking off her robe and placing it on the chair back.

I said it was hurting, but I had taken an aspirin. Since I was shirtless, she saw my shoulder right away.

"What a mess! I'm feeling so bad about it. Poor Jota! But we are going to put an end to your suffering".

Hearing those consoling words, I hoped she wouldn't kill me like the cowboys (in the films) do to their horses when they break a leg. She asked me to sit at the bedside and took from her first care "unit" what seemed to be a lotion within a strange-looking flask. Then, standing in front of me, she sprayed a little lotion onto both my shoulders and began massaging them delicately, just spreading the substance.

After this, she gave me a pill and asked me to swallow it. Then, she lowered the light on the dimmer knob and said I should lie down in the bed. As I did according to her "instructions," she knelt on the floor, just beside the bed and told me to relax. I closed my eyes. Antonina, then, began caressing my hair and my face, just the way she had been doing every morning lately.

The idea passed, briefly, to my mind that she was petting me. But, this time, she began singing in a marvelous voice some songs I'd never listened to. And, in a strange language. Her hands were so delicate, and the movements so certain that I began feeling such warmness and wellness I had never experienced. This feeling was in a crescendo, and I wondered when and where it would stop. But, then, I passed away. When I opened my eyes, it was morning and Antonina was seated at my bedside, caressing my hair and my face as if nothing different had occurred.

Chapter 27

An Expert Examines my Precious Stones.

Some days after the scorpion's episode I got a message from my brother saying I should come down to sign some important documents. My brother was 7 years older than me and took care of all family businesses, which means mine and his. And, this, he did much better than I could possibly do. This gave me the tranquility I needed to explore other areas of science, which satisfied my incessant curiosity for nature.

I told Yuri about my need to be away from the farm for some days and he had nothing against this and, on the contrary, encouraged me to spend some days with my brother. Then, I asked Antonina permission to leave the farm, which she granted. Of course, I would bring with me my treasure: the diamond, the emerald and the ruby-tanzanite.

I should have made it clear before that my brother, despite being an engineer, had been investing in the financial market with such expertise (and luck) that, in a few years, he could accumulate a small fortune. In this way, despite him and me sharing the same house and living a calm and modest life, we had a financial status that allowed us each to pursue our ways without permanent financial worries.

By sharing the same house, according to my brother, we could cut many unnecessary expenses and also help each other run the house. My brother was an obstinate bachelor and said he already had his "share of women."

After running through the documents and bureaucracy I told my brother about the gift I had received from Antonina, showing the stones to him.

"Ah, when I think you have had your share of women, you come down with this new lady," and, saying this, he laughed happily.

It must be said that my brother had many influent friends in the financial market. This included investments in gold and other precious metals, jewels, luxury watches and ... precious stones. He got curious about my new acquisitions and said he would call an old friend of his to take a look at the stones since I would stay home for 15 more days.

Next morning, just after breakfast, he said we would receive a visit from a friend, a precious stones broker/dealer. His name was Peter Andropoulos. Despite his name, Peter was an American citizen having also Brazilian citizenship. Peter spent his time between Brazil and the US, more specifically between São Paulo City and New York City. And, yes, Peter was Greek by birth and, not strangely, very skillful in business.

Not long after my brother told me of his arrival, Peter arrived, driving a nondescript old car. He was about 50, tall, very agreeable and extrovert, with a strong Greek accent. We soon were seated at the table and were served, by our cook, Maria, with fresh coffee, liquors, mineral water and orange juice.

"Well, Luiz, what do we have here today?" he asked my brother, laughing amiably. My brother nodded at me, and I brought to the table the whole lot in its original package, as Antonina had first presented to me: the 3 bags, each one with its corresponding stone.

Even before opening the bags, Peter widened his eyes and asked: "What kind of material is this? Can I feel it?"

"Of course!" my brother answered. Very calm, apparently no curious whatsoever regarding the contents of the bags, Peter analyzed the texture and color, sniffed at them, brushed his fingers on the material, then brushed the fingers together. He said he had never seen such packing for stones.

Then, Peter replaced the bags on the table and told me: "Jota, let's see what is inside."

I opened the first bag, where the ruby was partially included in the larger stone. The rock glued to the ruby was translucent, bluish in color but having violet tones and hues. Its shape was irregular. Peter took the stone in his hands and fingered all faces and ridges. Then, he took, from his pocket, a high power lens and examined, carefully, all sides of the stone. From another pocket, he took a flashlight and examined the stone from all angles and light incidences.

Then, taking from yet another pocket a laser pen, he said we should avert our eyes since the laser was too powerful. He pointed the laser to all parts of the stone.

Finally, still holding the stone, he said: "The red stone is, naturally, a ruby; otherwise, you wouldn't have called me here," he said laughing, "but what intrigues me more is this other transparent rock. I won't weigh it since the two rocks are glued together."

And Peter went on: "For the entire stone, just as it is, I can give you 500 thousand USD, no questions asked, no proof of origin. Of course you found it at your friend's farm, isn't it, Jota?" he said smiling at me. I made a vague, meaningless movement of my head.

"However, what really intrigues me is the rock to which the ruby is attached". I didn't mention it was a tanzanite taking for sure he would know it.

And, probably, he knew it was a tanzanite and, counting on our supposed ignorance chose not to mention it. And, Peter went on "I will be frank with you since I am an old friend of Luiz. This ruby, along with the attached rock, can be worth much more at an auction in New York. But I would have to regularize the stone, you see? And this costs money. But let's see the other stones now. I got curious!"

Then, I opened the bag with the uncut emerald, the one Antonina had exchanged with an iPhone. I handed the emerald to Peter. Before even examining it, he placed it back on the table and took a deep breath. He stood, walked briefly across the room, drank a cup of coffee and then drank a glass of orange juice and asked for one more liquor.

Then, he sat down at the table and looked at both of us and finally said: "Luiz, I have known you for a long time. Please, tell me: is there any dirty play in all this?"

My brother answered: "Look, I know Jota since he was born and took him in my lap so many times. It was only then that he has soiled me."

Calmer, after a generous dose of liquor, Peter breathed deeply and said: "I've never seen an uncut emerald this big and, yes, I've seen many emeralds."

In the face of Peter's reaction, I got a bit afraid of showing him the pink diamond. But I had no time to think about it before Peter extended his open palm and asked to examine the third bag. I had no alternative but to remove the "pinky" from the bag and place it on the table before him.

Surprisingly, Peter did not take the stone right away in his hand but just took a deep breath as if regaining some energy and looked at it.

"The first test is not definitive; I just want to see if it is harder than glass. I only need an old glass or bottle." I went to the kitchen and asked Maria to get me an old bottle. She looked suspiciously at me but got one.

"An empty wine bottle doesn't serve much anymore," I said, handing the bottle to Peter.

"For me, it serves all right," he replied, laughing. Saying this, he said to us: "don't you people worry, if it is a diamond, no harm done."

Finally, he ran the diamond along the bottle's surface. A high-pitched squeak filled the room, and Maria came running from the kitchen.

"Everything OK?" she asked. I nodded. Peter showed us a deep scratch upon the glass.

"Well, the basic #1 test was passed. It may be a diamond, all right. But, other stones do this."

Just after Peter's last words, Maria entered the room to take the coffee machine, but Peter asked her to take only the tumbler and leave the rest with the hot plate base, which was turned on. Peter placed the hot plate in the table center and touched briefly the plate, retrieving, immediately, his finger and blowing forcefully on it.

"Hot, it is!" he exclaimed, laughing. Then Peter, carefully, grabbed the diamond, holding it only from one of its extremities and touched the opposite side of the stone to the hot plate. Immediately, he put the stone back on the table, blowing furiously at his fingers. He sat at the table, breathing rapidly and blowing at his half-burnt fingers again.

Then, he closed his eyes as if regaining his thoughts. "The diamonds are known to conduct heat five times better than copper, which is one of the best heat conductors known," he finally said, looking ever more suspiciously at us and taking a good gulp of liquor. Then, he took from his bag a small scale the size of a cigarette pack. He placed the diamond on the balance plate:

"42 grams," he told us, closing his eyes again as if trying to recompose. Taking a calculator, he showed us the number 210 and said:

"Those are the beast's carats! And think that the famous Taylor-Burton stone had "only" 68 carats!"

Then, he sighed deeply and asked my brother for a cold orange juice. He looked at us for some seconds and, taking the stone from the table, blew at it with the mouth full open as if cleaning the lenses of a pair of glasses. Then, he blew again.

"My god, it doesn't keep the least bit of moisture on it! It conducts heat incredibly fast!" My brother and I felt that Peter was getting more and more perturbed as if trying to maneuver either a verdict or a buying proposal. Or, even, an educated withdrawal.

Following these performances, Peter took a powerful lens from one of his numerous pockets and began examining the "pinky" from all angles with the help of a small flashlight. He, then, grabbed the powerful UV laser pen from the table and asked my brother to turn off the room lights and close the curtains since he needed a dark environment.

At this moment, Maria entered the room to bring more coffee and a tumbler of orange juice. Luiz said calmly to her: "It's OK, Maria, you can come in, and we are just doing some tests." Maria left the tray on the table, looked at all of us and stepped rapidly out of the room, crossing her face and chest.

Peter then asked us to get farther from the table since there might be dangerous reflections from the laser. "I will throw the laser onto the stone in only a few seconds."

Saying this he first shone the laser onto the white towel that covered the table center. A very strong and beautiful bluish spot appeared upon the towel, so strong indeed that it made us avert our look. Then, Peter began moving the laser spot towards the diamond. Suddenly, the room lighted with a strong and marvelous green light.

The stone threw green rays so brilliant that it was impossible to look directly at them. Everything lasted a few seconds. When my brother turned on the lights, we saw Maria kneeling at the doorway with their hands in prayer.

"It's OK, Maria!"; my brother went to her and pulled her up to her feet gently.

"Well, my friends, this little guy got 210 carats and has an excellent overall quality. I can't define a money value for it right now. This isn't something that falls onto my lap every day, you know. Can I photograph the stones?"

"Oh, sure, take your time," we answered at the same time. Peter took a reticulate white plate as a size reference and photographed the stones, one at a time, over the plate, using a sophisticated camera and a special light fixture attached to it.

"In the meantime I recommend that you keep these stones carefully, but not in the safe if you got one. Try to hide each one in a different place and ... write down the location, please!" and he laughed, now, more relaxed.

"For my part I promise I will contact the right guys and will keep you informed. And ah ... Jota, I suppose you want to sell them, am I correct?" Luiz looked at me, and I said we could sell the ruby for the time being.

"Very good! And now I'll keep moving if you allow me."

Saying this, he took his utensils from the table replaced them in their different locations of his suit, raised, and dried his face with a big and colorful handkerchief.

"Sorry, I really have to go home, take a bath and process everything I saw here. And keep your mouths quite shut, believe me."

As soon as Peter left, my brother looked firmly at me: "Jota, I believe you owe me some explanations."

"Well, it is just as I said: I really got them as a present from the people of the farm where I'm spending some weeks."

"I can't tell you the diamond's proceedings because you wouldn't believe me. But the emerald came from Kenya and was exchanged for an iPhone, with a Masai warrior; the ruby came from Tanzania and cost a life." I'm not sure my brother bought my story, but he appeared calmer.

Chapter 28

Strange Talks with Antonina

About a month after leaving the farm, I returned sometime before lunch hour, having informed them of my arrival. The farm had experienced many changes during my absence. At the general parking area, close to the main dome, some cars and vans were there, parked along the many elongated clearings among the Eucalyptus trees. When I entered the dome, Antonina was alone at the table, expecting me. She said we would be having a special lunch to commemorate my return. Her eyes were wet and, upon seeing me, she embraced me long and kissed my forehead.

"I was afraid you wouldn't return," and her voice was choked with emotion.

And she followed me to my container, helping me carry my few bags. Then, she entered my room and closed the door behind her.

"Don't leave me, Jota," she said as she began to sob. "Promise me you will not leave me anymore!" And, recomposing herself, she suddenly left my container with a firm stride, leaving open the door after her.

As I said, I began noting many changes in the farm proper but also in our group. I remember that in the first few weeks after my encounter with them and even after Yuri came, the group's disposition seemed more or less of telling me of their life, their doings, and their aims. In other words, they seemed to be genuinely happy with my presence. But, after my one month leave and return, the group gave me the general impression that they were done with me. Their meetings weren't more at the table in the dome. It was quite clear they had frequent meetings in places I had no idea.

Also, sometimes, one or another of their race, unknown to me, was seen inside the dome at some activity, such as repairs or in talks with Yuri. The kitchen, now, had two girls working full time, one Brazilian and the other Landian. Breakfast was now available at the table only from 7 to 9. Anyone in need of food outside this period would go to the kitchen, which was now expanded and closed by new partitions. The homeliness of the place had vanished.

My only function in the farm seemed to me, now, related to Antonina. Even Greg seemed a bit distant. All of them seemed concerned with things I had no idea about but seemed to be part of something bigger and in constant change. Changes were in the air and, of that, I was sure.

When the lunch hour finally came on the day of my return, that initial atmosphere returned, Yuri appeared from nowhere and hugged me, saying he was glad of my return.

"Some people here were very concerned you would not return," he said loudly and laughing. But all this hit me as an adult receiving a boy who came back from a camp. At the lunch, Yuri made some general remarks, but I perceived that the important things were said and discussed elsewhere. As soon as the lunch was over, everyone departed to different places. Only Antonina and I remained and had one more dessert, followed by coffee.

Antonina seemed restless and invited me for a walk. Soon, we were upon a nice trail. However, Antonina remained quiet. Finally, she said:

"Jota, many things are in change here. Very important things. Soon, we have news, as Yuri will announce and I'm not sure they will be all good news," and looking at me, she continued:

"But do not be alarmed by the changes you see here. Remember, I will not change, and I will be with you. But, for this, for my being with you, it is necessary that you remain here with me because I can't leave this place. I must stay with my people. I'm not used to life on Earth, I would not survive outside and, most important, I don't want to return to Landa, and even if I wanted, I would be prosecuted and forced to leave the comfort of the colonies. And, as you know, it is very cold in Landa."

Then, as we continued to walk, she changed her mood, took my hand firmly in hers, and began pulling me and laughing like a child.

"I have so many things to show you so that I can see your surprised look, Jota. Come, come, she said, pulling me."

Then, she became serious and looked at me, menacingly:

"You know what? You have been a very naughty boy," and, saying this, she embraced me, kissed my forehead, and messed with my hair.

Then, she pulled me along and began to run. I, soon, got tired while she seemed to be making no effort. Seeing a flat stone, she stopped running and pulled me down onto the stone. And we lay there, I panting, and she silent, still holding my hand.

Then, the subject of my leaving the farm came up again to her, and she said; "Don't you ever go away from me, Jota, promise to me!"

"But what do you want me for?" I asked her, as we were still lying down on that stone. It was getting a bit cold, and the wind blew from the south, balancing the tops of the tall Eucalyptus trees.

And, after some thought, she said: "I need you so I can take care of you and protect you. And since it is my task to take care of and protect you, I can't let you stay alone."

"But, what would you gain by taking care of me?" I asked.

"What would I gain? What would I gain? I gain happiness, that's what I gain, Jota! Just to see you happy makes me even happier. Just to see your face when I caress you makes me infinitely happy! And, I need to be happy, Jota, I need so much to be happy!" and her eyes got wet again. "Don't you need to be happy, Jota?"

"But, I'm a man and I need to be with a woman," I said hesitantly.

"And am I not a woman? Am I not a woman?" She yelled, weeping, and lowered her pants and panties.

"Look, Jota, am I not a woman? Look at me, look!" and pulling strongly my hand made me touch her genitals.

"Am I not? Am I not?" she said loudly while my hand was forced to touch her body. She, then, let go of my hand. "Feel me, Jota, feel if I'm not a woman!" and, then, I moved my hand, all by myself, and touched her genitals. I was paralyzed by surprise, desire, and ... fear.

"Don't you think I'm naive, Jota!" she said, recomposing. "I know what your needs are. I can see right before my eyes," pointing to a slight bulge between my legs.

"But, don't you understand that there are other things that must come before that?" she said, poking me between my legs.

"We are not animals, Jota, we are superior beings. Do you think I don't need sex? I do need Jota, perhaps even more than you do."

"Don't you understand that there are different forms of love? There is a love that delivers, a love that receives, a love that protects. We belong to different races, Jota. For each of us, sex and love are different things. Even here, on Earth, certain forms of love do not allow for sex, and some forms of sex do not deal with love. You know all this, Jota!"

"Also, Jota, you must understand that we are not equal and, for this reason, our love for each other cannot be equal."

"What is going on between us, Jota, is an entirely new experience for me. I have never had someone to protect! I have never felt necessary and protective for someone. Being able to give love and certifying that my love is being delivered is entirely new to me, Jota!"

As Antonina was saying these words, we were still laying down on that flat stone. And Antonina began caressing my hair and face, as usual. And, I slept.

Suddenly, I opened my eyes, doubtful where I was. I looked up and saw a starry sky, an aggressively starred sky. Turning, I saw, vaguely, Antonina half seated, looking at me. It was very dark. And it was cold despite the stone still being warm.

"It's getting late, Jota, we must hurry home, they may be already looking for us!"

We stood up, and the cold air of the night suddenly got to me. Antonina then grabbed my hand and we hurried at a fast pace towards home. As we had left in clear day I hadn't brought a flashlight. All I could see, and badly at that, was Antonina's shadow pulling me. She did not vacillate and navigated through the trail as if she were walking along a sidewalk at noon. I will never forget that night, her glorious body pulling me along the pitch-black night, the cold air, the stars, Antonina's scent, and her hard breathing.

No, my macho ego wasn't hurt the least bit. Actually, I felt as if I was only a little boy being pulled by some deity, by some goddess. I simply let my body follow that wonderful woman. I didn't even feel my legs, I forgot about the cold, the darkness, my exhaustion. And, I felt cozy, protected, powerful, and complete.

We, finally, got home. No one was expecting us; the table with the dinner had already been cleared. Antonina pulled me to the kitchen, where the two servant girls got us some food and beer.

That same night, I dreamt of Antonina. We were lying on a large bed in a strange place. We both were naked. Then, Antonina embraced me, pressing her warm body against me. I felt her warmth, her breasts against my chest, her nipples hard. But I felt no desire, and it wasn't a wet dream. What I felt was relief, protection, love. I felt I was complete. As if what Antonina had said to me on that stone was real.

Chapter 29

Antonina Talks about Intelligence

After a few days from my return to the farm, Antonina apparently forgot our talks of a few days before and didn't talk more about the possibility of me leaving her. That small crisis of hers seemed to be a thing of the past.

As I have mentioned a few times, my walks with Antonina have been constant. I, from my part, took advantage of this activity in order to know her better and to get information on her life here and in Landa. I must have mentioned, in passing, that doubt had crossed my mind regarding the reasons for the Landians' migration to Earth.

At this point, it had become clear to me that a continuous process of immigration was plainly in progress, having begun many decades in the past. Seeing that my somewhat complicated relation with Antonina was getting stronger, I saw an opportunity to question her regarding the real motives of the Landian's arrival here. Another doubt that persisted in my mind was regarding Antonina's intelligence.

But why do I want to digress on this subject at this point of my narrative?

As it will become clear later, all my tribulations stemmed from a wide gap between Antonina's and my intelligences. And that is the reason

I have touched this subject and that I will come back to it a few times in the future.

Antonina had already provided me with some pieces of evidence that her intelligence was way above mine. But, just having won the chess match did not say much since I knew I was a poor player. Of course, there were subtle instances in which I perceived I was inferior to her regarding "brain power". I decided, then, to ask her if she thought I was an "intelligent person".

At the time of the present conversation, we were at some distance from the dome at a small clearing of the Eucalyptus forest. Antonina had brought, in her backpack, a big piece of tarpaulin that she opened in the grassy ground. Also, she had brought coffee, mineral water, orange juice and ... brandy. It was morning and the air had, still, some reminiscence of the night.

"What you mean by intelligence, Jota?" she answered after some reflection. She had bitten the bait.

"Well, there are many types of intelligence," I answered. "Nobody can deny that there were and are music geniuses: Mozart, Beethoven, Paganini, and recent ones such as Lang Lang at the piano. In art, no question there were geniuses like Dali, Picasso, daVinci. Also, in the abstract intelligence department, Newton, Einstein, and so many others," I concluded.

As this talk went on, I began to see that my goal would not be reached easily along this venue. I wanted to fathom her degree of intelligence and I was not getting any closer to that information. Then, I decided on a straighter approach.

"Antonina, do you think your intelligence surpasses mine?"

"Oh, yes, sure it does, but the question is not that. The question is: how much my intelligence surpasses yours?"

I answered that I had already perceived to be a great difference between our "intelligences" as if such quantification could be easily done. And I suggested that the comparison should be performed in the same type of intelligence at a time. I could have a greater spatial intelligence than she (I knew I didn't). She listened carefully my considerations.

"Yes, we would have to compare our bits of intelligence along a same type, no question. But chess playing is a reasonable test."

"Yes, but chess can be learned, and being a genius does not necessarily mean a chess champion. However, normally, chess champions are geniuses," I answered.

I remembered that all chess champions had high IQs, having been tested by psychologists all over the world. Garry Kasparov had 190, Magnus Carlsen 190, Bobby Fischer 187, Judith Polgár 170 and ... Jota 110", I finished.

We both laughed. And I followed with my arguments: "but you see that all this chess-oriented intelligence maybe just a great brain's processing power. This was evidenced by the famous match between the computer Deep Blue and Kasparov. Deep Blue won". Antonina heard my points with an indefinite expression and a rudiment of a smile in a corner of her mouth. Then, she said:

"I agree with most of your considerations, Jota. But, numerical calculations would be an intelligence index for you?"

"Without question, this is a good index," I answered.

"Then, test me Jota. But I must warn you that my knowledge of Earthian mathematics is still rudimentary."

"OK, do you know what a square root is?" I asked

"Sure, the square root of A is the number B that, multiplied by itself, returns A," she said.

"Then, what is the square root of 144?"

"It's 12, of course. Is this your test?"

I took my cell phone from the backpack and opened the Scientific Calculator App. Then, with some pomp:

"OK, madam Antonina, please tell me what is the square root of 65,245" and, looking at the screen, I saw the result: 255.431008

"Well, hummm, it is 255431008.Now, let me put the decimal point: 255.431008," she finally answered, after, say, 10 seconds total time.

"Correct! You are incredible!" I said

But, I wasn't to be humiliated so easily, and made the worst comment of my life:

"Well, OK, but this calculation you did any small calculator can do" I remarked.

"You are right, Jota, even a small calculator can do it." Then, she asked me to lend her my cell phone.

"Now, Jota, tell me what the square root of this number is," showing the screen to me: 555555?

"How can I know? You've got my phone!" and, still pointing the phone screen at me, returned my phone and said: 745.35556.

"Now, check if I'm correct. "Sure enough, she was correct.

"Now, Jota, it looks like this tiny calculator of yours is smarter than you," and seeing my pathetic look, she began poking me all over my body.

I threw myself down at the tarpaulin and, assuming a defense position, said, "I surrender, I surrender."

Not the least calmed down by my submission, she went down over my body and pinned my back to the tarpaulin, holding my arms down.

She, then, pressed her body against me, and our faces almost touched. I was completely immobilized. Then, I closed my eyes, waiting for a possible kiss in my lips. What a pretension! I opened my eyes, and she was staring angrily at me.

"Confess you lost, confess you have lost!" she repeated.

"I lost, I lost," I said, and she released me as she lay beside me. And then, she began caressing my face, saying, "Poor boy, poor boy, I love you so much! Don't leave me, Jota. If you leave me, how am I going to protect you? Tell me how?"

"What do you want to protect me from? This is my planet, and I should be the one protecting you," I said, looking at her lovely eyes.

Antonina didn't say anything. Then, she began sobbing.

Chapter 30

Antonina's IQ

After my humiliating defeat on numerical calculations, we walked along another trail looking for a place to spread the tarpaulin, as there were some persistent mosquitoes around our first camping ground. Soon, we found another clearing, and the ground was sand-covered. Numerous birds of all types were pecking actively at the ground insects. More birds, less mosquitoes. Antonina spread the tarpaulin, and we seated in order to have some coffee and ice water from another thermos. After we had rested some minutes, it came to my mind the talk with Yuri when he presented the report about me, including my IQ measured by the helmet.

"Tell me, Antonina, based upon the intelligence scale measured by Yuri's helmet what would be your IQ?" I asked, trying to appear casual. Antonina, apparently caught unguarded by my sudden question, remained silent for some seconds.

"You really want to know, Jota?"

"Yes, I really want to know the truth, painful as it may be."

"Well, as measured by the helmet, my IQ falls between 1300 and 1500. As a matter of fact, my IQ is the highest in the group, if this may interest you. But, remember, the helmet measures the processing power of the brain. As you know, intelligence is much more complex than processing power. Remember that your cell phone calculator is smarter than you!" she concluded, laughing.

"You are right, I said, but processing power is a good index of intelligence," I remarked.

"But, not always Jota. As you also know, some *"idiot savants"* can calculate the number Pi with a hundred decimals and make other complex mathematical operations. In addition to being able to memorize an entire telephone book,"

And we laughed and had more coffee. She hugged me and, messing my hair, said:

"But I still want to show you what my intelligence is capable of. Remember when you mentioned the ability of humans to dominate fire? And we all asked what would be the "fire" of a more advanced species? One day, we will talk about that, but not now that we are enjoying this moment."

Little did I know that the extraordinary intelligence of Antonina was not limited to just making number calculations. I never suspected that her superior intellect could interfere powerfully with the very essence of my own mind. With nefarious results.

"Tell me, Antonina, what is the expertise of your family members?"

"Well, Yuri is a doctor, as you know, Fred is an electronic engineer and communications, Greg is the navigator, and Marco is an ecologist."

"And, Antonina would be?"

"Ah, yes, I'm a physicist."

"And what is your area in Physics?"

"Nuclear fusion, lasers, quantum computation, and some other subjects. Do you want to hire me?"

What such a marvelous creature may want with a primitive being like me? A genius female, strikingly beautiful. Oh, yes she says she wants to protect me; that's her maternal instinct, probably Those, were my thoughts.

It was only sometime later that I discovered the real reason. And it was something I could never have imagined.

Chapter 31

Landian's Brain

Later, on that same day, after lunch, Antonina said she would bring me something. The lunch table had been cleared, and only the coffee machine was there. But for me, Antonina, and the kitchen girls the dome was empty. Antonina brought, a few minutes later, a beautiful book, a type flight manual, and the same metallic sheets as all other Landian books. She said it was an Atlas of Anatomy.

In the figure showing the general layout of a Landian brain, I perceived a very interesting characteristic. It is known that the human brain presents *gyri* and *sulci* in its external aspect. The initial impression one gets is that there is a great surface that needs to be accommodated into a relatively small volume, which is the cranial cavity. This impression corresponds to the reality. The brain cortex is where it is believed to be located the so called superior nervous activity that characterizes the human species and makes man the most intelligent species on Earth.

However, this "brain power" needs more surface area than that would be available on a uniform surface. For this purpose, the brain's surface folds into the gyri or circumvolutions. That allows more area with the same volume. It is known, also, that the more evolved intellectually a species is, the greater the number of such gyri.

What I saw in the picture of a Landian brain was an increase in the number of gyri and sulci (plurals of gyrus and sulcus). For each gyrus of a human brain, there were 10 gyri or more in the Landian brain. We know also that in the *neocortex* of humans are located the superior functions of the brain, such as language, learning abilities, memory, symbolic thought, and others.

These functions characterize humans as compared to other species. For example, the neural structures that allow humans to produce and control fire, create and use tools and weapons, paint symbols, have spirituality and other aspects are supposed to be located in the neocortex. The more animal functions are located deeper.

Antonina, then, showed me the *corpus callosum* of the Landian brain.

"This is a structure that connects the two hemispheres of the brain and exists, too, in the Earthians," she said.

"But, differently from the Earthians, the corpus callosum of Landians is more developed and carries out other functions, such as sophisticated processing of the information traffic between the hemispheres. We know very well the differences between Earthian and Landian brains since in Landa live thousands of Earth humans. And, of course, they die, and then we can study their brains".

In order to discuss here the particularities distinguishing the Landian brain from the Earthian's it would be necessary tens of additional pages and an enormous dose of reader's patience. It suffices to say that, in all brain structures that I saw in the book, the Landian brain was different from Earthian's.

I, then, asked Antonina what, I supposed, would be a tricky question:

"How can you prove that your intelligence is superior to mine?"

"The use of spoken or written language is a good index," she said.

"For example, I have no problem speaking, reading, writing, and understanding Earthians in Earth languages. But Earthians can't use our language since they can't grasp its essence. In the same way, a cat won't be able to read or speak the Earthian language."

Chapter 32

The Symbolic Thought

The present chapter summarizes one of my talks with Antonina after we had somewhat gotten to some understanding regarding her complicated relationship with me. So, this time, we just talked as two scientists or so, discussing. We were seated at the dome table, after lunch had been cleared and all people left for their tasks. I began to imagine what Antonina's task would be in their group in Earth. And what role I had in it if I had any.

But Antonina interrupted my thoughts and began lecturing me:

"Primitive men got bipedal, developed arms and hands, decreased teeth size and power. They began to increase their brain capacity and the dexterity in their arms and hands and fingers. But, at the same time, large carnivores began to perceive that there was an animal whose meat tasted good, and this animal had an added advantage for them: it was so easy to catch, subdue, and eat. This animal was a very bad runner, a very bad tree climber, and did not swim at all. And, it could not defend himself since he had small teeth and mouth and he had no claws. This animal was the primitive man."

"Surely, he had some abilities: he could make tools and could construct shelters because, having acquired a bipedal stance, his hands were now free for other nobler tasks. But these same hands were so bad for fighting since they had no claws. They couldn't do anything against large canines and powerful jaws and claws. And then, these intermediate man "projects" began to be annihilated by the less intelligent carnivores."

"However, little by little (centuries and centuries), man learned to make better tools and he, then, perceived that some tools could be used as weapons. At this period, a different man surged: surely, still a bad runner, a bad fighter, a bad tree climber, a bad swimmer, his clawless hands could not wound enemies. But, now, these same hands had acquired artificial "claws" like stone axes, stone knives so sharp they could make deep gashes in his enemies, spears that could be thrown at a distance, and heavy sticks that could crack heads. And that, made a huge of a difference. This made up for his body weaknesses. Also, he learned to hunt in groups, like wolves, hyenas, and savage dogs, which had been done millions of years before. And the use of weapons and group fighting or hunting made a huge difference."

"Now, man was superior to animals both in intelligence and fighting power. However, new problems emerged. A new and powerful enemy surged: other, better fighting men."

"This might explain why there is a gap between animals and modern men. The intermediaries were eliminated by modern man."

Then, Antonina abruptly changed the subject of her "lecture" since she saw I was not getting exactly her point. She remembered having promised me she would talk about the *symbolic thought*. And, she went on:

"Jota, now hear this. Let's take the symbolic thought as our case. This capacity to understand and create symbols is the hallmark of Earthian's and Landian's intelligence. This distinguishes them from other species. Apparently, animals do not possess symbolic thought," said Antonina

"But, after all, what is this symbolic thought of which you refer to so often?" I asked

"The answer to your question, Jota, the Landians have been studying for decades. There isn't a precise definition, however. Let's take examples using high-level language. If you read the word "banana" you immediately visualize this fruit in your mind. The word banana is the symbol for the real thing and the word makes the connection with the physical banana, which you can eat. In this way, if by reading the word banana, you visualize the real thing, then you have symbolic thought. Thus, the high-level language (spoken or written) would be the hallmark of symbolic thought."

My comment on this:

"OK, but then the picture of a banana would not also be a symbol for the real banana like the word banana was? And, a monkey could well understand this symbol despite not grasping the meaning of the word 'banana', "I said provocatively.

"Yes, here, you have a point, Jota. But tell me: have you ever seen a monkey drawing a banana when he wants one?" I was speechless.

And Antonina went on:

"The dawn of humans was characterized, essentially, by the use of symbols, maybe even earlier than tools or language. The pre-humans, before *Homo sapiens,* drew symbols in the cave walls. The drawing of an antelope, for example, is a symbol associated with the real animal. But, the primitive men went even further: picturing the antelope pierced by an arrow, the cavemen meant an action, and an action he desired to happen. And, going even further, the wounded antelope might mean a premonition of a successful hunt. Not counting that it might make things easier for that future hunt."

"It seems that future thinking does not exist in animals. Even some African tribes were related as incapable of future thoughts despite this being to be confirmed. In some drawings of primitive men, there are also evidences of *magical thinking,* one of the hallmarks of humans."

"What do you mean by this magical thinking?" I asked a bit irritated.

"As I said, Jota, in the drawing of the arrowed antelope, it might be that the painter believed that by drawing this or just desiring it, the hunt could be successful. That would be the magical thinking, Jota. Magical thinking is present in children as we all know, but disappears gradually as we grow up."

"One curious aspect of Landians, despite their intellectual superiority to Earthians, is that they preserve some magical thinking in adulthood. Landians are generally more spiritual than Earthians in many respects. For example, we believe in afterlife, at least during some period. Well, this is not quite new for humans too. But we, Landians, take this belief more seriously: when our loved ones die, we provide them with some essential items such as food, clothes, wine, and even utensils for their hobbies. The same did the old Egyptians with their kings."

"Then, you see, Jota, it may be a very simple thing to draw an antelope pierced by an arrow. A child does that. But no animal can draw things. Many can interpret symbols, even some complex ones. A monkey presses a button with a picture of a banana when he wants one. But he doesn't draw a banana when he wants one, despite having extremely delicate hands and fingers. You see? Do you see the limitation? That's the same limitation the gorilla has with the stick. He breaks the coconut with it but can't extend the reasoning to use the stick as a weapon."

"OK, you gave me a nice lecture, Antonina. But then what is the relation of your telling me of this symbolic thought of yours and what you call the superior intelligence (pronounced with some sarcasm) of Landians?" I questioned.

"I expected you to ask me this, Jota. Actually, I was certain that you would ask. Don't you understand that there is a huge gap between our intelligences? How many times do I need to tell you this? The answer to your question is very simple: in the same way animals do not comprehend the symbols of Earthian humans, also Earthian humans will not comprehend the symbols of Landian humans, our symbolic thought!" and, as if this were not enough, she went on.

"Look, Jota, remember how humans dominated the fire? And how does this require them to comprehend what the fire was? Now, Jota, someday I will tell you what the Landians' "fire" is."

"Yuri told you of our system of colonies in Landa, didn't he? He said that the colonies were specialized. But he didn't tell you everything, Jota. I, Antonina, will tell you two more things, and I trust that you will not propagate this."

"In Landa, we have colonies composed of Earthian humans or *Homo sapiens sapiens* as you know them. They live with the same comfort as the Landians and are free."

"And we also have 2 colonies of a species you may know of: *Homo neanderthalensis*, with 5 thousand specimens in total. Those are semi-free, however. They reproduce between themselves, build their shelters, but we provide them with raw materials and food."

"I want you to understand, Jota that we are not here for playing, we have purpose, and we work hard. The Earth is a laboratory for us and a precious laboratory at that!"

Chapter 33

Fabiana

The next day, I woke with Antonina at the side of my bed, caressing my hair and looking at me with maternal eyes.

"Come have breakfast, Jota, I will be very busy all day. You are going to be by yourself!"

Arriving at the table, I was surprised to see not only Antonina but also Yury, Greg and a beautiful girl of darker skin and black hair. Upon my arrival, Yuri greeted me amiably: "Take a seat and have your breakfast, Jota. I would like to introduce you to Fabiana, and she is Brazilian like you!"

They were at different stages of breakfasting and talking animatedly. Only Antonina was expecting me to begin breakfast.

"Fabiana has been recently transferred from another kibbutz in Rio Grande do Sul (RGS, a State of Brazil). She is going to be mentored by Isobel," said Yuri.

I learned that Fabiana was originally from the Brazilian state of Bahia, and she was 25. She was tall and lean, with green eyes, a really beautiful girl. She was a Forestry Engineer and would be working in the bamboo plantation. After breakfast, all departed, and I went back to my container to read. Later, I would walk and spend the day all by myself without the "protection" of Antonina.

Some days later, after breakfast with Antonina and having been released to myself (Antonina would be busy all day), I went for a walk, taking Greg's camera as usual. The day was sunny but a bit cool. After a few turns across a well-known trail, I saw Fabiana sitting alone on a flat stone, bathing in the sun. Approaching, I greeted her; she smiled and said she remembered me. However, I saw she had been weeping and used a tissue to dry her eyes. I asked her what the matter was and if I could be of some help. She answered that she was sad since she had to move from her previous kibbutz in a hurry.

"I worked there for more than a year!" she said.

"Why had you to leave the kibbutz in a hurry?"

"I had a problem with my mentor, and she is a "stranger", (meaning a Landian) called Sulamita."

"I will end up getting used," she said

"Getting used to working with Isobel?" I asked

"No, I will accustom to be without her," she said and began weeping again.

"To whom are you referring to?" I asked, offering her some cold orange juice.

"Without Sulamita," she answered and began sobbing.

"Look, calm down, and tell me what happened. Here, we are all willing to help you! I'll talk to Yuri about your problem," I said.

Calming down, Fabiana explained to me that Sulamita had been her mentor in the RGS kibbutz.

"In the beginning, she treated me quite well and paid me for my work. I could leave from time to time to visit my mother in Bahia and bring her the money I had earned in the kibbutz. I didn't need the money in the kibbutz since, there, I had everything I needed. They gave me clothes, a cell phone, and even a few jewels."

"Then, my mother passed away, and I began staying all the time in the kibbutz. My life was very good there, the work light, many hours off, a room with an exclusive bath, and my own TV. There were many Brazilians there, men and women, from many states of Brazil and many, many "strangers" (I don't know if she knew they were from Landa) that either didn't speak Brazilian or did it with strong accents."

Seeing that Fabiana had calmed down after releasing some words with me, I decided to go a bit deeper.

"And, what was your problem with Sulamita?

Fabiana seemed to think and sighed. Then she said:

"I disobeyed Sulamita and yelled at her. Sulamita then slapped my face. I got out of control and tried to pull her hair. But she moved, and my nail scratched his face, drawing blood. And, then, I was fired."

I began to feel that my presence was good for Fabiana since she was getting things out of her chest. But, saying this, Fabiana began to weep and, this time, sobbing. I offered her more orange juice and this seemed to calm her again. *What she needs is to talk her problem out*, I thought.

"But, if you have a job here, why so much suffering, and what is the reason for your sorrow?"

I wasn't prepared for her answer:

"What is my sorrow, what is my sorrow? It's that I love Sulamita, I need her, I suffer being away from her, that's my sorrow, "she said, sobbing.

That answer took me off guard.

"Fabiana, sorry, I didn't understand. Tell me, do you like women?" I asked this in a low and respectful voice.

Then, she laughed and dried her tears.

"No, no, nothing of the sort! I love men, all right. I even had a boyfriend at Bahia. No, it's different; it's something I can't understand. What I do understand is that I need Sulamita, and I need her badly. It hurts down here, and hurts a lot" and she touched her chest.

Then, suddenly, she looked at the time on her cell phone and said:

"I have to go now, thanks for your help, I feel lighter now, and I had to talk! I'll give you my cell number, and we talk more. Thanks for now."

We exchanged phone numbers and she went away, running. And, she wasn't weeping anymore!

I returned to the dome and had lunch and dinner alone, at the big table. Only the two kitchen servants were around. Then I went to my container, bathed and lay down to think.

I couldn't figure out what was Fabiana's drama and possibly not even herself could. However, slowly, I began to connect some points. What sort of feeling was that: certainly, it was not love between man and woman. Do my feelings for Antonina resemble the suffering of Fabiana? What happened between them? What sort of suffering is that? That hurts down inside the chest? Then, I slept.

I woke in the morning, and Antonina was at the bedside, caressing my hair and my face and looking at me with a smile. And, I began to weep.

Chapter 34

Life in Landa (Part 1)

"What happened, Jota, why you cry?" She kissed me in the head and messed with my hair.

"Let's have our breakfast, Jota, she said. Today, we are going to walk". Then, she left my container. When I got to the table, Antonina was alone, having everyone departed to their tasks on the farm. After breakfast, we left the dome into a sunny day. Antonina wore a short, sneakers and socks, a blue cap and the usual dark glasses.

As was her costume, she took a new trail to show me. We walked holding hands and she seemed anxious to show me something. This meant I was being pulled. After we had walked about 40 minutes at a fast stride we got to a glade where a large and flat stone formed the main accident. The stone had the right elevation to be seated on (as many other stones on the farm). Antonina took from her heavy backpack a thermos with coffee and 2 plastic glasses. We sat on the stone and drank coffee with cookies.

"I'm going to tell you, Jota, why many of our race are leaving Landa." This was one of my mysteries.

"Landa, despite the intense cold, has many positive points as a place to live: there aren't any of the great problems that plague Earth: such as famine, wars, diseases, crime.

"Landa's society is well organized; there are no countries, only one state. The habitable area is huge. As Yuri told you, we live in the Landa's half, eternally directed at the Sun. Of those 4 billion square km we inhabit only the area directly below the Sun where the temperature has acceptable levels."

"Our population is about 100 million, and, in this way, territory abounds. There are no oceans in Landa. Most of Landa is unexplored. In the half which is turned away from the Sun there is eternal darkness, ice and unknown territory. Only special flying crafts and tractors dare enter this region. In Landa's folklore, it is said that strange creatures inhabit there."

"In Landa, people live in colonies, which have a semi-military organization. Each colony has between 200 and 1000 members. The colonies have a council formed by up to 20 members, rotated each 2 years (Earthian yrs.) by voting. The council has absolute authority. The colonies aim at self-sufficiency but, frequently, change products between them. As you were told, the colonies are specialized, such as agricultural, technological, health oriented, etc. There is no private property, everything is communal and belongs to the corresponding colony. Each family lives in houses, not shared with other members of the colony. The houses must be kept in perfect order by the resident family. Everyone has quotas of food and expendables and the quotas are generous, but unnecessary expenditure is severely punished. Gluttony is condemned. Health problems are taken care of, old people and the unfit are treated with respect and affection. No one suffers with the cold or famine. No one is forced to live in a colony and follow its strict rules. But, living in a colony is a privilege that has to be continually renovated and paid for with work."

"From what you tell me, Landa is a "paradise lost!" I said.

"Now, to the drawbacks" said Antonina", ignoring my comment.

"Landa's society is extremely rigorous in customs. Marriage is indissoluble. If one of the couple dies, the mourning period is variable and depends on marriage duration and age of the widow or widower. There is a complicate formula that takes these parameters into account. During the mourning period all affective relations are forbidden. And, this period can get very long. Well, Jota, this is just one of the many problems"

"Work is a sacred activity. Everyone needs to work for the benefit of the colony. A lazy person is considered as a parasite and denounced by other members. The "parasite" is then evaluated by a board, and submitted to a readaptation process. In case he or she is considered difficult, the parasite is sent either to a readaptation colony or downright expelled from the colony. There are rigorous schedules for waking up, eating and going to bed. TV is only allowed as an efficient form of education, despite there being schools, absolutely obligatory. There are no recreational TV programs. Everything you do is watched and controlled. As an example, every evening after dinner, a 15 minutes TV program is shown where all challenges and conquests of the day are presented. The watching is compulsory and each TV set sports a frontal camera feeding the central office of colony with the images of the watching members. Once a month there is a meeting whose presence is obligatory and in which all challenges of the month are discussed and where the council board is always present. Joy and laughter are seen as bad behavior and excessive laughter is considered foolishness. Leisure is seen as a form of wrong behavior: the general atmosphere resembles that of an Earthian monastery. If all this were not enough, each colony member is obliged to watch other members, warn them if an inappropriate behavior is detected and, finally, denounce the "criminal" to the board. Sex for pleasure is considered inappropriate being subject to penalties. Only procreation sex is allowed."

"How is this "sex thing" supervised?" I asked, provocatively.

"Well, Jota, don't you know that sex has its characteristic noises? And that there are neighbors with good ears? And that there are, in Landa, excellent recording devices?"

"Music, dance, painting and all art are deplored officially since they are considered as futile".

Hearing this I remembered the extreme joyousness of the Landians here in the farm, especially, Antonina. Here, they are extremely extrovert, funny, playful, euphoric.

"Hypocrisy is a norm since all these rules are watched continually by the colony members, what creates an atmosphere of permanent discomfort, falseness and insecurity."

"If you do everything by the letter, don't laugh, don't have fun, don't make pleasurable sex, etc, etc, then you don't have problems. And, no one has privileges over others."

"The general result of this rules and benefits is that everyone has plenty of health care, plenty of food, plenty of education for the youth, plenty of thermal comfort. But the life loses meaning, all days are identical. Having things is forbidden and everything belongs to the colony. Food, clothing, cleaning products are obtained in the local markets. All items are controlled"

"Each member, at specified days of week, goes to the local market and gets everything he/she needs. But, there are quotas. All items are carefully recorded in the member's spreadsheet".

Chapter 35

Life in Landa (Part 2)

"In Landa clothing is Spartan. There are no nice clothes and all them are just necessary and not more. Clothes are divided into levels, in accordance with the roughness of their use. For example: Boots level 1, 2 or 3. Coats level 1, 2 and 3. The levels refer to degree of temperature, working conditions, etc. Let's suppose that your boot level 1 gets damaged. You take it to the market and exchange it for either a new one or a refurbished one, depending on your luck. But, if your boot level 1 gets "damaged" every month a tick in your spreadsheet is done."

"No one suffers from cold, hunger, lack of clothes or any other problem for that matter. Discontentment is something you have to keep for yourself. Never tell even your best "friend" that you are discontent, since it is considered a serious fault, and your "friend" will comment with others. If your discontentment gets known by many you are in trouble".

"And, what are the penalties for those "terrible crimes"? I asked, sarcastically, Antonina.

"The penalties in Landa are proportional to the gravity of the faults. The most severe are expelling from the colony and death. There are no long term prisons in Landa. Prison is inverted: the condemned can't enter the colonies any more. In other words, he or she is imprisoned outside. And, in Landa, "outside" is terrible."

"Despite all being accustomed to these rules since infancy, life in Landa is simply an exercise in survival. What makes things even worse is the knowledge that many of the rigid rules are, simply, unnecessary. However, the counselors, generally old people, fear that costume and rules relaxation may lead to anarchy and lewdness."

"And, what about the discontents, those that do not submit to the rules? What happens to them?" I asked

"They are free to live elsewhere, since it abounds territory in Landa"

"And, these discontents, are they many?"

"Oh, yes there are a lot of people that don't accept the rules. These, along with those expelled, live in alternative colonies, separated by the regular colonies by a wide exclusion zone. In the alternative colonies there are no rules whatsoever. Singing, dancing, drinking, smoking and pleasurable sex are allowed. There is no need to work, there are no obligations"

"And, going alternate, is it a nice move?" I asked

"Well, like everything in life there are good and bad points. Remember that Landa is cold. I lived some time in Siberia and Siberia is hot compared to Landa. In the regular colonies there are heating systems very efficient and available to all. As a matter of fact, heating is something not regulated in the colonies. You can set your home temperature to any point, even turn it to a sauna" and, at this, Antonina laughed: the energy centrals get energy from the magma and from nuclear fusion reactors, where the fuel is ... water"

"However, outside the regular colonies there is no heating. In the clandestine colonies where live those expelled or discontent, the heating is very poor and obtained by burning the few mosses or by making huge holes into the ground to be closer to the magma. Living close to a magma hole is an alternative quite dangerous due to the geysers expelling hot water mixed with lava. The clandestine have no provision of food, clothes and all the commodities provided for the regular colonies. They fish in the lakes and grab mosses. And, they have their own laws. The sentences are quite severe, death being a regular one."

"But about 200 yrs. (Earthian) ago some Landians went to reconnaissance missions about the solar system and found Earth; a planet that was warm, sunny, free, no rules for conduct, free pleasures, drink, sex, sloth and gluttony. And, returning to Landa, reported of a paradise called Earth. Truth must be said that in this paradise, you could die of hunger, could get easily killed, could get sick and you could suffer. But, if you didn't die you could ...live!"

Chapter 36

Migration Earth to Landa

It must be said that, despite my previous comments suggesting the contrary, we continued to have some meetings with Yuri. In one of these meetings, at the dome's central table, I asked of Yuri, if the continuous arrival of Landians to Earth did not decrease Landa's population.

"Yes, Jota, the migration from Landa to Earth certainly decreases Landians's population, but does not decrease much Landa's population"; he concluded with a smile and a look at the others.

"And, I think I have mentioned that there is continuous flow of Earthians to Landa. The mother-ships returning to Landa carry many Earthians."

"But what sort of Earthians want to go to Landa?" I asked Yuri

"You have employed the correct word, Jota, when saying "want" to go to Landa."

"We never forced Earthians to go to Landa. Many times we convince them". And, he laughed, looking at the others.

"In the same way there are discontents Landians, many Earthians want to leave Earth, seeking for a better life elsewhere. And, they are really many, I guarantee."

"Can you focus more on that, Yuri?" I asked

"As you well know, Jota, we have bases in many parts of the Earth. But, not all of our bases are in regions so nice as Brazilian southeast or north. As you also know, there are countries ruled by totalitarian governments, where the citizens live in terrible conditions. And to make things even worse, in many of these countries people cannot get out. Do I need to mention their names?"

"Oh, no, please don't, I know of these places very well!" I answered, laughing.

"And we have bases in these countries too, Jota. Our bases there are even more disguised and are continuously receiving people that want to run to liberty. Actually the only purpose of our bases in these "nice" countries is to function as an exit route for people who want to run".

"But where to?" I asked

"To any place where there exists liberty, Jota, simple as that"

"Of course, we do a selection. Our extensive data base allows us to identify those people with criminal past and those are excluded. There are many good scientists living in totalitarian countries that want "just to leave" no matter to where"

"A very important part, despite not numerically large, of our "passengers" to Landa are those paraplegics and tetraplegics that are seeking for a rehabilitation by the method I described to you, and which has been sent to us from the second planet of Procyon. You are going to watch the leaving of them to Landa and also, from the same craft, the arrival of those previously para and tetra, coming from Landa and, now, walking."

"And what are general rules for migration to Landa?" I asked Yuri.

"All Earthians wishing to go to Landa need to stay there for a minimum of 5 years, after which they can choose to remain there or return to Earth. The sick people, including the tetras and paras require 5 accompanying healthy Earthians that will provide care for the patients during the travel. The patients, once rehabilitated, however, don't need to obey the 5-year permanence rule."

"What we have found, though, is that few of the Earthians going to Landa want to return to Earth."

"Many medical doctors from Earth also want to go to Landa, for different reasons: some to run from totalitarian regimes, some to learn new forms of Medicine. We have found that many of these doctors prove to be excellent colleagues, especially the Africans and Indians who have remarkable qualities in diagnosis."

Chapter 37

The Earthians in Landa

Some days later, Yuri told us, during a lunch with all, that a mother-ship, from Landa, would arrive soon to Earth. And, many first comers Landians, as well as a few returning Earthians would disembark here in the farm. The farm routine had already changed appreciably due to this scheduled arrival. Apart from the family now being busier, many new "strangers" (Landians) were seen in the surroundings of our dome quite busy. In our dome, however, little had changed.

Antonina, also was very busy with frequent meetings (not in the dome). I saw her many times driving different cars and leaving the farm along with other strangers. But, what seemed to be her main business, "protecting me", continued at the same rhythm. Our walks together, holding hands, did not stop and, actually, intensified. Almost all mornings I was woken with Antonina at my bedside, caressing me and smiling, affectionately, at me. Antonina had been increasingly attentive and protective to me, despite her now busier schedule.

In one of the mornings that we went walking, Antonina took me to the trail that passed at the side of the cave's door. The two only times I have been there were in my visit to the cave, wearing the "infamous" helmet and also on the way to my terrible proof. Now, I couldn't even recognize the place. Many trucks were parked there and people were moving into an out of the cave, whose door was wide open. Some smaller trucks were even entering the cave, apparently loaded. According to Antonina, those were the preparations for the arrival of the mother-ship. What mother-ship was that? I had no idea. I only heard it was coming.

Antonina told me that about 500 new-comers Landians were to disembark on the farm. They were definitive migrants. Many came weak, some sick and all needed an adaptation period before they could be sent to their definitive destination kibbutz in many countries on Earth.

In this particular walk, we followed a new trail. I observed that Antonina, by the way he moved, seemed to be carrying a quite heavy backpack. I offered to carry it for her, exchanging for mine which looked way lighter than hers. She accepted with a strange smile. Taking her backpack and even before placing it on my back I perceived to having done a foolish act of machismo. Her pack was so heavy I couldn't even place it onto my back and, for this, Antonina had to help me. We walked some 50 min more and I was really tired. My legs were not obeying my central commands any more.

Finally, we came to a brook, whose banks formed a little beach of very white sand. Antonina placed my backpack onto the sand and I asked her if I could do the same with hers too.

"Yes, and I'll throw away the rocks"

"What rocks?" I asked, in surprise.

"The rocks I used as counterweight. I need to keep my legs strong! The low gravity here on Earth makes them turn to flaccid!" she said laughing and hugging me.

"What remains in my pack is our lunch. Today, we lunch here, in the open"

Then, Antonina went to the water, washed hands and face. From her backpack she took a large square piece of the same plastic tarpaulin, and one which was extensively employed in the farm.

"This plastic foil is the same used in that bag we placed the scorpions into. Remember, Jota? You were concerned that they might sting through the foil"

"Yes, I was very concerned indeed"

Taking a pointed knife from her pack she said:

"Now, I challenge you to pierce this plastic!"

Seeing that the sand beneath would dampen my strike with the knife, I found a hard piece of wood and placed it beneath the place where my strike should happen. I, then, tested, lightly with the knife's tip, the towel's resistance. My initial impression was that I was striking a steel plate. I, then, lifted the knife and looked at Antonina, who nodded.

Then, I struck. The knife's tip got bent immediately while the plastic foil showed no sign of perforation, not a single dent.

"This is the same material we use as a cover for our domes, in the bags, in everything!" she said, proudly.

"But, then, how you people cut this thing?"

"Nice question, Jota! The tarpaulins are cut with a special laser, in many standard sizes"

The lunch was finally spread down onto the tarpaulin; grilled pork, rice, scrambled eggs and a mayonnaise salad.

After eating we relaxed, seated on the tarpaulin.

Then, I took the chance to question Antonina a little more regarding the Earthians living in Landa. I decided to focus a bit more:

"What do the Earthians living in Landa do?"

"It depends much upon the time period they are living there" she answered after some thought. But, I felt she wasn't too secure.

"The recent arrivals go through an adaptation period, where we make their life very nice, as if you were touring in Paris", she answered, laughing.

"As soon as they arrive, they are distributed in colonies exclusive to Earthians. We try placing them in colonies speaking their own native languages. The new arrivals are introduced to their country fellows. Initially, they have a resting period, before being given light tasks. Earthians never work for Landians. The work they do reverts entirely to them".

She said these last phrases casually, but afterwards, I heard them, repeatedly. Casual as it may have seemed, this little information is of utmost importance to the understanding of many future events.

"In their colonies, Earthians receive, from time to time, the visit of Landians, many of them, curious to know of their habits. These visits also have purpose: very often, the visiting Landians invite chosen Earthians to spend some time in their homes. If both hosts and guests feel they like each other, the visitors are invited to live semi-permanently in the Landian household"

"But, what do Landians gain by having Earthians living with them? I just heard you tell me Earthians cannot work for Landians"

Antonina told me that there are many benefits, both for Landians and Earthians. For instance, Landian families receiving Earthians have larger quotas of food and clothes. It is understood that Landians receiving Earthians in their households do a service to all community. Antonina didn't specify what service, however.

"Can Landians marry Earthians?" I, soon, repented having asked this.

"Of course they cannot! What a question?! Jota" she answered a little upset.

"But, why not?"

"Jota, try to understand, please. This marriage you "propose" cannot generate children since Landians and Earthians, being of different species, cannot mate!" she answered, now, clearly upset.

And, even more upset, she said, loudly:

"And, even if it was possible having children, still would be an impure act!"

I perceived, immediately, to be crossing some line and entering a sort of philosophical quicksand.

"Sorry, I shouldn't have asked you such details"

Antonina smiled, hugged me, messed my hair and said I shouldn't be concerned since I wouldn't be going to Landa. However, Antonina's information was duly registered and catalogued in my mind, and ready to be processed along other pieces of data.

There were a few things that did not fit to me; for example, why Earthians going to Landa do not return to Earth, being free to and offered the means.

Chapter 38
Purification by Water

We were still seated on the tarpaulin, which had been laid on the white sand beach beside the brook.

I had given up asking more questions, since I perceived Antonina was a little reticent on continuing this subject. Then, I began taking some photos of the place, which seemed been brought from some paradise, such was the beauty of its geography. The flow of crystalline water, the white sand beach, the Eucalyptus forest surrounding the beach made the whole place seem surreal.

We went to the margin to wash the plates and utensils. Suddenly, Antonina took off her sneakers removed her dark glasses and entered the stream.

"What marvelous water, Jota, so cool, come here. We call this brook the Cool Water Brook (*Córrego da Agua Fria*)"

I went to the water, after removing my sneakers and socks. I was wearing short pants, above the knee.

"Come near me Jota and take off your shirt"

Saying this, Antonina removed her shirt and threw it onto the canvas. She was nude from the waist up.

"Now, Jota, kneel down and come closer to me, now, now!"

She had already knelt and we were facing each other.

The stream was shallow and its floor was soft sand. The cool water ran slowly, washing our legs. Very small fishes played around.

Being so close to Antonina bare breasts I got completely flabbergasted, and without action.

Then, Antonina scooped her hands and took some water from the stream. She began wetting my hair and my face and gently rubbing her wet hands over me.

"Jota, hear me, pay attention to what I say now; I am going to purify you with this water. Look at my eyes, Jota, and hear what I'm saying: this water is pure, sacred, it comes from the depths of the earth and this ground is sacred to us, Jota. This land is sacred to us."

Then, she began rubbing my neck, shoulders, chest, repeatedly wetting her hands with the stream's water.

"Now, Jota, it is your turn to purify me. Please, purify my body with this water!"

Then, I wetted my hands and dropped the cool water over Antonina's hair repeatedly until it was soaked. I then, continually soaking my hands, rubbed her neck and shoulders. Seeing my hesitancy regarding the "purification" of her breasts, she said:

"Why, Jota, my breasts do not deserve being purified?"

I, then, soaked my hands in the stream and began purifying Antonina's breasts whose nipples immediately got engorged and hard, and reacting, either to the coolness of water or to my touching.

"Now, Jota, don't move, let your arms down, because we are going to mix our waters"

And, saying this, she embraced me, firmly, pressing her wet breasts against my chest and moving her torso laterally side to side to "better mix our waters" as she said. Again, I was paralyzed and my desire for her, literally, was hurting me. She, then, scooped some more water in her hands and gave a further dose of purification to our bodies.

Now, I was certain this was a ritual, since absolutely no indication of a sexual content was in the air, coming from Antonina. She then, still pressing my body against hers, looked into my eyes and said:

"Jota, I love you so much. Never, never leave me" and, saying that pushed me, roughly, from her body.

"Now, we dry up" she said holding my hand and pulling me out of the water and onto the tarpaulin which was deliciously warm.

Then, Antonina said we should lie down to let the Sun further purify our bodies. And, we lay down, Antonina at my side and close to me. And, she still was nude from waist up. She, then, began caressing my wet hair and my face. And, she began to sing one of those mysterious songs of hers. Her voice was nice and very calming.

The combination of her nearness, the warmth of the Sun, the gentle breeze, made my desire disappear completely, to be replaced by a deep peace, coziness and completeness. We remained like this for some time.

Very slowly, I was learning her ways. *There were lines that should not be crossed. There were hidden protocols. There was some method, some pattern in all this,* I thought. But, still, I couldn't get the whole picture.

Still caressing me, she said:

"Jota, believe me, I will never abandon you, I will protect you and love you forever, until one of us die"

Saying this, she inclined her head above mine and kissed my hair and my face. At this moment, I think all factors summed up and a mixture of sensations invaded my mind. I remembered the caresses of my girlfriends, my mother caressing me, my father taking me by hand and telling me stories, I, on my mother's lap. I closed my eyes and felt.

I felt the scent of that wonderful woman at my side, that "would never abandon me and would ever protect me", felt her hands caressing me, the sound of her voice singing an extraterrestrial song. I felt the delicious warmth of the Sun, the scent of the forest, and the sound of the brook.

However, that mix of good sensations did not last long. There came the fear; the fear of losing her. For the first time I felt the fear of losing her love. And, remembered the suffering of Fabiana.

Chapter 39

Mayra

Next day I woke very early, with some noises and people talking, outside my container. I put on my clothes and went to the hall. Many people were helping to push a trailer into the dome. Yuri was there and called me. He was standing beside a brunette girl of median height, wearing glasses for myopia, some 5 degrees. She was discreetly attired. Then, Yuri addressed me:

"Jota, let me introduce our colleague. This is Mayra; she is an MD and will stay some period with us"

"Nice to meet you, I'm Jota, this is how they call me around here. What's your area?"

"I'm intensivist, but don't worry I'm not going to insert an oro-tracheal tube into you!" Hearing this, Yuri said:

"Well, that's not a bad idea; I think I'm in need of this, along some 100% oxygen and morphine IV"

We all laughed. Yuri then, called off the people who had brought in the trailer and, then, turned to me. He explained that Mayra would be helping in the reception of the new arrivers. I suspected that she did not know where these "arrivers" were coming from. The new trailer would be her quarters in the dome, Yuri explained. At the moment, some workers were connecting the trailer to the service pod, consisting of water, electricity/internet and sewer. I forgot to mention that those service pods were placed at various points in the dome, forming a radial disposition. And, my container had, now, a regular toilet, connected to the pod.

Chapter 40

Lost On Purpose

About 2 days after the arrival of Mayra I woke up, very early, with Antonina at my bedside, caressing my hair and face. I opened my eyes and we kept looking at each other. Without speaking, she went on with her caresses, from my hair to the neck, then, she circled my mouth, lips and said I should shave. I placed my hand over hers and felt the warmth from her hand.

Soon, however, she interrupted my reverie:

"Jota, let's have breakfast and today you are going to be all by yourself. I have meetings all day. They are arriving"

I washed, put on some clothes and met Antonina at the table. She asked what my plans were for the day and I said I would walk and take pictures. Then, she left in a hurry:

"We see each other later on."

Actually, my plan was a bit more complex than "walk and take pictures". I was planning an exercise of "survival in the jungle", as I had read in some magazines and books.

The plan was, essentially, getting lost and surviving. It wasn't the first time I had done this exercise in the farm. The plan ran like this:

I would first try to get lost along the labyrinth of trails. Having running out of my surviving "skills" and having not found my way, I would simply resort to Google Maps and other navigation apps installed in my cell phone. It was an interesting exercise and I was getting better at it. It is important to remark that the farm had 5 million square meters of area and a vast net of trails without any apparent (to me) logic. The trails were poorly signaled by a system of which I had no idea. And to make things worse, they were not rectangular forming blocks like in NYC. Also, the trees blocked completely any distant points of reference. In other words, it was a labyrinth and an extensive one at that.

It so happened that, on this day, I moved randomly taking different trails, entering and exiting bifurcations, avoiding known places. After about one hour of this exertion I considered myself "well lost". Then, I sat onto a stone, drank a coffee from my thermos, some water from a bottle, and began planning my return to civilization. The first rule in this exercise is trying to follow back your route, in other words to retrace your steps. If you succeed in doing this, then you end up at your starting point: in my case, the dome and lunch.

No, I hadn't brought bread crumbs like John and Mary. We were, now, in the 21st century. And, following the above rule, I began to retrace my steps. After about 300 meters I arrived at a bifurcation. Since I was distracted in my way to get lost, I didn't note the convergence of the 2 trails. Arriving at a bifurcation on your way back home is always a problem if you don't know the geography. What was the trail I came from?

I couldn't complaint since my aim was getting lost. But, so soon? I chose one of the 2 trails and walked for about 30 min on it. I couldn't see any familiar feature and concluded that I had not passed on that trail. The remedy was to go back to the bifurcation and follow the other trail.

In general terms, entering a bifurcation when you are going away from home it is easier to find the returning path, since you fall back where you came from. My problem now was that, after walking about 500 meters, trying to retrace my steps I came to another bifurcation. And, then, I was returning home. I had departed about 8 AM and my watch said it was 11. Lunch hour was approaching and all that walking increased my hunger.

I decided that, by the laws of random-walk, if I kept walking I would be getting farther and farther from home. So, time to be humble and reckon defeat. Enter Google Maps. I opened my backpack sank my hand in its depths and searched for the cell phone. Water bottle, thermos bottle, a towel, some old roller ball pens, folded sheets, a solar calculator I thought I had lost, Greg's camera of course, an old pack of cookies, coins, dental floss, tooth paste. There were more items. Then, the truth came: I had forgotten the cell phone upon my bed. *Try to maintain calm. Now, you have the real thing and you are really lost.*

Then, I remembered the camera. Maybe I could photograph any bifurcation and could verify, from the photos, what branch I had come from. My first target was the place I was right now. And, this place had some interesting features. Right beside my trail there was a glade, square in shape, about 30 x 30 meters wide. Covering the glade there was a low bush but, no trees. What called my attention was a sort of a tree trunk having the shape of an umbrella handle. Getting closer I saw it was not a natural "tree" but a metal tube, painted as to resemble, quite well, a tree bark. Some 10 meters away there was another.

They looked like ventilation ducts. I also perceived that such a clearing was quite level and regular, despite the ground being dirt, dead leaves, fallen sticks and dead dry branches. But, looking more closely, there was a definite air of artificiality to the whole place. I then made my preferred test which I learned from my father, civil engineer. I hit the ground with my foot. The impression was clear: the tympanic sound of a concrete slab with an empty space below. I, soon, found that this slab extended forming a square 30 x 30 m.

But, then, I remembered I was here not as an amateur engineer, but as a survivor candidate and tap-tap dancing wouldn't take me closer to my lunch. Also, it struck me I was lost for real.

But, then, to my plan: photograph peculiar places as references. And, this place was certainly very peculiar. Turning on Greg's camera I must have pressed some new button, and a menu appeared in the back screen: *Photo options*. I did not remember to have used this button before. *I just want to take a damned picture and this stupid button appears from nowhere!* I thought. Well, I pressed the button and then a list appeared:

Shutter speed, Aperture, ISO, Auto focus (Y/N), Save location (Y/N). The "yes" was already chosen in the last 2 options.

Then, without changing anything I pointed the camera to the place and pressed the shutter. Next step: to look at my photo. I pressed *Playback,* and another damned menu appeared: *View options.* Among the many "useless" options, one called my attention: *View location.* And, pressing this one, a pair of numbers appeared: -22.101119 and -47.911751.

These numbers I knew so well! They were the coordinates of my current position on Earth's surface! The first number was south latitude and the other was west longitude. I knew my position on Earth with 10 centimeter accuracy!

But what was the use of this information if I didn't know where my lunch was?! Then, I remembered that before I took to the trail I had seen the dome with a beautiful illumination and had taken some pictures of it. Hummm... what about some playback on those pictures? In the previous photograph there it was. The dome in all its glory, sun rays grazing its beautiful surface and, oops, not this crap now! In the dome's photo I pressed *view options >> view location* and there appeared the magic duet:

-22.102631 and -47.908145. Now, I knew the dome's position. I knew that each degree was equivalent to 111 km or 111,000 meters. By some lucky strike, my old solar calculator had been revived. Surely, dirty. But, working. Difference in latitudes: Dome minus Jota: 22.102631 -

22.101119 = 0.001512 degrees. Multiplying the difference in degrees by 111,000 we get 167 meters. The dome was, therefore, 167 meters at the south of Jota. Difference in longitudes: (Dome - Jota): 47.911751-47.908145 = 0.003606 degrees. Multiplying by 111,000, I got 400 meters east.

The dome was 400 meters to the east of Jota. I was not very far from the dome. Had I been in a desert, with free access to any direction and using the Sun as a compass, I would get easily to the dome even without seeing it. But, here, I had a problem: I couldn't follow the coordinates at my pleasure since I had to walk only along some trail. There was no trail following the directions to the dome. The Eucalyptus forest was impenetrable. Worse still, I couldn't see the dome.

I was seated on the stone, thinking of a way out, when I saw someone running really fast past me, like a blur. I thought it was Greg.

"Greeeg!" I shouted. The blur changed to Greg.

"Hi, Jota, what are you doing down here? You want to lose your lunch?" He was covered in sweat and panting.

"Hi, Greg, I'm lost. I was trying to get lost and I finally did it for real!"

Greg laughed loudly.

"I was doing a survival in the jungle training but forgot to bring my cell phone with the Google Maps"

"OK, then let's go to lunch and later you explain me this training of yours. It looks very interesting!"

We went walking together and in about 20 minutes got to the dome without any mistake. As I had calculated, I was close. In the way to the dome Greg said he was planning to talk to me and we arranged to meet after the lunch. He said, briefly, that he had been recruited to work as navigator in the mission Earth to Landa that would take place soon. One of the navigators was in sick leave and he was the only one available.

"In our missions the word "no" has no place, he said" lowering his eyes. And, then, considering all the travel times, he would be back only in 6 years.

"And, considering all things together, it is quite possible that we never see each other again, Jota". I saw his eyes getting wet. He pretended to be drying sweat drops but did not succeed.

"And I have a few things to talk with you before I leave, even if we will see each other a few more times before the mission. I am afraid of forgetting about you since I will be really busy in the next weeks"

After lunch, at which most were present, we had a coffee at a side table surrounded by some sofas. Greg approached me and asked if I could follow him to his container. We entered having Greg kept the door open. We sat down in some chairs.

"Look, Jota, I was thinking. It is almost certain that we won't see each other again. I have been talking with the others about giving you some presents and all agreed"

"One of my presents is already with you, the camera. And, here, are the remaining"; and he showed me an extra sized and very heavy bag clearly of non-terrestrial manufacture.

"Inside, there is a list of all presents, duly approved by all and a statement, signed by me, of the transfer of the items to you. Antonina and Yuri have a copy of the list and the statement. There is, however, an item which does not fit in that bag and it is already inside your container".

Greg's list of presents is a bit too extensive to be put here, but a few items deserve description:

The book of the cities, the infinite battery charger, a bag containing an assortment of precious stones (Greg didn't know about the stones Antonina had given me), the camera with all lenses and accessories and an English written manual, a powerful binocular from Landa (which I didn't know), a chess set, with beautifully crafted pieces made from a transparent material, the big Celestron telescope (not included in the bag). And many other items.

PART 2

Chapter 41

The Mother-Ship

Some days later I woke, as usual, with Antonina at my bed side. However, she was not caressing me this time. She was in a hurry:

"Jota, wake up. We are already having breakfast and there is some news, come, come!"

I was surprised to see everybody at the table since, as I have mentioned, it was rare to see more than one or two of them having breakfast. Surely, I thought, news were in the air. As soon as I have seated and filled my cup with some coffee, Yuri began:

"As I told you people before, we are expecting the arrival of a mother-ship to Earth. This will happen in 2-3 months from now depending on some minor changes in the program. At this moment our mother-ship orbits Ganymede while the transference-craft is presently on its surface collecting materials".

All this news was being transmitted from the mother-ship to our base, where Fred collected the transmissions and passed them on to Yuri and the others.

"Many Landians new-comers will arrive at our farm to be distributed to other locations over the Earth", continued Yuri, assuming a serious stance.

"They are our brothers and will arrive very tired and many, sick of body or mind. And we will have to take care of them before they are distributed to other kibbutz"

At this point of Yuri's briefing, I became aware that Mayra had already been informed regarding the nature of his new mentor and the group and wasn't showing any surprise.

What would be this transference-craft? I didn't know yet. Less, I knew what sort of materials was being collected in Ganymede. What I knew was I had one specimen, the diamond Antonina had given to me.

Later, in one of our walks, Antonina explained me what were the mother-ship and the transference craft. "The mother-ship never lands", she said. "It is too heavy and too big to land. It would crumble to pieces from its own weight. Like the International Space Station (ISS), it is either travelling or in orbit around some planet or satellite. On the contrary, the transference-craft, which is way smaller than the mother-ship, is a landing craft. I suggested that a comparison could be made between the ISS (as mother-ship) and the Space Shuttle (as landing or transference craft). Antonina approved my comparison and gave me tens of kisses, hugging and hair messing. She was getting very affectionate recently.

After Yuri had briefed the group with the main news, we relaxed at the table and a general talk ensued. I took the opportunity to ask Yuri some generalities:

"What is the propulsion system of the landing-craft?"

Joaquim

"Well, Jota, this is something I can't really explain very well. From what I know "they" use gravitational waves, both to neutralize local gravity and to accelerate in space. In reality the landing crafts are managed by an entirely different personnel and crew. We never have contact with their pilots. Suffice to us that they do their job with precision and safety. We never had a single problem with them". I felt that Yuri was not at ease in talking about the landing-craft crew.

Due to the frequent news of the mother-ship arrival, our lunches and dinners returned to be attended by all since many communications had to be updated. Also, Mayra had to be briefed on many details regarding health status of the arrivers.

It so happens that this same day, during lunch, Yuri explained a few more details of the big craft that was approaching us.

"The cruise speed of the mother-ship is about 300 km per second or one thousand of the light-speed. This, was a safe upper limit of velocity since there are microscopic dust grains in space that cause surface abrasion. These dust grains are remnants of comets and asteroids and exist throughout the solar system. In outer deep space they are much less abundant"

"Landa's distance to the Sun averages 10 billion km and Landa-Earth is a bit less, but depends on Earth's position. The travel duration averages 2 years give or take 6 months"

"The mother-ship, when comes near the Earth, never orbits Earth since it would be easily detected, even at higher orbits. Instead, it "parks" at Lagrange's point #1. This is one of the stable points that surround Earth. Lagrange 1 is located between Earth and Sun, about 1.5 million km from Earth, at a point where Sun's and Earth's gravity cancel each other. This means that the mother-ship, at this position, actually orbits the Sun"

"There are some advantages at Lagrange 1 point. It is relatively close to Earth to allow for a 10-15-hour travel time for the transference-craft and, at this point, the ship is permanently under the glare of the Sun, what makes its identification very difficult from Earth's telescopes".

The next briefing of Yuri occurred at dinner of this same day.

"There are, presently, two identical mother-ships. They alternate in their travels; one of them is always orbiting Landa. This is because these crafts are permanently crewed and contain many scientific laboratories, being permanent institutions. A third craft is being built. During their missions between Landa and Earth, the crafts make "stops" to explore many satellites in the solar system when these bodies happen to be in the approximate route. The big planets, Jupiter, Saturn, Uranus and Neptune are not visited directly since they have very aggressive atmospheres. Also, we never land in Venus since its atmosphere is toxic and acid and very hot to the point of melting lead"

During the days preceding the arrival of the mother-ship, Antonina was extremely busy. I, then, could see that she had a decisive role in the group, and that made me sort of proud of her. However, as to her attributions, she kept some mystery to me. Our walks were given a stop. Only at the mornings she still went to my bedside and caressed me, and she wanted to have breakfast with me. For my part I felt sort of free to walk through the farm at my leisure and photograph all I could. Despite not being able to transfer the pictures in the Internet, Greg gave me leave to use his "printer" and placed it at a corner of the dome, furnishing me with plenty of those metallic sheets, which no one seemed to be interested into.

At another lunch time, Yuri continued to explain:

"However, Pluto is one planet we do visit, since it is "close" to us. Among the various items we collect in those small planets and the big planets' satellites are crystals, precious stones, rare metals and precious metals. In their volcanoes abound diamonds that are ejected among the lava. Also some satellites have large fields of diamonds created eons ago from meteorite impacts. Those stones we get by the "carload" so to say. And, part of our organizations on Earth is funded with these collects. The kibbutz's are self-sufficient but require large amounts of money for their initial organization like buying of land, constructions and infrastructure."

"However, we can't sell the precious stones in large quantities since this disrupts the market and creates some suspicions as to their origin."

"And, what about Mars?" I asked Yuri

"We don't go to Mars" Yuri answered, in a concluding way.

Chapter 42

The Workings of the Mother-Ship

This time, Yuri's "lecture" was during a dinner when all were present. The reason Yuri intensified his "lectures" on the mother-ship was as a preparation for its impending arrival.

"Many experiments were done on Earth in trying to create an autonomous enclosure in terms of energy, water, atmosphere, food, etc. Those enclosures needed to satisfy a condition: sustain a group of people during a given period of time, with no contacts with the outside world. That means such enclosures needed to be *self-sufficient*"

"But before continuing, why am I telling you this? The reason is that the mother-ship needs to be self-sufficient. And it is projected, constructed and stored to sustain people's life for about 5 years, in outer space"

"On Earth, the most famous attempts at self-sufficient systems were Biosphere I and II, constructed in deserts in the United States. They worked for some time, despite many controversies and suspicion of fraud"

"During a long-duration interplanetary travel there are four things we consider as essentials: food, water, oxygen and energy. A great volume of water is stored in tanks when the ship departs. This water however must be recycled in order to last for some years, when the ship is travelling".

"Now, for the gases I will make a summary here. A comparison with the *carbon cycle* and *oxygen cycle* on Earth is very useful. On Earth, the carbon cycle begins with the atmospheric CO_2 incorporation into plants and sea algae. Then, CO_2, along with nitrogen, incorporates into the plants and algae. The herbivore animals eat plants and carnivores eat the herbivores. When plants and animals die they decompose, CO_2 returns to the atmosphere and the cycle closes".

"Oxygen (O_2) is produced by many sources, with many of them debatable. But, in what concerns life, O_2 is generated by plants and algae through photosynthesis. Then, when animals breathe they consume O_2 and generate CO_2. Also, decomposition of plants and animals generate CO_2 and fires in forests consume O_2 and generate CO_2. The oxygen cycle closes. A human being, be Earthian or Landian, consumes an average of 250 ml O_2 per minute, being CO_2 production essentially the same"

"Well, everything I said about these cycles hold in Earth's atmosphere. We say that Earth's atmosphere is an open environment. In a space-ship, however we have a closed system and both CO_2 and O_2 cycles differ from Earth's".

"O_2 must be supplied continuously, be it from stored O_2, from generated O_2 from water electrolysis and by photosynthesis performed by plants in the ship (in arboretums or plant nurseries and vegetable gardens). Such nurseries are illuminated by strong lamps that provide the necessary UV light for photosynthesis."

"Since the mother-ship is a closed environment the CO_2 produced by passengers and crew must be removed from the air. A small part of CO_2 is removed by the plants in the ship, by the process of photosynthesis. Another portion of CO_2 is combined with hydrogen that had been generated by water electrolysis, forming methane which is stored under pressure in tanks"

"Another important gas is nitrogen (N_2). Despite not being a respiratory gas, N_2 is important in maintaining the atmospheric pressure be it in Earth or in the mother-ship. Also, N_2 is part of the plants' function and structure. More recently, N_2 has been given important roles in animal physiology. All living beings are composed by carbon, nitrogen, hydrogen, phosphorus, sulfur and oxygen. The air in the mother-ship has 50% O_2 and 50% N_2. CO_2 has a very small proportion."

Chapter 43

Interplanetary Navigation

The following day, Yuri explained to us how the mother-ship navigates during its course between Landa to Earth and vice-versa.

"In its long voyage between Landa and Earth that lasts about 2 years, the mother-ship orients by the stars. Airplanes and ships on Earth used to navigate by the stars but this method has been replaced by the GPS (Global Positioning Satellites) system. However, in space, positioning by the stars works differently from what is done on Earth. Despite stars being too distant, when you move hundreds of thousands of kilometers through space, their relative positions change a little bit."

"As the mother-ship moves at 300 km/sec, in a few hours the closer stars change their apparent positions in relation to more distant stars. As such, for each location during the mother-ship travel there is a unique perspective of the star field. The powerful computers in the ship easily integrate this information and calculate the position and the velocity of the mother-ship."

"Additionally, in a manner similar to airplanes, the mother-ship uses a radio beacon emitted from Landa. This powerful and highly concentrate beacon of radio waves is projected towards the Sun creating a sort of space highway between Landa and the Sun. The mother-ship, then, inserts itself along this highway."

"The mother-ship has a cylindrical-conical shape. The bow is sharply conical in order to hit the dust particles at low angles and minimizing abrasion. The entire stern is cylindrical having 1000 m length and 600 m diameter. The total length of the ship is 2000 meters"

"The habitable sectors are pressurized and are formed by multiple cylindrical compartments to comply with Laplace's law. This law requires that the larger a sphere or cylinder the thicker its walls need to be to support the pressure. Since the ship is immense, this would require extremely thick walls. To work around this problem, the solution was subdividing the ship's interior into smaller habitable cylinders which are kept at the same pressure as in Earth's atmosphere. Most part of the ship is not habitable and contains the numerous equipments."

"Both crew and passengers live in small individual cabins having a width of 1 m, 2 m high and 3 m long. The cabins have a berth, below which are a toilet, a sink and a small closet. The toilet is portable and must be changed daily by a clean one. There is no sewer system and baths are taken with towels soaked in warm water. Daily, each crew or passenger takes his toilet bowl and used towels to a central and receives a clean toilet bowl and clean towels. Also, a passenger can change his/her used uniform for a clean one when necessary. All water is recycled. Excrements are boiled along with served water and enter the recycling process. The solid parts are burned and the water vapor collected from them. The solid residues are used in the vegetable gardens as fertilizer. During the long trips, deaths may occur. In such cases the bodies are cremated and their water (about 60%) is recycled. The ashes are used as fertilizer to vegetable gardens"

"However, if death occurs by act of heroism or bravery the body is "buried" in space, what is a great honor"

"The ship rotates around it axis in order to keep artificial gravity. It can accommodate about 10 thousand passengers and crew. Most of passengers are Landians migrating to Earth. Meals are served in numerous dining halls distributed through the ship".

"The mother-ship is a small city having a complete hospital with operating rooms and ICUs and many local dispensaries. There are many apparatus shops in different sectors of the ship. There is a prison and cult places"

"As I said, the mother-ship is a permanent institution where people study, courses are offered in different areas and scientific research is done"

"Food comes in different forms: frozen food, living animals are raised (rabbits, chicken) having been obtained on Earth"

"Passengers and crew wear uniforms, whose colors and insignia correspond to classes and functions"

"The passengers contribute to different services. Obligatory are cabin maintenance. But there are many voluntary services such as vegetable gardens, general cleaning, served waters, laundry and others that do not require specialized personnel. Voluntary work is always supervised by crew members".

Apart from these general data given by Yuri, I had the chance of learning of more details about the workings of the mother-ship and, these, I will present along the ensuing chapters.

Chapter 44

Mother-Ship Arrival Schedule

A few days later, during lunch, Yuri informed us that the mother-ship would be parking at Lagrange point #1 in about 2 months. Then, the transference craft would land in the farm, which is one of the HUBs for migration both Landa to Earth and vice versa. Once the immigrants, most Landian newcomers, land here they go for an adaptation process, treated if necessary and, then, distributed to the kibbutzes in Southeast of Brazil.

Yuri asked me if I would like to visit the transference craft while it was landed here in the farm. I immediately looked at Antonina who nodded. Then Yuri thought a few seconds and said that I might even be able to visit the mother-ship. But, in this case, I needed to disembark at the Northeast of Brazil. Yuri explained what might be a better arrangement for my visits to the crafts. (Why Yuri wanted me to visit the crafts??)

"The logistic of people's transferences are the following: the mother-ship, once arriving at Earth, stays parked at Lagrange #1 point. From this point the transference-craft brings the passengers to Earth's surface. They disembark at various countries. The transference-craft (which is a disc shaped craft) can bring to Earth a maximum of 700 people each time. Once the passengers disembark the craft receives Earthians going to Landa and replenishes stocks. Then the disc returns to the mother-ship, docks, and downloads passengers and stock. Now, the transference-craft (disc) fills up with more incoming Landians and lands again at different points of Brazil or any other country. The process repeats until all incoming people are on Earth and all outgoing people are in the mother-ship."

"As for you, Jota, your travel schedule will be: you take the disc here, disc to mother-ship, mother-ship to disc, disc lands in the Northeast".

"And what is this landing-craft that you mention, Yuri?"

"Jota, I will, for now, just say that the transference-craft is a double-convex disc, essentially a "flying-saucer" of which you people on Earth have been seeing for so many years. And, it is big, almost 150 m diameter."

"And, as for your visit to the disc, and mother-ship I will see this with Antonina since she has the last word in what concerns you. And, from what I know, Antonina will accompany you so that you don't do anything wrong" and Yuri went to laugh loudly and the others clapped hands. Antonina simply looked at the table.

More and more, I began to feel like I was a mascot of sorts for these people. And, maybe I should act as one.

As the date of the mother-ship arrival approached a crescent activity could be observed in the farm. Many unknown people, some Landians, some Brazilians and a few Earthians strangers. Trucks of different sizes and types brought boxes, cartons and livestock. Antonina told me that in a sector of the cave there was a full hospital, having ORs and ICUs where sick Landians newcomers were treated before being directed to their final destinations.

Chapter 45

Waiting for the Transference-Craft

Finally, the great day arrived. The mother-ship had parked at Lagrange point #1, two days before. The transference-craft (from now on we call *disc*) would be landing at the farm late in the evening.

5:30 AM: I woke with Antonina at my bed side. She was not caressing me but rubbing my hair.

"Let's have breakfast, Jota, today we have a lot to do! And we embark in the evening"

I had already told my brother of my trip, omitting details, of course. But I told him we would not be able to communicate for some days. However, I asked Fred if I could provide my brother with a number from the farm so that in case of some emergency my brother could contact him. We had breakfast in silence. Many of our group already had left. Outside the dome, many cars, vans, some buses, all vehicles parked along the many elongated clearings around the dome. Antonina and I approached to a car and I stepped inside on the passenger's seat. Antonina would be driving. The car moved in complete silence. An electric car. Antonina was a good driver, a little fast to my taste.

"Where are we going to?" I asked.

"You'll see soon" she answered while maneuvering the car with dexterity and hurry.

6:00 AM: It was a new route for me. I felt we were ascending. Finally, we got to a very large clearing in the Eucalyptus forest. A large dome, about double the size of our home dome stood at a side of the clearing. In the center of the clearing was a soccer field some 200 meters away from the dome.

"Here, the disc will land" she said to me, pointing to the soccer field.

Later, I was informed that the soccer field was a disguise since no one played soccer there. Not even the goal boxes were there. Right at the forest border, besides the dome was a huge water tower reservoir. Among the many cleared venues radiating from the central clearing there were many trucks of different types; most, were box trucks with refrigerating units at the top. From a plane passing overhead, they were, essentially, invisible.

"The box trucks are freezers" Antonina explained. Other trucks carried caged crates full of living animals, rabbits, chicken and turtles.

We parked and went to the dome.

"This dome was erected in three days and will be disassembled after the operation!" shouted Antonina, above the confusion of voices.

Entering the dome, its size impressed me. Inside, there was an ordered confusion. The entire group was there, along with many Landians unknown to me. Despite the dome being portable, there were permanent fixtures like service pods and other concrete platforms. Also, were visible a great deal of permanent cables, pipes and electrical installations. These, probably would be covered with a tarpaulin after the operation and dome removal. At the sides of the great dome hall were many containers. Antonina told me that the containers had sanitary, toilets, stocks, medical units. Others, were freezers, and one of them was a computer center.

Antonina seemed to have done most of his part in the operation since she was just going from group to group, and then she disappeared only to come back and see if I was OK. In the dome was all the support team, formed mostly by Landians. They had been brought from other kibbutzes, in order to help in the concentrated effort.

Also, in the dome were the passengers going to Landa. These, were 15 Earthian paraplegics with companions and 8 tetraplegics with companions. The paraplegics were joyous and almost exhilarating and were in the open, across the soccer field. Some were ball playing. The tetraplegics were also euphoric, some in special wheelchairs, some in portable beds or in special gurneys.

The euphoria among these disabled passengers could well be justified. If everything ran smoothly, they were to be returned to Earth in about 5 to 10 years or so and *walking*. In the air was happiness mixed with nervousness. It should be said that these 23 disabled Earthians going to Landa from our farm were but a small part of all disabled people about to embark to Landa in this same mission. They were to be collected at all places of the globe and were said to be more than 300 at this mission.

A few Landians were also returning to Landa. Yuri and Mayra were among a group of doctors and nurses organizing medical equipment and checking the health status of passengers.

6:30 AM: At a big table, at one side of the salon, a buffet is being organized with water, coffee, juices, and snacks. The main courses are to be placed there at 12.

7:00 AM: The passenger's uniforms begin to be distributed and explained by the ground team (blue uniforms). Earthians have green uniforms (inside the mother-ship these will be changed). Landians have white uniforms. Our shoes and sneakers will be left at the dome. From now on we are going to wear special shoes with soft impermeable soles. Each passenger can carry a handbag with his things.

8:00 AM: All passengers are already wearing their uniforms. The ground team (in blue or green) begins explaining the embarking procedures. The ground crew is composed by Brazilians and Landians living on Earth. They will function up to the embarking ramp. From the embarking ramp onwards, there assumes the crew (yellow uniforms). All passengers begin receiving their badges that should be worn around the neck, with the cards at the chest. In the badge are all passenger data, both written to all see and electronically identifiable.

8:30 AM: There begins a second round of passenger's identification. We all receive bracelets matching the information on our badges. The bracelets are comfortable and have colors. They are soft but cannot be removed. The bracelets will accompany us during the entire trip. The disabled passengers have light-green-red-line bracelets. My bracelet is light-green flat; Antonina's bracelet is white-red line. On board, all bracelets are monitored at checking points. We are not people anymore. From now on, we are bracelets.

9:00 AM: There begins some preparations at the landing point that will be at the soccer field. There are a few discrete demarking lines and LEDs which will light on only seconds before the landing. Remember that all operations are disguised or undercover.

9:30 AM: Yuri informs me and Antonina that the mother-ship has parked at Lagrange point #1 two days ago. Right now are being done the preparations for the passenger's transfer from mother-ship to the transference disc that will land here. There are 430 newcomer Landians, many with health problems.

12:00: The buffet is served, being super organized and well provided.

14:00: Another round of identification is performed. The use of the special shoes is better explained. They are elastic and comfortable. Socks are not allowed. Their soles are impermeable but soft despite being strong. We will learn that their soles are washable.

All passengers are told to sit down since a general explanation will be given by the leader of the ground team.

1. Inside the crafts (disc and mother-ship) there is military discipline and obedience is mandatory.

2. There will be no country rules; only craft rules that are a mix of Landa's rules and local craft's rules.

3. Problematic people will be restrained and brought to Earth if still in the disc or will be incarcerated at the mother-ship if on trip.

There were other items which I found of minor importance, like use of sanitary, use of cell-phones and other.

Chapter 46
The Disc Arrives

Up to 19:00: Free period for passengers. Support teams are working non-stop.

21:00: Passengers are told of disc landing scheduled to 22:50

22:45: Many people are outside the dome, looking at the sky. I look upwards but only see a sky full of stars. Antonina is beside me and I ask her what I should look for and if the disc is already visible.

"Try to see what you don't see" she says. I didn't understand but kept looking up and only seeing stars and more stars.

"Look there!" she pointed up.

I looked up and, then, I perceived that there were no stars in a small circular region of the sky. In a few seconds the circle without stars increased enormously and, soon, stars were visible only around the horizon. A strong and warm wind began blowing from the direction of the soccer field and then I saw it.

A gigantic black mass had almost stopped and was slowly coming close to the ground. Sparks came from it. Finally, about 10 meters from the ground, the enormous disc stopped abruptly as if having hit an invisible platform. The disc oscillated slightly, like a big boat in water.

A few seconds later, we heard a big boom and, soon after, a very brief but strong pressure shock wave. The big boom and shock wave were formed many kilometers above, when the disc crossed the sound barrier. It was the so called *sonic boom.*

From somewhere in the disc two chains were launched to the ground, creating large sparks. The disc was being discharged from a voltage of thousands of volts generated from the friction with air molecules during its passage through the atmosphere.

Soon after, about 20 balloons filled below the sides of the disc. The disc descended a bit more and rested upon the balloons.

The landing was over.

Only then I was able to observe more deeply the object in front of me. The enormous disc was entirely black, covered by spikes of about 10 cm. An intense heat came from it along with a slight ozone scent. A distinct humming seemed to come from the disc but permeated the entire place. Is size being about 120-150 meters across and maybe 20 meters high in the center. Its edges were sharp.

Soon after the landing a hatch began opening below the center and a large ramp descended slowly until touching the ground. As soon as the ramp touched the ground, a large number of crew, clad in yellow uniforms began organizing disembark. After about 15 minutes the Landian newcomers began descending. They had badges and bracelets and were clad in white uniforms. They formed a well-organized line as were descending the ramp. Their facial expressions were varied. Many looking surprised gazed at every direction, trying to grasp their new environs. Others were joyful and laughed and embraced each other. Some, were weeping. After this first wave, that lasted many minutes, there came the wheelchairs and gurneys carrying more Landians. Their descent was followed by hand clapping.

After the Landians had disembarked, there came the Earthians, returning home. This first wave was formed by the companions of the Earthian's patients that were returning from treatments in Landa.

After these, a surprise: descending along the ramp and walking slowly but firmly, were 14 Earthians, five women and nine men. They were escorted by yellow clad crew members. Soon after leaving the ramp, these people knelt to the floor and kissed the dusty ground. Taking some dirt from the ground, all rubbed it over their faces. And, they were all weeping. These, however, were a special group. They gathered with some members of the ground team, Yuri was called upon, talked with the newcomers and all went into the dome.

Since we were outside already preparing for boarding the disc, we just heard joyful shouts and handclapping coming from the dome interior. Then, Yuri came to us and told who these special arrivers were: 4 ex-tetraplegics, 10 ex-paraplegics. And, as we saw, they walked. Then, Yuri told to the tetras and paras that were in the boarding line, who the arrivers were. Later, I was informed that a reporter, disguised as accompanying a paraplegic leaked to the press the news of the walking ex-disabled.

While the passengers and newcomers were being handled, a conveyor belt had been deployed from another part of the disk, and empty trucks were being loaded with items coming from Landa. Afterwards, the conveyor belt inverted direction in order to receive items to be stocked in the mother-ship. Also a heavy hose was attached to a part of the disk and hundreds of thousands liters of water loaded into the tanks of the disk. Most of this water would be discharged into the mother-ship.

At the same time, the boarding of passengers was being handled by ground and crew teams.

Chapter 47

Earth to Mother-Ship

I will, in this chapter, narrate my boarding in the disc and the travel up to the mother-ship. For reasons related to my love for Astronomy, my readings on this subject, on space travel and even science fiction, the experience of boarding an alien craft filled my mind with nervous expectation and left an eternal impression in me.

Right in the lowest part of the boarding ramp, there was a double line of crew at the sides of the ramp. They were clad in yellow uniforms, all Landians, blonde, very light colored hairs. They didn't speak Portuguese, only Landian and English. The later was the official language from this point onwards. It became clear to me that the boarding was quite a different operation than disembarking.

Right in the beginning of the ramp, a series of different doormats were placed in series. The first one was wet with some liquid, probably a mixture of water and detergent. The second line of mats was a non-aqueous liquid and the 3rd line was a dry mat where a flow of hot air dried our soles. The crew had scanners and identified our badges and bracelets.

Having been scanned, our entry on the craft was allowed.

Finally, I would cross the doorway separating two different technologies, two quite different worlds. Suddenly, I was within an alien craft. There was a silence that only let some strange, low voices to be heard. A humming sound permeates all. There was a pervading smell of equipment that resembled to me some electronics shops in the USA. The temperature was cool but my uniform made me feel comfortable. Having observed the huge size of the disc, as looked from the outside, I imagined I would enter a cathedral-like hall. I was mistaken.

We went through a lateral corridor two meters wide by two meters high illuminated by a diffuse yellowish light. I observed that the walls, floor and ceiling were made of a material having the look of metal and plastic. All panel junctions were absolutely perfect. No sharp corners, everything round and flush. From some point on, all surfaces seemed padded. From the corridor, we entered a large room with about 40 seats, like those of a passenger plane.

Only 20 passengers were planned for this section, and we would be quite comfortable. That particular room had the shape of circle sector i.e. a room long and curved. I inferred the rooms should follow the curvature of the disc. They probably were all concentric. We were told to seat down. The seats were quite comfortable and well-spaced from each other. They had resting for the back, head, the feet and legs.

The angle between the back and seat was fixed to a little more than 90 degrees, while other sections of the seat had adjustable angles. Our room was entirely padded, walls, floor and ceiling. There were no hard protrusions. In our room there were 10 crew clad in yellow uniforms and organizing the seating of passengers and explaining the workings of the chairs. The crewmen oriented us to pay attention to the monitors which would be giving instructions for the lift off. The instructions were very clear and spoken in English. They were accompanied by very didactic diagrams.

We were informed, by the crew and by the monitors, that the lift off phase would create some relatively strong acceleration in order that the craft could clear rapidly the zone of observation. During this period, we would need to be seated. After 10 minutes' crew members oriented us to put the seat in horizontal position. Then, the monitors emitted a gong and changed configuration. Immediately, the crew began orienting us to change our seats to horizontal. We were told to fasten the seat belts, which were very complex but comfortable. The monitors sounded again, changing screens.

Lift off will proceed at 2G, then 3G, then 4G, in brief sequence. These numbers being the different values of the acceleration at lift off in terms of the normal gravity. A person weighing 70 kg would weigh 280 kg at 4G. However, in a horizontal position, this was bearable, as the monitors explained us.

The distance to the mother-ship is 1.5 million km and it takes, usually 10-14 hrs to get there. Close to Earth the disc must accelerate rapidly in order to diminish the chances of its being observed. But, outside observable distances, the travel is a sequence of accelerations and brief moments of zero gravity. This is a complex procedure, entirely performed by the powerful computers of the craft. The reason is that the travel extension is relatively short in relation to the speed capabilities of the disc. Too much velocity implies a long and uncomfortable period of deceleration at the final leg of the travel.

So, the computers try to find a best combination of initial accelerations at the beginning of the route and decelerations at the final leg of the journey. The result is that we are all the time feeling the effects of an artificial gravity of varying intensity. In order to decelerate the craft points its belly to the destination, while in accelerating, the top side points to the destination. This guarantees that we all are pressed against our seats during changes of velocity.

But, we were still on the ground.

Each minute, a different gong went off from the monitors. We were silent, expecting something big to happen. Something new to me.

Five minutes later, there appeared on the monitors, "Lift off in 5 minutes, stay calm and breathe deeply."

Then, "Liftoff at 3 min, 2 min, 30 secs, 10 secs 2 secs."

I closed my eyes. Suddenly, my body and my head appeared to be weighing a lot more. I opened my eyes and perceived my vision to be a bit cloudy and breathing more elaborate. Then my weight seemed to increase even further, and I had difficulty in seeing at the periphery of my vision field. I can't remember how long this took but suddenly, my weight began returning to normal.

Then, I began feeling lighter and lighter and finally, I wasn't pressing the seat any more. Exactly at this moment, the 10 crew members emerged from their seats. I saw, now, that they had been in the room all the time. And, the yellow-clad men began floating in the room. They loosened our seat belts and coached us to experiment zero gravity.

Now, I was able to look at the monitors the first time after our departure. Earth already looked as a complete sphere despite still very large. I could see, clearly, all of South America, even part of Antarctic continent. North America was partly visible. Both Pacific and Atlantic oceans were visible. What caught my attention also was that the Earth was receding perceptibly. The monitors also indicated our distance to Earth, to the mother-ship and ... our velocity at this moment: 45 km/second.

This, however, wouldn't last long. Half an hour later, we were told to sit again, but no need to fasten the belts. We would be accelerating lightly, about 0.5G for 1 hour. All changes in acceleration were announced in the monitors, and also explained to us by the crew members.

From that moment on, our trip was very nice, with acceleration periods, intercalated briefly with zero G. By the final 2 hours or so we would be decelerating all the time.

Chapter 48
Docking to Mother-Ship

As had been expected, about 11 hrs after we departed Earth, the monitors began showing images of the mother-ship. It was very far away but clearly visible. We were decelerating appreciably, at some 2 Gs, and were seated but not fastened. Our pushing onto the seat changed from now on, minute by minute, as the disc was finding the best velocity for the docking maneuver.

Rapidly, now the mother-ship image was filling, completely, the monitors' screens. What we saw was something the size of a city, rotating slowly. Then, the monitors stopped showing scenes and began showing procedures. Also, the crewmen (and women, as I forgot to mention) began instructing us how to proceed. We were asked to fasten our belts. Soon, our weights got to zero. But, then, we began to turn. The monitors explained we were rotating in order to follow the rotation of the mother-ship. The docking would occur at the stern of the mother-ship. According to the diagrams being shown at the monitors, the disc docks with its upper part.

Now, after about 30 min, the docking operation was over. We were told to unfasten the belts and to move carefully to the room's wall that was to be our "ground", from now on. We were being pushed, by the centrifugal force, toward the outer wall of our cabin. The crew members helped us travel, from our seats to the outer wall. And, soon were all standing on the outer wall, like those rides in pleasure parks. Above our heads were our previous seats. We were allowed a few minutes to get used to our new references.

Despite feeling a force pulling us toward the wall where we were now standing on, this force, or our weight, was really small. I felt I could easily jump upwards (I didn't do it though). From now on we were subject to different and funny gravity sensations. We were told to walk on the wall until we were below a huge shaft. Looking up I saw that the shaft went up some 60 meters and was covered with handbars, on which people were grabbing up.

Our gravity was really small so there was no danger in case of "falling". Also, we were being oriented now, by a much larger number of crew. Then, I began to move up. As I ascended the handbars I noticed that my weight was getting smaller and smaller. We finally came to a horizontal and wide tunnel. There, we had no weight whatsoever. I was floating and grabbed at a large number of handles fixed on the tunnel's walls. We were instructed to move along this tunnel until we arrived at a distinct threshold sided to many types of doors, which were all open.

We were, at this moment, entering the mother-ship itself.

From now on, there was a distinct change in our surroundings. Everything was different. We were told to wait at the entry hall of the mother-ship, where a different crew was awaiting us. This region was zero gravity. We were at the center of the mother-ship. Gone were the yellow uniformed people. This new crew was the mother-ship's crew. They were formed by Landians, clad in beige uniforms laced with insignia. They began reading our bracelets using hand scanners. They were very attentive and amiable and smiled assuring at us. They repeated at us: *welcome on board the Alpha.*

And we were being directed to the habitation quarters of the ship, which were located close to the external borders of the ship, 300 meters from the central reception hall where we had arrived. At present, our location was in the center of the cylindrical body of the ship. We still had to move about 300 m to our habitation space. At the hall we entered an elevator. Antonina, I and some 10 people more.

When the elevator's door opened and we exited, I was again feeling my normal weight, despite a little less. Actually, we were at the 0.8G level. We were directed to a corridor sided by numbered cabins. Cabin identification is a complicated business. They had sector and other alphanumerical codes.

Then, instructed by the crew, we were shown to our cabins. Antonina's was contiguous to mine. To open the cabin, we had to touch our bracelet to a lighted knob on the door. From now on, we would have to wear our new uniforms, already in our cabins. Mine was green (Earthians) and Antonina's white (Landians, non-crew).

We were told to meet to a certain hall, where some instructions would be passed to us, such as the regulations inside the mother-ship, available facilities for passengers, obligatory tasks etc, etc. The only obligatory tasks were cleaning of the cabins, exchange of sanitary toilets and of cleaning towels. Uniforms needed to be changed each 2 days. Daily bath was recommended but not obligatory. Highly recommended were exercises and attending to some lectures. However, there were numerous voluntary tasks: vegetable gardens, vivarium, served waters, water recycling, corridors cleaning.

For some complicated reasons that were not revealed to us, at least to me, the landing of the disc, scheduled to occur in a few days, was postponed for more than one month. This was not a bad news for me and not good too. Many strange things happened to me during this period. I suffered. But, I also grew.

Chapter 49

First Talk with Erika

Despite this chapter may look futile at first glance, it is necessary for the comprehension of the ensuing facts, which led me to suffer important crises in the following weeks.

Among the many voluntary tasks available to the passengers in the mother-ship, there was the work at the vegetable gardens. And, it was this work I chose as my first task.

There were many of those gardens distributed across the ship. And, some were placed at lower gravity to study the effect of low gravity on plant growth. At that morning I was at the vegetable garden closest to my quarters. The place was strongly lit in order to provide UV light for photosynthesis. Some people were even wearing sunglasses provided by the coordinators. As instructed by my coordinator, a Landian woman, my task was sowing broccoli seeds, applying some fertilizer and irrigating the soil patch with water: a very easy task.

Close to me was a brunette, about 20. By her looks she was an Earthian. However, she was wearing a white uniform, exclusive of Landians, instead of the green uniforms of the passengers.

"Shit, my fertilizer has finished!" I heard her talking in low voice, for herself. I turned and asked her:

"Are you Brazilian?"

She got surprised with my question.

"Yes, I am, but how did you find it?"

"I heard you talking, of course."

She laughed and answered to be native from the Brazilian Northeast without specifying the state. We were talking without too much looking at each other, in order to avoid being reprehended by some coordinator. Actually, as I learned later, this rarely happened.

"My name is Erika and yours would be?"

"Jota, nice to meet you!" I said, extending my hand.

She shook her head.

"We can't shake hands here," she said in low voice.

"Oh, why can't we?" I said

"Our uniforms, can't you see? Different colors."

"Huummmmm, I've got it."

It must be said that being ours a voluntary task, we had some liberty to maintain brief talks to one another. Other voluntaries were also talking without, however, interrupting their tasks. The coordinators oriented us very cordially.

Seeing her uniform was white (Landian, non-crew's uniform) I asked her if she lived in Landa.

"Yes, I live in Landa since I was 5, and I'm 21 now."

"But, can Earthians work as crew?" I asked

"In normal circumstances, they can't but my mentor is a crew, he is a pilot in this ship. And I came here as a companion to him. This gives me right to wear white," she said smiling and pointing to her uniform with some pride.

Erika told me she came to Landa when she was 5 and, at 8, she was adopted by her mentor.

Erika's first answers rang a bell in my mind. Some of my doubts might be answered now since I had in my "possession" an Earthian "specimen" living in Landa. And a very interesting "specimen" at that. I just had to tread carefully.

"And, is it usual for Earthians living in Landa to be adopted by Landians?" I asked.

"Oh, yes. And it is very nice to live within a Landian family!" answered Erika.

She told me that non-adopted Earthians, and they were the larger part, lived in colonies separated from Landians' colonies. They had their own schools, their own market, their own rules, and everything distinct from Landians.

Remembering what Antonina had told me about Landian markets:

"And are Earthian markets much inferior to those of Landians?"

"Oh, no, of course not! Earthian's markets are way better than the Landians'," she answered laughing as if my question was a non-sense.

"They have quotas like the Landian's but have a much wider variety of items!"

"How come?"

"As opposed to Landian markets, where things are stereotyped and unsightly, Earthian's have a much wider variety of products, they have colors and they are nice looking. Regarding food there are also more things to choose from."

Remembering Antonina's explanations regarding the strict rules in Landian colonies, I decided to explore a little more my new friend, Erika.

"And, do the people in Earthian colonies have tasks and strict timetables like Landian colonies?"

"Ok, yes, the Earthians, in their colonies, have many tasks, just like the Landians in their colonies. But in Earthian's there are basically maintenance tasks and foods farms. They don't have the big factories, for example."

"But Earthians, in their colonies, have strict timetables and they rotate among the many communal tasks," Erika added.

"Such as?"

"Oh, too many tasks to tell you here. The chicken coops, vegetable gardens, fish rising. Earthians make their own clothes. There are general tasks where all people work and specialized ones: mechanical, textile, medical, etc. But not big factories like the Landian colonies. And, Earthian colonies try to be as independent possible from the Landians."

Then, Erika, seeing that I was completely ignorant in Linda's life, gave some help:

"Look, let me summarize because this is important for you to know so that you don't make a gaffe. There are two categories of Earthians living in Landa: those living in Earthian colonies are called Type 1 and those adopted by Landians and living in Landian colonies are the Type 2. Very easy, eh?"

"Now, it's clearer to me! But, tell me Erika. Can the Type 1 Earthians visit Type 2 Earthians living in the Landian colonies?"

"Of course they can! Actually, the Landians often invite Type 1s to visit their colonies and interact with the adopted Earthians living there. And we, Type 2s, can visit Earthian colonies as well."

"Look, Jota, try to understand. The Landians love us and often visit Earthian colonies in their free time. They bring presents and invite Type 1s to visit their colonies. We are free people, Jota. But, there are rules and they are many."

"And, what about the Landian's homes? Are they better than the Earthians'?"

"No, they are neither better nor worse. They are different. The Landians' homes are stereotyped all the same, no colors, no decorations, no music. Everything is black, grey or white."

"I see, but why then the Type 1s Earthians like to visit them?"

"You don't know why the Type 1s like to visit Landian's homes?" and Erika appeared to be quite surprised at my question.

"I really don't know, but I'm curious!"

"Look, Jota, try to see this way. The Landians treat us, Earthians, very well, be Type 1s or 2s. They tell us stories, show us interesting things, play very nice games with us, they talk with us of nice things and they make us feel important, secure, protected and happy. It isn't easy for me to explain; they just make us feel happy."

"And, there is more, Jota. Sometimes, a Landian invites a Type 1 Earthian to live permanently in their home. When this happens, this Earthian gets adopted and becomes a Type 2. And, that's what I am, a Type 2" and, saying this Erika gave me a big smile.

"And, is this good?"

"Are you asking me if it is good? No, it isn't good, it is excellent, fantastic!"

OK, but tell me why is this so good, please."

"Well, Jota, there are so many reasons. Look this way: in the Earthian colonies people have to work a lot, everyone works. It's like the

Landians in their colonies. Also, there are many and many rules, many timetables. Living there is no fun. It's a survival."

"OK, I can see it, but when you are adopted by Landian family and become a Type 2, don't you have to work too?"

"Noooo, Jota! What a question! What a nonsense question! Type 2 Earthians never work. Just put this into your head. Haven't they told you that Type 2s can't work for Landians?"

"Sorry, Erika, I'm new here, please be patient with me. If I'm asking it's because I don't know."

"It's absolutely forbidden for any Earthian, be Type 1 or 2, to work for Landians. True, Type 1s do work hard but they work for themselves, not for any Landian. To summarize: Earthians of any type can't work for Landians. Period!"

"And, what happens if an Earthian is found working for a Landian?"

"That's easy, Jota. It's the Landian's crime, and I say crime indeed. They are punished and may even be expelled from the colony."

"But, why is that so?"

"The rules, Jota, those are the rules. And, rules must be followed."

Chapter 50

First Talk with Antonina at the Mother-Ship

This evening I had dinner with Antonina at the diner in our sector. She told me she was working in the served waters division.

"And the smell there doesn't bother you?" I asked

"Not much actually, since our olfaction is less sensitive than yours," she answered, a little upset. "We feel the odors but, for us, there are not so many gradations in smell such as Earthians do have."

"For us, the smell of things also hasn't the same meaning as they have for you people. This is one of the problems of us being intellectually superior," she concluded with a smile.

"But do you Landians feel the taste of foods?"

"Oh, yes, our sensitivity for taste is equal or superior to yours. But we find it difficult choosing food by its smell."

"Antonina, do you people use perfumes?"

"Well, I do like perfumes but in Landa using perfumes is considered vulgar or futile, despite not being forbidden. It is just considered as bad taste. In addition, our rudimentary olfaction does not allow us to appreciate their nuances."

"We, Landians, have less olfactory receptors, and our olfactory cortex is less developed as compared to Earthians."

"We use our brain cortex to nobler things than smelling," she said smiling malevolently at me.

"Yes, you are right, Antonina, it appears that olfaction increases as brain "power" decreases. This makes sense for me since animals, in order to eat, have first to find their lunch. And, they do that by olfaction."

"For example," I went on, "dogs have 10 thousand times the human olfactory sensitivity. And some races of dogs, like the *bloodhounds* have even more sensitive olfaction. These last dogs can follow the scent of lost children or fugitives with incredible accuracy."

And, I went on:

"I have a curious habit of smelling my books. When I smell an old book of mine, immediately the memories of that period come to my mind."

I've found it relevant to put here all this talk about olfaction, smells, scents, perfumes. Because I, myself, ended up by being a victim of this marvelous gift of nature.

After dinner and until the next day, there would be no more communal tasks but cleaning our cabins. Occasionally, an inspector would ask us to check our cabins. Since we would be free until next day, Antonina invited me to visit her cabin, where we could talk more freely. Remember, the cabins were a bit tight 1-meter-wide, 2-meter-high and 3 meter in length. The sleeping berth was located above all facilities, allowing for a space below the bed. Here, were the toilet and a sink/faucet.

No sewage system. The toilet had a hermetic lid to avoid smells and prevent leaking of waste in the event of a gravity emergency.

So it was that we went to her cabin and lay down in her bed. Then, as we were side to side holding our hands, Antonina began telling me some facts about her life.

"The last time I was in this mother-ship was many years ago when I moved to live on Earth. I couldn't stand anymore the austerity and hypocrisy in Landa. Our life was good if you consider material comforts. My husband and I had a nice home, no lack of food, no cold discomforts. Our home was excessively heated like all Landian's homes."

"I didn't know you were married. Where is your husband?"

"He is not on Earth. He is in Landa but dead and lost. Sergei was at an expedition across the dark side of Landa and their tractor fell down a magma crevasse. They melted within the magma and were lost forever." Her eyes went wet as she was saying this.

"We had no children."

She told me that, after losing her husband, she knew a man and they got in love with each other. But, since she was young, the mourning period was too extensive.

"But why did he not come to Earth with you?"

"He couldn't get the license to leave Landa since they suspected we were about to get married, what was forbidden during the mourning period. For me, life in Landa was becoming unbearable, such idiotic rules and such hypocrisy. My professional work as a scientist had been scraped and I was given a desk to process the interminable flow of information arriving from the Procyon system. My knowledge in Physics didn't mean anything more for them."

"And, there appeared this expedition to Earth, and they were looking for volunteers. I applied and was accepted. And, I'm here."

These revelations of Antonina, along with her sweet voice began relaxing me to the point I fell asleep. Strangely, the way she talked, her voice, her firmness stifled my desire for her that night. What proved to be a good thing; as I later would learn.

When I woke in the middle of the night, Antonina was embraced to me. Slowly, I disengaged from her body and went to my cabin.

I woke in the morning with Antonina caressing my hair and my face. We went together to the diner, where we had breakfast. I would be working again in the vegetable garden this morning.

Chapter 51

Second Talk with Erika

As soon as I got to the vegetable garden, I saw Erika. Our task today would be in another sector. We were to harvest lettuce leaves and sow seeds in their places. Then, we would add fertilizer and throw some water. The job was easy and, actually, relaxing and the monitors gave us a lot of room for talking as our work was voluntary.

I asked Erika if we could continue our talk from the day before. She acquiesced promptly.

"If you are so curious, why not?" she said to me.

"What about the learning of the Landians' language? Do you people learn their language in the schools?"

"We don't learn Landian language, period!" she said a little upset.

"How come you don't?"

"The reason is so simple, Jota. Try to understand this: we don't have enough intelligence for learning their language and this goes beyond just language. Earthian children do not learn their "things" and that is a subject I don't like to discuss. Next question, please?"

By some combination of factors, I was being shown three different perspectives of Landian/Earthian interaction given by three people on different conditions: there was Antonina, of course, and the Earthian was me. Then, there was my brief talk with Fabiana and then, Erika. These three samples were beginning to make some sense in my mind. However, the whole picture was still very fuzzy.

During my talk with Erika, I got the impression that she was getting bored with answering my constant questions.

"Erika, are you getting tired of our talk?"

"Not at all, Jota, but you know what? I'm curious too!"

"Why don't we do an exchange of questions?"

"What *an exchange* would be, Jota. Mind telling me?"

At this moment I perceived that a monitor was staring at us. I then harvested some leaves, sowed some seeds, fertilizer, water. And we changed our positions.

"Are you going to explain me this *exchange thing*, or what, Jota?"

"OK, OK. An exchange would be I asking you a question, and you answering me. Then, you ask me a question and I answer you. Just like that"

"I don't think I understood. You give me a question and I give you another question?"

"More or less, and the answers are included too," I said

"Hummm, I think you suggest that we ask questions alternatingly."

"Yesss, that's exactly it, and the answers also alternatingly," I said, giving a funny emphasis to "alternatingly."

And then, I thought I had got to my point. But no!

"But, this is not an exchange like you have defined it. We are just alternating questions and answers. And this means you haven't explained me what an exchange really is! Do you think I'm a sort of fool, Jota?" and she made me a funny menacing face.

"OK, let's do it different. Do you like chocolate bars?"

"Oh, I love chocolate, have you got one?"

"No, I haven't, it's only an example. Suppose you have an onion and I have a chocolate bar. I take it that you don't like onions, right?"

"Arrgh, I hate onion!"

"OK, then we are getting to do an exchange. I do love onions but haven't got one and you love chocolate but haven't got a bar"

"Then, if you give me an onion I give you a chocolate, and that's an exchange," and I concluded, with an air of victory.

"Hummm, but if you love onions so much, arrgghh, I can give you plenty of them. You don't need to give me a chocolate bar."

I began to feel I was wasting my time and, very soon, Erika would tire of my philosophical exercises. And, I would be depleted of additional information regarding their ways of life.

"OK, Erika, you are quite right. But, you are reasoning as if we both are "good" persons. But suppose I'm a bad guy. I don't want to help you. Just suppose, OK?"

"And, suppose you are lost and hungry and that you have got some onions. And, now, I approach you and perceive you are hungry and very sad and I have a bag full of chocolate bars. Are you getting the picture?"

"Yes, I get it. You are a bad guy. I think I'm getting it"

"Then, I say to you: hi, little girl, I see you are hungry. Do you want some chocolates?" and I went on:

"Ha, ha, ha, I can give you some, but only if you give me those delicious onions."

"Then, you give me the onions and I give you some chocolate bars. And I continue my way laughing at you."

Erika was looking at me, with wide-open eyes, as if in shock.

And, then, I concluded:

"Now, Erika, that's *an exchange*. Did you understand?"

"Yes, I think I'm beginning to understand: an *exchange* is something you do with bad guys. Am I correct? And, there is one thing more, Jota. Since you propose to make an exchange with me, this means you are a bad guy!"

Now, I was in deep trouble!

"No, Erika, nothing you said is correct. Look, how can I be a bad guy? No bad guys can be in this ship. Don't you know they know everything about each of us here? Look, when they chose me to accompany my mentor here, they had my doings since I was 12 years old!"

"I see. And who is your mentor?"

"My mentor is a Landian scientist called Antonina. Do you want to meet her? And she is now in the served waters, doing voluntary work."

"But, tell me Jota, how you people get things on Earth? Like, say, food, clothes?"

"Well, Erika, the Earth is very complicated. There are many countries, many languages, many religions, and a lot of bad people. To get things there, you have to work. Then, they give you certain pieces of paper having numbers printed on them: they call it *money.*"

"With this money thing you can get anything you want. Say you want 100 chocolate bars? No problem. Each bar is worth a money paper printed with the number 2. Then you give 100 pieces of that money. But there are "moneys" with larger numbers on it, like 200. And, having this money pieces you can get anything you want, nobody will ask questions."

Erika widened her eyes in surprise.

"In Landa, things don't function like that. I can get anything I want from my mentor. Not only he gets me things but also he does nice things for me."

"Nice things, like what?" I asked

"Well, besides giving me presents, he tells me stories, talks interesting things with me, caresses me, calls me nice names, takes me to see interesting places."

"And you also do nice things for him? Things that he likes you do to him?"

"Sure, everything I do he likes in a way or another."

"Humm, like what?" I asked

"What he likes most is that I stay close to him, that I rest my head on his lap, that I talk anything to him."

"Is your mentor married?"

"Sure he is what a question!"

"And his wife likes you too? Does she caress you?"

"Not so much, but I think she likes me."

"And, tell me Erika. You said your mentor caresses you. How does he caress you? I like to know because my mentor also caresses me and I love it. She caresses my hair, my face and my neck."

"Well, that's exactly how my mentor caresses me. How else could it be?"

Then, I made a question I was planning to make and only now found an opening.

"OK, but I've never caressed my mentor. Should I caress her too?"

Erika became quiet and harvested a few lettuces, sowed a few seeds, put on the fertilizer and watered the soil. She was thinking what to say, probably. Then, she looked down pensively.

"Jota, please listen to me. I see that they didn't tell you many things. What I can say is that you did well by not caressing your mentor. There are rules in Landa, Jota, don't you know? You never, and I repeat, never touch your mentor. And that includes caressing, does it not? The rule is: your mentor does the touching to you, he/she caresses you, kisses you, embraces you, protects you, takes care of you. You just receive. It is simple as that. Isn't it?"

Chapter 52

The Bath

I had been working all day in the vegetable garden, and I was tired. I don't know if it was because my physical exertions there or due to my talk with Erica. It might be both. At dinner, I met Antonina and we dined together and talked about our activities during the day.

"Tonight we are going to bath together. And we will stay together and talk," she informed me.

Antonina's "orders" caused me an enormous well-being feeling, and a mental lightness. Something in her certainty about the orders, as if they had been programmed in advance, in a sequence, gave to me finality as to their origin. And I loved that finality.

Also, I began to realize that Antonina, and maybe the others from her "family", gave a great importance to the water activities. Since the episodes of washing my car, the ceremony of waters, the purification bath in the stream, and even the jump amidst the falling water, I began to think: *Would all those water related events be part of some rites of passage? And, if so, was Antonina leading me, slowly but firmly, toward some end?*

In the ship there were many halls with TVs, game tables, chess. About two hours after dinner they served light food, snacks, juices, coffee or chocolate. Like we did daily, Antonina and I went to a dining hall closest to our cabins, had a few snacks and talked. Then, Antonina said to me:

"Now, we are going to my cabin, Jota. You came so dirty from the vegetable garden! I'll give you a bath before you go to bed. And bring a clean uniform, please."

As soon as we got to our contiguous cabins, Antonina said I should get some towels in my cabin and meet her in her cabin. When I got to her cabin, the sink was already full of hot fuming water and some towels were immersed, soaking.

"Now, Jota, take off your uniform and underpants, please. I'll teach you how to bathe in this ship," she said laughing.

I did as ordered and, as I turned, I saw that Antonina was nude. I had never seen Antonina nude, and her body perturbed me. I tried to think about sad things in order to stifle my excitation but to no result. Antonina saw my "complicated state".

"Jota, you are a very naughty boy, you know?" and then she threw cold water to my intimate parts.

"Now, turn your back to me, Jota, so that I can wash your backside."

She took from the sink a towel already soaked in hot water and began sliding it lightly onto me. Antonina was meticulous. Since the use of cleaning products was forbidden (water recycling rules) the bath with towels had to be more thorough. My backside cleaning had no particulars. After all, I was a receiver (as defined by Erika's rules).

Then, she turned her back to me.

"Now, Jota, you have seen how I did to you!"

I began to rub her body ever lightly. Firstly, behind her head and, then, to her neck. An inebriant scent emanated from her body, intensified by the warm water. I went down to the shoulders, back and waist.

"Now, careful Jota, I'm very sensitive here! Use your hands, Jota, no towel, please!" she said, separating her legs and pointing to her buttocks.

I soaked my hands in the hot water and began rubbing, delicately, her buttocks. She seemed to be enjoying since she turned her face sideways, eyes closed and a smile. However, no sign whatsoever of sexual arousal. Not even her breathing had increased.

"Now, Jota, let's go to our front sides. I'll wash you first so that you learn how to wash me," she began laughing and kissed the back of my neck before I turned. I breathed deeply, trying to suppress my arousal.

Then, she began. First, she soaked the towel in hot water and applied it to my hair. Leaving the towel on the sink she massaged my wet hair and my face. Taking the towel again she rubbed my neck, shoulders and arms. By doing this, she occasionally touched her body to mine, her breasts touching my chest. I inferred that the washing sequence would be from top to down. Then, she soaked the towel again and rubbed my chest, belly and lower belly.

After finishing my torso, she left the towel on the sink border, soaked her hands in the hot water, knelt down and began cleaning my genitals, periodically soaking her hands in the water. She was in no hurry and was meticulous. The touch of her hand on me was so good, so delicate, that I was afraid of getting off. But then, I imagined myself nude at an African savanna, surrounded by hungry hyenas. It worked. Antonina followed her cleaning, going to my thighs, legs and feet.

Partly following Erika's advice and partly my own survival instincts I just kept receiving Antonina's maneuvers on my body and kept absolutely passive. There was no space, not even a slight opening for me to embrace or kiss her. An invisible wall parted us.

I had survived this first stage.

"Now, you wash my front side, Jota, let's see how you perform."

At that moment, I had to act and, this, was not receiving. I knew I was treading dangerous ground, a forbidden territory according to Erika's rules. But, at the same time, I would be following orders. And, orders, well, you execute.

I began soaking the towel in hot water and twisting it over her head. Then I used my hands to wash her hair and as I was doing this I remembered never to have washed a woman's hair before. Oh, and not a man's for that matter.

"Soak well my hair and run your hands to remove the excess water" she commanded. So, I did.

Then, I soaked hands in water and began washing her forehead, face, ears. From her body emanated the scent of a female, slightly pungent, slightly sweaty, with no perfumes, and inebriant. She had her eyes closed and smiled approvingly. So far, so good, I thought. Next step was the neck, where I used the towel and passed to the shoulders. For her arms I used my wet hands. Then, I went to her hands.

She was passive, but now, her eyes were open and looked, inquisitively at my eyes. I then asked that she raised her arms and, using the towel and hands, washed delicately her armpits that released a slightly sweaty scent, which was extremely agreeable. And she kept looking at me as if trying to sense some emotion, or whatever. I was approaching a dangerous territory now: her chest. I soaked my hands and washed her upper thorax delicately.

"Jota, don't use the towel here; just use your hands. Towel is too rough," she said, touching one breast.

Just following her orders, I soaked my hands in hot water and began. I thought I would go through easily. No chance. Her breasts were so delicately firm and her nipples so hard and begging that I began to feel a bit dizzy as a result of my continuously repressed desire. Antonina felt I was in trouble and said:

"OK, Jota, that's enough here, move on downward, there is still much to be washed and we don't have all night!"

The next step was her belly and, here, no problem. My troubles rekindled at my approaching the lowest part of her abdomen. But, Antonina saved me:

"This part I wash myself," and, turning her back to me she washed her pubic region. But, very soon, she faced me again and asked me to continue. I washed her upper thighs with wet hands. In my doing this, Antonina covered her sex with her hands. For the remaining of her thighs and legs I used the towels. I was exhausted from the repressed desire and fear of doing something out of the "rules". I couldn't forget Erika's advice.

The bath was over. We dried ourselves with other clean towels.

"Let's go to my bed, Jota, don't put on your clothes yet"

We lay down and stood in silence for a while. Then, Antonina began caressing my face and my neck. Then, she kissed my neck affectionately.

"Do you like my caressing you, Jota?"

"I like your caresses very much, more than you think," I said, my throat slightly tightened.

"But, I have some need to caress you too; did you know it, Antonina?"

She stayed in silence for some minutes and then placed her head onto my chest, embracing me with one arm.

"I know you are afraid of me, Jota."

"Yes, I'm afraid of doing something you may not like."

"But, you don't need to be afraid, Jota. I'll never harm you"

"You are already harming me, Antonina; I'm suffering because of you."

"And, how is this 'suffering,' Jota?"

"It is anguish, a fear that you leave me, a desire of you. I need you, Antonina, and I need you badly."

At this moment, I felt I was going to cry, but I repressed it.

"And what you need me for, Jota? Tell me, tell me."

"That's my problem. I need you as a woman, but there is much more that I need from you. I suffer when I'm not with you. I feel that I need you all the time."

"And do you want me as a woman, Jota?"

"Yes I desire you badly, but I'm at a loss how to act."

"I know you desire me, Jota, I know very well, and I can see it also."

"But, it will go away, Jota, it will go away," she said tenderly, but with a firmness, a certainty, a finality, while caressing my face.

This last phrase of Antonina caught me like a blow. A tender blow. I had the feeling that she knew that "it would go away". Not because "it would go away" by itself but because she would see to that.

I couldn't imagine how my intense desire for her would go away by itself. There was, however, a possibility. That some much stronger feeling, some much stronger need, would either nullify my desire for her or make it insignificant.

And, in parallel with my "theories", I began to have a clear feeling that Antonina was conditioning me, maneuvering my mind, changing my perception of her. And, more than that: changing my perception of myself.

Her dealings with me seemed totally devoid of emotions, questionings, fears, hesitations. All that would be normal in a man/woman relation.

Could it be that those purifications, baths, caresses, and talks were part of a bigger scheme or plan? Involving many people like myself? Would it be a plan to conquer me, to make me dependent on her, to make me some sort of slave?

I felt that, from Antonina, there emanated a flow of intelligence, command and benevolence. All together. And, this powerful emanation inhibited me of acting toward her, of embracing her, kissing her. And what remained was ... receiving whatever came from her. I then remembered the words of Erika in the vegetable garden:

The rule is: your mentor does the touching to you, he/she caresses you, kisses you, embraces you, protects you, takes care of you. You receive. Simple as that. Isn't it?"

Chapter 53

Life In Landa, According to Antonina

After the first bath, my baths with Antonina became routine.

Not all evenings, but most. However, what we did on those baths did not progress to more intimacy. On the contrary, they fell into a very definite protocol. Sure, amid this protocol, Antonina said nice things to me and I to her. But, the protocol was there, sometimes disguised but, there, all right.

In one of those watery evenings, we had already bathed and were lying in her bed. In the impossibility of other activities, we talked. Antonina held my hand all the time.

"How you people get energy in Landa?"

"We have three sources of energy: geothermal, hot fusion and cold fusion. Still, for small devices, we use the graphite radioactive batteries that Greg has shown you in the farm."

I mentioned that in Earth, many scientists pursue the dream of cold fusion without any success up to these days.

"How could you make cold fusion to work?"

"Cold fusion is known from a long time in Landa. They use a porous alloy of palladium with the element 115 and feed this with deuterium and tritium. Sure, there are more details, but I don't feel like giving a lecture right now, Jota."

"And how you get this geothermal energy?"

"Well, the geothermal energy was the first form we used in Landa and is straightforward. We sink giant heat exchangers into the magma wells and input water. Water transforms into vapor and turns gigantic turbines that move the generators."

"This is, however, a very primitive form of using geothermal energy, but we keep it working since it functions well and the maintenance is minimal."

"But, more recently, we began using a process that converts heat directly to electricity. It is based in what you know on Earth as the effects Peltier and Seebeck."

"Energy is so plenty in Landa that we heat our houses more than necessary. That's our sole luxury and compensates the extreme cold outside."

"One positive side of the low temperature in Landa is that there is no need for refrigeration. We don't have refrigerators or freezers. Each home has cabinets on the external walls that make contact with the outside air. The external wall in these cabinets is made of glass to allow inspectors to verify our stocks. Overstocking is forbidden."

"And what about the schools?"

"Going to school is compulsory; each child is followed by a board of educators and has a detailed spreadsheet with his or her evolution. Education, in Landa, is taken seriously, and no child is left without a complete educational follow-up."

"How you people move on Landa?"

"We don't walk outside the buildings. It's simply too cold. All transport is done with cars and every family has one or two cars, depending of the family size. The cars are not one's property; they belong to the colonies and are leased to colony members through some protocols. Cars are used only for short distances, though. For larger dislocations, we use trains. For civilians, there is no air transport on Landa. Air transport is exclusive for militaries."

"What of kind of clothes you people use in Landa?"

"Oh, Jota, there is not much to talk about clothes in Landa. This makes me depressed. We don't have fashion, and clothes are antiquate, ugly, only functional. They are very functional, they are. I would say they are too functional. Each person is granted a basic wardrobe that varies according to his or her type of work. All clothes are comfortable, they keep you warm, and they are made to last. Oh, how long they last!"

"Oh yes, Antonina, Erika has been telling exactly the same story about the clothing and "fashion" in Landa" I said with a naive countenance. I think my comment hit some chord.

"Who's Erika?"

"Oh, I met Erika at the vegetable garden. She's Brazilian, but wears a white uniform. She has been telling many interesting things about her life in Landa," I said, in passing, feigning naivety.

"How come "wears a white uniform"! It can't be!" Antonina said, a bit upset

"She told me her mentor is a pilot here and she is with him."

"Humm, I see, that explains it," she answered, calmer.

"And what "interesting things" has she told you, Jota?"

"Oh, not many really. She only told me her life is so good there. She lives in a Landian colony and has been adopted when she was 8. And, she explained me how people get and wear clothes there." I decided to stop here and let Antonina ask for more.

Then, I would unload my "baits", piecewise, according to what she asked.

But I was mistaken. Antonina didn't ask for more details of Erika's life. She retook our previous talk about life on Landa as if what I told her of Erika had been a brief, uninteresting detail. However, according to Yuri's analysis of me, I was an excellent observer. And I felt her ways changed a little.

"So, Jota, it appears that you have lost your curiosity about our ways of life in Landa," Antonina said to me while she caressed my hair.

"I'm still curious, Antonina. How is the medical care in Landa? Everyone gets it?"

"Hummm, that's an interesting subject, Jota. Medicare is perfect in Landa. Actually, I call it excessive and intrusive. Medical checkups are compulsory once a year. No one can skip the annual exam. Treatments and surgeries are performed as necessary. However, elective surgeries are very difficult to be accepted, and a psychological report needs to be obtained. Also, the treatments and surgeries are compulsory. This is because a person which is not treated may become a future burden for Medicare."

"You want more, Jota? Aren't you fed up with Landa's costumes?"

Actually, I was well fed up, but Antonina's voice inebriated me. I had thought, a few minutes before, of doing a little game with her to get more information about what was destined to be my future. The talks with Erika seemed a reasonable bargaining chip since Antonina appeared to be genuinely interested in knowing what I knew through Erika's references. But I forgot one detail. I was deeply in love with Antonina, and I felt she loved me too, albeit in a different form. And, to bargain, you need a cold mind.

"Yes, Antonina, how do you people get things in Landa?"

"There is no money, nothing is in want. Everything that is needed is provided in adequate quantity. There are no delays, no mistakes. All your life is controlled and watched. Your minimal privacy is at home, with limits. Communication is through very sophisticated cell phone like devices. However, no privacy exists in communications. It is assumed you will not talk "wrong" things. Talks considered futile or unnecessary are intercepted and warned. Our life in Landa is dictated by survival, costumes, and by scientific and technologic advance. We do just what is necessary. Not more, not less.

Chapter 54
Religion in Landa

I asked Antonina about religion in Landa.

"There is no religion in Landa like you have in Earth. However, most Landians believe in spirits or beings without substance. They also believe in mysterious beings and terrible beasts on the dark side of Landa where night is eternal. Landians also believe in afterlife."

"And you, Antonina, do you believe in afterlife?"

"Yes, I do, but for me and most Landians, afterlife is a brief period, a transition between two states."

"And do you people have evidences for this afterlife?" I asked.

"Yes, we have as much evidence as you, on Earth, have evidence of God" she answered, pulling my hair.

"But, on Landa, like on Earth, there is evil! And, this you should know, Jota, looking deep into my eyes. In Landa there are bad people, like on Earth. And there are bad Landians living on Earth too."

And, then, Antonina began telling me some things I didn't quite know:

"After our communications with Procyon 2, we began to realize that not all communications arriving in Landa through Procyon 2 came, originally, from there."

"We found out that many blocks of data were being simply retransmitted from Procyon 2 and that these were coming from many sources in the Universe. Procyon 2 appeared to simply relay those data to us. And, since Procyon 2 stopped accepting our signals, the mystery went on."

"As Yuri told you, Jota, and I remember that "lecture", the third Procyon planet, known as Procyon 3, is inhabited by humans in the sense we know the term. They appear to have a same physical substrate as us and also they claim to have "emotions". But, also, these Procyon 3 beings, contact other planets, in other star systems. This, they inform us, continually."

"What is even more interesting is that these "contacts" they have with other systems are not all of scientific character. Also, they informed us that there are beings in Procyon 3 that lack a physical body and they call them *spirits*."

"Those spirits, despite lacking a physical body, can communicate. And, they are exchanging information with a special class of Landians that, probably, Yuri didn't mention to you."

"And what are those, Antonina, tell me, please. Do you know them?" and I began to get a beginning of chill down my spine.

"Those are the monks, Jota and I never saw one. But they live in Landa all right. And you don't need to be afraid of them," she said, messing with my hair.

"What about those monks, Antonina?"

"They don't live in the colonies; they live in isolated locals, like the Tibetan monasteries on Earth. Each group of colonies has its own monastery."

"What functions do the monks have?"

"Well, Jota, in what concerns the colonies, the monks talk with council members and give advice to them as to customs. They do not interfere with the administrative sector of the colonies."

"And whom the monks receive advice from?"

"From what is known in Landa, the monks communicate with the 3rd planet of Procyon. It is said that they receive advice from the Spirits that live in the 3rd planet."

Chapter 55

Third Talk with Erika

Next morning, I went again to work in the vegetable garden, where I soon found Erika. I asked permission from the monitor to work beside her. It was granted. However, I feared that our talks might be interrupted by some reason and decided to obtain more information as soon as possible regarding her life as an adopted Earthian. Seeing me, Erika smiled and asked me if we would continue with the "exchanges".

"Yes, Erika, we will continue the exchanges, but remember I'm not a bad guy."

"Erika, can you tell me how you interact with your mentor? You see, sometimes I feel insecure in how to deal with Antonina."

"But, before you explain me, I have one other question: do you love your mentor?"

My question made Erika lower her eyes and become quiet for a moment. She even stopped with gardening. Then, she looked right at my eyes.

"I love my mentor more than I love any other person. I just couldn't live without him! And now, it's my turn to ask:"

"Jota, tell me, do you love Antonina?" and she asked this with an inquisitive look straight at my eyes. Trying to buy some time, I diverted:

"Why you ask this?"

"Because you said she is your mentor, of course"

"Yes, Erika I believe I love her but still can't figure out how I love her and how she loves me. Yes, if love is to need someone badly, I definitely do love her."

"I thought you were a bit more intelligent, Jota!"

"I will tell you, Jota what, really, is to love someone."

"I'm listening."

"You love someone when you prefer to die rather than losing his/her love for you."

"So, again, Jota, do you love Antonina?"

"Well, according to your definition of love I think I still don't love Antonina up to the point of dying."

"Hummm," she grumbled

"But, each time it is getting more difficult for me to stay without her presence," I concluded.

Then, I felt she wanted to release some repressed feelings:

"I love my mentor so much that just thinking I might lose him makes me feel a pain right inside my chest."

"Tell me, Erika, do you love your parents the same way you love your mentor?"

"Nooooo, Jota, it is quite different! It's a different kind love."

"And what this difference would be, Erika?"

"There are many differences, Jota. One of them is that my mentor is a "superior being" and, thus, he loves me from above."

"But, Erika, who told you your mentor is a *superior being*?"

"At school, of course. All Landians are superior beings; didn't you know this, Jota? Haven't you learned that in school?"

"No, I haven't. No one in Earth knows about Landa or Landians. Only a few people like you, me, and the Earthians living here know about all this, Erika."

"How come, I can't believe this, Jota!"

After I assured Erika this was not an immediate problem, she recomposed. Then, I went on with my questioning:

"But, since Landians are superior beings, what about the Earthians?"

"Earthians are inferior beings, of course, Jota."

"But, if this is so, who are we, you and me, Erika?"

"You and me are inferior beings, of course!" she said with a smile and threw some water at me.

"And, is it bad to be an inferior being, Erika?"

"No, not at all! It is even better than being *superiors*."

"Tell me, Jota, do you feel bad being inferior to God?"

"Huummm, I don't think so." I grumbled.

"OK, OK, Erika, I'll buy this. But, if your mentor loves you *from above* how, then, you love him?"

"Oh, Jota, what a silly question! Of course I love him *from below*!"

"And what about your parents, are they superior beings too?"

"No, Jota, they aren't superiors, they are equal to me, they are good to me and their love to me is *level*, neither from above nor from below remember this: *level love*."

"Hummm, then you are saying that love can come from above, from below and level?"

I thought that my question was provocative and would cause her some reflection. But, no.

"Of course, Jota, loves are different depending to whom they are directed. Do you believe in God, Jota?"

"Yes, I do."

"Then, you should know that His love for you comes from above you! And do you love God, Jota?"

"Sure I love Him"

"Then, your love for Him comes from below, simple as that" and Erika made the gesture of obvious.

"And, what about *your* love for God, how is it directed?" I asked.

"This is obvious, Jota, my love for Him comes from below, since I am inferior to Him." And, seeing no monitors looking at us, she threw some dirt at me.

"I am beginning to understand, Erika. But, what about the love for a man, for example the love, say, for your boyfriend or his love for you. What kind of love is that?"

"Oh, that's a more intelligent question, Jota. Logically, this is a quite different kind of love and we call it *carnal love*. It involves sex and possession and also egotism to some extent. And this love can also hurt. And, sometimes, it involves no love at all!" and she said this with a smile.

"And, what about the love between a Landian and an Earthian? Can this love be of the carnal type?"

Erika's face reddened immediately. She looked at all sides.

"This question I shouldn't even answer, Jota, how dare you formulate such a nonsense question to me?" she said with a semi-closed mouth and an indignant look, stifling her anger. But then, she saw sincerity in my eyes.

"Don't you know, Jota, that this "thing" you mentioned, and that I don't even dare to word it, is a grave crime?"

"I didn't know really, Erika. I'm so sorry to have asked this. But whose crime is it, since there are two parts involved?"

"Naturally, the Landian is the perpetrator in this case" Erika answered, unwillingly.

"But, if both parts are involved in a consensual sex, why is it that only the Landian carries the fault?"

"Hummm, there is so much you still have to learn, Jota. Look, Jota, please, pay attention. Aren't Earthians inferior beings? That's the reason, Jota. Earthians are *vulnerable*, not only regarding sex but in all relations with Landians. In principle, Earthians are considered as *victims*. Of course, there are nuances that need to be evaluated case by case."

"Wow! How you happen to know so many things, Erika?"

"School, Jota. We go to school. There, we learn things. Isn't so on Earth?"

"Not exactly so, Erika, not exactly."

But then I went on:

"OK, I see it now, Erika. But suppose an Earthian wounds or kills a Landian. Who's the criminal?"

"Don't try to confuse me, Jota, I'm no child! In this case the Earthian is judged by an Earthian court according to Earthian' s laws. And those courts are severe, Jota. Expelling from colonies or even death are common penalties."

"Erika, you have mentioned God's love. But who is God to you, Earthians, living in Landa?"

"Well, Jota, I suppose that you were taught that God is the Creator, a being infinitely good, wise and powerful?"

"Sure, they taught me this, but I wanted *your* view. Thanks."

I went on with my task for the day in order to arrange my thoughts. Then, I asked Erika what I believed would be a crucial point for me.

"Erika, tell me, do you consider your mentor also as a god?"

And I expected also some reflection from her, some delay. But, no. Her answer came immediately.

"My mentor is my god in Landa. But there is another god, the God of all men."

Chapter 56

The Bridge: 1st Visit

After he knew I would stay about 1 month in the ship, Greg invited me to a visit of the command bridge of the Alpha, which was the name of our ship.   The sister ship, Beta, was in orbit around Landa. A third ship would be operational soon and was in construction, already orbiting Landa.

Greg was one of more than 20 navigators operating in the Alpha. The command bridge was a marvel of technology. Different from what one sees in sci-fi films, the bridge didn't have those gigantic windows where the crew sees "the entire Universe".

All the seeing was done by means of cameras placed at different points. What caught, my attention immediately were the big monitors: 2 monitors on the front side with view of the bow, 2 monitors at starboard (right side) with a view from the ship's right side, 2 monitors at port side (with view from the left side) and 2 monitors with view from the stern.

Also, 2 monitors were located on the roof and 2 more at the floor. These last showed the view of cameras on the top and bottom sides of the ship. For each set of 2 monitors, there was a big console with seats at the front. Today, there were 12 navigators at the bridge, 2 at each console. At present, there were a total of 24 navigators on board. At each console, the monitor images remained static during 10 minutes then all 12 panels changed images simultaneously.

Greg told me that the Alpha, when going between Landa and Earth, cruises in the ecliptic plane, which is an imaginary surface defined by Earth or Landa orbits, which are in a same plane.

Greg explained me that the Alpha keeps turning permanently along its central axis. This rotation provides artificial gravity and stabilizes the ship due to the gyroscopic effect. Due to this permanent rotation of the ship the stars appear to be rotating around the ship and the navigators can't get a good view of them. To work around this problem, the cameras take photos of all sides exactly when the floor plane of the bridge crosses the ecliptic plane. This set of photos, that feed the images on all monitors are taken each 10 minutes. These photos cover all views of the sky.

"Jota, seat here by my side," said Greg after having introduced me to the other navigators in the bridge.

"I'm going to explain you how we calculate the ship's velocity. We are, presently, at the Lagrange 1 point, moving at 30 km/sec. However, en route to Landa, our cruise velocity is 300 km/sec. During an interval of 100 minutes, or after only 10 photos we move 1,800,000 km. This is enough to see a change in the positions of the nearest stars in relation to the more distant stars. This change in position we call *parallax*."

"We have a base of the 20 nearest stars, of which Proxima Centauri is the closest one, at 4.3 light years from us (Identical distance to Alpha Centauri)."

"But how does this method work?" I asked

"Jota, suppose you are in a train and you look at the window. The poles at the sides of the line zoom past you super-fast. The homes and people a bit farther from the tracks don't seem to move so fast. Finally, the mountains very far, appear to be immobile. Now, fix your attention is some small house that you know to be at 400 m from the train. And you see that the house moves a certain angle in relation to the mountain far away in some time interval, say 10 seconds. Using some mathematics, you can calculate the distance the train has moved in 10 seconds and, then, its velocity."

"As a matter of fact, despite we are almost "parked" here at Lagrange 1, we are actually moving at 30 km/sec and our cameras and computers can calculate our velocity. I can show you the parallax of Alpha Centauri. Look at this photo taken of Alpha Centauri a few minutes ago. Then, look at a photo we took 24 hrs before. We will amplify the photos."

"Look, Jota, are the 2 photos identical?"

I examined carefully the 2 photos. They were similar but Alpha Centauri appeared to have moved a little bit, relative to the stars at the background."

"See, Jota, from that small drift of the Alpha Centauri, our computers can calculate how much we had moved in 24 hrs and then our velocity. These two data are important: position and velocity."

"OK, Greg, but wait. You said Alpha Centauri is 40.6 trillion km from here. But, how you know this distance? This seems to me a circular argument," I said a little upset. At this moment a few navigators were watching Greg's "lecture" and my questions. And they were having a lot of fun.

"Hey, Greg, now, Jota has caught you ehhh!" one of them shouted to Greg. And others came to see the cause of such a commotion.

"Jota, the way we calculate the distance of Alfa Centauri is exactly the opposite of the method we used to calculate the distance travelled by our ship," and saying this, Greg laughed loudly looking at the others.

Seeing my upset features, Greg invited me to the kitchen and we had a delicious coffee. He and another navigator went to a blackboard and patiently explained to me the intricacies of the calculation. And I spare the reader of this boring explanation.

Chapter 57

1st Lecture: Water Control in the Body

As I mentioned, every day we had lectures in the ship, covering many different subjects. Many took place simultaneously, and some were considered more relevant. Still, others were fundamental, compulsory for the crew, and recommended for passengers. The lectures had a proper calendar and were not postponed or altered by the different phases of the trip. Such as was the case we had now, being the end of one leg of the trip and the beginning of another.

Who attended the lectures? These were usually open to all, with the exception of the very specialized ones. The lectures dealing with health and medical subjects were attended, in great part, by the medical students aboard the ship. I may have mentioned that the mother-ship was a permanent institution. As such, getting an internship at the mother-ship was a dream of many medical students. The demand was indeed so great that there was an examination or board to select the 500 or so medical students for a 2 way trip of the ship from Landa to Earth and back, a journey taking, easily, 5 years.

The medical students, during these long periods, were, actually, progressing in their careers. I'm telling these details to justify that lectures by renowned doctors were very coveted by future doctors. Also, these doctors were extremely useful in helping the graduate doctors, both in clinical and surgical procedures.

Back to the lectures.

Some lectures were recorded in studios and presented in high-quality videos. Others were live. The presence was monitored since, for some groups, such as the medical students, some classes were compulsory, as I said. The lecture I was about to attend today was considered the number 1 priority: *The water control in the body.*

The lecturer would be the famous professor Antonin Rochavsky, MD, PhD, one of the many Landian doctors serving in the ship. I didn't know Professor Rochavsky in person but had heard about his notable career. He was a bachelor, 65, and lived in the ship. His life was his patients and his students, and he loved both of them. I'm afraid of digressing too much in this notable person and so we begin. As I said, the lecture was live.

The lecture hall had 200 seats and was full; many people were seated on the floor and many standing. Such was the fame of Dr. Rochavsky. As soon as he entered the hall, all stood and clapped hands.

And, Dr. Rochavsky began;

"The reason for such a theme being a priority here in this craft is that water is considered one of the few substances absolutely essential during the trip."

"From the water depends: the maintenance of vital functions of the body, oxygen production, cleaning of the body and the excrements, irrigation of the vegetable gardens, substrate for the fusion reactors, production of H_2, necessary for CO_2 removal from the air, along with the many types of cleaning procedures."

"But, among those many roles, the water is essential for the vital processes of the body. And, for these to occur and be maintained it is necessary that the body maintains its water reserve at an approximate constant level. Since our body loses water continually it must receive, continually, an input of water. Like a bank account, there is a balance describing the deposits and withdrawals. But, different from the bank account, the body must maintain a constant balance."

"Let's see how our body keeps the balance of water" he began.

"Our first question: how much water do we have in our bodies?"

"There are 2 means of discovering that: one is cremating you and weighing your ashes. Knowing your weight when you were a walking creature, the difference would be water. No, we never did this experiment but the Nazis did. Our scientists did that also using rats or mice" (This is not exact however since fats and other non-water based structures do evaporate as well).

The second method is more precise but more elaborate. The body is cremated and all water evaporating from it is collected. This is what we do here in this ship, with the dead passengers. We recycle their water and keep their ashes as fertilizer and give a small sample to the relatives. But, if you die here as a result of heroism, we don't keep your water or ashes.

We bury you in space, what is an honor. The water recycling in the dead is described in the Earthian movie "Dune", a planet that lacks water. At this point, all clapped hands.

"Well, from what is known from these methods (not recommended) we know that water constitutes 60% of our weigh, as an average. Lean people have more water and fat people less water since fat contains very little water. But fat weighs as you all know. Let's take an average adult male weighing 70 kg. This average creature carries 42 liters of water in his body. That's a lot of water!"

"But all this water is not free in the body like it is in a bottle. The body water is restricted to *compartments*. There are 2 main water compartments in the body: the *intracellular* and the *extracellular*. The intracellular is the largest, having 2/3 of the total water. This means 28 liters in our standard guy of 70 kg weight. Consequently, the extracellular has 1/3 of the water or 14 liters. The extracellular compartment has subdivisions: *intravascular* (within the vessels, 4 liters) and *interstitial* (outside cells, outside vessels, 10 liters). The interstitial compartment is sometimes considered a renegade. However, this is the water region that bathes all cells. This means that the cells "talk" directly with the interstitial medium.

"All this water and its distribution among the compartments are "managed" automatically by our body. The only thing the owner has to do is drink water when he/she feels thirsty.

The body water can distribute among the compartments according to many factors such as water ingestion, temperature, and, more importantly, the hydration degree of the body."

"Forty-two liters is a lot of water and in order to maintain this volume approximately constant we need to do what you do with your bank account. Let's consider a 24-hour period: a table was shown (volumes in ml):

Inputs of water: by drinking 1500, input from foods 500. Water is consumed and generated by the metabolism in more or less the same amount (zero balance).

Outputs of water: urine 1000, feces 200, respiration 700 and sweating 100. These values are averages and hold for a cold climate. The numbers can vary depending on many factors such as exercise, temperature, humidity.

As you can see input and output must match, and they usually do.

When input and output match during a period of time the body is said to be in *water balance*. This is like a well-organized man that keeps his balance at the bank approximately constant by daily examining the gains, deposits and withdrawals. But, differently from our friend financier, we don't do *savings* of water. But camels do.

"This matching between input and output is not exact, however. There are factors that increase water loss from the body: The pathological ones are: fever, diarrhea, vomiting and the physiological are: exercise, sweating, water restriction. As such, we need to be alert when these factors occur. If you run a marathon, for example, plenty of water must be replaced, literally on the run"

"When you drink too much water the kidneys eliminate the excess and when you don't drink water the kidneys save it. We are going to see that later, but for a primer, the kidneys work in 3 main modes: eliminating excess water, saving water and neutral.

"Many students ask me if the opposite, drinking too much water, is dangerous. Well, in principle, not. But if you really exaggerate there have been described cases of water intoxication. Sometimes, this occurs in mental patients."

"However, and this is a big *however*, there are some conditions in which all this equilibrium can be deranged:

Case 1: *Coma.* In this situation the patient must be provided with care. He/She cannot depend on the thirst sensation to ingest water. As such, the inputs and outputs of water must be computed by the intensive care unit. A daily weighing of the patient is indicative. The best information about the hydration status is the central venous pressure (CVP). Normally it is very low, close to zero mmHg. Hypovolemia may have a negative CVP.

Case 2: No access to water.

This case is very interesting and creates life-threatening situations.

Let's take the classical example of the individual lost in the desert.

There are phases in this situation:

The first phase is called *hypovolemia* when there is deficit in water volume of whole body. In this phase all organs are still functioning. The kidneys detect this decreased volume and save water by decreasing urinary volume. Here, we have 2 problems. We are breathing and this eliminates water from the lungs. Also, in order to function, the kidneys need to eliminate a minimum of 500 ml water/24 hrs. This urinary minimum is necessary to eliminate the body substances which must be excreted, the so called waste substances."

"The ongoing restriction of water increases the osmolarity of the plasma since more water than solutes are lost. The plasma becomes more concentrated and drags water from the interstice by the phenomenon of osmosis"

"This helps keep the blood volume sufficient to allow the heart to continue pumping and maintaining the blood pressure at levels necessary for cell perfusion and kidney filtration."

"But, as the water restriction continues, the interstice, having lost water to the blood, increases its osmolarity and begins pulling water from the cells by the same phenomenon of osmosis. Inside the cells, there is the greatest water reservoir in the body, 28 liters, in our standard subject. For some hours, the cells sacrifice their own water in order to maintain blood pressure and their own supply of oxygen and nutrients"

"At this point, things begin to get complicated. Because now, the problem gets to the cells proper. From this point on, we begin entering what is called *dehydration*. This is really serious since the function of the cells begins to get deranged. One important group of cells that get deranged are the brain cells. At this moment, an intervention may still reverse and save the subject. But, this is a delicate point between life and death. Other problems begin to appear, and positive feedback cycles begin to be created. For example, a decrease in blood volume and pressure decreases the pumping power of the heart. The blood flow to many organs begins to decrease. One of these organs is the heart itself. Heart cells, receiving less blood from the coronaries begin to lose efficiency and the pumping power of the heart is further impaired. This creates a positive feedback cycle.

"Other perverse cycles also begin. At the kidneys level, blood filtration decreases, and waste products from cell metabolism begin to accumulate in the blood, such as urea. Mental deterioration comes from cerebral dehydration, decreased blood irrigation and increase in urea. Cells, in many organs, begin to die. At this point, things are irreversible. They end with death."

"And to finish, here is my reminder that our trips between Land and Earth or back may last, easily, 2.5 years. This ship, during interplanetary travel, is a closed system. Our water here is entirely recycled, but this doesn't mean it can be wasted. We just have to remember to use the water consciously.

"Thank you!"

Chapter 58

Antonina's Dramas

One night, after my routine bath with Antonina, I was already in my cabin, trying to sleep. She had said to me that my desire for her would "go away". In reality, my desire still existed but was a bit more under control. Other feelings were entering the arena of my complicate dealings with her. Some of these feelings were of an unknown nature for me.

In this night I was trying to fall asleep when I heard a weak weeping sound coming through the wall that separated our cabins. Since the berths were all placed at the same configuration I knew I was separated from Antonina by less than one meter. Between us, a thin wall guaranteed our privacy. I forgot to mention that among the items I could bring with me to the ship was my faithful stethoscope.

I placed the stetho against the wall and began to listen. It was as if I were inside Antonina's cabin. Probably, the high technology of the engineers hadn't anticipated this situation. Antonina's weeping was mixed with words, spoken in a strange language but, clearly, her voice. The sounds stopped for some minutes, only to start again, this time with a different context. The weeping had given place to moans. I placed the stetho against the wall and listened. I never imagined that moans could carry so much suffering. However, they began to increase in intensity and began to convey a clear sexual content. The moans went on in a crescendo both in intensity and frequency. Then, they stopped abruptly to be followed by trepidation of sorts. Then, a sobbing. But it wasn't simply a sobbing. It carried so much distress and suffering.

Finally, the silence.

This "audition" impressed me strongly. For the first time, I could sense a 'weakness' in Antonina in the sex department. Something told me she had her dramas, that she had emotions and conflicts on that area too. Sure, I had seen her weep many times but what I heard this night was something that appeared to be coming from a tormented soul. Up to now, I had seen Antonina as an inflexible, dominating, powerful woman who was insensitive to human and worldly passions. Now, Antonina revealed to be fragile and fighting with internal demons. After all, I thought; *she was a woman, another brain, super intelligence but still, a woman.*

My difficulty in getting sleep increased now. I couldn't clear my mind of those sounds coming from the soul of a possibly tormented woman. That increased my love for her and gave me a feeling that I might or should protect her. Then, I remembered Erika's words: I was a receiver. And, I wept. Finally, I went to sleep.

I woke up with Antonina lying at my side in the bed. She was caressing my hair and my face and looking at me with maternal eyes. Her eyes had some signs of sadness and weariness.

"I see you haven't slept well, Antonina. Am I correct?"

"Yes, you guessed well, Jota, I wept all night, I was so sad!"

"And, now are you still sad?"

"Not any more, Jota, now I am with you and I'm happy again" she said caressing me.

"You should have called me when you were sad, Antonina. I would be with you and talk to you"

She looked long at me. Then, she laid her head on my chest and began sobbing quietly. I embraced her head and began caressing her hair. I had never caressed her hair. I was crossing lines. Instead of calming down she grabbed my head and began sobbing violently. Slowly she began calming down and we stood quietly.

Suddenly, she recomposed.

"Let's go Jota, we have breakfast ahead."

Chapter 59

Respiratory Gases

The second essential lecture was ministered by another Landian, doctor Thiagus Liebov, MD.

And, he began:

"This ship is an isolated system, as opposed to a planet's atmosphere."

"We have, here, an artificial atmosphere containing 50% O_2, 50% N_2. CO_2 is present at 0.1%. This atmosphere resembles Landa's but has much less CO_2."

"In order to illustrate what can occur in a closed system, I will give you an example of an accident that occurred on Earth. A mini submarine, with two men, was servicing a submarine line when a problem with its hoisting operation led to an overflow of water into one of its tanks. The sub went down and crashed onto the ocean floor, 500 m below the surface. There, she stood for more than 80 hours"

"This incident was related in the book "No time on our side" by Roger Chapman, one of its 2 crew."

"A rescue operation was put underway. There were two minisubs in different parts of the globe who could go down and attach cables to the distressed sub. The rescue subs were thousands of miles away, though.

They would have to be brought by air and then by sea, up to the site of the wreck."

"The entire problem rested upon the distressed sub's oxygen reserve, which was good for little more than 80 hours. But there was another problem. The two men were breathing, what was good news. However, the downside of breathing is that you generate CO_2, and excess CO_2 is toxic. They were advised not to move or even think too much in order to save oxygen."

"The men were rescued alive when they had only a few hours left of oxygen. This accident illustrated, in dramatic style, the dynamics of respiratory gases in a closed system"

"Well, since our body needs oxygen badly, what is oxygen necessary for?"

"I asked a candidate this question when I was part of the board selecting candidates. This particular candidate gave a lecture as part of the selection steps. The subject of his lecture was how the body dealt with respiratory gases during physical exercise."

"Sure, his lecture was good, he was firm and the lecture was well structured. But, this candidate had a problem. He was a bit too secure. And, having attended to lectures of great scientists, some of them Nobel Prize winners, I remember well that most presented their subjects in a modest, even naive manner, letting his doubts and questionings come to surface. And, we know well that in science, as opposed to religion, there is no absolute truth."

"Well, as I said, I prized his lecture, said he had a good knowledge, and made the question:

"What is the role of oxygen in respiration?"

"The candidate couldn't answer. The answer, in very general terms is: oxygen is the final acceptor of electrons generated along the respiratory molecular chain in the mitochondria. Without oxygen to accept them, these electrons accumulate, clogging the entire respiratory process. In a few minutes' death ensues."

"One of the most famous poisons, in part due to Hollywood, is cyanide, supposedly employed by high Nazi officials to kill themselves before being tortured. Cyanide interferes with the respiratory chain by blocking the electron transfer. The death is painful but preferred to torture in case of capture."

Then, Dr. Liebov gave sequence to the main body of his lecture, of which this was only a summary, in order that the reader gets the spirit of lectures on board the ship.

"Inside our ship air pressure is 500 mmHg and lower than the 760 mmHg in Landa or Earth. Here, O_2 is at 50% proportion so its partial pressure is 250 mmHg. In arterial blood, however, O_2 pressure falls to lower values. On Earth, the O_2 proportion is only 21% and its partial pressure in the atmosphere is 150 mmHg. In blood plasma it is around 100 mmHg. Hemoglobin saturation is between 95-98%."

"Well, we saw that oxygen is our "hero". Now, I present you our "villain", CO_2. CO_2 is, essentially a waste product, but a necessary waste. But how can it be that a villain is necessary? It happens that there is another villain in our body and, this one even more dangerous than CO_2: H^+ or the proton.

Protons are formed during cell metabolism and they need to be maintained at a constant and very low concentration in the blood: $10^{-7.4}$ Moles per liter, or pH = 7.4. Protons are so reactive that they have to be kept "at bay" at all costs. Increases in proton concentration can wreak havoc in the body and, so, the pH must be kept between 7.35 and 7.45. CO_2 helps keeping the pH at more or less constant level because our "villain", CO_2 is part of a *buffer system* that can capture excess protons and keep them in the form of carbonic acid, which is a weak acid and so keeps protons linked to it. The buffer system acts like a reservoir of protons. When there is an excess of protons the reservoir captures them, keeping them at bay. When protons are in deficit, the reservoir liberates them."

"However, CO_2 must be eliminated from the body since this gas is continually generated by the cell metabolism. CO_2 elimination is performed by the lungs as we breathe."

"In our ship, the only item we have in unlimited quantities is the energy. Energy is used in the ship's propulsion, water heating and in all operations that demand electricity".

"In what concerns this lecture, energy is used to generate oxygen from water by a process known as electrolysis (splitting by electricity). In this process water molecules (H_2O) are broken in its constituent elements, O_2 and H_2. The energy needed comes from electric power. Using a high temperature, H_2 is combined with CO_2 forming methane gas. This last reaction removes the better part of CO_2 from the ship's air. A smaller part of O_2 production and CO_2 removal comes from photosynthesis performed in the vegetable gardens scattered across the ship."

Chapter 60

My First Crisis

I believe it was 2 days after my episode of listening to Antonina's dramas through the wall. After our evening customary bath Antonina told me she would be busy all next day, at meetings with some crew members. She didn't tell me but I suspected she was engaged at some administrative or technical work, apart from her voluntary work at the served waters section. She told me we wouldn't see each other all day long and perhaps also in the evening. After the bath we talked for about 1 hour, lying at her bed, and then I went to sleep in my cabin.

However, I couldn't get the sleep I needed. I had the feeling that some delicate balance between downward and upward forces in the workings of my brain had been broken. Right away I began experimenting strange thoughts and scenes of my childhood; I, wearing diapers, crying for my mother, alone in a large cradle. Finally, I slept. But, then, came the nightmares. In one of them I was in a strange country, alone and didn't remember if I had a home. I wanted to walk but my legs weighed too much.

Finally, I woke, sweating profusely, a terrible headache. Despite being awake, I couldn't figure where I was, couldn't determine if I was awake or still into the nightmare. I curled down my body and pulled the cover over my head. A terrible feeling of void invaded me. I couldn't even remember who I was. I perceived I was crying and then came the fear. I feared getting out of bed and didn't know what was outside my bed. For an instant, I got to myself and didn't know why Antonina hadn't come to my bed to wake me. It was then that the smells came.

Everything smelled. Not that they were phantom smells. No! They were real but ten times more intense. The bed presented to me a variety of scents, my pillow and the sheets. During some instants, I felt I was in another person's bed. My hands had the usual scent but amplified ten times. My body was a mélange of different scents. These weren't new for me but amplified enormously. I couldn't imagine myself walking through the ship's corridors without Antonina. As it appeared to me, everything was hostile and meant harm for me. And, I wept and wept.

Finally, after I didn't know how long, there was a knock at my door. Since I didn't answer, after some more knocks, a crew woman entered my cabin and seeing me crying and curled, she asked if I was OK. My answer was more crying. She smelled strongly, and such a variety of scents I could make a list. Disinfectants, sweat, her clothes smelled, her hair smelled. The woman closed the door and went away. Soon after, two male nurses and a doctor came down to my cabin.

The nurses were pushing a gurney. The doctor was very kind to me, he knew I was an Earthian and said this was quite normal I shouldn't get worried. The doctor smelled disinfectant sweat, his breath smelled of some past meal. Since I kept crying one of the nurses gave me a shot. Then, I "passed away".

When I opened my eyes I was at a hospital room, well illuminated. I was lying on a technical bed that seemed more a Formula 1 car. There were more beds, all empty. The smell of disinfectants was strong as well of clean sheets (yes, they smell too) and drugs. The same doctor that saw me at my cabin was seated at a chair beside my bed. He smelled clean clothes, sweat, hospital things. He asked how I was but, trying to answer, my throat tightened and I began to weep.

Soon after, I saw Antonina hurrying down into the room and asking questions to the room staff and talking in a strange language. Antonina came to my bed and held my hand. I pulled her hand against my face and began kissing her hand and weeping and sobbing. Slowly I began calming down. Then, the scent of Antonina came to me. She sat beside my bed. I couldn't let go of her hand and kept holding it against my face and kissing it. And, then, sniffing it.

Slowly, a feeling of peace descended over me, not from the tranquilizer I'm sure. It was a peace that was giving me a strange feeling of power. I then got out of the bed and knelt on the floor. Two nurses came to grab me but Antonina asked them to let go. I then placed my face between her knees and wept profusely. She caressed my head saying this was going to be over very soon. This gave me again, an incredible feeling of peace and well-being. Looking at the sides, I perceived that there were more people watching my performance. They were doctors and medical students as I could identify by their demeanor. Some doctors were discussing, apparently, my case. I had the clear impression that I was being the object of some medical debate.

Then, a warm liquid began leaking into my legs. It was my urine. Soon, two nurses put me onto the bed and cleaned me, applying me a diaper. But no shots were given this time. I was so peaceful, so happy and calm. I slept. But didn't know for how long.

When I woke, Antonina was seated at a chair beside my bed. I got of the bed again and knelt down on the floor, placing my head between Antonina's knees. An exact repetition of what I had done before. At some distance from my bed I saw many doctors and students. They were now seated in some ordered array. The other beds had been displaced at the sides of the large room to give room for the "audience".

I said it was a repetition. Not exactly. Now, I was "powerful". I was laughing, still with my head between Antonina's knees. I lifted my head, looked at her eyes and laughed and kissed her hands. Antonina was talking to me in a low voice, telling me she would never abandon me again, she loved me, etc. I was euphoric. I was complete. I also looked at the medical group watching me, and my look at them was defiant. *Can't you see now who I am,* I thought of them*: How can't you see how powerful I am! What are you looking at? Can't you see I am with Antonina?* Those were my thoughts.

Then, I slept.

When I opened my eyes, I saw a woman nurse seated on a chair beside my bed. She asked me if we could talk. Her name was Rita Velo and she was a Brazilian living in Landa with her mentor's family, who was a Landian doctor, working in the ship. She told me that she had been adopted by his mentor when she had come to Landa as a companion to a tetraplegic.

(I chose not to mention the smells I felt in order not to disrupt my narrative.)

Rita told me that Antonina had asked her to talk with me.

"What you are experimenting now, Jota, is a normal crisis that is part of a normal mental process in which *"your wild personality conflicts with another personality which is being gradually shaped by the influence of your shepherd"* in your case, Antonina (those were her terms).

"Can you explain to me what this *wild personality* is all about? Am I a savage by some chance?" I asked a little upset.

"No, Jota. This term "wild" means your native personality, the one you always had. And no need to get upset. I'm here to help you"

Then, Rita went on:

"You are probably going to experiment some other crises, less intense than this first one since the first is normally the strongest"

"The crises can be triggered by any negative experience even a simple cold"

"But, Rita, have you undergone all this process yourself?"

"Yes, I had, Jota. All Earthians that begin creating strong bonds with a Landian mentor go through the same process. However, the crises are not all equal from people to people. There are common features, but there are many variations. There are cases in which the *cognitive conditioning* can generate psychosis, suicidal thoughts and even physical aggressions at the mentors"

"What this "cognitive conditioning" means, Rita? Am I being trained or what?" I asked a little upset.

"No, Jota, you are not "being trained". This is just a term we use to describe how Earthians go through their evolution as they interact for long periods with a same Landian.

"Jota, I will repeat in part what I said before. This conditioning I refer to is a slow process in which your wild or original personality is being, slowly, shaped by your conditioner or shepherd, who, in your case, is Antonina"

Rita, seeing my unsettling face:

"OK, OK, Jota, let me explain again a little differently. You don't need to be upset since no harm whatsoever is being done to you"

"When an Earthian begins interacting, continuously, with a Landian, a bond begins to form between them where the mind of the

Earthian gets continually influenced by the Landian's mind, in this case your *shepherd*, Antonina"

"This influence, acting continuously during some time, begins to modify, to change, to mold, the personality of the *lamb*, I mean the Earthian" and she corrected "lamb". However, I registered the pair, *shepherd* and *lamb*.

In rare cases, the influence is not completely oriented from Landian to Earthian. Sometimes, the interaction can strongly influence the shepherd's mind, too. But this is rare.

"But why is it that the Earthian's mind gets influenced by the Landian's and not the opposite or even both personalities get changed by their mutual interaction. Shouldn't this interaction be bilateral?" and I was still a little upset.

I began to realize that Rita, despite her willingness to either help me or Antonina, was following a sort of protocol in her explanations.

"No, Jota, the interaction is not bilateral" she went on, patiently, and lowering her voice. A shadow of smile appeared in her mouth.

"The *superior* mind dominates the *inferior* mind and that's why the interaction can't be bilateral. You see now, Jota?"

I immediately remembered Erika's explanations.

"Rita, but tell me, why is it that the Landian's mind is superior to that of the Earthians?"

"That's so easy to explain, Jota. It's because Landians are way more intelligent than Earthians. The difference between Landian and Earthian intelligences is way greater than the difference between Earthians and chimpanzees"

"But this is not to say that the shepherd does not get influenced by the lamb, Jota. No, shepherds are emotionally linked to their lambs and they can suffer from their love too"

Now, Rita began to employ, freely the terms *shepherd* and *lamb*.

"Now, I begin to understand, Rita. It's like a mother and her child. The mother dominates the child by her love and care and by her superior intelligence but the child also has the mother in a leash, isn't it?" I said winking one eye and smiling.

"That's perfect, Jota, you have put it into a nice way of explaining!" and Rita smiled effusively at me.

Gradually, I began perceiving that I couldn't stand a discussion with Rita since I saw she followed well established protocols. And, that, she did well. I also became aware that my "case" was not a novelty. And it appeared to be progressing according to what was expected from Landian psychiatry. I remembered I was one among thousands of Earthians interacting with Landians on Earth, Landa and ... in this ship.

But Rita was still at my side.

"Can you tell then why my olfaction is so sensitive? It began with the crisis."

"This is not so common but is well described and observed. I, myself saw some cases of *olfactory liberation*."

"And, tell me Rita, what would be this olfactory liberation?"

"What happens is that your olfaction is losing some inhibitory influences and it is getting freer. In some sense, and in terms of olfaction, you are descending a bit down the animal scale."

I was about to say things I would repent and decided to laugh amiably to Rita. After all we both were Earthian, we both were *inferiors*.

"I'll have to go now, Jota. But, try to see this way: there's nothing wrong at being inferior, Jota, really it's OK."

"Yes, Rita, it's better to be a receiver, isn't it?"

And Rita, being caught by my remark, decided to sprint away from the room.

Chapter 61

Crisis' Aftermath

I stood, bedridden, at the Medical Center for two more days. Despite not receiving any medications I was feeling very well. My impression was that those strange things with me had never occurred. To be entirely sincere I was feeling better now than before the crisis and, much better at that. My olfaction had lost much of the initial potency and was still quite sensitive but well-behaved, so to speak. I was feeling lighter, calmer, and more confident. My impression was that a big weight had been released from my head. I was less concerned with my things on Earth, with the future, with my brother.

However, I continued to have a special interest in the smells of things, of the bed sheets, of the persons dealing with me. But it wasn't an obsession anymore. Later, I began to realize that my necessity to sniff at everything came from a better perception of smells in general; I mean a better processing of the given smells. Like when you process the images you see and connect them with past images and situations or experiences.

I was alone in the room and it would be 10 in the morning since I remembered having had breakfast. The room was particularly silent this morning. Then, I heard, in the corridor, some movement of people, some voices, and felt, immediately, the scent of Antonina, quite distinct above other smells. Antonina's smell was so intense for me, that even before she hadn't entered the room I detected it.

Soon after she entered I heard her talking to someone at the door, and then she came to my bed. She came smiling at me and kissed my face, caressing briefly my face and my neck.

"How you feel today, Jota?"

"I feel OK, Antonina" and immediately took hold of her hands, kissed them, and began sniffing at them in an impulse. I couldn't stop sniffing and kissing her hands, and moving my face against them. I, then, began sniffing at her arms and she, perceiving my necessity, came closer and offered me her face, which I began to sniff avidly. I rubbed my face against hers, continually sniffing at her face, at her hair.

Molecules coming from her face, hair and her breath entered, in profusion, through my nostrils and were processed by my newly developed "sniffing apparatus". Those scents were processed in my olfactory bulb, and sent to higher centers like the limbic system.

The olfactory signals were combined with those from past olfactory memories and past images. The result? I began forming in my mind Antonina's signature, triggered by smell. The possibility came to my deranged mind that now I could follow Antonina by the molecules she shed to the environment. That gave me enormous security.

All those obscure thoughts were unraveling at my mind, while I had Antonina touching me. I came to myself and found my face immersed between her knees. And Antonina caressed my hair. Then, it happened again. That warm liquid dripped to my legs. My urine. Antonina saw it and I was hoisted to the bed, cleaned, new diapers. I never felt so well in my life; I was euphoric and was planning now how I would follow Antonina, just by a tiny amount of her dead cells shed from her skin. Just like the bloodhound dogs do to follow lost children and like the thousands and thousands of pets do to follow their masters.

This gave me a new capability. So many new sensations began invading me that I looked through my "rearview mirror" and saw one of them: my desire for Antonina. She was right, it would not go away, nor by itself. Now, it was being supplanted by many new and stronger sensations.

After lunch, I slept feeling a great peace, and without having taken any drugs. Toward the end of the afternoon I opened my eyes and saw, seated at the chair beside my bed, what should be a doctor, bearded, gray hair among the blonde. A Landian doctor, certainly. He looked at me with a mix of curiosity and affection. And, he didn't smell so bad.

"Hi, Jota, I'm Doctor Alten Felder psychiatrist. Look, I know you are a doctor too and Antonina told me about your problem. I'm here to help you. Can we talk?"

"Sure we can talk" I answered.

"How are you feeling today? I was told you had some crisis, was it so?"

"Look, doctor, now, I feel very well actually. It appears I could get through. It was very bad indeed; I've never felt so bad like last days. Now, I feel light, like some weight had been taken out from my mind."

"Jota, your case is typical as I will explain you better. But we are in no hurry. Actually, we have been observing your reactions in the past days. You know you did a remarkable performance?"

And he laughed and tapped my shoulder lightly.

"First of all. You may have been told about Landa and its customs rules and laws. This ship is not Landa, that's the first thing I want you to know. Second, your case is very interesting for many reasons. Firstly, because you are a doctor, secondly, you have been brought here from Earth and thirdly Antonina told me about your relationship with her. And, finally, fourthly, your performance was remarkable! And, adding to that I, personally, want to learn from you a few things"

"I think you already know this ship is a science laboratory, running independently from Landa's rules. Science has been scraped in Landa. They just follow recipes coming from Procyon. But here is no Landa. Here, we are masters and do not follow stupid rules. But, there is more, Jota. I heard that, besides being a doctor you are also a scientist. Did I hear correctly, Jota?" I nodded, smiling at him.

"Let me tell you that your case is very interesting to me because you are returning to Earth and your shepherd also. We don't have many cases like yours! Quite frankly I, personally don't"

I saw he was repeating what I've heard. It was if he was blurting out the repressed feelings of scientists in Landa.

"Well, but now for our case. This crisis of yours stems from a conflict between two sides of your personality. Your relationship with Antonina is changing your wild Earthian personality and your wild side is fighting back. I know that the nurse Rita has talked with you and I will repeat some of her words with a bit more science, since you are a doctor" and he laughed amiably.

"OK, I was told of that, but this wild side of me. What is it that it is fighting with? Tell me, please, Doctor!" I asked him.

"Sure, I will explain. Look, Jota, Earthians have 3 elements in their personality: the *id*, the *ego,* and the *superego*. The id is your animal part, that one who will kill an enemy, will rape a girl that attracts you and so on. The ego links the id with the world reality and exerts control over the id. The superego establishes morals and keeps instincts at bay. This, however, is a crude summary"

"Well, when Earthians establish a prolonged interaction with the same Landian, like what happens with you and Antonina, a *bond* is established and these 3 parts of your personality are modified in different degrees"

"Thanks to the research done in this ship, we know now what is the basis for these changes, and I will show you in due time.

These changes that are, presently, occurring in your brain, are reversible up to a certain point and this is one of the reasons we are having this talk and that I want to help you. And, at the same time, you will be helping me in a way to be clear later on"

"Jota, for some reason, your bond with Antonina grew much stronger and faster than what is usual"

"But, first of all, let me guarantee you that your crisis in not a mental derangement in the pathological sense. It is a "normal" process we call *"neural remodeling"* induced by your contact with Antonina. Tomorrow we will have you tested by our imaging laboratory and, for the time being, I prefer to keep you in this unit. And take care of yourself!" Saying this, Dr Felder was gone from the room.

Antonina came to visit me in the evening. She was very attentive and I, this time, behaved very well. No performances. I was calm. Antonina's presence gave me the customary peace and well-being feeling. But, not much more.

I slept all night.

In the morning I was given a slight sedative and soon after Dr. Felder came to my bed.

"Jota, we are going now to the imaging center and we will make some scans of your brain. I want to be sure everything is OK"

Joaquim

I remember being driven on a gurney, into an air-conditioned room, at a somewhat lower temperature. I was, now more heavily sedated, but remember being introduced into a narrow tunnel similar to a Nuclear Magnetic Resonance (NMR) machine. Then, I passed away.

I woke at my warden bed, with Dr. Felder at my side.

"Jota, your exams are OK but they have shown us very interesting things. Nothing you should worry about, no pathologies. We will discharge you for now and very soon we will talk again". He gave me a light pat at my shoulder and went away.

Chapter 62

More Revelations of Antonina

After my recovery I went back to my routine with Antonina. However, things were not the same and I couldn't figure out what was different. Despite this I felt OK and, this was what mattered.

Our baths had been resumed as if nothing had happened.

One night, after we had bathed as usual:

"Antonina, what are the *bonds* between Landians and Earthians?"

"Who told you of the bonds?"

"Many people mentioned to me the term bond. Dr. Felder, the nurse Rita and others told me that I was forming a bond with you"

I didn't mention, however the other terms I have been told: *cognitive conditioning, wild personality, superior intelligence, shepherd and lamb,* and other complicate terms employed to explain my crisis.

Strangely, Antonina seemed to not have been informed of what had been said to me. Would this be a standard protocol to avoid biasing my case by Antonina's interventions? Or would it be simply something that happens in some (dis)organizations, where the left hand is not informed what the right has done?

"Jota, this so-called, bond is not more than a strong link that is establishing among the two of us. A link of confidence, love and goodness that, now, exists between us.

What an extraordinarily simple explanation for so complex case as mine, I thought.

"Jota, Yuri hasn't told you everything and I told you only a part, also."

"I have said to you that Landians migrating to Earth are those that can't stand anymore the life full of rules in Landa. This, in part, is true. But the real reason for the migrations is not this"

"OK, Antonina, what, then, is the real motive for the migrations?"

"We have a mission, Jota. A mission on Earth" and she held my hand stronger. But, I won't tell you all today. For now, I just want you to know that there is a purpose, a purpose, Jota"

She, then, embraced me tenderly, caressed my hair, and kissed me on the head.

"I'm part of this mission, Jota and you are too"

"However, I'm afraid I won't be able to keep my word to the regulations and purposes of my mission" and, this, she said more to herself, in a lower voice.

And after this we parted and I went to my cabin, trying to sleep with all that information turning inside my head.

I woke in the middle of the night hearing a weeping that seemed to originate from Antonina's cabin. Repeating my "écuteur" performance, I placed my stetho against the wall. The sounds were effectively coming from Antonina's cabin. It was a weeping, interspersed with unintelligible phrases. And, then, began the moans, loaded with such suffering tones. This time, something in the sounds carried a sort of repentance.

Despite the sounds denoting a sexual background, the weeping and the phrases revealed a profound bitterness and suffering. Soon after, the moans became louder and more frequents, some vibrations were felt, and then the sounds stopped abruptly, only to be followed by sobbing. But, what a sobbing! It seemed to me that a great sorrow was being released. It seemed to me that Antonina was expressing the sufferings of the entire world.

My head twirled with all this. *What mission would be that and what would be my part on it?*

Finally, the sleep took hold of me. I woke in the morning, with Antonina at my side, caressing my hair and my face.

Chapter 63

Synaptic Connections

I think that, two days after my exams, Antonina told me, in the morning, that Dr. Felder wanted to see me. I should go to his room in the medical center. Following instructions, I finally came to the medical center and Dr Felder's room.

"Hi Jota, how are you feeling today?" he asked me shaking my hand and patting me slightly on the shoulder. In the room were 3 more doctors, two males (Drs. Valentin and Montagna) and one female (Dr Svetlana). Dr Svetlana was strikingly beautiful.

"Jota, I have your exams and I want to show them to you. Seat here at my side, Jota."

He, then, pointed us to a large screen:

"The images you are about to see, Jota, are confidential and first-hand results. I think you were told that this ship is a closed system in terms of materials and air. But it is also closed in terms of science. This ship is not Landa and some of the results I will be presenting, now, cannot leak to Landa at this phase of the research."

And Dr. Felder went on, addressing, now, the 3 doctors:

"This is our colleague an Earthian, let me present you, Jota. As I told you a few moments ago, Jota is being conditioned by his shepherd

Antonina Neina, who is also in this ship. And, I have the pleasure of showing you, perhaps in firsthand, some results we obtained with the analysis of his brain. I will be talking in English as a special attention to Jota who, of course, does not understand our language."

"The images you are about to see were obtained with our neuro-imaging system, at a cellular resolution."

And, a big screen began showing what appeared, to be scans. My scans. And, Dr Felder went on:

"These synaptic groups were activated, reversibly, by introducing in the subject's blood, pheromones from his shepherd. The controls, without pheromone pulses, are at the left panels. The pheromones were also introduced by having the subject sniff at vaporized pheromones. This later procedure caused the same synaptic activation"

"As you clearly see, these synaptic clusters "lighted up" as they began secreting transmitters that were synthesized from the pheromones from his shepherd. A sequence of images indicates that these synapses are not established permanently yet"

"As you can see, they are still sort of trying to connect; they connect and disconnect periodically, as experimenting, as shown in these sequential images. We know, from previous studies that, once they connect, they stabilize in this new arrangement. There is no more reversion and the lamb is said to be a *permanent lamb*."

"In this other figure, you can see the same imaging of an Earthian who had been interacting for 5 years with his shepherd. It is clear that the corresponding synapses are not visible anymore, having been replaced by *tracts*, which means permanent neural pathways. This is a permanent condition and the subject is an example of a *permanent lamb.*"

"Please, look at those connections, how they are established and firm. They are anatomical now and, before, they were only functional. Now, it is irreversible."

"Now, if the shepherd abandons the subject or dies, this Earthian lamb is doomed, since those connections only hold to function with that specific shepherd. They have matched with the brain of the shepherd."

But, asked Dr. Svetlana: What do you mean when you say the "the lamb is doomed"?

"The lamb is doomed in the sense that there is no reversion. The lamb cannot anymore live separate from his or her shepherd" Dr. Felder answered.

"Our theory is that the shepherd exhales continually pheromones from evaporation from their skin. The lamb, sniffing at those pheromones reacts to them and slowly, very slowly begins making synaptic connections matching to those hormonal signals. Those signals are specific to the shepherds'; they have a signature!

"Is this sniffing mechanism the only one, in which the lamb gets the pheromones?" asked Dr Montagna.

"No, the pheromones may be introduced into the lamb's blood through the skin. This occurs by the shepherd caressing periodically the lamb, in the face or neck. However, we have no indication that a shepherd knows this and he/she does this caressing purely by an act of love"

"Have you seen how a baby reacts to the mother's scent? How the baby calms down as soon as he feels the mother's scent? And, how also the mother reacts to the baby? Probably, those same pheromones. And, that, is a quite promising field for our future research" continued Dr. Felder.

"We are about to propose a theory linking all this. And we have data to prove it. It is going to upend the knowledge of the brain. And, it did not come from the Procyon system! This theory is ours. Ours and only ours!"

Then Dr Alten Felder dismissed the small audience and asked me to stay. But now, it was my turn to ask questions:

"Who asked you to tell me all this Dr? Are all Earthians in my situation told of these alterations in their brains?"

"No, Jota. By all means no. They don't know about this. For the Earthians living in Landa and adopted by Landians, this is a nice arrangement of course, since they live happily, no need to work. They have food, housing, heat, all comforts a person may want. They can date, make love, marry, and have children. Also, for the Landians this is a nice deal since they are very happy having one or two adopted Earthians in their homes. I think Antonina told you how Landians benefit from this. Isn't it a nice arrangement?"

"Well, now to your question, pardon my digression, Jota. I was only justifying that this arrangement is beneficial."

"It was Antonina, your shepherd, who asked me to explain all this to you. She loves you so much she wants you to be free to decide before it's too late, before the connections on your brain close forever and you are turned into a permanent lamb."

"We are very interested in your case, Jota. This is the first time I know of, that a shepherd asks us to tell his/her lamb what happens and to stop the process. This is because Antonina does love you, maybe more than you love her. Your case is very illustrative, Jota. We have been discussing it with much interest in this ship"

Then, Dr. Felder got emotional, I believe, from the importance of his discovery and its future impact:

"Antonina loves you, Jota, she told me that and she was weeping all the time she was telling me. She wants to stop the conditioning before it's too late. She loves you as a man, not as a Lamb, she told me."

"Also, while she was out of herself, she said a phrase to me that I repeat to you since I really could not understand:"

"Through love, I have been conditioning Jota and, through love, I will stop it."

"But, Jota, it is remarkable how you are reacting to all this. Now, your olfaction increased tenfold or more. A coincidence? Not at all. The synaptic connections are now "in a hurry" to close down and become permanent. For this, they need an extra boost of pheromones obtained by your sniffing your shepherd. Remember what I said about the shepherd's hormones? You are now, by means of increased olfaction, increasing your capacity to absorb and react to those pheromones and to close down those synaptic connections. In other words, it looks like your brain is in a hurry to make you a permanent lamb."

"But, we believe there is another process occurring in parallel and this one rests more heavily upon the olfactory system itself and is not dependent on pheromones. Remember that your synapses are experimenting, so to say, with new connections. Well, we saw that many of those synapses are forming with neurons of the limbic system, a region strongly connected with emotions. We believe that the olfactory impulses act here in a non-hormonal fashion: those olfactory signals *facilitate* the synaptic transmission by lowering the membrane threshold for action potentials at the post-synaptic neurons. As such, fewer mediators (pheromone-derived) are necessary to fire those synapses. This is, we believe, the cause of your super olfaction at this moment. And, I repeat:"

"It is as if your synapses are in a hurry to close down the circuits and turn you into a permanent lamb"

"And, this is dangerous, Jota. Once the circuits close down no reversion is possible and you are dependent from Antonina forever. But Antonina wants you to reverse, she wants you to be the same Jota she knew, and the one she loves as such. She doesn't want you to be a permanent lamb, Jota. See that?"

"And, that's why she is pleading to me to try to reverse this all. This could easily be done by your distancing from Antonina. Then, you would slowly revert to your original wild personality. But, there is a problem, Jota. If you interrupt your contact with Antonina you will succumb, you will not stand it. This reversion needs to occur slowly, in reversible steps. And, her love for you must change from the *dominant* to the *level type*."

"And what would be this "level type" of love, Dr. Felder"?

"That is simply the normal love between two Landians or two Earthians, and the "level" word means the couple has the same intellectual level."

"But, Antonina thinks there is a way, Jota. No one knows about this. Remember your desire for her? And that she said it would go away?

She told me everything. You see, no secrets to a psychiatrist! I will not say any more Jota, let things happen. We will see."

"Ah, before I forget: Antonina said to me another phrase I can't understand the meaning:"

"She said she would sacrifice for your sake."

"But, how can you do all these tests here and tell me what's going on with me? Could you do that in Landa?"

"Nooo, not at all, Jota! This ship is not Landa. I didn't tell you this: this ship is a laboratory. Landa's rules don't hold here. There are no idiotic counselors, no monks' rules. Here, we are free people to think freely, without hypocrisies. Here, we are scientists with free thought. We follow our moral rules!"

"And, before I forget. Remember those tetraplegics in this ship, going to Landa? Well there is one that will stay here, Jota. The same apparatus that imaged your synapses is being used to probe into the lesion zone of the spinal cord. We are trying a different approach with this patient. We will induce synapse formation in the lesion region. If this works we can obtain some form of contact between the proximal stump and the distal stump. And, then, action potentials, Jota. Actually, we have 3 patients under this program."

"And there is more, Jota. Earthians are not as dumb as Landians think they are. Not at all. We have a theory that we are testing here in this very ship. And our theory may upend psychiatry. Our theory is that Earthian interaction with Landians is an evolutionary adaptation of Earthians. A survival strategy so to say. Look, not only the adopted Earthians suffer changes in their brains. No, also Landians who are shepherds show changes; we have seen those changes at cellular level. Look, this can't leak, I could be prosecuted! They show some forms of bonds with the adopted Earthians. This is to say that the shepherds also need their lambs. And, I tell you, they need them badly. They also can't live without them. Do you know how is this called in biology? Symbiosis, Jota, symbiosis."

Chapter 64

The Mission

In the evening after my interview with Dr. Felder and after the usual bath with Antonina, we lay down in her bed. Then, she began explaining me:

"Our mission is dominating Earthians, not through force but by the way of love. We are going to be their shepherds and we will protect them against the wolves."

"And who are the wolves?" I asked

"The wolves? They are few but as happens in the wild, a few wolves dominate many lambs" she said, but nor explaining who were wolves or lambs despite I knew who were the lambs.

"There were previous attempts of doing this, Jota. Everything is registered. But, what makes our mission the more difficult is that many lambs defend and protect the wolves, even knowing they will be eaten by them!"

"This is the most difficult part; to protect who does not want to be protected."

"For this reason, we need to dominate the minds of the lambs by way of love and, then, make them understand our role."

"But, how is this domination by way of love? I can't understand how is that possible." I asked.

"Jota, domination through love is the most powerful one. It's more efficient and more lasting than the domination through force."

However, Antonina did not answer me what this "domination by love" was all about.

"And who is directing the noble missionaries in their noble task of dominating by way of love?" I asked, satirically.

"We don't know where the directions ultimately come from, Jota. What we know is that the monks orient us."

"And is this an ongoing process, Antonina?"

"Yes, it is, and from a long time. And you are a part of it."

"OK, but if the Landians have this mission on Earth what is then the role of Earthians living in Landa?"

Antonina thought a little as if trying to navigate through some delicate questions.

"Look, Jota, don't you think that Earthians are being forced to go to Landa. Their migration to Landa is spontaneous, and Yuri told you about that; I was there when he explained. So, what is your concern?"

"What happens, in fact, is that once the Earthians are in Landa, they establish colonies there. Many, are invited to live with Landian families. And Landian families love to have Earthians living with them."

All that, of course, I knew, since my talks with Erika. But I had to listen to the other side. I had to know how Landians viewed this interaction.

"And why is it that Landians love having Earthians living among them?"

"Now, Jota, you touched an important point. Look, you remember I told you how rigid are the rules imposed to Landians? How uninteresting their lives were, without leisure, without fun, no laughing, no singing, etc? You remember that, Jota? Here is the catch, Jota. Earthians don't need to follow those stupid rules, more fit for a monastery. Earthians, being considered inferior beings, are free to sing, to have fun, to laugh. And all this "happiness and fun" can be watched by the Landians who, not only watch but take some part. And, this is considered as an accepted Landian behavior, Jota. You see now?"

"Yes, I see all right and I didn't like the least bit. For what you say, Earthians are clowns, aren't they?" I said clearly upset.

"Not that, Jota, you read it wrongly. Remember that Landians can't express happiness, they can't sing, dance, laugh? However, if these manifestations are directed to an Earthian they are accepted as correct, and the pretext is that they are an act of goodness and love, directed to an inferior being."

"I see now; it is a way Landians found to go around those stupid rules. Am I correct now?" I remarked.

"Yes, Jota, you have put it very well!"

"But there is more, Jota. Earthians have a very important role for the Landian children. Earthians are very receptive to acts of love and kindness and the Landian children learn to respect and care for them. It has been demonstrated that in households having Earthians, children present a better intellectual development."

"And, I was almost forgetting, Jota. Earthians are very important for the elderly too. They function as receptors for the love elderly people need to express."

Chapter 65

Second Talk with Greg

I think it was one day after my talk with Antonina that I went for a second visit with Greg at the Command Bridge. I was sort of curious how crime was dealt with in Landa.

"Greg, tell me, in Landa can regular citizens carry guns?"

"No, Jota, there is no need for guns since crime as you know on Earth does not exist in Landa. Look from that point: robbery or theft doesn't make sense since there is no private property. Thus, the few crimes deal with assault, murder, and crimes against honor and corruption. The penalties are very severe in general. Murder and corruption have death penalty. The other crimes are simply annotated in the citizen's spreadsheet. And they summate. Getting to a certain scale, the citizen goes to a recovery colony. Having no recovery, the citizen is expelled from the colonies. Crimes against honor can be dealt with by dueling. But this is quite rare indeed."

"Do those laws apply to Landians living on Earth?"

"No, Jota, on Earth there apply each country's laws. This is one of the advantages of living on Earth, where leisure is allowed, and you can express your happiness or discontentment. Not in Landa."

"But you people do not have rest periods in Landa?"

"Oh, yes, of course, like work, rest is compulsory! Rest is a part of the work," he said laughing is a satirical fashion.

"How is that?" I asked

"Every day there are periods of rest, and then, you must rest"

"And, what about leisure? Is this allowed?"

"Well, we consider leisure as any activity which is not considered work or rest period and, then, you have to justify. But if you are interacting with an Earthian, either playing with him/her or laughing or singing to him/her, or music listening, then it's OK."

"OK, Greg, I think I'm beginning to get the taste of it. But, tell me. Do you, personally agree with those rules?"

"No, Jota, I do not agree with those stupid rules. Unfortunately, they have to be followed. The social system is too fragile in Landa and hinges on strict obedience to those rules. It works like a human pyramid, where the failure of one can mean the collapse of the entire pyramid."

"And, how about the capitalist system in some developed countries on Earth? How would function such a human pyramid?" I asked.

"There would be hundreds of thousands of smaller pyramids, more or less independent from each other, some decreasing in size, others increasing, and yet others crumbling down."

"Do you know, Jota that about 80% of air travel on Earth are leisure?"

"But, is this bad?" I asked.

"Well, in average, not good or bad, but no good for the climate, for the ozone layer and for atmospheric pollution."

"But, without pleasure travels, many people would lose their jobs, a lot of fringe benefits would disappear," I said.

"Yes, Jota, you are right in this point. But this brings us to the capitalist model"

"And, what do you think of the capitalist model, Greg?"

"Well, in my opinion, capitalism, despite being conceptually wrong, attracts me because it works in real life and works for many people. Sure it does not work for all. That's statistics isn't it, Jota?"

"But, Jota, capitalism is also perverse, since it excludes a lot of people."

"And, what about the social model in Landa? Doesn't it exclude too? I asked.

"No, Jota, no one is excluded in Landa, except those that do not fill the requisites. Those are excluded from the colonies."

"OK, Greg, but now tell me; if everyone has all they need why aren't they happy?"

"I will give you an example, Jota. You know that, on Earth, there is abundance of oxygen in the air. Not only that but all have the right to breathe it freely. Does that make you happy, Jota?"

"Doesn't make me happy, but would make me unhappy hadn't I been able to breathe this oxygen!" I concluded, laughing.

"There, you see Jota. Differences in things we have and others don't, give us the illusion of happiness. Differences in things we can do and others can't, give us the feeling of power"

"So, Jota, it's all about feelings and illusions, isn't so?"

"We have, in Landa, an index to measure the degree of *physical discomfort.*"

"And what would be this 'physical discomfort'?"

"Cold, hunger, and diseases are examples of direct physical discomfort. Over the centuries, physical discomfort has been decreasing on Earth and that does not depend on social strata. And this is a consequence of science and technology evolution. Only 300 years ago, or less, even kings suffered great physical discomfort. Hygiene was rudimentary; no one took baths since it was believed that baths were bad for health. There were no sanitary installations. Even at the palaces filth was generalized. To hide smells from lack of baths perfumes were used throughout. Itches, as consequences of skin infections, parasites, allergies were routine in the life even of kings and nobles. Chronic venereal diseases were the norm. There was no scientific medicine, everything was empirical."

"Nowadays, even the poor have a better health care than kings on Middle Age had. Earth is a great laboratory for us, Jota and we study Earth since a long time ago, and I mean centuries at that."

"And how is life in Landa, I mean how you people get things?"

"In Landa there is no economical law. The social system is very similar to Earth communism. All people are equal in terms of material goods. There is no law of the market as in capitalism."

"And how is wealth generated in Landa, if this wealth is to be divided equally?"

"Wealth is generated through the collective work of all and is divided equally by all. Contrary of Earth's communism all are equal. There are no people "more equal" like on Earth's communism."

"OK, Greg, but since wealth is equally shared by all, what incentive has one to work more or better or simply, work at all?"

"There are no incentives for work in Landa. You don't work more or work less. You work in the necessary measure to do your job. Your work is constantly watched by your own colleagues. If you work more than the others they denounce you as seeking some privilege from the boss. If you work less you are denounced as lazy. See what I mean?"

"Look, Jota, on Earth, according to the capitalist model, you need to work to have a home, feed your family, provide health care, and have a car."

Some navigators were watching, now, attentively, my talk with Greg and none of them had been on Earth.

"In Landa it is the opposite. They give you all you need, but you have to do your part, and your part is the work"

"But, who defines *what you need*, Greg? Tell me, please. How can one define what I need and what I don't need?"

"That is a good question, Jota!"

"Yes, that is a good question!" some navigators said to Greg."

"Yes, Jota, a good question indeed. Who decides are the counselors and the counselors consult with the monks. And the monks are minimalists."

"The monks define a minimum you need to live. According to them if you don't suffer then you are happy."

"As many have repeated to you the only luxury in Landa is the heat. That, you can use at your will, no limits."

And the navigator nodded approvingly:

"Oh, the heat is so good."

"Well, I'm minimalist myself. I want to have a barebones Ferrari and a barebones yacht." I said to Greg.

And the navigators: "What is a Ferrari, what is a yacht?"

Greg laughed and said we should have a coffee in the galley of the bridge.

There, away from the indiscrete ears of the navigators, I asked Greg.

"And, were you happy in Landa, Greg?"

"I wasn't happy in Landa and now, I am happy on Earth," he said flatly.

"Living in Landa is unbearable, Jota. Hypocrisy is general. As I said, heat is our only luxury, our baths, sauna, etc. All houses enjoy the heat, there are no limits."

"The pleasure given by the heat is the only one accepted in Landa."

"Now, Jota, try to understand this: during the work period you can talk to your colleagues, this is not forbidden. But you need to constantly measure your words. Everything you say or even you don't say can cause you problems. I'll give you an example of a typical (and "correct") dialogue during work hours."

A: Good day, colleague. How was your rest yesterday? Did you enjoy the heat in your house?

B: Yes, colleague, the colony provides us with this marvelous luxury, the heat. Today, I will work carefully for the progress of our colony!

A: That's very nice of you, colleague. I will also work for our progress and will always thank our counselors for their wise advice, and for the good things the colony gives me.

B: You said very well, colleague. Today I'm particularly happy for dedicating all my day to the progress of our colony.

"Can you see what I mean, Jota? Imagine enduring this, day after day and never knowing if some colleague is talking badly about you to the boss."

Greg explained to me that discontentment is considered a grave fault since it propagates and decreases the general efficacy of the work.

"You never should say to a colleague that you aren't happy or you are upset with something. And, usually, you are."

"Everything you do or do not is evaluated by all and twice a year you are given a mark. Low marks, repeatedly, can mean a reprehension and too much reprehension can mean expelling from the colony."

"So, it isn't enough that you do your work correctly. You need, all the time, demonstrate to the others that you are doing so. And also you need to demonstrate that you are happy with your work. There is no end to that, Jota."

"And what about if you have a family, and then you are expelled?" I asked Greg.

"I don't know how to answer that Jota it just gives me the creeps!"

PART 3

Chapter 66

The Medical Center

I think it was one day after my long talk with Greg that he asked me if I would like to visit the Medical Center (MC) of the ship. Actually, I had been there recently as a "patient". But, this time, I would be a visitor. Despite my talks with Yuri about the notable advances in Medicine in Landa, there was more that I was curious about. So, I promptly accepted the invitation and since Greg had his morning off, there we went. Greg was friends with Dr Olaf Anders, one of the directors of the MC. Greg introduced us and left.

The impression Dr Olaf Anders caused in me was most favorable. He had the typical physical constitution of Landians, relatively short, strong-built, blond hair. He was extremely extroverted, which let me guess he was still feeling the liberty from a temporary "vacation" out of Landa.

My first contact with Dr Anders revealed a great affinity between our lines of thought regarding Medicine. Dr. Anders was the opposite of those physicians restricted to the *guidelines* or *mainstream medicine.*

"I'm very glad to have you here, Jota! I've heard about you in recent days and I hope you can get through the crisis!

But, I would like to hear some of your opinions on Medicine."

"Look, Jota, let's suppose you are obese. Our mainstream *medicine* will recommend some drugs, a diet and some exercises. However, what I call *rational medicine* will guide you to a complete change in lifestyle. Now, you will be told to "think lean". Sure, some drugs, surely diet, but now, true exercises. Not those 3 times/weekly walking around the block."

Since the beginning of our talk I let it clear that I had the same opinion regarding mainstream medicine and that the guidelines were OK up to a certain point. But, to my surprise, Dr Anders seemed more interested in Earthian Medicine.

"How do you people treat bacterial infections on Earth, Jota?"

"Can I call you just Olaf? Well, we use antibiotics. However, more and more infections and bacteria are getting resistant to antibiotics."

"Oh, yes, that was what I imagined and, actually, have read about. But, in Landa and in this ship we don't use antibiotics anymore, Jota."

"We use, now, bacteria genetically engineered. These, have a programmed lifetime and destroy pathogenically bacteria with great specificity. Then, they suffer apoptosis, what is a programmed cellular death," he concluded.

"Also, these "good bacteria" are generated from the very bacteria present in the infection. In this way, they are immune to bacterial resistance."

During our talk I noticed that Dr Anders had, hanging from his neck, what appeared to me as being a stethoscope. His instrument had a larger than normal "bell" and had a flexible tube, with the usual bifurcation and the ear pieces.

"Olaf, is this, by any chance, an electronic stetho?" I asked, pointing to the instrument.

"Well, Jota, it depends on what you consider as "electronic". Sure, it has some electronic hardware inside here" he said, tapping the instrument head and looking at his assistants, who nodded.

"This little guy here, differently from your Earthian stethos, is not *passive*. It's *active*; it seeks the sounds and not only listens to them."

"Also, this stetho takes advantage that we have two ears and captures sounds from two distinct directions: it is stereophonic."

"Come with me, Jota. I have to see some patients and you will have chance to use this stetho in the real world," he said, smiling and leading me to the wardens, being followed by his 6 assistants.

We came to a room where 4 male patients were laying in their beds.

"This "boy" here is Andres, Jota," he said as he tapped affectionately the patient's chest.

"He is one of our navigators and is here because he felt a bit dizzy and his heartbeat wasn't regular. We have identified an arrhythmia, and treated it. He seems to be OK now and is waiting the doctor in charge to discharge him. Sorry for the pun", he laughed. The assistants also laughed in unison.

"Jota, here, take my stetho and serve yourself," he said, indicating that I should auscultate Andres. And, he looked at the assistants.

I sat on a chair beside the bed, said hello to Andres and introduced myself as a doctor from Earth.

"How are you today, Andres? Can I examine you?"

"Sure you can! But, am I going to Earth?" said Andres, a little concerned. Everyone laughed.

"No, Andres, you are going to stay right here on this ship," Olaf told him.

I asked Andres to breathe normally and relax. And, I began to examine him. I observed his face, eyes, tongue, neck vessels and thorax. I held his fingers, pressed them, and checked the color, the nails. I should have measured the blood pressure, palpated the abdomen, etc. But, this first observation was enough for me. After about 5 minutes and many curious looks from Olaf and his assistants:

"Jota, weren't you going to test the stetho?" Olaf asked me with a bit of impatience.

"Oh, yes, I was going to," I said

"But then, what were you doing?" Olaf asked, already slightly irritated and looking at the assistants, who nodded respectfully at him.

"Oh, I was examining Andres and then, I would auscultate him."

"I'm sorry it took some time. But I think Andres needs oxygen urgently. He is cyanotic, has elevated respiratory rate and intercostal retractions. And, he looks dyspneic." I finished.

"What!" shouted Olaf loudly. There came two nurses and the warden doctor while the assistants began eagerly examining Andres.

"I want a gasometry now and then oxygen 100%," shouted Dr. Olaf Anders at the warden staff.

And we all went to a side of the big room.

"How did you find all this, Jota?"

"Well, I was performing the patient's examination before auscultating him," I answered humbly, justifying my delay.

Soon after, Andres' results came. In fact, he had low blood oxygen and a resulting respiratory insufficiency.

Then Dr. Anders addressed his assistants:

"Now, you see the importance of the patient's examination. We sometimes forget that and go straight for the tests. And, we forget to *observe* the patient, as our Earthian colleague here has done."

Then, Olaf invited me to a coffee in the doctor's room.

"Coffee is the only good thing around here," he said to me and then looked at the assistants, who nodded.

"Well, Jota, I was really impressed with your *second* performance (the first he was referring to was my crisis). And everyone laughed and clapped hands at me."

"But I know you preferred the first. Am I correct?"

"Yes, your performance with Antonina was unforgettable. And just to think you were not performing at all! Sorry again for the pun." And, now the laughing was complete!

Olaf, it appears, was good at creating puns, which his assistants were very aware of.

"OK, my dear colleague and *observer*, did you forget your stethoscope?" said Olaf as we reentered the warden. Then, Olaf approached another bed.

"This is Mario and he has chronic heart disease," he said as he was introducing me to a patient who was reading at the bed.

"Now, Jota, please use the stetho to auscultate Mario. Do me a favor and do not "observe" him this time."

I sat beside the bed, applied the ear tips to my ears and placed the stetho head against Mario's chest.

"Can't hear anything," I turned to Olaf. Mario, the patient, looked at Olaf quite scared.

"Calm down, Mario, you didn't die yet," said Olaf tapping his shoulder. "Our doctor here didn't turn on the stetho!"

"OK, Jota, you are ready to go!" said Olaf, turning on the stetho.

Then, another problem. The instructions were in Landian. Olaf changed the language to English.

As I approached the stetho's headpiece to Mario's chest, even before I touched the skin, I began listening to sounds and instructions: *Configuring filters*. I perceived the stetho was making some adjustments.

I, then, placed the stetho's head against Mario's precordium, which is the chest region immediately over the heart.

Suddenly, I felt myself amid mystic surroundings. It appeared to be some sort of battlefield. Then, as the stetho was adjusting, I felt myself within a hydroelectric plant, machines working and giant masses of water gushing. Little by little the sounds began to fit in, to make sense, as my ears were getting synchronous with the sounds. Then, there began new instructions: *move to the mitral area*. I moved the stetho to where I believed the mitral valve was located down the chest.

Immediately, I began hearing the sounds of the mitral valve, opening on diastole and closing on systole. In this configuration, the filters were set to hearing the valve walls vibrations. Instructions appeared to other valves, the tricuspid, the aortic and the pulmonary. And, I followed them. Then, the stetho began setting the filters to hearing flows of blood, to identify murmurs, for example. Finally, new filtering and adjustments for hearing heart wall vibrations. There was much more than this but only interesting for a cardiologist.

Then, Olaf and his assistants, having observed my "open mouth and dropped jaw," decided to have a bit more fun with me.

"Let's see one more patient, Jota, and this one will surprise you, I guarantee!"

We then moved to another wing of the MC, quite separated from the one we had first entered.

"Here, we have Earthian patients. We need to separate them from the Landians. Different bacteria, you see," said Olaf, maybe expecting some reaction from me. I didn't say anything. Who was I to argue?

"Jota, this is Francesco he came from your planet and his only problem is being Italian," said Olaf, tapping Francesco's shoulder.

"Francesco was a tetraplegic on Earth and came to Landa for treatment. He now walks and uses his arms and hands better than I do. But, his heart "took some revenge" and needed to be replaced."

"Listen to Francesco's heart, Jota, and tell me what you think."

I took a seat on the chair beside Francesco's bed and began the auscultation of his chest. Now, the stetho appeared to be a bit confused. No more instructions. What I heard, now, seemed to me two pumps driven by electric motors.

"Does he have two mechanical hearts?" I asked Olaf and his assistants. But, when I turned to them I saw that some other doctors had entered the room and were observing me.

"How do you know there are two hearts?" asked Olaf with an inquisitive look at his assistants.

"Well, it seems to me that there are two pumps, but I'm not sure, of course."

"Yes, Jota, Francesco has two mechanical hearts, you have heard correctly."

"But, tell me, Jota, why you do you think we use two pumps instead of just one more powerful?" Olaf asked me, and looked at his assistants who nodded approvingly.

Now, there were some 15 doctors and I was being viewed as a curiosity. An Earthian doctor examining an Earthian patient inside an Earthian infirmary. Not something that happens every day! What an Earthian doctor having an IQ of 100 was doing in the middle of doctors having an average IQ of 1200?

However, I was not shaken by my numerical and intellectual inferiority.

And I answered:

"Well, the reason for having two mechanical pumps in Francesco is that the heart has, actually, two mechanical pumps driven by a same muscle."

Hearing my answer, one of Olaf's assistants, Nikita, said:

"It is obvious that the heart has two pumps, but Olaf's question wasn't that. He wants to know why the biological heart has two pumps" and he appeared to be a bit upset. Olaf, himself didn't seem to mind.

"OK, and that's why I'm trying to complete my answer," I continued, unabated.

"The circulatory system of Earthians has three main territories: arterial, venous and pulmonary. And they have three different functions. The arterial territory, having a high pressure, works in the distribution of nutrients to cells. The venous territory, of minimal pressure, absorbs the fluid that has been filtered by the arterial capillaries. Finally, the pulmonary territory, with intermediary pressure, serves the pulmonary circulation by means of uptake of O_2 and eliminating CO_2.

"OK, OK, but can't you be more specific and more to the point, we can't stay here all morning!" said Nikita, visibly altered. Olaf asked Nikita to be more patient.

And I went on:

"Now, regarding the pressures. The arterial system has a high pressure, which is needed for capillary filtration. But the venous territory, in order to absorb fluid, needs to be kept at a very low pressure." Nikita, at this point of my explanation, was sending inquisitive looks at the others as if something had to be done to stop me. Olaf, undaunted, was listening. And, I went on:

"OK, we all know that central venous pressure is close to null; we measure it routinely"

"But why does the venous pressure *need* to be so low, why, why?" said Nikita and I sensed he was trying to confuse me.

"If the venous pressure is not very low, the Starling forces will be no favorable to fluid absorption by the venous system and edema may occur"

"OK, but you haven't explained why it is necessary having the second pump: the right heart, the right heart," said Nikita.

And, on I went, unabated:

"Now, we come to the pulmonary vascular territory. We should remember that the venous blood, arriving at the *venae cavae*, has lost most of its pressure and most of its velocity. This means it has lost, almost completely, its energy."

"But, now, we have a problem: this same blood needs to traverse the pulmonary circulation and close the circuit by arriving at the left heart. And, for this, the blood needs energy."

"And, here, enters the second pump, the right heart. It is the right heart that gives the blood the necessary energy to cross the pulmonary vessels, exchange gases with the atmosphere and complete the circuit."

And I said this, looking firmly at Nikita.

"So, it is not possible to solve this with just one pump, powerful as it might be."

As I finished, all assistants remained silent and looked at Nikita. Olaf thanked me and Nikita left the room, in silence, without looking back.

Chapter 67

First Night

After my tests with the brain imaging apparatus and the findings of Dr Felder concerning new synaptic connections in my brain, Antonina changed, perceptibly, her interaction with me. The first indication I had of this was after the third bathing "session" we had after her talk with Dr Felder.

Initially, the bathing "protocol" seemed to me as a regular one, exactly the same sequence we had had in our very first bath. But, when came my turn to bath her at the front and I had cleared down the lower abdomen, Antonina did not turn her back to me. Instead, she embraced me and began caressing my chest while her eyes were locked into mine. Then, she asked me to clean her genitals using my hands. Up to now, despite my desire, I was following her instructions to the letter. And, so, I began cleaning her down there. This time, however, Antonina began breathing faster and moaning imperceptibly. As I went on with my task, she touched my chest with her face and touched her lips to my chest. Then, I could perceive her breathing was really more intense and her moans intensified.

"Touch me stronger, Jota, I'm beginning to like it," she said as she began to moan and rub her lips to my chest.

"How good it is, Jota, don't stop, don't stop," and, saying this she began caressing my genitals so gently and naively. And, clearly insecure of what exactly she should do and where.

"Do you like it, Jota? Do you like my caressing you? Tell me, please!"

"Yes, I like very much!" and she could see and feel it.

Antonina pulled me down and went tip top so as to make her face level with mine and, for the first time, for the first time ever, she touched her lips to mine, so lightly, so gently, as if she was probing a new territory. And, as she kissed me she embraced me so strongly I felt I couldn't even breathe.

Inevitably, her genitals had to touch mine and she began rubbing hers against mine. Her breathing increased and her moans intensified. Then, abruptly she pushed me from her and began sobbing.

"I can't Jota, I shouldn't. Let's dry ourselves."

We took clean towels and wiped our bodies dry.

"Let's lay down, Jota, I can't go on with this, I can't!"

We then went up to her bed and lay down, both of us facing the roof.

"Don't ever leave me, Jota, I love you so much!"

And, saying this, she went over me and, pressing me against the bed, began kissing my lips and rubbing her body against mine. As she went on with this, she began moaning and rubbing forcibly her sex against mine. Then she turned abruptly and returned to her side of the bed. Immediately, however, she pressed her face against my chest and began sobbing and shaking her body as in a convulsion. Then, she stopped.

After this, Antonina fell into a sleep. I, slowly went down the bed, put on my clothes and got to my cabin. That night I had her scent all over my body and I slept like a baby.

I woke with Antonina at my side in the bed. She was looking at me.

"Jota, forgive me for what I did to you! I was out of myself." And, she began caressing my face as she ever did before, every morning.

"Of course I forgive you, but you haven't done me any harm"

She didn't say anything but only looked at me, tenderly, and caressed lightly my hair. Her eyes were wet and conveyed a deep sadness, like something was coming to an end. Then, she recomposed and came back to her firmness.

"Let's have breakfast and I will be very busy today. In a few days we go back to Earth, Jota. And, I don't know what expects me there."

My day was routine, I was still at the vegetable garden but never saw Erika again. What I've learned from her was more than enough.

The approach of our return to Earth made me think that this was a unique experience in my life.

Next evening, after our usual supper before night, Antonina told me to wash myself in my cabin and then go to her cabin since she wanted us to talk. This was a clear break in our bathing routine. I took it as being a message that we should stop the intimacies and that Antonina had crossed some line with me.

However, I was not correct in my guesses.

We went up to her bed. We were both naked, according to Antonina's instructions. Antonina embraced me right away and began kissing my lips.

"I love you, Jota, and I want to give you pleasure, I want to quench your desire. But, teach me, Jota. Teach me how to give you pleasure!"

"Anything you do to me will give me pleasure, Antonina. Just being here with you is enough for me."

Then, Antonina began rubbing her body against mine and her sex against mine.

"Tell me, Jota, how to do it, teach me, so I can give you more pleasure," and she began trying get penetrated.

"Will it hurt, Jota? Please teach me."

Then, I discovered that Antonina was a virgin. Not only was she a virgin, but also, her sex experience was null.

And, after three consecutive nights of experimenting, we finally did it.

"How come you never did it Antonina? And your husband? Didn't he want to?"

"Jota, you don't understand. Had nobody told you that sex in Landa is only to procreate? My husband was a strict follower of rules. According to him, sex should be respectful, and no pleasure should be derived from it! Rules, Jota, those damned rules!"

The night following the one we had finally completed our sex relationship, we were again lying together in her bed. Antonina was pensive, looking at the roof while her hands caressed my face. Then, she turned to me and placed her face in front of me:

"I shouldn't be doing this to you, Jota!"

"You don't need to blame yourself, my love. You aren't doing me any harm."

"But, still, I shouldn't do these things to you."

"You are not "doing things" to me, Antonina. We are both "doing things" to each other."

"No, Jota, it doesn't work thus. I'm the one responsible! I'm the one to carry the fault on my back."

"Why is that so, why are you saying this Antonina? In this case I'm at fault too."

"It can't be your fault because you are pure, Jota, you are innocent!"

"I'm not pure, Antonina, I've done my share of bad things."

"No, Jota, you don't understand. It's not just you. All Earthians are pure beings, they may do wrong things to themselves, they may kill each other, they may enslave each other, they may rob, but they don't know what they are doing, Jota. They don't know, I assure you, they don't!"

"But, if this is so, then why you are doing those "wrong" things to me, my love?"

"I'm doing this to quench your desire, Jota; I want you to have pleasure with me. And also, I want you to give me pleasure, Jota."

"Because seeing you are having pleasure gives me double pleasure. I also need pleasure, Jota. And I need so much. But, my pleasure is wrong and I shall pay for it. Still, I need to do it, Jota. I began it with you and I have to finish it. I can't leave you now, Jota. You wouldn't survive. I will sacrifice myself for you."

Only some months later, I would be able to understand what Antonina was saying to me, what she was trying to explain. And, then, it was too late…

The monitor in our cabin was showing, now, Earth and Moon. Earth had the size of the Moon as viewed from Earth and the Moon looked way smaller than we see it from Earth. Comparing with those images in former days I noticed that both Earth and Moon appeared always as "full". They never showed phases. The Universe continued its rhythm, oblivious of our dramas.

Chapter 68

The Ferals

On the second morning after my last meeting with Antonina, I was told that Dr. Felder wanted to see me.

"How are you, jota? How you feel today? No more crises eh?"

"Oh, yes Dr Felder, I'm feeling very well."

"Well, the reason I called you here is to ask you for one more contribution to science, just one more scanning of your brain. Do you mind doing me this favor?"

"No problem Dr Felder, we still have a few days left before returning to Earth. But, I got curious, Dr. You were telling me about what you call the *permanent lambs* and that those become irreversibly attached to their shepherds."

"That's right, Jota, once the neural connections stabilize and give rise to permanent tracts, there is no reversion and it gets to a permanent condition. And there is more, Jota. It seems the connections are shepherd-specific".

"Yes, Dr, that's what I understood. But, are those permanent connections free of say, some "maintenance," so to speak?"

"Oh no, Jota. Not at all! The connections need to be kept "working," and I repeat yours "so to speak". Do you know of anything in the body that does not need to be kept permanently working in order to function? Probably you don't know, eh?"

"In order for permanent lambs to continue to be stable, they need a constant interaction with their shepherds. Please, this is dangerous territory and I'm sure you keep this talk between us."

Actually, it was a forbidden talk, but Dr Felder wasn't the least concerned about me leaking it. He knew that Earthian talk was usually considered nonsense. And, he went on.

"What happens is that this permanent conditioning or "maintenance" of their lambs is done unconsciously by the shepherds. Actually, the shepherds don't know it, since this a new study. This is done, in a most natural way, by the constant caressing of the lambs by their shepherds and the constant sniffing of the shepherds' pheromones by the lambs. Also important are the talks and nice words exchanged between shepherds and lambs. It's like the conditioning you received from Antonina which, in your case, is reversible, up to now, we hope so! Now, we know from the studies done here in this ship, pay attention, Jota, here in this very ship, that a permanent neural connection cannot be left unassisted. It needs to be continually maintained by those maneuvers, we call them *love actions*. These love actions are essential to keep things running, say, smoothly."

"But, Dr, what happens if, by any chance those *love actions* are interrupted, say, permanently?"

"Ah, Jota, I sincerely desired you would not ask me this. But we are scientists, aren't we? Science must have no secrets!"

"However, what I'm about to tell you, Jota, is no secret in Landa, despite the mechanism has not been revealed up to now. Permanent lambs that stop receiving love actions and hormonal conditioning revert, Jota. They revert!"

"They revert to what, Dr Felder? Do they revert to their previous wild condition, the condition they lived previously on Earth?" I asked, feeling a slight fear creeping along my spine and a tightening in my throat. *I might be among those*, I thought.

"Jota, pay attention to this. The permanent lambs that interrupt their interaction with the shepherd and stop receiving love actions enter into an irreversible *feral state*, Jota. Essentially, they turn into beasts. We call them *feral lambs*."

"We have three of them in this ship at present and will receive two more from Earth in the following weeks. Do you want to take a look, Jota? But, I advise you, you may not like it!"

"I would appreciate very much to see those feral lambs, Dr Felder. I've seen many strange things in my life, Dr, and I believe one more will not topple me over."

"Well, I need to visit them today, it is my turn. And you can come along with me. Let's go."

We went down a corridor that ended at a heavy door with bars. At the door was a guard carrying a sort of gun that, to me, appeared a sort of stun gun on steroids. Seeing my surprise at the looks of that strange gun, Dr Felder:

"It's a phaser Jota, a paralyzing gun. Non-lethal. Those specimens are quite rare. We can't afford to have them killed!" Dr Felder said smiling at the guard.

"It's OK, Boris, I've brought a visitor, please open up"

Upon which words the guard opened the heavy door. Then, we entered a lateral corridor faced, from one side only, by cells with thick transparent walls. The first 2 cells were empty. At the 3rd cell was another guard, seated on a chair. Also, in the corridor were some backrest chairs, very comfortable. From that cell on, there were transparent and thick walls closing the corridor.

"Those chairs are for observation, Jota. We learn much observing what is inside these cells." And, then, I saw it:

He was sleeping on the floor despite having a berth. At the movement he woke up and came raging and banging at the wall.

"Go away you crap, go away, let me sleep" Despite his clothes were changed every day he was filthy. And he spat at the wall, leaving a slimy trace of saliva.

"What does he eat?" I asked

"Well, he has to eat everybody's food, but what he likes most are rats."

"Rats?! But are there rats in this ship?"

"Jota, c'mon, do you know of any ships having no rats?"

"Yes, there are rats here and we trap them. In this ship there are places no one has entered for many years. Unpressurized, essentially no oxygen, very cold. There, the rats thrive. Most captured are cremated to be used as fertilizer but some we give to them ferals. And they like to catch and eat them alive!"

"And, how you clean them and change their clothes Dr?"

"That's easy, Jota. See those tubes in the roof? We inject a mixture of carbon dioxide and nitrous oxide and those beauties get very docile."

"Do you like to see one more, Jota, or should we pass on?"

"OK, let's pass on, Dr, I've seen enough."

Then, we moved along the corridor and after crossing two more cells and two more transparent walls we came to a cell at the end of the corridor.

"Now, Jota you will be introduced to Calypso, our muse in this ship. She is a feral lamb, but a very special one as you will be able to verify."

We entered a hall which faced a large cell with a huge and thick transparent wall pierced by numerous holes the size of a finger. A guard was seated at a backrest chair, semi-sleeping. At our entry he stood and said hello to Dr Felder. In the hall facing the cell, there were some 4 backrest chairs.

"Please, don't touch the wall, Jota, just don't touch it"; Dr Felder said as we were facing the cell interior.

The cell looked like a beauty parlor. Walls painted a light pink, a gigantic and beautiful mirror at a side wall, a closet, a vanity desk, complete with mirror and drawers. On a berth was lying a woman, apparently sleeping. Her face was turned away from us. Hearing the movement in the hall she seated at the bed.

"What a marvelous scent of a fresh lamb," she said, probably, referring to me.

"Go away you all that I want to be alone with this fresh lamb!" she said loudly and commanding.

Dr Felder whispered to me, "We will be watching you at the cameras. Don't touch the wall or look firmly at her eyes. She will try to hypnotize you. Remember she is very cunning. Take your time because this is going to be fun". And, saying this, he left with the guard.

I was alone in the hall.

Calypso descended elegantly from the berth and came close to the wall. She was a very beautiful girl of about 20. Brunette, long hair down almost to her waist. She didn't walk. To my eyes, she floated across the room. Coming close to the wall and placing one hand on it she said:

"What is your name my fresh lamb?"

"They call me Jota"

"What a marvelous scent you got Jota, so fresh, so innocent. You want to feel my smell? Come near sniff me at your will."

My olfaction, despite having lost much of its "power" was still very sensitive. And the girl's scent was something I've never experimented. It was a combination of delicious and mysterious fragrances. Her voice sounded like music. It didn't seem to come from her mouth but rather from some distant magic place.

"Tell me, my boy, how do you like me? Do you want to have me? I can give you so much pleasure. Just say you want me and I'll be yours."

I didn't say anything. I was completely mesmerized by her looks, by her voice, by her scent. She didn't move she seemed to float.

"Tell me how you like my body. Does it please you? Have you ever seen a body like this?"

And she pulled up her shirt revealing her breasts. Approaching the wall near me she pressed them against the wall.

"Touch them and feel how firm they are. Touch my nipples"

Seeing I wouldn't touch her breasts and not even the wall, she made a sad face.

"How bad you are, and I was so eager for your touch. I'm so alone here Jota, and I have so much love to give. Why don't we run away from this place Jota?"

"You want me to sing to you, my love?"

"Yes, please do sing to me," I said, timidly.

"Then, sit down in that chair and listen."

And then, what I remember was she beginning to sing. Her voice was so melodious, so captivating and gave me a sense of completeness. As if listening to her was the only and obvious thing to ever be done. I just closed my eyes and listened.

"Hey Jota, time to go now!"; Dr Felder was shaking me by the shoulder.

"Where am I?"

"You are OK, Jota, let's go, you have been here for almost an hour!" Then, I came to myself and saw I was seated at that chair. Inside her cell, Calypso was sleeping, her face covered.

When I came to the main hall of the cells, I was met by a few doctors and three guards. And they all clapped hands at me.

"Congrats, Jota, you have survived Calypso. Not everyone survives her!" said Dr Felder, laughing loudly.

I was still a bit dizzy and disoriented when we came to Dr Felder's office.

"She is a beauty isn't she, Jota?" Too good there was that wall. You know what? Once she managed to seduce a guard, had him make sex to her, hypnotized him, killed him and when the guards arrived she had already eaten her face and neck."

"Her IQ is 300, Jota, and she is very cunning."

"Well, Jota, I want to show you the scanning of those feral lambs."

Then, Dr Felder began showing me a few scanners from permanent lambs that had gone feral.

"See, here, the region of the limbic system, Jota. Can you see that it presents numerous glioses (plural of gliosis), which are scars of regions of cell death? In most of those feral lambs there is extensive damage to the limbic system and associated areas. But in Calypso's brain, as you can see in this other scan, it is different. There are no signs of previous cell death. Instead, there is cell proliferation. But, abnormal cell proliferation. This finding will give me a science prize, Jota!"

"I am very impressed Dr Felder, but what happens to those feral lambs at Landa?"

"Oh, yes, Jota, very good question and a simple answer. We euthanize them Jota; there is nothing else to be done."

"But, now, their brains are being sent to us for a more detailed analysis to be done here in this ship and in my laboratory!"

"But, tell me Dr, about those permanent lambs in Landa. Do they know what happens if their shepherd dies or abandon them?"

"Yes, Jota, they know and that's a great concern of them. But, most lambs live in households with many family members and these multiple acts of love blunt the conditioning, making it more diffuse, more spread, so to say. This makes the connections less shepherd-specific, you see what I mean? The real danger is when the lamb is exclusive of a single shepherd."

"Like my case, Dr?"

"Yes, Jota, like your case, you got it! And since you and your shepherd live on Earth, your chance to interacting with another Landian shepherd is essentially zero."

"Do the monks also have lambs?" I asked, as if trying, unconsciously, to change subject.

"Ah, that's a very interesting and very intelligent question, Jota. Yes, the monks do have lambs, all right, and also the counselors. Life is very difficult on Landa without the lambs, Jota. Very difficult indeed. I think someone may have explained to you the role the lambs have in Landa's way of life."

"And, look, Jota, one more thing. Those monks are not that good people they make you believe they are; you know?"

Chapter 69

Artificial Gravity

The date for our return to Earth was getting closer now. I, Antonina and Greg would land at the Brazilian northeast, along with some hundreds of people.

My last lecture on board would be "Artificial gravity" to be ministered by Dr Boris, a Landian physicist. But, before the main lecture, Dr Olaf Anders would present a brief lecture: *Long term effects of zero gravity.*

"Effects of zero gravity began to be observed in Landa since the beginning of space exploration in the years corresponding to 1850 on Earth. But, since there are many Earthians in this ship, I will concentrate in the effects beginning at the 1960s on Earth."

"Initially, it was observed that long stays in space led to cardiac problems, loss of muscle mass, osteoporosis, edemas, mental changes and other smaller alterations. These deleterious effects were observed in greater scale in the ISS, with longer stays at zero gravity. But, how to minimize those effects?"

"One of the first approaches was to implement a rigorous program of physical exercises. But despite this, the deleterious effects of zero gravity still continued to occur."

"The result of these experiences was that no amount of exercise could substitute for gravity. And thus, the necessity for implementing artificial gravity in space travels or long stays in space stations. And, to explain this, no one is better than Dr Boris Zelenko."

And the audience clapped hands.

After this short live lecture, there entered, in the monitors, a recorded lecture by Dr Boris:

"After all, what is gravity? Despite many advances in physics, both in Landa and Earth, gravity still defies the minds of physicists."

"It was Albert Einstein, an Earthian physicist, who, for the first time, postulated that gravity is not a force but, instead, a deformation of space caused by the presence of a mass. A large mass strongly deforms the space-time around it. A given object near this mass will follow the line of least energy and the result is equivalent to a force acting in the object. These ideas are part of the General Relativity Theory, proposed by Einstein in the beginning of the Earthian 20th century. Of course, I will not dwell on this theory because I want you to remain in this hall," he said, and everyone laughed.

"Now, what would be the difference between natural and artificial gravity? The answer can be found in the concept of *acceleration*, with is the change in velocity with time."

"And, more important, can we feel acceleration? A good example of acceleration is to be seated in a sports car that can get from zero to 100 km/hour (28 m/sec) in 2.8 seconds."

"When the car starts to run we are going to experiment an increase in velocity of 10 m/s each second. This is equivalent to an acceleration of 10 m/s^2.This acceleration is numerically equal to the so-called *acceleration of gravity* on Earth and the same acceleration you get if you jump from a plane before you open your parachute." (g, on Earth, is actually 9.8 m/s^2).

"In both examples, you accelerate 10 m/s^2. But there is a difference. In the sports car you feel a force pushing you forward. That force applied to your body is your mass x g. Suppose you weigh 80 kg. The force you feel on your back and buttocks will be 80 x 10 = 800 Newton's."

"But, when you jump from a plane and accelerate down the same 10 m/s^{2}you don't feel any force at all because, now, you are undergoing a natural acceleration or natural gravity."

"And, there is a third case. Suppose you are standing over a scale that marks the number 80 (your weight). You feel a force on the soles of your feet, pushing you upward, and this force is 80 kgf. In this curious case you feel the gravity force, but you don't accelerate."

"But, suppose this same scale is placed inside an elevator and suddenly you see the number zero on the scale you are standing on. And you don't feel any force on your soles. I'm very sorry to say your elevator is falling down."

"Now, what really is necessary during space travel is that your body feels a constant force applied to it all the time. And that is what prevents (or minimizes) the "zero gravity" diseases."

"We, then, see that natural gravity creates that condition of a constant force applied to the body. However, we feel that force only we are not falling (fortunately). And, in this case, we are not accelerating. However, to simulate natural gravity we must be accelerated by a force that we can feel. And, I know this seems quite confusing."

"To increase a little bit your confusion I will add a little summary:

In natural gravity, when you accelerate means you are falling, and you feel no force acting on you. But when you are standing on Earth (or Landa) you feel a force but then you don't accelerate.

"But, in artificial gravity, in order to accelerate, you always feel a force pushing you."

"From what we saw we can postulate that, if our spaceship accelerates continually with 10 m/s^2, we are going to feel like we are on Earth. But there is a problem, and actually two. The first problem is that in order to accelerate you need thrust and that means energy. The second problem is that with continuous thrust the ship's velocity keeps increasing. This is good up to a certain point, but when the velocity gets too large you need to decelerate and, again, use thrust and energy."

"But there is a way around this problem: rotation. And by rotating, we can get the *centrifugal acceleration*. There is, here, a great advantage over linear acceleration: there is no need for thrust and so, no need for energy. Once your spaceship gets rotating it keeps rotating. You want an example? The Earth."

"So, the gravity you feel in this ship is artificial and caused by the rotation of the ship around a central axis. Here, we have different levels of "gravity". The greater gravity is at the ship's border. At the central region or axis of rotation, we have zero gravity. This ship turns at 1.56 revolutions per minute and we have a maximal gravity of 80% of G at the borders. There, are located the habitable parts, like the cabins, restaurants, hospitals, etc. But there are many levels approaching the axis of rotation, where the gravity is also adequate for longer stays."

Chapter 70
Return to Earth

While we were at the mother-ship, the transference disc had performed many landings at different parts of Earth. On each of those landings many Landians disembarked from the mother-ship, to stay on Earth permanently. In one of these landings a new navigator was incorporated to the mother-ship and Greg was released to go back to Earth with Antonina and me.

Our return went on without incidents, and we landed near a small city of the North of Brazil whose name I wasn't allowed to reveal.

During the disc descent we experimented a brief period of 8G deceleration and I lost consciousness briefly. We landed close to a dome, like the one at our farm. After going through a brief medical check-up we took a bus to Teresina, from where we embarked upon a flight to São Paulo City and, from there, by car, to our farm.

The farm hadn't changed, but all movement related to the mission to Landa was gone. Yuri, Marco, Frederico e Mayra came to meet us affectionately. I was told that Mayra had moved permanently to the farm and was now part of the "family". Her mentor was Yuri. A new container had been added to be her new quarters.

From my perspective, Mayra had changed. Her joviality and spontaneity had given place to a calmer, more respectful and contemplative attitude. The influence that Yuri had exerted upon her was all evident. His comments were studied and followed by glances at Yuri as if she was expecting some feedback. Also, before answering some questions she looked briefly at Yuri.

With this and other small changes, life had returned to normal in the farm.

My relationship with Antonina had now changed to a different level. Now, we were lovers and her domain over me seemed to have disappeared, or at least, was not as explicit as before. No more orders. We had reached a sort of stable process.

However, her dealings with me were a bit different here in the farm, as compared at the mother-ship. The ship was a sort of neutral territory, more liberal. This might have contributed to a faster development of our relationship.

The night after our return to Earth, the "family" offered us a welcome dinner. Presents were Yuri, Marco, Frederico, Greg, Antonina, Mayra and me. Also, Isobel and Fabiana had gathered for us. I was told that the other occupants of the farm, as well as the occupants of Dome 3, which had been dismantled, had been removed to other kibbutzes. Also, I was informed that there were now only two domes and that Isobel and Fabiana were the sole occupants of Dome 2. Also, someone told me that the wood processing plants have been moved elsewhere.

I had the clear impression that the pace of activities was way lower than before. Maybe as a foreboding of new facts on the horizon.

Fabiana, too, was different and seemed, now, to have established a firm relationship with Isobel, a sort of bond of which I had a clear and negative remembrance. Like I saw with Mayra, Fabiana, despite joyful, also sent occasional glances to Isobel as if seeking some sort of approval or questioning or acquiescence. Isobel hadn't changed and, from time to time, stared at me with that curious and inquisitive look I had observed at the first meeting with her. My impression was that she was studying me. When she stared at me I felt transparent or like I was nude and I felt a creeping sensation down my spine.

The welcome dinner was excellent and had the supervision of the family girls, along with the two servant girls. Many special foods, wine and beer. There was a musical background playing Landian music, which was prohibited in Landa's colonies but is current in the clandestine colonies.

After dinner and dessert, we were served coffee and liquor. Yuri then announced that Mayra had passed the test of trust. She had jumped "to death".

"It was a bit different from Jota's case, however, since Mayra was afraid to jump. But after she had been assured that there was a net below, she jumped. Even so, she gave us proof of trust because the net below wasn't visible from the top of the cliff. However, it wasn't proof of craziness like Jota's jump," and everyone clapped their hands.

Mayra remained silent as if insecure of what to say, and after an assuring nod of Yuri said:

"I thank everyone for the clapping despite not knowing whom it was directed to: Me or Jota," and all responded:

"To you!"

Afterwards, Yuri said that he had received praise from his colleague, Olaf Anders, about my visit to the Medical Center in the ship.

"And, to prove that, here is a gift for you, Jota, from Olaf," said Yuri and he handed me a box. I was asked to open the box and did it; there, was the stethoscope of my dreams. A brand new one, sealed pack, instructions in English.

Then, it was Greg's turn to speak, and he said he was doubly happy about not having to go to Landa and for going back to Earth.

"I couldn't even imagine how terrible would be getting back to Landa after having known this fantastic planet!" and he pointed downward.

More hand clapping to Greg.

Then, Yuri asked me to tell Mayra and Fabiana about my visit to the mother-ship and my trip in the disc, since both had never left Earth.

I said that everything impressed me, everything was new to me. Of course, I didn't mention all the negative or strange experiences.

And, I said also that the landing back on Earth I couldn't experience because I had passed out due to the 8G deceleration. Greg explained that the disc descent had to be fast in order to avoid detection.

"But, why is it necessary disguising the disc since the *flying saucers* are making so many exhibitions for all to see?" I asked to Yuri and Greg.

Everyone looked at Yuri trying to see his reaction to my question.

"Look, Jota, we don't know where these crafts come from and even less do we know who pilot them."

Chapter 71

Second Talk with Fabiana

My life on the farm went to its normal pace. My walks with Antonina returned. One day, while we were walking, we passed by the place where I had lost my bearings. The strange concrete floor with the umbrella handles sticking out.

"What are those "umbrellas" and what is this concrete slab below our feet?" I asked Antonina.

"Look, Jota, this farm is not a typical colony. This is actually a base of operations. There is more below ground than above. And, in some places there are many levels underground."

Not always I walked with Antonina. Many times she was busy with new tasks. There was something in the air, something telling me of imminent changes. Also, my dependence on Antonina had decreased to levels close to normality. Our love was now level, not from below, not from above, according to Erika's definition.

But I knew this was only an illusion. I knew that Antonina, despite demonstrating genuine love to me, was still trying to revert something that she knew was not going to be good for me. What mattered, as I was concerned, was that I could stay long periods away from Antonina. And that during our love encounters we felt happy.

Joaquim

It was on one of those solitary walks where I always carried Greg's camera (now mine). I had left the dome soon after breakfast with Antonina and was exploring new trails.

Turning a curve of the trail, I suddenly was facing Fabiana.

She was closing the trail so as not to let me pass.

"I knew you would cross this place when I saw the trail you took," she said, laughing.

"I've lost your phone number and want to talk to you. Let's go to that stone where we can sit."

Such stone I didn't know. Like many on the farm, it was a large, flat stone at the right height to be seated on.

Fabiana had changed, as I had commented before. But now, in daylight and at a closer range, I could perceive that she had lost that sad look I had observed some time before on our first encounter. Her eyes appeared now to be more focused and secure. But her gaze had lost some joviality and freshness and spontaneity they had then. Fabiana thanked me for my nice words when she had broken up with Sulamita.

"It was a difficult period for me but now, I'm feeling better. My bond with Isobel is much stronger than with Sulamita."

Hearing the word "bond" once more I was surprised and Fabiana sensed it.

"What's wrong with you, Jota? You look strange!"

"Oh, nothing serious, but tell me about this "bond" you refer to."

"You don't know what a bond is Jota? They didn't tell you yet?"

"Well, I have heard many mentions to this word recently, but I would like to hear from you."

"Jota, the word *bond* here means *domination by means of love.*"

"But then, Fabiana, you have been dominated by Isobel?"

"Not necessarily, Jota. It can be said I have submitted myself to her."

"And how come you have submitted yourself to Isobel? Was it by your own will?" I asked with some tones of sarcasm in my voice.

"It was through love, obviously, Jota," and she gestured it.

Fabiana understood my sarcasm but didn't react to it.

"Don't you know where the word *dominate* comes from, Jota?"

"Yes, I think I know the origin, Fabiana. I have studied Latin at the school and remember that *dominus* means master, lord, owner, the one that exerts power command over one or more individuals. And that *dominate* meant exerting this power. And I also remember the phrase *dominus vobiscum* that I heard at the catholic masses. It means *the Lord be with you.*"

"And who would be this *Lord* you have mentioned, Jota?"

"The Lord I mentioned is our God, obviously!" I said, imitating the "obvious" gesture Fabiana had made.

"That's it, Jota. You, yourself, have answered your question! And isn't God your Lord, your *Dominus*, Jota?"

"Yes, Fabiana He is my Lord."

"And doesn't He by any chance dominate you, Jota?"

"My Lord doesn't dominate me. I'm the one who submit to him, who allow him to dominate me."

"And what kind of domination is that, Jota?"

"I always knew God had us under His domain through His love to us, to me, to all."

"Then, Jota, do you reckon that God exerts his domain over you by means of His love to you and not by any force or power that we all know He has?"

"Yes, Fabiana, I always understood this."

"Then, Jota, why can't you understand that Isobel dominates me through her love for me?"

"And what form of love does Isobel exert upon you?"

"That's a difficult question, Jota. To understand this love of Isobel to me, I would need to be able to understand a being that is superior to me. And that is not possible, Jota!"

"And, is Isobel superior to you?"

"Yes, Jota, she is superior to me, like Antonina is superior to you," answered Fabiana giving a deprecating tone to Antonina's name.

"And why is Antonina superior to me? Why isn't she equal to me?"

Seeing that Fabiana remained silent, I went on.

"And what does Isobel mean to you?"

"She is my shepherd and I'm her lamb, Jota. Can't you see this? Where have you been?"

"And why have you mentioned that Antonina is dominating me?"

"It was Isobel who told me. She said you are a "poor lamb" and that she pities you."

"What?!"; I said, indignantly. But I couldn't even argue since Fabiana, looking at her cell phone, said:

"I have to go now, Jota, but before going, I would like to kiss you!"

"What type of kiss would be that?"

"This type!" she said, grabbing me by the neck and kissing me long on the lips. And then, she ran, laughing loudly and mockingly.

Chapter 72

Talk with Antonina

That night, after dinner, Antonina came to me.

"Jota, there are a few things I need to talk with you. Please come to my container that I want to give you a bath. I've already took my bath today."

I changed my clothes to cleaner ones, went to the mirror and, seeing my face reflected, asked to my reflection: "What's going to be this time?"

"Let's go to my bed to talk," said Antonina as I entered her room.

We went to her bed and lay down without touching each other. Antonina went directly to the subject:

"I saw you and Fabiana kissing today, Jota," she said calmly and in a low voice.

"Yes, you have seen it correctly, and have you heard her asking to kiss me too? And that I didn't know it would be a kissing on the mouth?"

"Yes, I know of this, Jota, I was listening you talk with Fabiana. Do you know that I've got a very good hearing and that I can walk unseen?"

"Look, Jota, let me tell you. You are entering a very dangerous territory. Not in what concerns Fabiana, she is an innocent. I refer to Isobel, to Isobel, Jota!"

"Isobel and Yuri were a married couple down in Landa. They had to run from there, did you know that?"

"What wrong have they done, Antonina?"

"Impure acts, they were condemned to be expelled from the colony."

"What kind of impure acts?"

"What do you think those acts were, Jota? What do you think? They did impure acts with their lambs. This was what they did, Jota!"

"And why I should be aware of Isobel? Can she do me any harm?"

"Yes, Jota she can do you a lot of harm. She can destroy you."

"How come, Antonina, is she going to kill me? What for?"

"No, Jota she will not kill you. As I said, she can destroy you. First, she dominates you, like she has dominated Fabiana. Then, she uses you for her fun, for her pleasure and then she leaves you, she abandons you, Jota."

"Dr Alten Felder told me you went to visit Calypso. Did you like her? Did you find her beautiful? Did you know where she came from, Jota?"

"I saw Calypso; Dr Felder took me there to see her. To see what happens to a permanent lamb that is abandoned. He said I should see with my own eyes since I might one day tread Calypso's way."

"Did Dr Felder tell you that Calypso is very cunning, that she has incredible seducing power, and that she hypnotizes?"

"Yes, Antonina, he told me all that. And that she sings also. I've listened her singing and couldn't resist!"

"Good, Jota, you have been well instructed by Dr Felder, who is my friend and who has been counseling me regarding your problem, Jota."

"Do I have a problem, Antonina?" I asked, as again, my throat tightened. Antonina saw it.

"Yes, you do Jota. Probably, Dr Felder explained to you your situation. And it's a delicate one, Jota."

"Dr Felder repeated your scan. He told me you are stabilized but he would prefer that you had reversed a bit more."

"Am I still in danger, Antonina?"

"Dr Felder said to me that you probably will get back to normal, Jota, but for this we are both changing our ways to each other."

"I will sacrifice for you, because I love you Jota."

"Did you know who Calypso's shepherd was?" Antonina asked me.

"Yuri was her shepherd in Landa," she said, before I answered...

"Then, he met Isobel and they got together, but outside marriage. And that was one of their crimes, Jota. But, it didn't stop there. Calypso seduced Yuri and they became lovers secretly. And that was the second Yuri's crime."

"It happens that Isobel discovered and demanded that Yuri abandon Calypso. The problem was that Calypso had become a permanent lamb and, being abandoned by Yuri, she went feral and poised to be euthanized. However, Yuri knew an important member of the Transplanetary Corporation and they managed to get Calypso into the mother-ship, which, as you know, is a neutral territory."

"When they need to euthanize a feral lamb that is not too aggressive, they bring him to Calypso. Calypso is a nymphomaniac and seductress."

"That's why Calypso thought you were one of those lambs and tried to seduce you. And, Jota, I tell you, it is very difficult to resist Calypso."

"Calypso is a Middle Ages princess, have they told you, Jota?"

"What!? How come she is alive?"

"A clone, of course, Jota. She is a clone of Princess XX of late Middle Ages. A clone of one Princess XX of YY who was executed in 1495 in ZZ."

"And what was she executed for?"

"Vampirism and cannibalism"

"Are there clones of important people here in the farm, Antonina?"

"Yes, Jota, but this is restricted and I trust you. There are clones of Kings, Emperors, Indian chiefs and many others."

"But, if you don't mind can I finish with Calypso?" Antonina continued.

"Calypso was cloned from the remains of that princess on Earth, and sent on to Landa as a frozen embryo. Her embryo was impregnated into a Landian woman who died after giving birth to her. She was then adopted by Yuri when she was ten. And then, Yuri abandoned her because of Isobel. And that was the third Yuri's crime."

"But I don't think Yuri's a criminal. He appears to be an honest guy to me."

"You are correct Jota; Yuri is a good person. But he was weak he didn't do his crimes on purpose."

And Antonina went on:

"Calypso is now a mascot in the ship. Actually, she was placed into the mother-ship, illegally, by a high official who had been seduced by her."

"And now, they give to her some lost lambs who are going to be euthanized in any way. But she doesn't kill them. What happens is that she gets fed up and needs a replacement, you know how those things work, don't you, Jota?"

"And, then, you were shown to her and she thought you would be "served" to her".

"And, how about this cloning; where is it done Antonina?"

"In this very farm we have a complete laboratory of molecular biology and, among other procedures, we do cloning, "downstairs," she said referring to the underground facilities.

"Now, Jota, let's get back to Isobel because I think you are going to be invited to her Dome very soon. Isobel can easily dominate you. Actually, right now, this wouldn't be all bad since it may help reverse the process, according to what Dr Felder told me today. Oh, yes, I keep in touch with him every day."

"Look, Jota, Isobel isn't a good person. She is evil; she almost destroyed Yuri's career, and she destroyed Calypso by having Yuri abandon her."

"And what will happen to me in case she dominates me?"

"You will not be able to live without her. Have you already forgotten your crises? Multiply them by ten, and you will see what Isobel can do to you!"

"You are going to be a permanent lamb; your brain will be synchronized to hers'. You are going to crawl at her feet. Because she is evil, Jota, evil. And when she gets fed with you she either may abandon or kill you."

"But, can't you dominate me too, Antonina?"

"I almost dominated you, Jota. Remember your crises?! I wanted to dominate you to turn you into a better person so that you could be my lamb and I would protect you and give love to you. Because you still need my protection, Jota. Don't you forget that!"

"But, I was weak, I have put myself in your place, I had pity of you, and then, I discovered I loved you not as a shepherd loves her lamb but as a woman loves her man. I am a woman, Jota, remember this, I am a woman."

"But, then what do you want of me, Antonina, I am lost, I don't know any more what I am!"

"I want you as a man, Jota; I love you as a woman loves her man, that's how I love you!"

And then, she embraced me and kissed my mouth long. And, then, began to sob. And how much she sobbed.

"Why are you crying, my love?"

"It won't work, Jota, it won't work, I'm so sorry!" and she embraced me strongly and sobbed convulsively.

Chapter 73

Domination According to Antonina

I have described, in my narrative, my talks with different persons and their views of the domination process. Many common points I have seen, but I think it is instructive to relate here Antonina's view of this fascinating mental process. But what new information may come from her view? Not much, but her view is somewhat different from others.

"What happens during the domination, Antonina?"

"Domination occurs when a superior being begins exerting some mental influence upon an inferior being and ends up by modifying its personality."

Up to this point no news.

"But what would be a superior being and an inferior being, Antonina?"

"In the Universe there are beings with different intelligences. When beings with very different intelligences interact, there may occur certain domination of the less intelligent by the more intelligent being."

"For example, Jota. I am a superior intelligence as compared to you and, as such, I have a *domination potential* over you. But this does not mean I will be able to dominate you. It means just that domination is possible.

"Did this domination occur when the European colonizers encountered the Indians in America?"

"No, Jota, of course not. Europeans and Indians were both of the same species, *Homo sapiens* and had, essentially, the same intelligence. The difference was just in the cultural varnish of Europeans and their more powerful weapons."

"But, when comparing Landians and Earthians there is a difference. Landians are not *Homo sapiens*, as you know."

"OK, but you were telling me of Isobel. What about her interaction with an Earthian?"

"Well, with Isobel, the domination does not occur spontaneously and naturally by the way of love. Isobel is wicked and obtains pleasure in modifying the personality of the unfortunate Earthian to which she bonds."

"And, what does Isobel gain with this perverse domination?"

"Nothing too special, Jota, just the pleasure to feel superior and have the company of an inferior being."

"OK, but in the case of a "good" domination of an Earthian by a Landian. Is this a good arrangement for him/her?"

"Oh, Jota, I think Dr Felder already explained this to you"

"Yes he said something to me along this line, but I would love hearing this from you, Antonina."

"If the process occurs naturally, it is generally a good arrangement for the Earthian, having a shepherd. His/her personality becomes shared to that of the shepherd and many of his/her conflicts are transferred to the shepherd. What I'm telling you are the opinions of the Earthians themselves, note that."

"I think I understand, Antonina, and I found it very good of you telling me all this. I knew most of it, of course, because I use to talk to people."

"Oh, yes, so you talk to people, eh? And can you tell me which people have you talked to?"

"Sure, I have talked with Fabiana two times here on the farm, with Erika on the ship, with Greg, with the nurse Rita on the ship, with Dr Felder on the ship."

And I went on:

"But there is something I haven't been told yet, Antonina."

"Hummm, and that "something" would be?" she asked me.

"How does the domination process in Landa differ from that on Earth?"

"Well, Jota, the process itself is the same. What differ are the purposes. And they are very different at that."

"On Earth, the Landians have a mission, as I already explained to you, which is the domination of Earthians by way of love and then orient them on the path that will prevent their demise."

"On Landa, the Earthian presence is accidental, a consequence of the exchanges of people that you are aware of. As a result of this, there are lots of Earthians in Landa and this is good for both Landians and Earthians."

Chapter 74

Isobel and Fabiana

On a certain morning, I had just woken up when my cell phone rang. It was Fabiana inviting me to have lunch at Dome 2. During the breakfast there were only me and Antonina at the table and I commented with her my invitation.

"It's OK for you to go, Jota, but remember what I've told you regarding Isobel."

I confirmed my presence to the lunch. I should be at Dome 2 by 10 AM and bringing my camera.

It was an easy and agreeable walk of 800 m up to Dome 2 which was at an elevation some 20 m higher. The morning was sunny and agreeably hot with a slight wind.

Fabiana met me at the dome entrance since she was already outside. She wore a bikini and told me they had arranged the things at the back patio, whose access was through the dome itself.

"Jota put on some shorts left by the guys," she said leading me to a room formerly occupied by the boys.

I changed clothes and left the room wearing only the shorts and followed Fabiana who was waiting me seated at a sofa in the hall. We left the dome through a back door and into a patio whose floor was made of a smooth material resembling plastic and was very nice to my bare feet.

This part of the dome was new to me. The patio had some beach chairs, a small bar under a roof and some other amenities. A strange music was playing low.

Isobel was lying on a beach chair beside two more empty chairs, one of them probably Fabiana's. I said hello to Isobel kissing her at the face.

"It has been a long time since you don't visit us, Jota! Fabiana tells me a lot about you!"

Fabiana pulled another chair to me and placed it beside hers.

"What are you having, Jota?" indicating her glass.

"The same as you."

"We like scotch on the rocks, I will prepare one for you."

As soon as I got my drink, I lay on my chair. It was at this moment that I saw the Jacuzzi bathtub, from which very nice bubbling sounds were coming.

"Hey, Jota, we were just waiting for you to arrive before we went to the water, c'mon everyone to the water," Isobel shouted at me and Fabiana.

Isobel stood up and moved for the Jacuzzi

"You two, come to the water," commanded Isobel.

We all went to the pool's border, Fabiana pulling me by the hand. Then we entered the water while I was still with my drink and left it at the border.

The pool was relatively deep since, as I sat, the water reached to my middle chest. The water was deliciously warm and exhaled a nice scent of essences. I closed my eyes for a moment and felt the warmness of the water, the heat of the Sun on my face and shoulder, and the delicious scent emanating from the pool, which blended with the perfumes of Isobel and Fabiana. Underlying the perfumes' fragrances came to my still sensitive sniffing apparatus, the unmistakable scent of the girls' bodies. The combination from all these odors impinged on my olfaction and my brain, a unique message: sex.

Then, when I opened my eyes I saw the girls had taken off the upper part of their bikinis and Isobel was spreading an oily cream on Fabiana's breasts. Looking sideways to the pool's border, I saw the lower parts of their bikinis, which were also strewn to the floor. The girls were nude.

"Now, Jota, it's your turn. Please remove the shorts. In this pool, clothes are forbidden!" shouted Isobel, over the humming and bubbling sounds of the Jacuzzi, as she stared at me with a strange smile.

I was "forced" to strip myself of my shorts.

"Your skin is too pale, Jota. Haven't you people sunbathed at the ship?" said Fabiana to me. And as she was saying this she began spreading the cream over my face, neck and shoulders. Then, she took a more generous portion of cream and began applying the cream to the underwater parts of my body. She was meticulous and showed no emotions while massaging my lower parts with the cream. Isobel laughed interminably, glancing at my confused features. And, confused, I was!

"You are too selfish, Jota; now you have to apply the cream on me!" Fabiana shouted at me. And saying this she embraced me and kissed my mouth.

I breathed deeply and began my task.

I began by the face, then neck and shoulders. Seeing my indecision regarding her breasts:

"Now, Jota, don't forget those, Isobel did not apply correctly," pointing to her breasts.

I began spreading the cream to her breasts and she closed her eyes and soon began massaging me down there.

"Do you like that, Jota?" she said, laughing irreverently and intensifying the massaging. But Fabiana was not looking at my eyes. She looked at Isobel as if waiting some instruction.

"Now, Jota, don't make me suffer, I also want some massaging and more cream there," and she pulled my hand to her genitals. As I began massaging her, Fabiana pulled my body to her and embraced me pressing her breasts to my chest.

I was "saved" by Isobel who shouted at Fabiana:

"That's OK Fab, now give Jota to me, please," and saying this Isobel said I should apply cream to her body. She took another tube of a different brownish and thick cream.

"Here, Jota, I'm waiting," and she motioned to me to apply the cream onto her breasts.

Fabiana, who was between Isobel and me, changed position so that I was, now, just beside Isobel, and our bodies were touching each other.

As I began massaging Isobel's breasts and chest with the cream, she spread the cream to her own neck, shoulders and face. Then, she began reapplying the cream onto me. Onto my neck, my face, my shoulders and my chest.

"Don't stop, Jota, it's so good. I want to give you the same pleasure," she said as she continued to transport the cream from her body to my skin.

"Go lower, Jota, I want this cream down there, you know?"

I got more cream, from the tube, into my hands and began massaging her lower abdomen. She had a firm and muscular abdomen that had a delicate firmness. At her command of "lower, lower, Jota!", I, finally, got to the desired location. I will never forget the feeling of massaging Isobel's genitals. I couldn't stand my confusion and desire. Seeing my confused expression, Isobel took a generous portion of cream and began massaging me in my lower parts. Forget Antonina or Fabiana! Isobel's massage was unbearably good. I was on the left side of Isobel. Sorry, some geometry is necessary here. With her left hand she was massaging me.

Then, I perceived that using her right hand, she continually removed cream from her body and applied to my neck, chest and shoulder. In other words, I began to perceive that Isobel was transferring cream, from her body, to my skin.

Then, she began the kisses. She embraced me and began kissing my mouth with a sort of perverted kiss more appropriate for a prostitute.

When I turned to look at Fabiana, I saw and empty pool. No one at was the chairs. Seeing my confused look, Isobel:

"Fabiana is finishing our lunch, Jota. You know, she cooks so well!"

Suddenly, Isobel changed. Instead of the perverted behavior she had a few minutes before she was, now, a tender and innocent woman. Her kisses became tender, shy and passionate. She began looking at my eyes.

Instead of the sensuous massaging, she began caressing me delicately, my face, my mouth, my chest, going down, down, but gently, as if she was an amateur. At the same time that all these transformations were taking place in her demeanor, she never stopped to transfer cream from her body to mine. But now, gently, as part of her caresses.

And, she began to talk.

"Do you like being with me Jota? Do you like my kisses? I'm so insecure when I'm with you. Am I behaving badly? I'm not what you think, Jota."

While talking those void phrases, she didn't stop her caresses on me. However, how delicate she was now, how innocent she looked.

"Jota, I liked you the first time I saw you, but then Antonina took care of you, took you for that travel to the mother-ship."

"Look at me, Jota; look how sad I am. It's because of you because I'm beginning to think I love you."

As I looked at her eyes I began to feel a sort of fear mixed with desire. She was strikingly sensuous. Her voice was so calming now; her voice tone was of a plea. And, she looked really sad; her eyes were pleading with something.

And, then there was her smell.

She sensed I was sniffing at her body.

"Do you like my scent? Come closer, sniff me, feel how excited I am. And she pulled my face gently to hers, let me sniff at her neck and pulled me down to her breasts.

"See, Jota, how excited they are, sniff at them, Jota."

And, she moved my head to make my mouth touch her breasts.

"Feel them, Jota. Kiss me here, please kiss me," and as I began kissing her breasts she made me put the nipples into my mouth.

"Taste me, Jota, taste how they are begging for you!"

And, as I looked again at her eyes, they were wet. Soon, she began sobbing and pulled me strongly to her, pressing her breasts to my chest.

"How I need you, Jota, how badly I need you."

Then, she stopped the sobs and recomposed. As I looked again at her eyes, I saw another woman. The same face, the same beautiful and sensuous looks. But, now, her eyes were showing that same look I had seen the first time I saw her. Now, she seemed to be preying on me. I tried to look away but she gently moved my face and made me look at her eyes.

"What's it Jota, what happened, are you afraid of me. No, Jota, I won't bite you. See, how fragile I am!" And she kissed, gently, my lips.

Something evil emanated from Isobel's eyes. The expression on her eyes matched her facial expressions. I began seeing, in her eyes, a great force of command and, from them, there appeared to emanate an enormous flow of intelligence. At the same time, her eyes seemed to convey cruelty, malice, and deception.

A variety of facial expressions began to parade, matching her eyes' expressions. She seemed to fear me, then, poised to kill me. In seconds, pleading, imploring. Imperceptibly, this changed to a look of desire.

Also, these facial expressions seemed to be synchronized with her caresses in me.

Her mouth had an incredible arsenal of expressions. It was capable of transmitting enormous sensuality and, in seconds, contempt, then plea, then, fear. From fear to goodness. It was becoming to me very difficult to stand this.

My mind was getting confused and overloaded with the multiple sensations Isobel was impinging on me.

But, then, it all began to clear up. Somehow, I managed to reason, to try to make sense of all this. I began to analyze the sequences. The cream, sticky, oily and warm. Her skin, my skin. From her skin to my skin. It began to make sense. She was transferring cream from her skin to my skin. She was making me to smell her body, her breasts and nipples. She made me taste her nipples.

I was being impregnated by her fragrances. Fragrances or hormones? Pheromones!! Isobel was conditioning me! The cream was a vehicle!

But how did she know the pheromone process? This was recent finding of Dr Felder. Not even on Landa they knew this. Non-authorized research, by Landa's rules. Clandestine research and punishable. But Antonina had contact with Dr Felder from the farm. They were following my evolution. They were trying to prevent me from getting to a permanent lamb. How was this information exchanged? Who, on the farm, relayed messages from Landa or from the mother-ship. Who could do that?

My God! Frederico! Isobel had co-opted Frederico!

In an instant, it hit me. And I looked to my side. Isobel was staring at me with an inquisitive look.

"Jota, come with me. Do you know they all are moving from here? Do you know this, Jota? Antonina can't live in a city. She can't even open a bank account! She doesn't even know what money is. Antonina is such a naive! They are going to abandon you, Jota! They need to move, believe me, Jota!

Look, Jota, I'm very rich. I have hundreds of precious stones. We can live happily in the city. No work, only pleasure! We can buy a nice apartment."

My thoughts were:

Among so many lies, there might be some true facts.

Truth is scaffolding for lies.

She is rich and she is smart. No question she is evil!

The more I listened to Isobel, the more convinced I became that Antonina was a good person and that she was sincere and loved me.

"What about Fabiana? Are you going to abandon her?" I asked her.

"Oh, Fabiana? She will come with us. She's so useful!"

"I was introduced to Calypso; you know?" I said in a passing way.

"What??!! Where's Calypso? Here on the farm?"

Immediately, Isobel stopped pretending and assumed her (probably) real features. And they weren't nice!

"I don't know if she is here. I've met her at the mother-ship and I don't know if she has disembarked here or in China or if she is still in space!"

More thoughts:

The family may actually be leaving the farm. She may be telling the truth.

She may be more informed than Antonina. Frederico may be telling her of the messages between the operation centers and from Landa also.

Now, I remembered Fred's warning me against Antonina.

His warning might be a favor to Isobel in order to keep me far from Antonina so she could make me her lamb.

I began to feel tired. So diverse sensations began to give me a sense of desperation and fear. I closed my eyes for a few seconds.

"Are you OK, my love?"

Joaquim

I opened my eyes, and Isobel caressed my face tenderly!

"I've got a headache, I think" I said

At this moment, salvation!

Fabiana: "Lunch is ready, everyone out of the water."

Immediately, I felt an enormous relief.

I went to the bathroom to take a shower. Surprise. No soap.

I didn't get concerned about removing Isobel's pheromones from my skin. I already knew something. And, I knew more than Isobel, probably.

I put on my clothes and went to the hall.

Fabiana had changed to a tunica and was smelling of fragrances. She was wonderful!

The lunch table was already set. And, it was wondrous.

The food was delicious. We drank wine. Then there came the dessert, liquors and coffee.

We went to the sofas.

Fabiana looked often to Isobel.

It was 5 PM.

Isobel excused, saying she had a headache and left the room.

And, I wasted no time.

Saying I needed to go back to the dome to help Greg, I excused myself. Fabiana, having got unprepared for my sudden leaving kissed me goodbye.

Finally, I was free to go back to my dome. I walked briskly and the cool air helped me recover my bearings. I thought I had survived Isobel. Not bad. I had also survived Calypso!

During my pensive walk I tried to make sense of Isobel's eyes. I finally reached a conclusion: they did not look human.

As I entered the dome, I saw Antonina in an armchair. She had her eyes closed. Without opening her eyes, she said:

"How was the lunch, Jota?"

I told her of my encounter without, however, entering in some details.

Now, Antonina had opened her eyes and was studying me.

"Too good Isobel didn't hypnotize you, Jota, too good she didn't lock her eyes onto yours!"

I didn't answer but my blood froze.

"She locked her gaze onto you, didn't she?"

"Yes, Antonina, what's going to happen to me now?"

"I don't know. Probably nothing. For now."

However, I didn't mention the cream swapping between Isobel and me. I didn't want to concern Antonina with something she couldn't remedy. And, actually, this creaming thing might have been beneficial by blunting the effect of my conditioning by Antonina.

As to Isobel's intentions regarding myself, I had no doubt. She wanted me as her lamb. But I spared Antonina of all that part of my meeting.

Chapter 75

Antonina's Farewell

A few days have passed since my fateful encounter with Isobel and Fabiana. Things seemed to have gotten back to normal. My relation with Antonina was entering into a normalcy and our mutual respect and friendship had surpassed the carnal aspects. I felt that what Antonina had done in that area was more for my sake than due to her sex desires. I became conscious that Antonina, deep in her soul, was not sexually minded, was not driven by desires. She was timid and sex, for her, seemed not to be an obsession. I even had some doubts as to what kind of pleasure she derived from sex. Antonina was returning, slowly, to that initial care for me, an almost maternal, protective care. I believe that was the real essence of what she felt for me.

But now, I perceived that she was suffering from some foreboding of what I couldn't conceive. The way she looked at me told of an end, an outcome unimaginably bad. I sensed she was enjoying her last days with me, her last days with the world.

Also, among the many evident lies Isobel told me in our encounter at the Jacuzzi, there were some that, to me, seemed to be facts. Firstly, Antonina might not be able to live in a city on Earth, as she had no malice or experience with worldly things. That, outside her group of Landians, she was lost. Secondly, the group would move from the farm. This, I could sense from numerous small changes which, individually, might not be important but, in the whole, indicated an important change in things. Most of the transport was out of the farm. Many trucks were leaving the farm, loaded. The only things coming in were of grocery type. Dome 3 had been dismantled; the wood processing facilities had been scrapped.

On top of all those changes, a fact that may have precipitated things was that my brother needed to suffer a delicate and risky surgery and he asked me to give him some support. From what he told me, I would have to stay about 2 months away from the farm.

As soon as I was informed of my leaving, I told Antonina, Yuri, and Greg. Yuri didn't object to my leaving and offered help in case I needed something. I promised to come back as soon as I had cleared my duties with my brother.

I left my address and my cell phone number with them.

All this happened in the morning, and I would be leaving the morning of the next day.

The Last Supper:

Yuri and Mayra organized a dinner for my departure.

Presents were: Yuri, Greg, Marco, Frederico, Antonina, Mayra, Fabiana. Isobel wasn't there.

The dinner went normally, no news whatsoever of changes in the farm. But the hints and signs were all over the place. During the dinner, despite the happy atmosphere, a hidden shadow appeared to hover above everything. Something suggested the end of a party.

Last night with Antonina:

This night, Antonina and I slept together. No sex things.

We embraced each other. Antonina wept and wept.

Things that she repeated to me:

"Jota, I want you to know that I will always love you and protect you. Please remember this, please."

"I'm sorry, Jota, I'm so sorry," and she wept.

"I think you will be all right. Listen, whatever happens to me, remember it was in the name of my love to you," and she wept.

This did not last long. Antonina slept, embracing me. I, myself, couldn't sleep.

Despite saying those sad things to me at no moment during this night, she said things like:

"Come back soon, I will be waiting for you."

"When are you coming back?"

As I will comment in another part of my narrative, I am very perceptive of "non-said things". These, were equally important to me as the "said things". Things people didn't say when they should. Things people didn't ask when they should.

Joaquim

The morning of my departure was incredibly sad. Antonina seemed dazed. She moved from place to place without purpose. Her eyes always wet. When I was about to leave, already in my car, she stayed at the car window, only looking at me. She didn't say anything, only looked at me. I began to weep but kept going. I had to go.

Chapter 76

Letters and Crates

About one month after my leave from the farm, I received a letter from Greg:

"Dear Jota, my friend, we had to leave this farm. Orders from above. We can't stay too long at the same place. Rumors began to spread. We were directed to another region of Earth, another continent. We won't see each other again, Jota."

"It was a pleasure to have you among us. You brought joy to our group. Your curiosity, your questions, and your remarks. You brought joy to Antonina, and she needed it badly."

"But, do you remember Yuri told you that you would be given a mission?"

"Well, the time has come, Jota. That mission was the reason we brought you into our family. First, we checked your past, then your courage and your trust in us and, especially, your character. You passed all tests, Jota".

"Your mission will be to finish a few things for us. Things we had no time to do. And they are important. I will not mention the details of what you need to do. That's because we trust your power of observation, your curiosity. And we trust your character. This is the most important to us."

"Also, we trust that you will preserve this place; this is sacred territory for us, Jota. Remember that it is sacred ground, and someday you will understand why. Try to explore the place, don't leave anything unexplored. Don't forget the underground. There, you will see strange things. You will learn much Jota. Very soon, we will give you our new address. In case you have any problems, you may contact us. Remember, we are a strong organization.,"

"And, so that you may accomplish this mission, we are giving you our farm. Well, not quite giving. You will need to buy it but, for this, we are transferring you enough valuables to buy this farm many times. We are very rich in terms of material worth. This is not all that is worth but it helps maintain the other things, you see. You will receive 8 crates. Instructions on how to open them and a description of the contents will be sent along with them. As soon as you obtain 4 million dollars from the stones, and you have the amount deposited in a bank, please contact Dr Jonas Almeida, lawyer, telephone xxxx, address xxxx."

My brother's surgery went without problems, and he recovered in about 2 weeks. About 40 days after my departure from the farm, a van arrived at our home bringing a registered delivery in my name. There were three men from a well-known delivery firm. I was asked to identify myself, and they needed a witness, which was my brother. We were identified, photographed, and had to sign many papers. After these procedures, they began to unload 8 crates which were loaded, one at a time, onto a cart and moved into our home. Each crate had my name, address, and weight of 50 kg. Accompanying the crates was a note from Greg: "Open the crates, but do not throw away anything before checking the contents. Many valuables are disguised in the padding."

After the delivery van went away, my brother and I began unpacking one of the crates. There were many items, most alien and very interesting. Sculptures made of strange materials, books, and artifacts. Gold objects. Hidden inside the padding were stones. And, what stones!! It would be tiresome for any reader if I described all the contents. Just the stones in the first crate were enough to buy a few houses like ours.

Peter Andropoulos was called again to make an evaluation of some stones. A part of the stones was sold in New York, from which we got 10 million USD. Peter got 5%. One of the purposes of this donation from Greg was to legalize the money, their money, according to my brother's conjecture.

Once we got the amount deposited and part converted to Brazilian money, I called the layer Jonas Almeida, who represented a Mr. Joe Smith (fictitious names). We did the buying transaction, having received the farm papers. From now on, the farm was mine and my brother's, as partners.

My brother was not convinced of the facts I had related to him. He suspected, particularly the alien nature of my friends. Worse than that, as I could check later on, he suspected my mental sanity. But being discreet and prudent said nothing.

Chapter 77

Antonina's Letter

Some days after Greg's letter and the delivery of the crates, I received a letter from Antonina with a programmed delivery. On the envelope was her name handwritten, with the Courier New font: Antonina Neina. Opening the envelope, there was the letter itself, entirely handwritten in Courier New font.

"Jota, when you get this letter, I will be dead."

"I will jump from the same cliff you jumped, but I will clear the net. I couldn't live with that guilt. I had broken my oath. I couldn't have had sex with you. You are a pure and vulnerable creature according to our laws, Jota. Lambs are pure, they are sacred. This is what our laws determine. I couldn't have befouled you, since according to our laws, and, I repeat, lambs are pure."

"But, I didn't do it for my satisfaction; I didn't do it for my pleasure. I did it to quench your desire. However, this does not lessen my fault."

"But, there was another reason, a more pressing one. You were about to become a permanent lamb and to become permanently dependent on me, Jota. And that, on Earth, is a big problem."

"There was only one way to prevent you from becoming a permanent lamb, and Dr Felder instructed me; our love needed to become level. Like the love between a man and a woman, of the same species. Not anymore the love of a shepherd to her lamb, like it was."

"Then, we became level Jota; I became your woman, and you my man. But, for that, I had to break my oath, and was, accordingly, a criminal under Landa's law. And, even more serious: I fouled you, since from my perspective you were pure."

"My dear, when I began interacting with you, my plan was to make you my lamb. You now know the details of the process. I never imagined that I could be more than your shepherd. You seemed ideally fit to be a faithful and very satisfying lamb. Always curious, inventive, happy and obedient."

"But, then, I forgot one detail. We were not on Landa. We were on Earth, and our permanence on the farm was not definitive. Things began to change, pointing out that we should move to another continent. There was a chance that you and I would have to part. I could have told you before about this, Jota. But I was weak, I couldn't imagine leaving you. I began to need your company so that I could protect you. And, how much protection you needed! You seemed so fragile and innocent."

"And, after I had fouled you and became your woman, I discovered I couldn't live without you. And our group had to leave Brazil, and we would separate. I couldn't stand this. There was no way for me but death."

Chapter 78
Return to the Farm

Dr Jonas Almeida, the lawyer of Greg's "family," has left me all the keys to the different doors of the Dome 1. Each key had a label on it.

Soon after the papers had been cleared, I returned to the farm, now mine, bringing my brother with me. Dome 1 was intact, with no apparent modifications. The main door was a heavy steel contraption, with 2 panes, heavily hinged to steel pillars. It opened through 3 sturdy locks, of a type new to me. Actually, I never had to deal with those locks since that door was never locked during my stay on the farm.

The dome's interior was unchanged, and all containers at the same place. The container's doors were closed but unlocked. They had only books and empty boxes of diverse types.

My brother and I decided to spend a few days on the farm to get things arranged inside the dome. I took one container for myself, and my brother took another one beside. The containers were plugged onto the service totems and had water, electricity, and sewage.

Antonina's container was also there, with an unlocked door. I entered it. Immediately, I was transported to another "dimension" of another era. That era when we were together. I sat in a chair and wept. Her bed was unmade, her scent pervading all parts of the room. Some clothes, sneakers, and boots. On a pile of documents, I saw many photos. I went through some of them and found some of me; others, were selfies of me and Antonina. On the wall, there were a few pictures, of which one caught my attention. Antonina, with her husband Sergei, shot on Landa. The day was "sunny" and shadows were cast almost vertical. Despite sunny it was semi-dark, and a desolated landscape. They were embracing each other.

Then, there was a notebook full of Antonina's annotations written in Landian language.

On a shelf, there were perfumes, creams. In a closet, all of her dresses, shorts, and skirts.

In another notebook, spiral bound: there, were her drawings. I didn't know Antonina used to make drawings.

I opened the book:

On the first page, the Dome 1: so realistic, it seemed a photograph.

The pages were followed by drawings from various aspects of the farm.

One beautiful drawing was of the transference disk at night, a background of tall Eucalyptus trees. A starred sky. It seemed fantastic, surreal. Even some constellations were drawn correctly.

There were more pages with drawings.

A beautiful drawing called my attention: the woodpecker, like I had photographed it. But in the drawing, the bird seemed alive.

Another one was a drawing of me, hyper-realistic and seeming like a photograph.

On the next page, the same subject: I. But this one seemed to be her view of me. It was me all right, but like an idealization, probably like she saw me, all blurred.

On other pages, there were drawings of her, looking at a mirror.

My God!

In yet another drawing, there was my car and I standing on top of the car's roof, a scene that did not occur. I was waving at her, my hair all wet.

On another page, I was in the air, upside down, arms extended, and in the middle of a somersault (another imaginary scene).

She was drawing things from her imagination.

In another scene, she was sitting on a stone, the setting sun behind her. I was kneeling with one knee on the ground, and the camera in hand. I was photographing her.

In yet another drawing, we were playing chess. Everything seemed real, the chessboard with the pieces. But something was amiss. I was checkmating her!

Antonina was mixing real scenes with her fantasies.

In a very beautiful drawing, Antonina was wearing a long dress, jewels, and bracelets. She was in front of a mansion that looked like a Beverly Hills-style mansion. Behind her could be seen a Jaguar car, resplendent.

Another group of drawings: The first drawing was of my face, zoomed in on my left eye. In the second drawing, there was just my left eye spanning the entire page.

Third drawing: my pupil, enormous, the iris super detailed. Inside the pupil was a woman wearing a long dress. The woman was upside down. As I turned the book upside down, it was Antonina. She had drawn me, as my retina was seeing her.

Another series of drawings were of her, nude in front of a mirror. Then, she was nude at the brook where we bathed. Then, she was nude, floating on a dark background.

I then jumped many pages.

In another drawing, the last one, Antonina was in the air, open arms, upside down. Her gown was being dragged by the air. Her features were so real, she was smiling. Probably she was jumping to her death.

I was overwhelmed. I lay down on her bed, put my head on her pillow. Her scent was vivid, as if she had left the bed a few minutes before. And, I wept.

When I came to me my brother was sitting at the bedside with a glass of brandy.

Joaquim

"Take this, Jota, it will calm you".

In the refrigerators, a total of 4 of them, and freezers, also 4, there was a lot of food.

After we had settled down at the table and had some fast food, I took my brother to see some parts of the farm. Since we were inside the dome, I wanted to show him, first, the basement. After some research, I found the hatch on the floor between the internal and external domes. It was disguised below some garbage, pieces of tarpaulin, and other discarded items. We opened the hatch, which, by itself, was a masterpiece of engineering, according to my brother, an engineer by education.

The basement was empty except for 2 big freezers, still working, and a few shelves leaning against the wall. Since the walls were free of items, I could see a wide two-leafed door very well built. The door had no lock and just one bolt. We opened it and entered a rectangular room. There was a light switch that turned on many strong lamps. We were hearing a loud and high-pitched humming. It came from a cylindrical contraption, the size of a car. A small porthole on it was slightly open, and opening it, we saw another cylindrical structure, clearly of terrestrial origin. High vacuum, do not open, high RPM, Danger, etc, were some inscriptions.

Then, I remembered Greg's mention of the flywheels as an energy storage system. There were two other systems like this, but they weren't turning. In this room, in addition to the flywheels, there was a big diesel generator and fuel tanks.

My Friend Greg

On the other side of this room, opposite the entry door, we saw a short tunnel that gave access to another room. This clearly was the control centre of the big water reservoir that Greg had mentioned to me and was below the floor.

We left the two rooms and came back to the main basement. It was then that I remembered the bunker below the basement. The problem was that I couldn't remember where the opening to the bunker was located. I only remembered it was near the circular wall. We began testing the floor by hitting it with our feet until a hollow sound revealed the hatch position. So precise and discrete was the transition of the lid with the floor that we couldn't see it at first glance. Now, how to open the hatch? There was no handle or hole where a tool could be inserted to pull it open. In one of the dust covered shelves I saw what appeared to be some rubber suckers like those used to handle glass panels. *That will be the hatch's handle*, I thought. With the sucker we easily opened the hatch. Then, I remembered Greg's letter. I remembered he mentioned me as his friend and, as such, he also was **my friend Greg**. I already knew the well-built and high-tech ladder descending to the bunker below. It had a security tube and descended to the blackness. My flashlight, directed below, could barely show the floor. When I touched the floor, I groped and found the light switch fixed to the ladder. The bunker was empty and looked way bigger than when Marco had shown it to me. The lateral wall was circular and seemed to match the wall of the basement above. Where, before, was an enormous computer center; now was an empty space. No question that the

419

equipment of this room should be removed in its totality.

The material of this wall intrigued me. I got the feeling that more things should be there. Actually, unconsciously, I was looking for a door in the wall. However, the wall was absolutely smooth.

"And what if the door is on the floor?" my brother suggested. We then began hitting the floor with our heels. It sounded solid all over. We gave up on this search and decided to go upstairs, actually, "up ladders". As we got to the foot of the ladder, on our way up to the basement, my brother hit the floor with his foot. It was hollow. We cleaned the dust on the floor and found a very thin line indicating a separation between the main floor and a small square. It was the hatch leading below. But, like the first hatch, it had no handle to pull it up.

"Look, Jota, the hatch is fixed to the last rung!" shouted my brother, as if we were 100 meters apart. That was it. Very ingenious indeed! Actually, there was a single ladder all the way from the basement floor, the bunker, and to?? I pulled the rung upwards, and a black void appeared below. Now, I was entering unknown territory, and the words of Greg kept coming to my mind, **my friend Greg**, he was.

I threw the light down, and there was another floor some 4 meters below. We descended. As I got to the floor below, I hit the floor at the ladder's foot. It was solid. At least from this ladder, we were at the bottom. The same type of light switch was fixed to the ladder end. I switched on the light, and my brother came down. It was a circular room, way smaller than the bunker above. We were, now, more than 15 meters below ground. The wall of this room was perfectly circular and very smooth, like some sort of plastic. Hitting the wall with a clenched fist, I could sense the firmness of thick concrete. However, the surface seemed plastic. Something told me that we might be inside the water table, and this room would work as an inverted pool.

Easily visible, leaving from the wall, there were two tunnels, perfectly circular, 1.9 meters in diameter and lined by metal plates. Along our exploration, we would encounter this type of tunnel many times.

Since we had only one flashlight and no reserve batteries, and fearing an interruption of the lighting system, we decided to go back to the dome and return on the following day with more equipment, beverages, and food. We went to the city and bought a few things for food and some more gear.

The next day, we had a solid breakfast and checked our exploratory equipment: flashlights (4), batteries (many), candles (20), ropes (1), two compasses, cell phones, sandwiches, water, orange juice, and coffee. The candles had a special task: to test air currents. Having read most of Henry Rider Haggard's books, I knew the importance of determining air currents and the role of candles for that.

We rapidly came to the lowest room whence exited the two tunnels. For some reason, our compasses were working. Probably they wouldn't work inside the metallic walls of the tunnels. One tunnel exited to the west and the other to the southeast, forming an angle of approximately 130-140 degrees from each other. We decided to begin exploring the west tunnel. Right at the tunnel entrance was a light switch that, turned on, illuminated the entire visible extension of the tunnel. I was very careful about bifurcations since our Google Maps would be of no help here. I repeated the rule to my brother: entering a bifurcation guarantees your return. The problem is exiting one on the outgoing leg of a trip. In any case, if we left a bifurcation, we would leave a mark on the way we came from. After some 100 meters, we did the candle test: a clear wind came from the "end" side. After 200 meters, a surprise: a bifurcation. The left tunnel went southwest and downhill. The right side tunnel went northwest and discreetly uphill.

We decided to follow the left tunnel. The downhill slope was about 15 degrees, perfectly navigable, since we had rubber soles in our boots. The tunnel curved a little more to the left, but didn't bifurcate. Some 100 meters more and we saw, in the distance, a disk of daylight. About 150 meters more and we arrived at an iron door. The door had a locking bolt that could be opened only from the inside. We were very careful now in guaranteeing our return. As we opened the door, I left a dead and thick branch preventing its closure. It was clear that this door was meant to be opened only from the inside and to prevent any unwanted entry from the outside. It had some small holes to guarantee a minimum of air exchange in the tunnel. Finally, opening the door, we got to open air.

The first thing we perceived was the roar of falling water. We were in a dense forest of native trees. The door we came from exited from the face of an enormous cliff. From the top of the cliff came down a waterfall that ended into a natural pool. As soon as I distanced myself from the door, it all came down to my memory. It was here that I ended my jump from the top of that cliff. I then took many photos from the local using Greg's super camera. However, I couldn't see the protection net, where I had landed that fateful day.

We were at the bottom of a great valley, covered by a dense native forest. A permanent mist enveloped the place, giving it a surreal and mystical appearance. From the big pool where the water fell with a roar, a brook went down.

On that terrible day of my proof, I hadn't observed all these details. In addition to my high adrenaline and my previous fear, there were many people laughing and celebrating my feat of courage, or insanity. I don't even remember how we got out of that valley. Sure, it wasn't through that door and that tunnel. However, today, I was being a good observer, the way Yuri had described me, and how I did my performance in the medical center of the mother-ship. I mean, the second performance, of course.

Something was out of place in that scenario. It was a black object, round and shiny. It was lying at the border of the big round natural pool, where the water was falling in roaring gushes. We came near. It was a helmet, similar to the one I had used in my visit to the cave, and also similar to a motorcyclist's helmet.

Joaquim

I took the helmet into my hands and raised it from the rocky ground. The helmet presented a big crack on its back. Inside, there was old blood and a lock of blond hair, soaked in semi-dry blood. In the rock where the helmet was resting, there was also a pool of dry blood and blood mixed with water droplets. I sniffed at the helmet interior, and the scent of Antonina came rushing to my nostrils.

Immediately, I felt dizzy and nausea invaded me. I sat on the rocky ground and began to weep and sob. I don't know how long I stood there. I only remember my brother holding my shoulder with his left hand, assuring me. In his right hand, he had a cup of hot coffee laced with brandy. I gulped it all and felt better. My brother pulled me up and we returned slowly through the tunnel. My brother placed the helmet in my backpack, and he carried both packs to relieve me. I will never forget the return to our dome; I had lost all sense of location and was just following my brother, like a zombie.

My desperation lasted 2 days, during which I slept in Antonina's bed. Actually, I remained there, feeling her scent, rubbing my face on her pillow, and weeping and weeping. During this period, my brother took care of me, preparing the meals, bringing me food and whatever I needed.

Slowly, I recovered. There was nothing to do. Antonina had done what she had said in her letter.

Chapter 79

Northwest Tunnel

On the morning of the third day, after I found Antonina's helmet at the waterfall, I was able to reason normally. Then, my brother and I decided to explore the other arm of the West tunnel. This one went to the northwest direction.

We easily got to the West tunnel, since we knew the positions and how to open all the hatches. After 200 meters, along the West tunnel, we came to the bifurcation from where the Northwest tunnel began. It went uphill on a gentle slope. After about 100 meters, a surprise: a circular gate, certainly waterproof, was closing completely the tunnel. We began examining it. It was formed by a metallic and ribbed disk, having three levered bolts securing the gate at a steel border. Writings in Landinese were all over the non-ribbed regions of the door. It was easy to perceive that the gate opened in our direction, and our initial impetus was to open it immediately. But we found it better to give it a more detailed look. In the lower part of the gate there was a handled screw.

My brother then suggested that we removed the screw or unfastened it in order to probe the existence of water on the other side. It might be that the screw was some sort of valve for equilibrating pressures.

We supposed this gate served to block any flow of water coming from above. I even suggested that the other side might already be flooded and, if we opened the gate, the water gushing through the opening would prevent us from closing it. And, worse, we might be drowned.

We unfastened the screw and, then, removed it. A strong air jet came in our direction. After a few minutes, it disappeared, indicating the pressures were equal across the gate. We then moved the levers, opening the three bolts. Pulling the gate in our direction, it opened with a very smooth movement. Each lever had a corresponding one at the opposite side of the gate, indicating the gate could be opened from the two sides. A very sophisticated sealing ring, lodged into a channel, ensured a complete blockade of both water and air flow.

After about 200 meters from the gate, we came to a square hall 30 x 30 meters, 5 meters in height. This hall was full of different items. Big and heavy crates, dimensioned to be moved by a forklift, which was in a corner. Many items could not have been moved there through the tunnel. Without question, this big room deserved a more detailed inspection. In addition to the crates, there were many smaller items scattered at the corners or even in the middle. There were many equipment parts, books, 2 carts.

At another corner, a tall ladder went directly from the floor to the roof. The ladder seemed to be firmly fixed both to the floor and to the roof. We went to the ladder's foot and I kicked the floor there. Hollow. We knew the scheme. I pulled the lowest rung, and a hatch opened, revealing another big room below. We went down into it. This room was circular with a diameter of about 20 meters. In this room, there were smaller crates stacked against the wall. From the wall emerged a small pipe terminated by a high-tech faucet. Attached to the faucet was a hose that went into a round water reservoir of about 1000 liters' capacity. The reservoir was almost full.

Again, the texture of the walls caught my attention. By percussion with my clenched fists, it was solid concrete. But it was covered by some plastic material.

Then, my original suspicion resurged. We were amid the water table, inside an inverted and gigantic tank! We were completely surrounded by ground water! I opened the faucet and took the hose from the water tank. Delicious water gushed from it.

At this moment, my brother remarked that the ladder went up all the way to the roof of the square hall, and we went up the ladder. I saw that it was fixed firmly to the roof and terminated at a circular and domed hatch. My brother brought up a heavy piece of wood with which I hit the hatch, and it moved a bit, letting some dirt and wood sticks fall. The lid was hinged, and with a strong push, it opened, revealing to us a beautiful blue sky. The lid fitted perfectly with the frame and had an O-ring preventing water entry.

When we got to the open air, I checked our coordinates: -22.101111 and -47.91175. The "umbrella" handles were there also, and we verified their correspondence with ventilation shafts, opening from the roof. No question that this was the place where I got lost during my "getting lost" exercise.

While the lid was open and more light entered the square room, we saw two identical big machines whose general format resembled a big armadillo, and what we call a "tatu" in Brazil. A short description of this interesting equipment we will give now, since it would have a decisive role for us.

These "tatus" were cylindrical-conical machines supported by rollers at their entire circumference. Their length was about 6 meters. At what appeared to be the nose, there was a conical structure that gave it the general aspect of an immense armadillo. This conical nose was formed by a thick metallic armature. On it, there were, firmly fastened, numerous metal bits suggesting having a rock-cutting function. The nose looked as though it were capable of rotating and also of being extensible from the main part of the machine. The general impression was that of a formidable boring machine. On its rear, there was a sort of shelf where we could see curved plates. These plates seemed to match the covering of the tunnels. Also on the rear, an immense instrument panel indicated that they were the control buttons and levers.

Every aspect of the machine led us to conclude that its function was to construct the tunnels. It seemed capable of boring and walling the tunnels in a single operation. One question remained open to us: where was the earth or rock removed? This would be answered to us in a practical and terrifying situation.

Chapter 80

Southeast Tunnel

The following day, soon after breakfast, we proceeded to explore the southeast tunnel. We were well equipped. This time, in addition to the flashlights, batteries, and candles, I took with me 2 small printer motors coupled to tiny LED panels. These tiny motors, being turned by hand, create a very decent illumination. From a physics point of view, this is an interesting contraption. These motors, normally, work to produce mechanical torque when fed by electrical voltage. But, they also work in reverse: when forced to rotate, they generate voltage and the voltage lights the LEDs.

According to my brother, bringing them was an exaggerate precaution.

The southeast tunnel presented the same general architecture as the others. Perfectly cylindrical, 190 cm diameter, metal plated. The wall was formed by the welding of 3 identical curved plates, 1-meter-long in the tunnel direction and about 2 meters wide, measured along the curvature, with a flexible tape measure. Each 1 meter of tunnel length had 3 plates soldered with extraordinary precision. As such, each meter along the wall presented 3 longitudinal lines of welding. The segments were welded together, forming the wall. Also, the use of three sections allowed the panels to be transported along the already welded sections of the tunnel.

Joaquim

The tunnel went on with a slight uphill slope. We were very cautious with bifurcations. After about 150 meters, a surprise: a shaft 90 cm wide went up from the main tunnel. On it, a fixed ladder was leading to a possible exit. I noted that the air was stagnant and lit a candle in order to see if there might be an air current. The flame stood perfectly vertical. As we moved a few meters more, our feeling was of really stagnant air, and the candle extinguished. Trying to relight the candle, not even the matches lighted up.

"There is a lack of oxygen here, let's move out!" I shouted.

Then, I remembered the shaft nearby and decided to open it to the exterior. As I went to see this with my brother, I saw him lying down on the floor, gesturing as not being able to breathe. We were almost below the shaft, and I went hurrying up the ladder and forced open the lid above the shaft. It fell to the side with a bang, and immediately, a very strong wind began to blow from the side we came from. Probably, there was a fast wind above the shaft and a low pressure had established there sucking the air from the tunnel.

I came down the ladder to help my brother, but he was already OK, despite still lying down on the floor.

I went again up the ladder and got out to the open air. A glorious and sunny day greeted me. The top of Dome 1 was clearly visible some 300 meters northwest. I repositioned the lid, leaving a small opening, and came back to the tunnel. Since my brother was still feeling the effects of hypoxia, we decided to scrap the expedition for the day. We went back, retracing our steps, along a now super ventilated tunnel.

The next morning, we returned to the southeast tunnel. I had left a small opening at the shaft lid, and today, a light wind blew, coming from the hall where the 2 tunnels departed. We passed the vertical shaft and went on. Now, the uphill incline was a bit accentuated. I supposed that the tunnel slope followed the ground above in order to keep the tunnel at a constant depth. However, after some 100 meters, the tunnel leveled off. Soon, we came below another wide and laddered shaft, and this one had about 20 meters in length, being quite longer than the first one.

I went up the ladder. There was also a circular lid that was a bit loose, indicating a recent opening. I left this lid a bit dislodged in order to provide some additional air flow. On our way back, I would reposition both lids firmly.

Not very far from this last shaft, we came to a gate like the one we saw at the southwest tunnel. Again, there was the screw for pressure control on the lower part. I opened the screw: no wind or water. We, then, opened the gate, moving the three levers: the same smooth and precise hinge mechanism as the other gate had. This time, however, there was a difference: after about 1 meter apart, there was another gate, and this one was quite different and seemed to open away from us. Furthermore, this gate was not ribbed, its surface being smooth all over. There were many signs in red and some painted arrows. The written signs were in Landinese.

I opened the lower screw and a strong gush of air came in our direction. Like the other, this gate was hinged on our left. The gate had three bolts, like the previous ones. One bolt opposite to the hinge, at 3 hours, one at 12 hours, and yet another at 6 hours. The gate also had a horizontal bar that could be moved to the right, along three guides. A careful exam showed us that this bar was not a bolt, but had the function of preventing the inadvertent closure of the gate. On the proper bar, there were many written signs in red. The bar could only be moved to the right after the gate had been opened.

Despite a counter wind, we opened the gate, which revealed to be a massive metal disc about 8 cm in thickness. The gate was circled by a heavy O-ring running inside a very precise groove. The general impression was of a very heavy and strong gate; whose function was not all clear to us.

I passed the gate without problem and held it open in order for my brother to go through. However, as soon as he passed the gate jamb, my hand slipped, and the gate slammed shut with a bang. We initially weren't concerned since, up to now, all gates had a bilateral access to their bolts. Another tranquilizing factor was that we thought that the gate had banged closed by the action of the air pressure difference and, certainly, could be opened as soon as the pressures equalized on the two sides. Also, there might be more shafts with ladders, opening to the outside. We kept walking and, soon, got to another shaft. However, this one was only 20 cm wide. Putting my hand below the shaft, there came from it a weak breeze and a strong smell of bush. Certainly, it was a ventilating tube with an umbrella extension to the outside air.

Our tunnel went on level.

It was at this moment that the lights went off. Suddenly, we were in total darkness.

"Let's keep calm!" I said to my brother, and remembered, from the many adventure books I have read, that on these occasions it is necessary to think outside of the problem. Something I call a literary experience on survival.

"Let's go back to the gate," my brother suggested. Of course the gate was closed, but now, from the screw hole, there came an air flow in our direction.

"Now, the pressure is greater on the other side, and the gate should open!" we both exclaimed. Question was it didn't.

We gave up, temporarily this way of exit and went back to explore the tunnel. We weren't explorers anymore. Our only aim, now, was to get out of this place.

In order to save batteries, I suggested to my brother that we used only one flashlight, which was more than enough. Actually, even in total darkness, it was possible to tread along the tunnel by groping at the smooth walls.

Some 50 meters more and we came to a great hall. My flashlight immediately illuminated one of the boring machines, one of the giant "tatus". The big room was perfectly circular, about 30 meters in diameter. Scattered about were infinity of crates, boxes, and empty cartons. Many items were strewn onto the floor, as if signaling a hurried moving. From the hall, not counting the tunnel we came from, there were two tunnels at 90 degrees from each other. One tunnel was in the same line as our incoming tunnel and was leveled. It seemed to be a continuation of our incoming tunnel. The other tunnel, at 90 degrees to the right, was short, about 20 meters long, and went up at an accentuated slope. We went up this short one and arrived at the end of a boring machine, one of the big "tatus". That was the first time we saw one of those boring machines in its working position. It gave us a clear message that its service had been interrupted.

We supposed this tunnel was unfinished and had been abandoned during the hurried moving out of the "family".

We sat down on some mattresses scattered across the floor, ate one sandwich each of us, and one half-glass of orange juice. Then, we revised our not very nice situation. We would try to find our exit at the next tunnel.

Chapter 81

Trapped!

Now, our aim wasn't anymore a curious exploration but a desperate search for freedom. We divided our actions into three categories: look for an exit, look for items that might help us survive here, and, finally, tools for opening the gate that had betrayed us. In addition to the many crates and boxes, we found what seemed to be tunnel plates carefully stacked. We took three plates and found out that they formed a circle of 190 cm in diameter or, exactly, one of the 1-meter-long sections of the tunnel. There was a huge stock of those plates. We examined, once more, the tunnel wall and concluded that each one-meter-long section was formed by three curved plates welded together, forming a cylinder. The welds were so precise that, at first glance, they were not visible. From the wall of the big hall, there exited a beautiful and sophisticated faucet from where a short hose terminated at a 500-liter water tank covered by a tarpaulin. Moving the tarpaulin, we checked the water inside. I drank some and found it delicious. This gave us good news and bad news. The good: we had an unlimited supply of fresh water. The bad one: we were at the bottom of a water table. What protected us from drowning were the hall's walls and the tunnels' metallic shells that, ironically, were trapping us inside!

"Well, from thirst, we are not dying," I laughed at my brother.

Then, we proceeded to do some research. We began opening crates and boxes. There were many types of equipment, electronic devices and parts. In another crate: manuals and many books. In yet another: many tools of different types. This last crate we separated from the others. It might prove useful for our escape. I was looking for some drill or cutting machine with which we might tackle the massive gate that had betrayed us.

On my watch, it was 4 PM, and we began to get hungry. Our backpacks had some more sandwiches, chocolate bars, orange juice, a bottle of brandy, and coffee inside a thermos. We were already wearing our coats since our surroundings were cold.

By a conservative calculation, assuming no shortage of water and a sparing diet, we would eat for about 4 days more.

We had a "lunch" by candlelight to spare the batteries. After eating, we did an inventory of our light-producing gadgets. Each of us had 3 candles and a matchbox. Our flashlights had one more stock of batteries each.

Light seemed, now, to be a precious commodity for us. We began searching for alternative sources of light. Among our plans was searching the hall, trying to find items useful for our escape and exploring the ongoing tunnel in search of an exit. We decided to move to the unknown tunnel since we could always come back to the hall.

We, then, took to the new tunnel which was on level; what I

checked by pouring some water on the floor. The water ran in both directions. Twenty meters away, one more small bore ventilation shaft brings a scent of vegetation. After 20 meters, another identical shaft.

Since the traitor gate that had imprisoned us prevented any airflow and we were experimenting with constant ventilation from the shafts, we concluded that there should be another air passage.

"Well, we also won't die by lack of oxygen!" said my brother.

We went on and passed by one more ventilation shaft. By a wrong step, my brother let his light fall to the floor. It immediately went off: the lamp was broken. We took off the batteries and stored them in my pack.

Finally, a few meters away, we came to a gate. This one, however, was entirely different from all others we had seen up to now. Perfectly circular, seemed solid metal, and had a 10 cm wide hole, right in the center.

Placing my hand in front of the hole, I sensed it was sucking air strongly.

"That explains our ventilation. The other side of this gate must communicate with external air," I told my brother.

The door had many inscriptions, probably in Landinese, and all of them were engraved into the metal. Not written.

Probing the central hole in its depth I found the gate was about 8 cm thick. The gate had no other features aside from the central hole and the inscriptions. Also, on the gate margins, there were absolutely no features. No welds, no hinges, no bolts, nothing. The gate seemed to fit perfectly and firmly with the outer jamb, also in metal. There was no indication whatsoever of how to open this gate if ever it was to be opened. From the way the door fitted with a metal rim, it was clear to us that it was placed from our side. The central hole seemed to us to function as a ventilation mechanism to assure air circulation and also to equilibrate pressures.

One detail that called, again, our attention was the inscriptions. Also, the general idea to be inferred was that this gate wasn't meant to be opened. Like the lid of a sepulcher.

"Look, Luiz, the inscriptions are formed by groupings of points, like all other writings we had seen. Also, like the writings in the many books I had seen in the dome."

"But, there is a difference. Here, the inscriptions were not printed. They were engraved, carved, sculpted into the metal," my brother remarked.

"They were, certainly, carved with a very hard point or even with a high-powered laser," Luiz added (Luiz is my brother).

I got hold of my Buck folding knife, hard 440 steel, and tried to scratch the gate's surface. It was absolutely impossible.

"Yes, you are right, Luiz. But why all the trouble of using a laser if a good printing would do?" I asked Luiz.

In response, Luiz said we should drink some old coffee to fix our ideas. We got our thermos, and I remembered that mine was formerly Antonina's. Luiz's thermos was inherited from Greg. In passing, I told Luiz of the origin of our thermos.

"Wait, there is something written in my thermos," Luiz said.

"And, also, in mine! But does that matter anything to you?" I said ironically.

"It matters a lot, Jota!" he answered with more irony.

"Look, here is Greg's name" and he pointed to a group of points engraved on the gate, matching exactly the ones in Luiz's thermos.

Greg's name was carved onto a column of symbols along with other 4 groups of points. We began "reading" the symbols. There was a symbol way bigger than the others that matched exactly the symbol on my thermos, previously owned by Antonina. Besides that bigger symbol, there was another symbol that we easily identified: a beautiful flower deeply engraved in the hard metal!

Chapter 82

The Tomb

In an instant, the reality came to us. We were facing the tomb of Antonina. What appeared to be a gate was, in fact, a tombstone. And, like a tombstone, it was resting onto the rim or jamb and fixed there in some way we couldn't determine. It would be out of the question, forcing the stone toward the inside space. If there was any way of removing that stone it would be pulling it from the inside out, in our direction.

However, all that activity began to drain my flashlight's battery, and we decided to return to the hall as soon as possible while we had some light. We still had the batteries of the broken flashlight and two more candles. After this, the deepest darkness was waiting for us.

While still having light, we needed to explore the contents of all the crates and boxes in the hall in trying to find items either to free us from this other sepulcher or at least provide some more time for illumination. The perspective of being in the dark was terrifying! Adding to our concerns was the fact that we were amid the water table. Actually, we were submerged. The same barriers that were restraining us were also protecting us from the water surrounding us.

And, we were hungry.

We ate one more sandwich each and the remaining warm and old coffee from our thermos. I apologized to Luiz for having brought him to this predicament.

"Don't worry, Jota, we will be out!"

Before we were in total darkness, we decided to turn over all the crates and boxes and scramble all items to the floor without any care and in a hurry.

Most items were electronic parts, books, and manuals. In another crate: many types of clothes, winter coats, boots, caps, sunglasses, backpacks. Another crate had plastic jars with wide openings and big conical-shaped stoppers of a silicone-like material; a bit harder, though. The stoppers, of different sizes, matched to the jars' mouths. We were looking desperately for lanterns, candles, anything that could provide light. Some boxes had sleeping bags, portable camping mattresses, but not a damned kerosene lamp!

My watch showed 8 PM, and hunger came back with a vengeance. We drank plenty of water. I knew that water ingestion deceives hunger and is always beneficial. We decided to give a wide interval before eating our last sandwiches.

My flashlight began to blink at about 9 PM. We were looking for any flammable and well-behaved material that could sustain a flame since our candles were getting smaller by the minute.

By 11 PM, we were exhausted and hungry. We ate our last sandwiches. My flashlight was gone. When the last candle went off, we would be in the deepest darkness. Before that occurred, we gathered mattresses, sleeping bags, coats, and boots and went to sleep very warm. The silence and exhaustion made us soon get to sleep.

I opened my eyes at 10 the next morning and called Luiz to wake him. I knew well that hunger would soon establish as our metabolism went from sleep to the waking state. We had still to scramble the crates and boxes, of which there were many unturned. In some crates there were tents, still in their boxes and more mattresses. We concluded that our death would be by starvation since we had water, oxygen, and clothes.

I, then, returned to explore the tools' crate and turned it over, scattering all items onto the floor.

It was then that the candle extinguished. We were now in complete darkness. And, this, becomes terrifying when you are trapped.

"Let's see the good side. Here, there are no beasts, no bad guys. We have plenty of water, clothes, and blankets. We just have no food!" I commented.

"It would be very nice if we had some orange juice left in those empty jars we found in the crates," said Luiz.

I remembered that we might have some juice left in my pack. I found we had 60 ml and gave half to Luiz. That was our last food.

In complete darkness, I continued to grope at the floor. Then I came upon the big rubber stoppers. One of them had about 10 cm diameter at the middle of its conical length. It was rubbery like silicone but a bit harder. And it was long, about 25-30 cm. I tried it on the jar mouth, and it fitted perfectly, allowing for a perfect and very firm sealing.

Immediately, I remembered the hole at the center of the tombstone. And I commented on the coincidence with Luiz.

"OK, Jota, very nice. Now you want to deprive us also of oxygen!" he said, laughing.

Luiz was right. When we were at the tombstone, there was airflow through the center hole coming from the tomb side and into our direction. This confirmed my theory that the central hole had the function of ventilation and pressure equilibration. Certainly, the tomb had its own ventilation shafts. It might even have a man-sized shaft! Then, things began to make sense in my mind.

I remembered what Antonina had said about the Landian beliefs in the afterlife. Of course, I thought, the dead need oxygen, at least at the beginning of their journey across the River Styx.

But if they need oxygen, then what about food during their journey? Those were my thoughts, and, of course, I didn't dare to share them with my brother. Not now.

"Let's go, Luiz; I want to try this stopper on the tombstone hole."

"But, tell me, Jota, how are we going there in the dark? How are we going to find the tunnel exit?" A very pertinent observation!

I had an idea that the tunnel leading to the tomb started beside the water reservoir. We groped along the hall wall until we came to the reservoir. Indeed, beside it, we found the tunnel entrance. Along the tunnel, it was easy to tread since there was no mistaking. Passing below the ventilation shafts, we felt they were now sucking air from the tunnel. The vegetation smell also had disappeared. Some other scents were in the air. After few more steps, we felt a horizontal wind coming from the tomb.

"It's coming from the central hole in the tombstone. We are near it!" I shouted, since, now, the wind was a bit noisy.

Then, we came to the tombstone. The wind, coming through the hole and from the tomb, was now decidedly stronger. Some atmospheric changes had occurred, probably.

I had put the stopper inside my backpack. Now, I had to find it. Well, despite the stopper being big, my backpack was still bigger and, sometimes, inscrutable. I began groping inside in order to grab the stopper. My hand navigated among the many items I carried unnecessarily. Then, I saw a brief flash of light spreading from the pack interior.

"What's that?" my brother shouted at seeing the light flash.

Now, the howling wind made it difficult for us to talk normally.

I continued to grope inside my backpack, forgetting the stopper momentarily and now in search of the mysterious light flash.

It was then that I remembered the printer motors connected to

LEDs. Casually, I had moved the motor, flashing the LED. I then took one motor and began turning it and illuminating, provocatively, my brother's face.

"Excess precaution, eh Luiz!" I said, handing Luiz the other motor.

"While we have muscle energy to turn these motors, we have light!" I said triumphantly.

"Yes, you are right, Jota. But, for this, we need to eat something!"

These two new sources of light uplifted our spirits!

Now, we went back to our research about stoppers and holes. Actually, there was some germ of an idea brewing, very deep, in my mind, saying we needed to do the experiment.

Now, with my new lantern, I illuminated the backpack and grabbed the stopper. Trying it into the hole, it "fitted like a glove". The hole was completely sealed.

"Very good, Jota, now you really did it! It was a "good idea" because we are now going to die by anoxia before we die by starvation!" and he clapped his hands at me.

"Let's keep the stopper there, and we will test the airflow at the ventilation shafts," I said in a lower voice since the silence returned.

Too bad we hadn't the candles anymore. I found some cotton threads down inside my pack and put them under the shafts. Not a breeze was passing. Complete stagnation.

Our conclusion: Not counting the small hole left by the screw at that traitor gate, ventilation only occurred between the ventilation shafts on the tunnel and the tombstone hole, now closed by the stopper. Inside the big hall, there was no air passage. Having concluded this "brilliant" aerodynamics experiment, I removed the stopper from the hole, and Luiz, immediately, began breathing more happily.

"Let's now observe the direction of the airflow," I said to Luiz.

"OK, Jota, but do we intend to get out from here, or do you want to write a thesis on "air flows between tombs and tunnels"?"

Luiz had no idea about my purpose in this experiment. And, worse, neither had I.

"Do you think the airflow might invert direction, Luiz?" I insisted on my divagations.

"The airflow depends on the pressures at different places up there," he answered, pointing up and giving me a menacing glance since he was fed up with my theories.

After establishing the feasibility of sealing the tombstone hole with the stopper, we came back to the hall and continued the search for items that could help us get out. My watch showed 8 PM. The intense hunger made it difficult to reason adequately.

At 10 PM, we began hearing thunders. A thunderstorm was brewing outside. The sounds came from the tunnel. Certainly, the thunder sounds were passing through the ventilation shafts. Along the way toward the tomb, we came below one of the shafts, and I perceived that it was sucking air with enormous intensity. The same was occurring with the other shafts. We came to the tombstone and verified that, through the central hole, the glare of the lightning was plainly visible. This indicated that the tomb had a sort of communication with the exterior. Approaching the central hole of the tombstone we felt the air gushing violently toward us and making a terrible and desperate howling sound.

No question that the tomb should be explored as an escape route. The storm, instead of calming down, was growing in intensity.

All those isolated pieces of information began to add to my mind, and then, everything made sense to me. My obsession with that stopper as a means to close the hole, my checking the pressure differences, while the air was gushing violently. Many things that were concocting in my mind began to take shape.

My thoughts: *We could use that gigantic wind force to dislodge the tombstone.*

"Luiz, what happens if we close the hole with the stopper?"

"I think it will create a pressure difference large enough to dislodge the tombstone" and, this time, Luiz did not seem angry at me.

"How large would be the force, Luiz?"

"Humm, let me see:" he said.

The radius is 90 cm. The area is: Radius squared x Pi = 90^2 x Pi = 8,100 cm^2 x 3.14 = 25,400 cm^2. If we have a pressure difference of 1 atm = 1kgf/cm^2, then the maximum force would be 25 tons. We may have easily a 15-ton force acting upon the lid, from inside out," he said and took the stopper from my hands, ready to push it into the hole.

"Wait, wait, if the tombstone falls down, it may rupture the tunnel wall, and water will come in," I said.

"We need to pad the tunnel floor with some mattresses so that the falling tombstone will do no damage to the wall."

"And also get the mallet to force the stopper into the hole," said my brother.

We took everything we needed, placing the items near the tomb's door. The air, gushing through the hole, made a sound so intense that it even baffled the thunder.

"Luiz, hold the stopper into the hole, and I will hit with the mallet."

At my first strike, the stopper got firmly into the hole, only to be ejected violently out at a great speed. It missed my brother by a few inches. We found the stopper 50 meters down the tunnel.

"We need to keep hitting the stopper with the mallet until it gets firmly attached to the hole. Just one strike is not enough," I said, shouting over the howling sound of the gushing air.

We then brought the stopper for a new trial at the hole.

Outside, the tempest was raging and increasing in force. The interval between lightning and thunder was getting smaller and smaller, indicating the lightning was coming closer.

The air jet through the hole was so strong now that we might not be able to insert the stopper into the hole.

"Keep the stopper into the hole, Luiz. When I do the fourth strike, we run away," I shouted at my brother.

Using all his forces, Luiz finally could get the stopper into the hole. As soon as the stopper had positioned, I gave the first strike and, without waiting, gave the second, then the third, and the fourth. The air jet disappeared immediately, and we ran away at full speed. We entered the hall and went to a recess, lest the tombstone rolled down the tunnel and smashed us.

But, as we were crouching there, I illuminated my brother's face. Terror was stamped in his look.

"We are going to die, Jota!" he shouted.

"It's not the pressure that is increasing inside the tomb. It is that the pressure is decreasing here! We are being vacuumed, Jota!" and he was shouting desperately.

He was right; the air inside the hall and the tunnels was being sucked out through a phenomenon described by Daniel Bernoulli, a Swiss physicist and mathematician. The incredibly fast wind outside created a zone of low pressure at the external openings of the shafts, and this pressure difference was sucking the air from our place. We were already feeling the effects of low pressure. Our ears were popping. Worse still, we were not getting enough air to breathe. We were, now, struggling to breathe.

"Let's remove the stopper before we die here!" I cried desperately. And, we were about to do that. The question was, we had no forces, even to stand up. The effects of anoxia were already being felt in our bodies.

Then, after about half a minute, we heard a terrible bang and a clang. Immediately, we were invaded by a strong gush of air, fresh air laced with humidity, and a strong smell of vegetation.

We weren't going to die anymore, at least not now. We went to the tomb's direction. The tunnel end was illuminated with each lightning. As we approached, we saw that the heavy lid had fallen over the mattresses. No damage was seen to the tunnel linings. Also, we weren't going to drown!

We passed the threshold into the tomb. The vision we had was that of a gigantic circular nave, like that of a church. At each lightning a brilliant light focused at the middle of the hall. About 10 meters from the middle, we saw a beautiful and sophisticated low table. On the table there was a transparent box, rectangular in shape. It measured about 2 m in length, 1 m in width, and about 70 cm in height. The box seemed like a technical structure, a sort of chamber. The walls were thick and precisely built. We approached slowly, and my throat already got the usual lump I used to experiment in very stressful situations. My brother, sensing my trouble, held me gently at my shoulder.

We got beside the box, and I illuminated it with my motor lantern.

Inside was lying Antonina, with a serene expression, maybe a suggestion of a smile. From my medical experience, no indication of death came from her features. She seemed to be sleeping. Certainly, she had been embalmed by a very sophisticated and perfect process to give her the appearance of a living person. *That was one more example of the Landian technology, probably a century ahead of Earthian's*, I thought.

Her blond hair was well arranged very natural looking. A blue mantle covered her body. Her features seemed to change with each lightning. We looked up at the ceiling: an enormous transparent cylinder pierced the rocky roof. It seemed to me a gigantic optical fiber leading the day light into the hall interior. At each lightning, a flash of light entered the hall, brought down by the light cylinder.

We stood in silence; my brother placed his hand on my shoulder.

There was not much to do now concerning Antonina. From my view, she was OK.

We, however, were not OK. And now, the hunger came, implacable, indifferent to my feelings.

We began to explore the big hall in search of some food. At the wall, carefully hung, were dresses, mantles, scarves. At a low table, many beautiful dolls. And, there were the shelves along the curved wall. On one shelf, there were big and beautiful books. Another shelf had boxes. We counted about 20 big boxes the size of a microwave oven. Another shelf had folded clothes, blankets of all styles and colors, and pillows. On a lower shelf, close to the ground, many shoe pairs, sneakers, and socks. On the hangers, there were skiing clothes, glasses, sticks, and boots.

"Let's see the closed boxes," I said to my brother.

As we opened the first box, a surprise: the box was full to the brim with chocolate bars and cereal bars, all made in Brazil. Without waiting, we began to eat.

"Go easy, Luiz, let's do it slowly!"

I then remembered the clinical cases where trying to revert too rapidly certain conditions led people to death: starving people given too much food; people deprived of water for many days, given plenty of water; hypothermic patients warmed too fast; dehydrated people given too much IV fluid.

I was, clearly, exaggerating since we were not starving … yet. Anyway, not to cause an intestinal derangement, we ate 3 bars of chocolate and 3 bars of cereal each.

Then, we saw closed boxes lying on the ground, below the shelves. The first box had beer cans. The second box had wine bottles.

Then, it came to my mind, again, the Landian belief in the afterlife and all the comforts it should carry.

This reminded me of the Egyptian pharaohs who were buried with their horses, valuables, food and, also, their preferred concubines.

Another box had various types of nuts, Brazilian nuts, and almonds, of which we tasted a few, along with some cans of beer and an entire bottle of wine.

Having filled our stomachs, we turned back to planning our escape. But, with less hurry.

We decided to bivouac inside Antonina's tomb since we had ample stock of camping mattresses, blankets, and sleeping bags.

Also, we would not look at Antonina anymore in respect for her.

The next morning, the weather appeared to be clear since the light fiber gave a very luminous glare throughout the hall. We spent all day exploring the tomb. Some closed boxes still remained on the higher shelves. As we had no ladder, I tiptoed and pulled one box out. However, it slipped and went down, throwing to the floor an enormous quantity of many types of nuts. Among the nuts were stones. There were many emeralds and rubies, all uncut and with different sizes and shapes.

One day more had passed and we, despite having eaten and drank a lot, hadn't progressed in the way of getting out. Evening came and, then, the night. We went to sleep after another bottle of wine. In the middle of the night, I heard my brother dreaming: "It's the tatu, it's the tatu," he repeated. The "tatus" (armadillos) he was referring to were the boring machines.

Chapter 83

Saved!

The next morning, I asked my brother if he had dreamt of a "tatu". He didn't remember. We ate some bars and drank a couple of beers.

"Let's take a look at the boring machines; maybe you remember something of your dream, Luiz."

As soon as we got to the "tatu" inside the hall, the first thing we did was examine the control panel of the enormous machine. The panel was at the rear, above the tray with the tunnel plates. There were three red levers placed horizontally on the panel. The right side lever had a circle with rays at one side and an identical circle without rays at the other side. Now, the lever was pointing to the circle without rays.

"I suppose this lever turns on the machine," I said.

And I moved the lever to the circle with rays. Immediately the machine lighted the panel and began to make some sounds.

"But, wait, Jota, let's see the other machine inside the tunnel. That's the one useful for us since it is already in a boring position!"

We went up to the inclined tunnel. Despite the slope being accentuated, it was no problem for our rubber-soled boots. This other boring machine was identical to the first. On its tray were 6 tunnel plates, enough to pave 2 meters of tunnel. As I turned the right side lever to the circle with rays, the machine lighted up and began emitting sounds. But then, the machine stopped the sounds, and, above the middle lever, which was horizontal, a light began to blink, and some buzzing sound began intermittently like the rear beeping sound of trucks.

"Turn the lever to the light," my brother said

As I did this, other sounds began. Now, began a sound of compressed air being injected. A mechanical arm grabbed one of the plates on the tray and moved it into the machine's interior. Then, the arm grabbed another plate and then another.

Silence.

A few seconds after the last plate went inside the machine, it began shaking and seemed to be forcing the tunnel wall backward with tremendous force. It seemed that the nose had been extended forward. A grinding sound began, intercalated with a small stepwise progression of the machine up the tunnel. While this occurred, the entire tunnel seemed to shake. Some smoke appeared, and a smell of welding invaded the air. Then, the machine stopped, and the arm grabbed three more plates, leaving the tray empty.

"Let's put more plates in the tray, I shouted to my brother."

We began a frantic run back and forth between the stack of plates on the floor and the machine up the tunnel. We had to provide plates at the same rate the machine was placing them at the tunnel wall.

We brought more plates but the machine had worked faster than us. It had stopped, and a strong light blinked inside the tray.

"It "wants" more plates!" my brother shouted. We placed 9 plates on the tray and the machine returned to operate.

"But, wait, Luiz. Where does the machine dump the earth as it moves on?"

"Probably, the machine keeps pushing the earth sideways with a brutal force as it moves forward. That's what the conical nose is made for. It's like driving a pointed stake into the earth."

Engineers. They always have an explanation.

"Yes, you are right, Luiz. The conical nose rotates grinding and at the same time pushing the earth to the sides. And if it finds rocks, the machine probably melts them with the lasers."

"But, in order to push forward, the machine needs to employ a tremendous force. Where does it get fulcrum?" I remarked.

"It locks its rear to the tunnel walls behind and extends the nose forward. This explains why the tunnel behind shakes so much". That was my brother's answer. No questioning...

In effect, observing the already constructed parts of the tunnel, it was possible to see small indentations where the rear part of the machine locked itself with the metal plates of the already formed tunnel.

While we discussed the workings of the machine, it kept working, oblivious to our opinions about her. However, we forgot to feed the tray with plates. The machine stopped and "asked" for more plates. And we put more plates onto the tray. As I came back, I placed my hand on the just-formed tunnel, and it was very hot. The welding between the plates was perfect.

"Let's do some calculations, I cried to Luiz: the tray had 6 plates, and we put 9 more, totaling 15 plates. Since it uses 3 plates for 1 meter of the tunnel, it has bored 5 meters since we turned it on."

We placed 9 more plates on the tray, and the machine went on at an approximate rate of 30 minutes for each meter. After about one hour and a half, the machine stopped and asked for more plates. And we put 9 more plates.

My watch showed noon. We put on 9 plates more and returned to the tomb. The light coming from the optical fiber fixed to the roof was intense, revealing a sunny day. We had decided to let Antonina rest in peace since I felt that, just by observing her, I wasn't being nice to her.

We ate and returned to the hall. The machine was quiet. By our calculations, it had bored 14 meters in addition to the 20 meters it had done before we came.

Then, a doubt came to our minds. How do we know if the tunnel already got to the surface? To prevent any inflow of water, the machine sealed the tunnel completely, making it impossible to see the other side.

"But, wait, Luiz. If the tunnel got out, it will make a different sound as we strike it". And, now, my medical instincts went to the scene: the patient's percussion.

I got hold of one of the many hammers scattered on the floor and began testing the tunnel wall. Beginning at the tunnel exit from the hall, the sound was dull, revealing that the other side was compressed dirt with no empty spaces. Then, I kept hammering higher and, about 3 meters before the machine, the sound began to change. While we did this, the machine kept working. Two meters up, the sound was that of a cracked bell. Also, the "behavior" of the machine was different. Now, in advancing, the machine did not push the tunnel back like it did before. The tunnel walls neither moaned nor writhed as before.

Conclusion: the machine didn't need to push the earth ahead anymore because there was no more soil ahead.

"Let's stop the machine. The tunnel is off-ground!" I shouted.

"But, wait, Jota, if we stop the machine, how do we get out? The machine is blocking our exit!" Luiz shouted.

It was an argument very convincing indeed. The machine held to the tunnel walls with such a force that it would be impossible to dislodge it. Eager that we were to allow the machine to work without stopping, we had placed 9 more plates on the tray. This would allow the machine to build 3 more meters of tunnel.

"Let's stop it now, and we decide afterward what to do," I suggested.

I, then, turned off the middle lever. The machine did a few more welds, as we saw by the smoke and strong reflections of the lasers. I hit the tunnel wall with the hammer; cracked bell sound. The tunnel was off the ground.

The solution, now, was moving the machine out of our way. It had done its job. But, now, it was blocking our exit.

"Let's turn on the leftmost lever. It may make the machine only move without building the walls", I said.

We turned on the leftmost lever. The machine began to creak but didn't move. Suddenly, it began to move forward.

A few seconds later, a bright circle of light blinded us temporarily at the same instant that a loud banging sound came from the open mouth of the tunnel. The machine had left the tunnel and fallen to the ground below. We came up to the tunnel border and looked down. We were about 5 meters above ground, in the middle of a Eucalyptus forest. On the ground, a terrible scene was taking place.

The machine, as in revenge for having been "deceived", had turned on the plate welding mode, and the soldering lasers were wreaking havoc. The laser beams were so intense that it was impossible to look directly at them. The beams were now cutting everything on their paths. The cut

Eucalyptus branches, some very heavy, were falling to the ground and catching fire. The machine had to be turned off at all costs.

But the first action was to block the lasers. We began throwing down tunnel plates at the machine. After about 10 plates the lasers did not emerge and began cutting and melting the plates violently and randomly.

We then got some ropes and went down to the ground. We were risking now being caught by the lasers. The problem was, now, to locate the control panel behind the machine in order to turn it off. Finally, with the help of my brother, I could turn off the machine. So many branches had fallen down that they extinguished the fire. Now, we had to close the tunnel mouth in order to prevent the entry of bats and birds.

The following day, we returned to the tunnel exit and cut out the excess tunnel part using a torch. We needed, now, to cover the tunnel mouth with concrete and throw some dirt above. For this, we needed the crawler tractor I knew was stored at the cave.

I had not returned to the cave after my first visit wearing that helmet.

The cave's heavy sliding door was not locked, and I found a disguised button that, pressed, opened the door. We went down the cave corridor leading to the main hall and, arriving there, we switched on the lights. Anyway, we had our own lighting equipment. In the enormous hall, all the equipment I had seen on my first visit was there. And, many things more. The big crawler tractor, made in Brazil, was there all right, parked against the wall. It was in working condition and also fueled. My brother knew how to drive it. In order to better examine the tractor, we had to pull aside a big tarpaulin covering it. As soon as we moved the tarpaulin and, later, the tractor, there appeared the entry of a tunnel. Since our priority was now the covering of that tunnel we exited from, we decided to return another day and explore this new tunnel.

The next day was employed to cover the tunnel with concrete and soil. Not far from there we found the upper part of the big optical fiber, which was protruding about 1 meter from the ground. It was a marvelous piece of technology. A solid transparent plastic rod measuring about 30 cm in diameter pierced the ground. I checked its coordinates and took note: South 22.106445, West 47.90135.

We came back to our dome, riding in the tractor. The next day, we returned the tractor to the cave and began exploring the "new" tunnel, beginning at the great cave hall whose exit had been hidden by the tractor.

This tunnel was not paved by the metallic plates. It was concrete all over, and the floor was flat and broad, about 3 meters wide. Its height would also be about 3 meters, and the roof was arched. The floor had clear marks of small gauged tires. The tunnel was about 40 meters in length and had no ventilation shafts. We supposed the ground would be way above.

Chapter 84

Negative Mass

Moving out from the main cave hall, we entered the new tunnel. I don't remember how much we walked there, but we ended up in a circular hall, about 30 meters in diameter. There, a curious scene awaited us: maybe 40 four-wheel carts, flat-bottomed, possibly electric-driven, were parked side to side. The loading platform was low, about 50 cm from the ground. Each cart was carrying 12 big concrete blocks, 3 lines abreast and 4 lines along the cart length. The concrete blocks had a 50 x 50 cm base and 80 cm height and should weigh roughly 500 kgf (kilogram-force) each, considering a concrete density of 2.5 grams/cm^3. As such, each cart should be loaded with about 6 tons. And, the four narrow gauge 12-inch radius and 8 cm wide tires should be absolutely overloaded and flattened. But they were not. Something was, evidently, amiss.

Then, I saw what was above the concrete blocks. Since it was somewhat dark, I first saw a strong chain fixed to a steel loop at the top of each of the blocks. Then, it seemed to me that the concrete blocks were hanging from the roof, and that explained why the small carts were not overloaded with 6 tons each.

I called my brother's attention to this and, then, we saw it.

The blocks were not hanging from the roof. They were hanging from metallic cylinders that were simply suspended in the air.

Actually, the cylinders were "hanging" upwards from the concrete blocks! And they were hanging upside down like inverted pendulums. I went up to the cart's platform and pushed one cylinder sideways. It moved, oscillated for some time, and stopped. Hitting the chain, it was possible to feel the great amount of tension it was submitted to.

Looking at my brother, I saw him suspending one of the concrete blocks from the cart platform by holding the chain and using one hand for that.

"It must weigh about 2 kilograms, Jota!"

I then took one complete system (concrete block + chain + cylinder) from a cart and put it on the ground. It was easy to hold the block by its chain using just one hand. But, in trying to move it up and down, I felt an enormous inertia. Like you moving a big boat in the water. Since the concrete blocks weighed in at about 500 kg and they felt like 2 kg in our hands, the cylinders were pulling upward with about 498 kgf.

I was trying to organize these new findings in my head when I looked at my brother. He was weeping. Then he came to me, embraced me, and, still weeping, he said:

"How happy I am now, Jota. I was sure you were crazy. And, now, I know you are not!!"

This view of the inverted pendulums, his being an engineer, convinced him of the truth of all the "crazy" things I had told him about my friends on the farm.

"These cylinders must have a *negative mass*," said my brother.

"Yes, they may be used as counterweights in the disc," I remarked.

I, then, took some pictures of the carts and their strange loads.

But, our surprises did not stop there. From the carts hall, there emerged a tunnel, this time of a type well known to us: metallic plated, 190 cm diameter. Certainly, they were also built by our friendly but temperamental boring machines. This tunnel was discreetly downhill and was well-lighted. It had many written inscriptions on the walls. Many measuring instruments were hanging from special hooks fixed to the walls. Most symbols were of the type I knew well. A central circle surrounded by 3 wide rays: the international symbol for radioactivity.

Chapter 85

Isobel and Fabiana

Despite my relatively long stay on the farm and my short stay at the Landian space crafts, I hadn't, up to now, seen anything relative to radioactive materials.

As a scientist, I had worked on many projects employing radioactive substances, and I knew something about the related instrumentations.

As such, the instruments I saw, hanging at the tunnel, clearly denoted their function. They were radiation counters, despite being a type I still had not used. Fortunately, their instructions were in English. A digital display with well-defined and brilliant numbers expressed the radiation dose in milliSieverts, or thousandths of Sievert. There was a warning that the instrument should be checked and calibrated at a standard radiation source fixed to the wall nearby.

There are numerous units to measure radioactivity, but, for us, the milliSievert was ideal for measuring the dose of received radiation. To get an idea, an X-ray of the thorax loads the patient with 0.1 milliSieverts. Some tomographies (CT-scans) can reach a dose of 10 milliSieverts. A dose of 5,000 milliSieverts, or 5 Sievert, is lethal, at 30 days, for 50% of the exposed individuals. All this information was written on many cards fixed to the walls.

The counters should be attached to the waist, with the readout looking up. Also, it was necessary to set the instrument to zero. From now on our counters (mine and my brother's) began summing up the received dose and the exposition time, both appearing at the readout.

Immediately, our counters began showing the numbers in milliSieverts. Also, the radiation intensity was measured by sound clicks, the higher frequency of clicks indicating a higher intensity of the source. Even at the point we were, our counters were clicking, and the numbers were increasing slowly. From this point on the tunnel had no lamps and was becoming darker as we progressed.

Then, close to the end of the tunnel, we began seeing a greenish luminosity. Finally, we came to another circular hall (all were circular, probably to stand the water pressure from the water table around). This hall was being illuminated by a set of glass ampoules containing what seemed to be a glowing powder. The ampoules had a flat bottom and were supported by small tables at a height of about 1 meter from the floor, and formed a half circle, being equidistant from the circular wall behind them. There were 15 of them.

At about the circle center there was a big table.

Even before we entered this new hall our counters began clicking with a higher, but not "alarming" frequency. My display read 0.005 mSv.

We could get to about 10 meters from the central table before our counters began increasing the clicking rate. My display showed now 0.02

mSv.

The central table was about 60 cm high and had the approximate dimensions of a king-size bed but without the head and feet rest. On the table was a large padded mantle. And, covering it, there was a beautifully adorned white sheet touching the floor all around the table.

On the sheet and at the middle of the table were two women embracing each other.

One had blond and short hair, almost white. Her skin was white too. The other, brown-skinned, had black and long hair hanging from the table, almost touching the floor. Each wore a white and beautiful gown. The brunette's attire was very well arranged. Her hair was also carefully arranged as falling from the table. The blonde woman was not so carefully attired. Her arms seemed to be embracing, forcefully, the brunette. Her beautiful and white legs were partly uncovered by the gown which had fallen from one side. Also, her legs were spread as if she had been kicking the covers.

A slight, pungent odor pervaded the place.

As we approached the table, our counters began to increase the clicking rate. We receded slowly from the table and almost bumped into a ladder fixed vertically at the floor and running up through an aperture on the roof, 4 meters above. I went up the ladder and from up there, took many pictures of the hall and, especially, of the two women.

"Let's move from here. There is too much radiation!" I said to my brother.

We then moved all the way up the ladder and through the aperture above. The aperture went through a thick concrete slab that formed the floor of a hall, which was empty and dark, except from the glow of another aperture, to which the ladder top was, apparently, attached and protruding about one meter above the floor.

Going all the way up the ladder, we finally came to a place that I knew well. We were at the central hall of Dome 2, where Isobel and Fabiana were, previously, living.

Dome 2 was intact. In the dining room, there were many pieces of furniture and the table where I had lunch with Isobel and Fabiana. In the kitchen a working refrigerator, well provided. Many foods were getting bad, but in the freezer, there was a large stock of frozen food.

The bedrooms were also intact but disordered. Clothes were scattered on the floor and beds.

We took from the refrigerator a carton of orange juice, which seemed OK, and, from the freezer, a large lasagna and micro waved it.

And, we went to look at the many photos I had taken of the girls. My brother still didn't know Greg's super camera. The first photo showed the scene as we had seen it. The two women embraced.

Now, the details:

The sharpness and quality of the photos were unbelievable. The first zoom made it clear that the two women were Fabiana and Isobel. Fabiana had her eyes closed and a serene expression on her face.

It was clear that it was Isobel who was embracing Fabiana, who had her arms extended, her left arm over Isobel's neck, and the right arm extending from the "bed's" head and hanging down.

Their lips were forcibly touching.

Isobel's features weren't serene. Despite having her lips touching Fabiana's there was a clear contortion in her features. A creamy pinky substance was seen frozen and dripped from her mouth's lower corner. Her eyes were open, looking at infinity and still carrying the evil look that she used to give me. Her left hand was hidden below Fabiana's torso. Her right was clenched as if in a spasm.

No question whatsoever. They were quite dead.

Now, for our theories:

It became clear to me that they had met a ritual death planned by Isobel. Probably, Fabiana was poisoned after being hypnotized by Isobel. And, then, Isobel took, herself, a rapid action poison.

The radioactive ampoules may have had two roles. Firstly, some ritualistic ones and then sterilize the bodies, preventing their decay by bacteria. I suspected that the bodies were, slowly, being mummified.

My brother raised a question: what to do with their bodies?

Leaving them there was out of the question. Calling the police would be foolish since an investigation would be done into the entire farm. We would be incriminated surely by actions we had not committed. If we explained everything, we would be interned at a lunatic's asylum.

I suggested closing the cave's door and covering it with dirt. Our entry to the cave would be, in this case, through Dome 2.

But, before putting in effect that plan, I had another idea.

"Let's send them to space, Luiz!"

"How come, Jota, I can't see it!"

We, then, left the cave by its external main door. In passing through the hall with the negative masses, I took a good look at the chain that connected the cylinders with the concrete blocks. The chain was permanently fixed to the cylinder, but its fixing point with the concrete block was detachable through a screw mechanism. It became clear to us that this arrangement had the purpose of allowing the handling of the negative masses. Without the counterweight of the concrete blocks, the cylinders would be unmanageable and very dangerous to handle. That meant that the (cylinder + concrete) block system could be disconnected when it became necessary while being easily moved as a 2-kilogram load.

We went back to our Dome, rested, and had dinner. After dinner, I explained to my brother the plan I had in mind, in order to send the two girls to space.

Chapter 86

The Launching

My plan was to wrap the girls with a tarpaulin, forming a sort of coffin and attaching it to the negative mass cylinder.

The next step would be disconnecting the chain from the concrete block. Then the (coffin + cylinder) would go up, taking the two girls to the space.

However, some calculations would be necessary.

Remember that the concrete blocks weighed 500 kgf, and the cylinder would weigh a negative 498 kgf. A complete set cylinder + block + chain weighed 2 kgf, as we verified by a scale at the hall.

Two extreme cases were considered.

In the first case, if we put too much weight on the coffin, the system would simply not go up.

The second scenario was more of a concern: the combined weight of the two girls would be 120 kgf. Summing up the tarpaulin, the chain, and the ropes to secure them together, the coffin could reach 150 kgf. In this case, the system would have an ascension force of 498 - 150 = 348 kgf or 3480 Newton's, considering $g = 10$ m/s^2. On the other hand, the total mass would be 498 + 150 = 648 kg. The upward acceleration of the system would be 3480 Newton/648 kg = 5.37 m/s^2. What would be the problem with such acceleration?

In one minute, our coffin would attain a velocity of 322 m/sec or 1150 km/hour. Of course, the air resistance would retard, but the air resistance itself would be our problem. We know that an object passing through the atmosphere at a high speed will burn due to friction. We see that in the meteors, which may attain speeds in excess of 20 km/sec.

In the case our girls attained too large speeds, the coffin might catch fire, the ropes would burn, and the girls would fall to Earth. The solution would be increasing the coffin weight in order to guarantee a slower rate of ascension. However, a too-slow rate of ascension would also be a problem, making the launching apparent to a casual observer. In other words, the girls should go up fast but not too fast and not too slow.

We decided to prepare everything at the carts hall, where all the necessary materials were in abundance. This, we would do the next day in the morning, with the launching scheduled to be done at night.

After dinner, my brother came up with an excellent idea:

"Jota, since they have died in a ritual, we should launch them in style too, ritual and everything else, the complete pack."

Fabiana would be sent with some soil to make up for the fact that she was not going to be interred in her natal country. As to Isobel, we would add some comforts like some jewels and food.

Next day in the morning we went to the carts hall where all we needed was there. What caught my attention there were some strange garments of orange color, hanging to hooks fixed to the wall. Each vest was composed of a body part and a headpiece. Thick gloves and boots completed each set. I removed one from the wall and could hardly raise it; such was its weight. No question they were radiation-proof garments, impregnated with lead.

"Luiz, I know how to remove the girls without being exposed to the radiation."

We put on the garments and went to the hall where the girls were resting. The first thing was to drag the table with the girls as far from the radioactive ampoules as possible. Then, in a hurry, we put together the 15 ampoules and formed a protection wall in front of them using lead bricks that were strewn on the floor. I knew those bricks well. They are called "lead castles" and are V-sided so that they fit together without leaving open crevices. And, they are quite an effective protection against radiation.

Then, already well protected against radiation and with no hurry, we wrapped the girls, temporarily, into a tarpaulin and brought the bodies to the cart's hall.

We took off our special outfits and got our attention to the materials available in the hall.

Firstly, we removed all the concrete blocks with their attached cylinders from one cart, leaving it completely empty. The carts were electric-driven, and their handling was quite simple. Using this empty cart, we went to the cave exterior and took some soil, placing it in robust plastic bags, along with a few pieces of grass. In the hall, we weighed the bags to 80 kgf. The material accompanying Fabiana was ready. Now, for Isobel's baggage. We went to Dome 2 and found Isobel's quarters. In contrast to her complex and malevolent personality, Isobel's quarters were simple and sparely furnished. We took some clothes that we thought to be nice ones. From the many boxes strewn onto the floor there were gold bracelets, necklaces with precious stones, a great variety of rings, many with precious stones. Another box had the usual assortment of food bars. We chose a variety of items and brought them down to the cart's hall.

"The remaining jewels we keep for our coffins!" my brother remarked.

The total weight of Isobel's items was 40 kgf. We then placed the girls onto the cart's empty platform and opened the tarpaulin. Their bodies were flaccid. We first tied the two girls together, face to face, using ropes. Then we wrapped them with a first layer of tarpaulin and, then, one more layer of ropes. While we were doing these procedures we kept a respectful demeanor. The second layer had the earth bags of Fabiana and Isobel's items. Then, we wrapped everything using a bigger tarpaulin. Finally, more ropes wraped the pack. Now, we weighed the complete "coffin" with the girls: 280 kgf. This, plus the chain weight, would be the load the cylinder had to carry into space.

Now, for the calculations: 498 kgf upward - 280 kgf downward =

218 kgf or 2180 Newtons. That was the ascension force. Total mass was $498 + 280 = 778$ kg

The upward acceleration: (Ascension force)/Mass $= 2180/778 =$ 2.8 m/s^2. We decided that this was a reasonably large acceleration but not large enough to the point of burning the girls by friction with the atmosphere.

Having done these preparations, we went to our Dome to rest. After dinner, in the dark, we would launch the girls to space.

Then, after dinner, came the moment. We were very nervous thinking about what we hadn't thought. Sometimes, obvious things are left aside.

We went to the carts hall, where everything was ready. The final preparation: we fixed a very strong rope to the chain hanging from the cylinder. The other extremity was made to do many turns around the coffin and many knots were done to guarantee a firm connection.

First, we had to move everything out of the cave into the open air of the night.

The night was very dark, with no moon. A cloudless sky gloriously starred. A cold wind blew from the south. The smell of the Eucalyptus trees, the sound of nocturnal animals and birds. I felt fear mixed with nostalgia. Two women that I knew, that I had exchanged caresses and kisses with: one innocent, the other perverse, united firmly together, poised to travel during millennia through the space. I remembered my talks with Fabiana and how much I had learned with her. With Isobel, I had experimented with seduction, had been introduced, briefly, to evil, and had suffered a beginning of domination.

Now, for the disconnecting procedure: it consisted in removing a screw that connected the lower link of the chain to a steel loop embedded into the concrete block below. That step seemed to us the most dangerous one. The screw was impeded to get loose by means of a nut and its friction with the chain.

The nut, preventing the screw from sliding from the loop on the concrete block, was carefully unscrewed. Now, to remove the screw, a rope was fixed to its head. I was to give a firm pull on the rope, loosening the screw. The coffin would be, from that moment on, connected only to the cylinder.

A fatal problem would be one of us getting entangled in the system and going up along the coffin to meet a terrible death.

My brother sprayed a lubricant onto the screw and the retaining loop on the concrete block. All our movements were, now, very slow and careful. We did a big knot in the rope extremity I was to pull. The idea was to give a big pull to the screw in order to remove it in a single strike.

My brother would be scanning the sky in search of planes that might collide with the coffin. The last thing we desired was a coffin with two girls, bags of earth, jewels, and food entering the turbine of a passenger jet.

"Now, Jota, in the 3, you pull the rope!" my brother shouted.

"1, 2...3"

I pulled the rope with all my strength. The screw escaped from the chain and the loop, almost hitting me. There was a strong bang, and everything shook.

I didn't look up. When I finally had the courage to look up, I saw nothing.

Fabiana and Isobel had gone on their voyage to infinity.

PART 4

Chapter 87
The Demon's Heart

It was an enormous relief for us to have sent to space the bodies of Fabiana and Isobel.

However, we still had another problem and also one which could put us in confrontation with the law: storage of radioactive materials requires many licenses in Brazil. Without those licenses, it is illegal.

I'm referring to the luminous capsules or ampoules that surrounded the bodies of Fabiana and Isobel. Our suspicion, regarding the luminous powder, was that it was Radium 226, one of the isotopes of the element Radium, which has a half-life of 1,600 years. This isotope became famous since it had been the main subject of Marie Curie's extraordinary scientific career, and that gave her one of her 2 Nobel Prizes. Her laboratory notebooks, exposed in some Parisian museums, are still quite radioactive. Radium 226, despite being radioactive, is not among the "dangerous" elements since it emits, essentially, alpha particles, which are not the most penetrating ones.

So, our concern was not relative to its risk to health. That we could handle. Our concern was regarding the law and the risk of our being put behind bars.

With all these questions in our minds, we decided to investigate deeper the regions annexed to the "radioactive hall".

My Friend Greg

The next day, in the morning, we went down to the "radioactive hall" and passed through it in search of the protective garments that were stored in the "carts' hall. "Wearing our heavy suits, we came back to the radioactive hall. We, immediately, improved the lead barrier around the radium capsules and, then, removed our garments, now not necessary anymore, since our counters were clicking at base level.

We could now explore more leisurely the hall, which seemed to be bigger than our initial impression. Its format was circular, like many others. To our surprise, there was at the wall the opening of another tunnel, at about 90 degrees from our entry tunnel, which we knew well. There was a light switch that we turned on, illuminating all the extension of the tunnel. This tunnel had no ventilation shafts, possibly being deeper. A rough estimation indicated we were 20 meters below ground.

We, soon, walked the whole length of this tunnel, about 50 meters. Then, we came to an enormous hall whose darkness added considerably to its apparent size. Switching on the lights it revealed to be some 45 meters in diameter and, also, perfectly circular. As opposed to the radioactive hall, which was essentially empty, this new hall was full of the most varied items. Two boring machines absolutely identical to our previous "friends" were resting against the wall. The circular wall was completely taken by shelves containing a great variety of objects.

We began keeping our attention to radioactivity signals, since we were "wearing" our counters. Our detectors, up to now, were giving only the baseline clicks. As we were following the circular wall we came to a small room protruding from the main circular wall. Even before entering this room, our counters began increasing the clicking rate, but not alarmingly so.

We entered the room.

Inside, there were many scattered items, some on the floor and others on small shelves close to the walls.

But what really caught our attention was a singular assembly.

A flat platform was mounted on an axis indicating, clearly, that it was meant to rotate around that axis, passing from its present horizontal position to a vertical one, in a clockwise fashion from our frontal perspective. On this platform, there were two metallic plates united by 2 robust and well lubricated hinges. As we were facing this contraption, we saw that the right side plate was firmly fixed to the routable platform by way of well-placed screws. The left side plate was not fixed to the platform. Its connection to the right-hand plate was only through the two hinges. Thus, this left-hand plate was free to rotate around the hinges. What was preventing this rotation was only the fact that the platform was, now, horizontal.

Attached, firmly, to each metallic plate was a metallic hemisphere. They were identical and gray-colored. The hemispheres were attached symmetrically at the outer border of each plate. Their flat faces were turned upward, but not exactly so. It was quite evident that if the left plate, by any chance, rotated over the right plate, the 2 hemispheres would match, forming a perfect sphere. Even the small angling of their flat surfaces suggested that each hemisphere was slightly inclined in the direction of the central hinge.

Since our counters were clicking faster but not alarmingly so, I dared to touch one hemisphere. It was decidedly warm. Approaching the counter to each hemisphere the clicking rate increased but, still, not much. There were two stools in the room, and we sat down to think.

Suddenly, I got it all. My heart rate increased, and my mouth dried as nausea invaded me, followed by a terrible fear.

I took some pictures using Greg's camera so that we could analyze the assembly without getting radiation.

My brother sensed my reaction and asked if I was feeling well.

"Let's get out of here, Luiz, and I will explain to you what I think this is."

We passed our known sequence of tunnels and ladders and got to Dome 2. We took some beers from the refrigerator and sat down on the sofas.

I handed my brother the camera with the photos.

"Look, Luiz, what we have here are the two halves of a sphere, possibly made of Plutonium 239. Being in the position they presently are, they can rest there for many years, even thousands of years. However, if they are joined together, forming one whole sphere, the two hemispheres attain a *critical mass* and, then, if the system has been designed correctly, we have a chain reaction and the sphere may explode as an atomic bomb. I'm not sure how fast or strongly the hemispheres must collide to create a "full" atomic bomb. Also, I don't know if what we have there is Plutonium 239 or Uranium 235. It may well be another element unknown to Earth science. But, if this was projected by Isobel, what I suspect, I suppose the idea was of an explosion, and a big one at that."

Then, I continued to describe to my brother what I knew since this subject has always interested me.

"The atomic bomb in the Trinity experiment and those thrown over Hiroshima and Nagasaki used this same configuration. The difference was that the sub-critical hemispheres were thrown to one another more violently, using a smaller non-nuclear bomb.

But, one such artifact was left unused and, even without exploding as a bomb, it caused the deaths of two scientists."

"Let's see it on the Internet, Luiz".

I found something on the Internet and we synchronized our cell phones to read. It was my brother who read to me. And I also put on some of my observations:

"In the months following the first atomic bombs, between 1945 and 1946, another group of scientists was trying to attain the critical mass without colliding two sub-critical hemispheres to one another, like it had been done in the Trinity experiment and at Hiroshima and Nagasaki bombings. The scientists had, in their hands, a subcritical complete sphere of Plutonium 239 that would be used as a bomb in Japan. But having Japan surrendered, this sphere was left over and available for experiments. This was a smaller sphere and could be left without causing problems. It emitted only weak alpha particles and low-energy neutrons.

But, there was a means of waking up this innocent sphere: by placing, around it, a neutron reflector. Now, the neutrons emitted by the sphere, that would calmly go away, were reflected back into the sphere, hitting plutonium atoms and fissioning them. The fissioned atoms liberated more neutrons that, instead of going away, were stubbornly reflected back to the sphere, generating more fission and more neutrons, creating a chain reaction. The effect would be the same as putting together two subcritical hemispheres.

The first accident with this sphere occurred on August 21, 1945. Harry Daghlian, a physicist, was experimenting with reflecting the neutrons with blocks of tungsten carbide. Accidentally, Daghlian let slip one of the blocks, which caused a non-explosive chain reaction that generated a flash of blue light and a strong heat wave. Behind these innocent effects was a fatal neutron burst. Daghlian died 25 days later from the radiation effects.

The second accident occurred in May 1946 with Louis Slotin in the same place and with the same plutonium sphere. This time, the neutron reflector was formed by two beryllium hemispheres arranged at some distance from the plutonium sphere. Slotin was regulating the reflector position using just a screwdriver. He was also showing off, wearing jeans and cowboy boots. His screwdriver slipped and the neutron reflector moved to a "wrong" position. The result was the same: a blue flash and a heat wave. Slotin died nine days later from radiation effects.

Due to these two accidents, the infamous Plutonium sphere was nicknamed the *Demon's core* or *Demon's heart.*

The famous American physicist Richard Feynman, a Physics Nobel Prize winner in 1965, compared the above experiments to

"tickling a dragon's tail."

While we were reviewing this interesting subject on the Internet and I was telling my brother some other information I had, Luiz looked at me with wide-open eyes. We got one more beer to calm down. And, I went on:

"Luiz, someone, probably Isobel, assembled that system in order to explode part of the facilities in the farm. Some form of revenge, maybe," and, I kept talking:

"Anyway, whatever had been her aim in assembling this "bomb," her project has been interrupted with her death. The two halves of the "Demon's heart" will cause no harm while they remain on that platform and the platform remains horizontal. In order that the hemispheres join and explode, it would be necessary that the platform rotated to the vertical position". And, I went on:

"Not even too radioactive the hemispheres are since they emit only alpha particles and low energy neutrons," I concluded.

Luiz began looking fixedly at me. Then, he threw his beer can to the floor and shouted:

"Jota, you are wrong! Let's go there immediately!"

We rushed down the ladders, through the tunnels, and got to the room where the two halves of the Demon's core were innocently lying down on the platform. We didn't even take the radiation counters with us. As we neared the platform, my brother said:

"Listen, Jota, just listen!"

Luiz was right. I was, now, hearing a tic-tac, which seemed to be coming from a big clock.

Probably, when we were here with the counters, the clock's tic-tac got mixed with the counters' clicks and, this, confused me.

But, it didn't confuse my brother.

Then, I remembered that Luiz, having had a problem with his left ear, lost much of his hearing on that side. Curiously, his right ear developed into a much more sensitive hearing apparatus.

"Yes, Luiz, you are right. There is something keeping the time."

Then, we saw it.

Partially hidden behind many pieces of shelves, piles of books, manuals, and dirt was an old and dusty pendulum clock. The face, however, hadn't the hands. A weight was hanging from a delicate chain. The other side of the chain seemed to be connected to an escape wheel, whose frequency was controlled by an enormous pendulum, which was oscillating slowly. All that paraphernalia was connected to another gear system, now visible to us, behind the mobile platform. The gear system acted on the clock's single hand: the rotating platform!

"Look, Jota, the platform is set to turn on a clockwise direction, like a clock's hands!" shouted my brother.

"Don't take your eyes off the platform, Jota!" shouted my brother again.

Nothing happened.

We kept our eyes locked to the platform.

Then, after 20 minutes, we saw it! The platform gave a popping sound and turned almost imperceptibly. Without the sound, we wouldn't be able to see the change. But it had changed!

"The system is armed, Luiz!"

We could see that the rotating platform was already some 5 degrees deviated from the horizontal position. However, we couldn't verify when the system had been set to work or, in other words, armed.

"Look, Luiz, as soon as the platform gets to the vertical position, the left-hand plate, carrying the left hemisphere, will be above the right hemisphere. With one or two clicks more of the platform, the left plate, along with its hemisphere will rotate rapidly on the hinge and will smash into the right hemisphere. Then, the 2 hemispheres will be joined into one supercritical mass. And, then, booooommmmm!"

"Let's disarm the system!" shouted my brother, running to the pendulum.

I held him by the arm.

"Luiz, don't do that, please! You don't know, Isobel! Her IQ is 1300! And she is very cunning. When you have that IQ, and you are bad, then you can be really bad!"

"She was expecting us to do something smart; to disable the workings of the mechanism, something she would do herself. But we are going to do the opposite, Luiz."

"She, certainly left a trap, for anyone trying to disable the mechanism. We are in no hurry; this thing will not go off now!" I insisted.

Then, we calmed down and began to examine the system. I was right: the mechanism was more complex than one might think at first sight.

We found a strong spring, cocked behind the table, which would be released if any of the many parts of the system were touched. This spring was directly connected to an independent mechanism able to rotate the platform instantaneously. And, then...

"Luiz, we need to act on the final step. We have to prevent the platform rotation."

We decided to make many changes to the system. Firstly, we moved some concrete blocks beneath the right side of the platform to the right of its axis of rotation. And, we did this without touching the underside of the platform. This would prevent further rotation of the platform.

Then, we began looking for some strong iron bars in order to attach the 2 plates to one another, preventing their folding at the hinge. For this, we had to comb the main hall.

My attention was caught by a great number of 200-liter plastic barrels with screwed lids. They were all dusty, revealing not having been handled recently. One of the barrels, however, was not dusty, and a viscous and clear fluid seemed to have leaked from the top. I rotated the lid counterclockwise to release it and pulled it off. The barrel was full of a clear viscous and inodorous fluid. Its interior was dark due to the low illumination of the hall. I shone my flashlight to the inside. Immediately, I let off the lid and shouted at my brother. He came running. We illuminated the barrel interior with our combined flashlights. Inside, the face of Frederico, open-eyed, looked at us. It was entirely covered by the liquid.

"Well, Luiz, in this packaging, he will last for centuries. No worry with him now!"

The other barrels also had glycerin, but we decided not to examine their insides. At least not now! The first sample had been enough.

Resting against the wall of the main hall, there were many shelves. Scanning them, I found a box labeled: *High-performance silicone glue*. That was what I was looking for. I took many tubes of that glue and went back to the small room. The first thing I did was to glue the left plate to the rotating platform, preventing it from folding. Then, my brother came with many iron bars, and we glued them to the whole extension of the plates. Now, they were fixed to one another, and this was one more impediment to their folding.

Our plan was to return more times to this small room and see if we had not left something undone.

We were now exhausted physically and emotionally. We made the entire trip back to Dome 2 and, from it, to our dome. On our way through the fresh evening I told my brother of the things I knew about Isobel and of what I suspected of Frederico. I remembered Frederico's warning: "Watch out for her!" Her, who? Isobel? Had Isobel planned everything? The destruction of the buildings using a bomb? Might the two of them, Isobel and Frederico, act in concert? Had Frederico relayed to Isobel the communication between Dr Felder and Antonina regarding my case? Why had the family left the farm? Why didn't Isobel follow them? Had Isobel eliminated Frederico? We probably would never know!

Chapter 88

The Embryo's Lab

The next day, we came back to the large hall where we had found the armed "bomb" and Frederico's body. The low and unequal illumination of the place prevented us to fathom the big dimension of this hall. It was way larger than we initially perceived.

Hitting the curved walls with clenched fists, I found that they did not seem to be massive concrete like all the circular halls we had encountered up to now. Rather, the wall seemed to be more like a divisor wall. And, this divisor wall seemed to surround the hall in its entire curved perimeter.

The idea coming immediately to my mind was that this sort of internal wall delimited a curved room that surrounded the main hall. As such, the main hall would be delimited by two circular walls. One of them being internal and only divisor and an external one, structural.

But, how to access this compartment between the two walls?

We, then, began to walk along the wall, searching for an aperture or door. Behind some displaced shelves and disguised as part of the wall, we found a massive door, more appropriate for an industrial freezer.

The door was closed but not locked. Actually, it didn't have a keyed locking system. Instead, what kept the door closed was a massive bolt, lever type, fitted to a rail at the jamb. We moved up the lever, freeing the door. Pulling it open we saw that it was thick and thermal insulated. There wasn't, however, a mechanism for opening the door from the inside. Since the episode of the traitor gate, we have been very cautious regarding "temperamental" doors. As such, before entering the compartment, we put many pieces of wood on the door jamb to prevent the door from closing behind us.

As we entered, we saw a huge curved corridor. It was dark but, as we turned on the lights, a very long and curved laboratory was revealed. Its width would be 5 meters, but its extension was unfathomable from our position. The room was occupied by an immense lab bench at the external wall. The bench was well constructed in what appeared to be inox steel. It supported all that is found in a biological lab. There were sinks of many types: faucets, Bunsen burners, vacuum inlets, and oxygen and nitrogen outlets. The opposite wall, or the internal wall of the corridor, was essentially either for storage materials or for large equipment like big ovens, deep freezers, and refrigerators. Also, at the internal wall, were large glass covered closets containing glassware. The internal wall also had other big equipment, like HPLC, DNA sequencers and spectrometers.

This curved lab was very long and appeared to surround all the extensions of the main hall.

And, we continued to walk along its curved extension. Some 60 meters ahead, we began to see large Dewar flasks, certainly containing liquid nitrogen. These tanks weren't new to me but, these, in particular, had enormous sizes. Dewar tanks contain, usually, liquid nitrogen at -196 degrees Celsius and are employed as a storage medium for many types of biological preparations like semen, embryos, cells, etc. I counted roughly 20 big Dewars. Their height was 1.5 meters, and their width was some 60-70 cm. They were supported over robust wheeled platforms. The Dewars were closed at their tops by big and sophisticated lids.

Some of the benches nearby had microscopes, stereomicroscopes, ultraviolet microscopes, and inverted microscopes. Sophisticate micromanipulators were also distributed over the benches. Many types of elaborate lamps were seen, fixed to the ceiling or supported above the benches.

"What do those tanks hold?" my brother asked, pointing to the big Dewar flasks.

"Let's take a look, Luiz"

The Dewar flask I was about to open was closed by means of a big screwed lid. Below that, there was another lid pressed down onto a big O-ring at the border. At its center, this lid had an aperture or valve of sorts, whose function seemed, to me, to regulate the pressure inside the flask. I opened this internal lid by lifting it around a hinge. Inside, there was liquid nitrogen. Hanging from an internal circular shelf, there were metallic wires with a looped head. The wires were dipping into the liquid nitrogen. I took one wire and, on its end, there was a basket containing many glass ampoules.

Using a large tweezers from a nearby bench I took one ampoule and returned the wire with its basket to the Dewar, closing both lids.

"We are going to discard this ampoule probably, but we need to know what we have here," I said to my brother.

I took the ampoule to one of the big stereomicroscopes on the bench. I adjusted the power to 80 X and illuminated the ampoule with a focus lamp. The loupe was connected to a small monitor display at its top, and my brother could see, through it, what I was seeing at the eyepieces.

What we saw was a human embryo, semi-translucent under the strong lamp. It seemed to be dead but, about 10 minutes later, its heart began to beat. I knew it wouldn't be long before the heart stopped because of a lack of oxygen. And it wouldn't be possible to return the embryo to the nitrogen, since the deep freezing process goes through steps that can't be reversed.

After about 20 minutes, the tiny heart stopped beating. The small creature was dead.

We went on through the lab. It seemed endless. As we moved along, the lights were sparser and the lab appeared to be less used, with many items stacked on the benches, some below. After some meters, we had to resort to our flash light, so bad was the illumination. Finally, we got to the end of the long laboratory corridor.

Chapter 89

The Indian Cemetery

At the end part of the curved laboratory and at the external wall, there was a steel door with three bolted levers. The door was clearly locked from the inside since the three levers, one at 12 o'clock, the other at 3 o'clock, and the last at 6 o'clock, were firmly hooked at their corresponding supports at the jamb. Judging by the size of the hinges and the door size itself, 2 m wide and 3 m tall, the door seemed to be quite heavy.

We opened the door but remained inside the lab. A light wind came in our direction, bringing the smell of earth, soil, and rotten things. My olfaction, still rather sensitive, signaled something bad, terrifying. The door opened to what seemed an enormous cave since our flashlights didn't reflect on any wall. Also, it was pitch-dark.

Now, we turned our attention to the door. There were no levers on the other side: the door couldn't be opened from the lab's exterior. Then, before we went through the doorway, we collected all sorts of things to block the door closure. This wasn't difficult, given the amount of discarded items strewn across the lab's floor.

In order to get to the outside ground, about 2 meters below the door, we descended down a well-constructed ladder, fixed at both extremities. We, then, stepped onto the ground below, which was not paved. A terrible feeling invaded me. The darkness and enormity of the place and that smell of decomposition gave me a feeling of death. My brother was silent.

As we moved our flashlights along the walls and roof, it became clear to us that we were inside a natural cave. The walls and the roof formed a single natural and rough rocky surface. The cave was elongated. In the region where we stood the average width was 25 meters and the height about 15 meters, the roof being approximately domed.

My brother was now terrified and suggested we got out of that place.

"Let's walk a little more and, then, we get out, Luiz," I remarked.

Then, my brother suggested that we left some lighted candles to mark our way. The only reference we had to our back journey was the weak light coming from the open door which was becoming smaller and smaller as we moved on.

We had brought about 50 candles and some tens of matchboxes.

We placed lighted candles at every 10 meters. The ground was like rammed earth and was damp. Without sunlight, no plants grew, only mushrooms.

We did not walk much, maybe 7 candles before the first ceramic urn appeared. It was a big one, more than a meter high and about that as wide. It was decorated with beautiful indigenous motifs. The urn had a robust lid, fitting with its aperture on the top. We threw our lights, and more urns became visible. There was some order in the way the urns were placed over the earthen ground. They were arranged in two rows, leaving a broad passage between them. The urns weren't identical, though.

"Let's take a look inside, Jota!"

"Are you sure you want to look, Luiz?"

"Well, you suggested looking then you look first!" I said, laughing and tapping Luiz's shoulder.

I lifted the urn's heavy lid and placed it, carefully, on the ground.

My brother threw his lantern's light inside.

"Let's get out from here, Jota!" he shouted.

I illuminated the inside with my lantern.

What I saw wasn't nice. Luiz was right. A mummified male Indian with noble features and a beautiful headpiece was crouching inside the urn. Even crouched and mummified, it was possible to discern the haughty face of an Indian chief holding his weapons.

It was necessary to have a coffee laced with a generous portion of brandy to calm down my brother.

We decided not to open more urns, at least today.

The urns were, certainly, remains of an old Indian cemetery reserved for chiefs. The ordinary members were probably left to be eaten by the forest's animals.

As we were preparing to return to the laboratory, my brother said:

"Wait, Jota, keep quiet for a minute, will you?"

Then, Luiz began to move among the urns. As he kept distancing from the door of the lab I stacked two more candles into the ground. I heard nothing but knew Luiz did.

Fifty more meters and 5 candles, Luiz stopped and crouched behind an urn. I threw my light to the ground. A woman was lying down, moaning feebly.

I took from my backpack a thermos with coffee and approached the cup to her mouth while my brother lifted her head. She drank, slowly, the coffee with brandy and, then, began to cry. She was very dirty and emaciated but I clearly recognized her.

It was Mayra.

We managed to carry Mayra into the laboratory. We went to the well-illuminated portion and lay her down on an empty bench. I gave her more coffee with brandy, water, and orange juice. I also cleaned her face with a towel soaked in warm water. This fortified her enough to let us help her walk to the great hall.

There, we found a stretcher and laid her down on it.

I went to Dome 2 and brought down clothes and solid food. We needed to feed her well in order that she could climb the ladders to Dome

2. Then, we took care of her during all that night.

The next morning, Mayra was strong enough to follow us up to Dome 2. There, she rested during all day. In the evening she was able to have dinner with us at the table in Dome 2. She had recovered well and was another person, laughing and talking. We all slept at Dome 2. The next morning, I brought my car from Dome 1, and we took Mayra to our Dome and accommodated her in her own container. Mayra slept all day. In the evening, we all had dinner together.

Chapter 90
Mayra's narrative (Part 1)

The next day, very early in the morning, Mayra woke us. She had prepared a nice breakfast.

Then, after breakfast, I asked Mayra to tell us what had happened to her.

"I was already dominated by Yuri and didn't have any more initiative. He placed me with the cloning team in that lab close to the Indian cemetery you have found me."

"I was happy, since I had been transformed into a sort of zombie. My internal conflicts seemed to have disappeared. But, deep inside me, something was shouting out. Yuri had been perverse since he made use of his domination over me to use me sexually. Actually, this didn't hurt me much since he was kind and delicate."

"Things, for me, went by like in a movie. I had reached a point where I couldn't do anything by my own will and, actually, I appeared to have lost my will. At the same time, I needed Yuri at my side. I couldn't stand being away from him."

Hearing this, I remembered my crises but didn't say anything.

While describing her predicament to us, Mayra began to get emotional, and her eyes got wet.

"What will be of me now? I have no more my job and have no home!" she said while, now, decidedly weeping.

"Calm down, Mayra. Now you are family and will be living with us. You have a container here, all to yourself. The one you are occupying right now."

"And, here, there is a copy of the Dome's keys. You are free to enter and leave without giving us any explanations."

Mayra thanked us, stopped crying, and went on with her story:

"Since to access the laboratory we needed to go through Dome 2, I often met Isobel and Fabiana. We got friendly and I began having lunch and even dinner with them. This was when Yury allowed me.

Later, as I got more intimate with them, we often bathed all three of us in the Jacuzzi. After some time, I perceived that Isobel began taking some special interest in me"

"I had the impression that she wanted to dominate me in order to revenge Yuri or to just have me under her domain. She said bad things about Yuri and that I would be better off abandoning him and staying with her. However, my work and relation with Yuri weren't modified by this."

"And what exactly would be your work, Mayra?" I asked.

"I'll tell you about my work later since, now, I want to continue on with my story."

"Everything began to change with a rumor that police would be investigating the farm, that there had been a people's traffic suspicion. And Yuri assembled us and told us that we would need to abandon the farm in a few days."

"The next day began an intense activity here, many trucks being loaded with equipment and leaving the farm. I couldn't follow this operation closely since I had to stay in the lab all day long. Some days later, Yuri said that everyone needed to leave the farm and that I would have to follow him. I got scared but didn't say anything. Silently, I got a big backpack, loaded it with cereal and chocolate bars, and my personal things, and ran into the Eucalyptus forest. I hid there for two days."

For some reason, founded in my instincts, I got the impression that Mayra was not telling the whole truth. However, I couldn't identify the false from the true parts of her narrative.

And, Mayra went on:

"Slowly and cautiously, I began moving from my hiding place to check things. I was afraid of approaching Dome 1 and, since I was closer to Dome 2, decided to check things there. Even from a distance, I saw there were people living in the dome. Fabiana, who was outside, saw me and called me within. There, was also Isobel. They asked if I had run away, and I confirmed. They had also hidden among the Eucalyptus trees when they knew they would have to move out of the farm."

"Isobel invited me to stay living with them in the dome, provided I would help with the house chores. I promptly accepted since I had no home, no job, and no money. I shared the bedroom with Fabiana. But, soon, things began to turn badly. Isobel was treating me like a servant and giving me orders. Then, she changed and got friendlier with me, only a bit too friendlier as the days went on. She began taking some liberties with me, invited me to sleep in her room, and treated me so well to the point that I felt Fabiana was getting jealous.

During the Jacuzzi baths, that we took daily, Isobel insisted that I took all my clothes. Soon, she began touching me and spreading sunscreen onto my body. And, then, telling me to do the same with her body. During those cream-spreading sessions, Isobel looked, fixedly, into my eyes. I had no energy to repel those advances and feared that she would expel me from the farm in case I refused. Isobel had absolute control of all things on the farm and in the dome. She used two cars that were left abandoned. She had plenty of money, and we often went to the city to buy things. She had bank cards, and I suspect she had an apartment there. And she bought me presents, and some expensive ones. Other presents she gave me were from her own stock of jewels and precious stones.

Then, during the Jacuzzi baths, began the kisses. Isobel began caressing me and kissing my arms, then my shoulders. I had no initiative to refuse. Soon, in the following days, Isobel began kissing my neck and massaging me down and down. In the next few days, she began kissing my mouth and, kiss, she did, my God. That woman was a kissing machine!"

"Slowly, I felt I was surrendering to her, and I began to feel pleasure too. My head began to light up, and my necessity of Yuri was growing less and less."

"During those "loving" sessions, Fabiana kept smiling at me and. repeatedly. looking at Isobel as if waiting for some orders or instructions. And, she advised me to accept the situation since it would be good for me in the long run."

My God, I thought, *I've seen that movie before!*

"As I told you, I had no place to go and decided to adapt to the "house rules". After dinner, in the evenings, we talked: me and Isobel. Fabiana was always silent and only talked with me when she and I were alone."

"Many nights, Isobel slept with Fabiana, and I was free to go out and walk. Also, I had the key to the dome and could have some time for myself, no questions asked. I could go in and out at any time. That was one good side of the arrangement I had put myself into."

"However, I was taking my precautions and, under the pretext that I had things to do in the lab, I was almost everyday there. In my backpack I carried foods in the form of non-perishable. I stored everything in the freezers, which were working normally there. In this way, in case Isobel and Fabiana left the farm, I had a few weeks of survival."

At this point in Mayra's narrative, my brother said:

"You wait please; I think there is some leak of water."

Soon, he called me to help him "with the leak."

I went to see what Luiz needed, and when we were out of range from Mayra:

"Jota, Mayra didn't mention Antonina's death! And she certainly was present at the farm!" he whispered to me.

"Yes, Luiz and she doesn't know that we know of Antonina's death!

That was it. I sensed that Mayra was not telling all the facts. And, I was probably right.

"Sorry, Mayra, those water leaks, you know," I said.

And, as we resumed our talk, Mayra went on:

"However, things began to get sour. Isobel insisted in an approximation, even more intimate than the kisses and caresses, and she appeared to be insatiable. And, also, she began resenting my refuses."

"One day, as I was going from the lab to the dome, I passed a small room and saw a light inside. I went to take a look and saw Isobel, Fabiana, and Frederico assembling some equipment there. Seeing me, Isobel got furious, took an iron bar, and went after me. I managed to hit her with my backpack and while she recovered, I went running back to the lab. I entered the lab and slammed the door against her. She got hit in the head and fell momentarily to the floor. Without waiting a second, I ran through the lab. But she didn't follow me. And I heard her shouting:

"You, ungrateful bitch! You want to stay there? Then, stay forever and rot there!"

"And, I heard the door being slammed shut in the distance."

"I kept very quiet and tried to calm down. I had food for many days and an unlimited supply of water. Then, I began to think. I knew well the other door of the lab, the one leading to the Indian cemetery cave where you found me. This cave is long and a bit tortuous. The cemetery is only the initial segment, having about 150 meters of extension. Then, the cave ramifies into three arms: the central segment ends at the main cave hall and opens there by means of a heavy door that opens only from the side of the great hall. This door, as I remembered, remained permanently open. I knew well the cemetery cave since I went there almost every day to collect material from the Indian mummies for the DNA. Many times Yuri went with me. The cemetery cave has no illumination, and we can't change the positions of the urns. Those were conditions that needed to be respected for preserving Indian traditions."

"As I rested, and ate a chocolate bar, I began to think what Isobel would or might do with me. Certainly, I had seen something I shouldn't and the three of them might want to eliminate me. Also, Isobel knew I could go to the Indian cemetery and, from there, arrive at the door to the great hall. Once in the great hall, I knew an escape route that I was sure Isobel didn't know."

"An annex of the great hall was our hospital, where I had worked many and many hours treating the sick Landians arriving to stay on Earth. And I knew some exit shafts from there. The hospital was my territory! And, there, I knew how to deal with Isobel!"

"So, I became almost certain that Isobel would anticipate me and try to close the door from the cemetery cave to the main cave hall. Then, I took some emergency lights, loaded my backpack with food, and hurried to the cemetery and, from there, to the door to the main cave. The route was long, dark, and slippery up to the final portion, which was paved. Running the fastest I could I, finally, arrived at the door. It was locked from the outside. Isobel had run ahead of me; either she or Frederico. I don't think Fabiana would be trusted with that task."

"Then, I returned in the direction of the lab in a hurry since there was no way I could stay in that dark and gloomy place.

Getting back to the Indian cemetery I saw, at a distance, the illuminated doorway of the laboratory, and I ran desperately to there."

"As I got to about 100 meters from the door, I saw, against the light rectangle delimiting the doorway, the silhouette of Isobel; and she shouted:

"Die there, you bitch. I'll come later to put you into an urn!"

Then, she slammed shut the door and I heard the heavy lever locks being engaged to the jamb."

"I was, now, imprisoned in the cave."

"My backpack was full of food and water was no problem since it dripped from the roof. I didn't risk exploring the ramifications of the cave since I feared getting lost."

"I had been a Girl Scout in my teens and took it seriously. I knew how to survive in the jungle and desert. But what I needed now was how to break down some doors. However, I knew their solidity. Not to count that Isobel might be waiting for me."

But, then, Mayra abruptly stopped her narrative and got frightened:

"But, wait; where are Fabiana and Isobel?"

"Mayra, we were just waiting for you to ask this!" I said, looking firmly into her eyes.

Mayra blushed immediately and lowered her eyes. But she didn't say anything.

"Isobel and Fabiana are dead. And they were launched to space," I said.

I then explained to her the details of how we found them and the launching of them to space using the negative mass.

Then, I explained to Mayra the terrible contraption that Isobel had assembled in that small room.

It was getting late, and we saw Mayra yawn many times. Thus, I suggested that we should go to bed, and the next day, Mayra would continue her narrative.

The next morning, I woke up earlier than usual and went to the kitchen to get some water. It was then that I heard a key turning in the dome's door and Mayra entered, panting, carrying a backpack. She said she had left early to do some jogging before preparing our breakfast at the regular time. However, I clearly saw that this was an excuse but said nothing. At the breakfast, Mayra looked tired, with the typical countenance of someone who hadn't slept well. In effect, as soon as we finished breakfast, she excused, saying she had a headache and that she had trained too strongly; and went to her container.

In the late morning, my brother and I were talking in the main hall when Mayra came out from her room, carrying a renovated and happy face.

"If you want, I can continue my narrative, and later, I will make a nice lunch for us!" Mayra said.

"And, what about Antonina; had she left with the others?" she asked in initiating the talk.

I had the clear impression that this question was not sincere, but didn't say anything. I looked at my brother, and he nodded discreetly.

"Mayra, we have bad news to give you: Antonina is dead. She left a letter to me saying she would kill herself, jumping from the cliff."

However, I didn't enter in the letter details, of which not even my brother knew.

"And, Mayra, we saw Antonina dead...." and, then, I explained to her everything we saw at the tomb.

Mayra's reaction to the news of Antonina's death, our finding her in the chamber, the tomb, etc, was quite strange. In none of his comments and questions regarding our information, I saw sincerity and correspondence between the related facts, her questions asked and her facial expressions.

Despite Mayra denoting surprise and consternation with the news we gave her, my impression was that she was acting, at least in part of her reactions. Also, Mayra didn't do the questions that were supposed to be made.

I need to repeat, here, something about me, regarding this sort of questioning. I give importance to all people say to me. But I give the same or even greater importance to what they don't say when they should say. And also to what they don't ask when they should ask. In the special case of Mayra, the questions she didn't ask when she should ask were:

How did you find Antonina's body?

Where is her tomb? How did you find her tomb?

How did you know it was Antonina's body?

If you saw her body, in what state was it? Decomposed?

Was she disfigured? Was her face covered?

However, the questions Mayra did were:

"But how did you find the entry for Antonina's tomb?"

"How did you certify she was dead?"

Another very curious fact was that after this talk Mayra didn't ask more questions regarding Antonina.

Chapter 90

Mayra's narrative (Part 2)

"During my prison in the cemetery cave I rationed food and saved the batteries of the lanterns. Fortunately, there were no rats or bats there since there were lots of traps containing poison. Also, there were no holes or apertures for animal entry."

"After some period there and with no cycles of day/night, I lost count of the passage of time. Depression came, and I lost my will."

"Each day, I was weaker and weaker, and my initiative abandoned me. I feared to explore the other branches of the cave since I could easily get lost."

When we found Mayra she had, in her backpack, only 2 bars of chocolate and 2 bars of cereal.

"Mayra, what specifically was your work at the group?" I asked

"My basic formation was Medicine and, then, I had training in Intensive Therapy. Later, I specialized in Molecular Biology."

"My work on the farm was to produce embryos from the genetic material obtained from the Indian mummies. From this material we produced clones. The technology for cloning came entirely from Landa, be it equipment, protocol or personnel. I just followed protocols under Yuri's supervision. There were many researchers working in the lab. I, also, attended at the farm's hospital, but that was a minor part of my duties".

It became clear to me and Luiz why Yuri kept Mayra under close vigilance. And, Mayra went on.

"The Landians have registers of all births and deaths as well of marriages from all notary houses, churches and parishes in the entire world. With this information, they can generate false papers for most Landians. These data also helped in finding genetic material from some famous figures."

"I'll give you an example: this Indian cemetery is very old and has been studied for more than 100 years by Landian scientists. The bodies in the urns are important chiefs. One of the Yuri's projects, helped by other Landian researchers, was producing clones of these chiefs and sending the embryos to Landa by the thousands. These embryos are implanted in Landian women who desire to have Earthian babies."

"And why do those women want Earthian babies?" I asked.

"I thought they had already told you about this, Jota!"

"This is part of a project to increase the population of Earthians in Landa. The Earthians are eventually adopted by Landians to become Lambs and then they go to living in Landian households."

"But, Mayra, tell me, are those Lambs a sort of slaves in Landa? What is their role there?" I asked while my brother looked at me open-eyed.

"That, I was not informed of, Jota. What I know is that Landian women who give birth to Earthian babies get many benefits from the system. Anyway, I'm not going to Landa so how should I be concerned with this?"

"Well, Mayra, I sort of thought that you had talked with Fabiana during your stay at Dome 2. You said you had got friendly with her. What things did she tell you about the Lambs?"

"One of the things Fabiana told me was that they sell embryos to specialized clinics here on Earth. In Landa, the embryos either will be Lambs or live in Earthian colonies."

"And what about me, Mayra, what did Yuri say about my function here?" I asked Mayra: no answer.

"You got friends with Fabiana, right?" "Yes"

"What things did she tell you about Lambs here and in Landa?": no answer.

"What did Fabiana tell you about Isobel? She told me she loved Isobel". "Yes, Fabiana told me this same thing."

"Did they tell you, Mayra, about the *Permanent Lambs*?" "No, no one told me this."

Then, Mayra went on with her narrative:

"At each voyage from Earth to Landa, thousands of Earthian embryos are sent, frozen, inside the Dewar flasks. And, once there, as I told you, the embryos are implanted into Landian women who want to have Earthian babies."

"Also, those embryos cloned from Indian chiefs are quite valuable even here on Earth. We had numerous meetings in a special room at the lab where those subjects were discussed in English since many Earthians participated. I was informed that embryos cloned from famous dead people are quite valuable here on Earth. The reproduction clinics scattered over our entire planet offer them at high prices. What about having a baby cloned from a movie star, a Nobel Prize winner, a war hero, an astronaut, a King?"

Chapter 91

Launching Number 2

I told Mayra that we had found the body of Frederico and that, probably, he had been killed by Isobel.

"Mayra, there are three things that we must eliminate from the farm since these things can complicate our lives:

"The "bomb", Frederico's body and the embryos."

My initial idea was to bury Frederico along with the embryos. However, the hemispheres of the Demon's heart might be a problem.

"Let's solve all three problems at the same time and in the same package. We just send them all to space!" said Luiz.

"Frederico and the embryos will have a dignified burial, and the bomb may explode anywhere in the Universe."

The idea was approved immediately by all.

The next day, Mayra knocked at my door:

"Time to wake up. Breakfast is ready!"

She looked well-disposed and happy.

At the breakfast Mayra was talkative and gave suggestions on how we should organize our launching.

Well-fed and in high spirits, we went to Dome 2 and, from there, to the great hall that was encircled by the laboratory. The room with the "bomb" was there. The rotating platform, coupled to the pendulum clock, had moved, maybe, 1 degree.

We took Frederico's body from the barrel and extended it on the floor, having put a tarpaulin before. At his chest, there was a hole that continued all the way to his back. It was a typical shot from a laser rifle. We then wrapped the body with some layers of tarpaulin, of which there were stacks of all sizes. We chose adequate ropes and wrapped him firmly. On the shelves, there was a great assortment of ropes of many types.

Our idea was to make a single pack with Frederico, the bomb, and the embryos.

While my brother and I were preparing Frederico, Mayra went to the laboratory carrying many bags of super-resistant plastic. She would remove all ampoules from the Dewars and place them into the bags along with plenty of Styrofoam beads to prevent their breaking.

With respect to the "bomb," we simply removed the screws that were attaching the right plate to the platform. Then, we had the two plates with their hemispheres. The plates were already fixed to one another by iron bars and could not fold.

After those preliminaries, we began the assembling of the "payload" for the launch.

Frederico's pack was tied firmly to a stretcher so the body would not fold. On the opposite side of the stretcher, we tied the package with the bomb. The bags with the embryos were now assembled into a larger bag, which was tied firmly on Frederico's legs. The whole package, plus a counterweight in the form of a bag of soil, hit 300 kg on the scale. The calculation of masses and accelerations was performed by my brother, and I chose to spare the reader from this interesting exercise.

Fortunately, the tunnels linking the great hall to the carts' hall allowed the passage of carts.

In the carts hall, we took a concrete block plus its negative -mass cylinder and loaded it into our cart.

Then, we all mounted onto the cart and my brother drove us up to the big cave hall and from there to the external sliding door. We left everything in the corridor, exited from the main door, closed it, and went home to rest. The next day, in the evening, we would launch.

Launch day.

We had dinner as usual and went by car to Dome 2. There, we went down to the radioactive hall, carts hall, great cave hall, cave corridor, and external door. There, our cart with the payload was awaiting us. Opening the cave's sliding door, we came to the open night. The atmospheric conditions were: starred sky, no moon, and weak wind from the southwest. The usual scent of the Eucalyptus forest and the chorus of the night animals brought to my recent memory the launch of Isobel and Fabiana. Where would they be by now?

But, back to business:

We would launch directly from the cart platform. Mayra was scanning the sky for airplanes. Luiz and I were at the business end of the launch. This time, Luiz was to pull the rope, and I would follow the ascension.

I'm not sure how Luiz did the mathematics for the launch. This time, the payload climb was calmer. But it accelerated fast, and in about 10 seconds, it merged with the night. Frederico, along with some hundreds of embryos, were becoming mere specks in the Universe.

Chapter 92

The launching platform

One morning, after breakfast, we asked Mayra to tell us about the geography of the cave system.

"What we know as the cemetery cave is, actually, a complex of 3 different caves", she began. "Beginning with the exit door from the laboratory, we emerge into the cemetery itself, which is non-paved and contains the urns. Some 50 meters after the last urns, there comes the paved part of the cave, which goes all the way to the door separating from the main cave hall. But, this elongated cave has 2 arms: a left arm and a right arm. Both arms are caves themselves, being part of the same cave complex, which includes the main cave hall and its corridor leading to the external door."

"The cemetery part of this cave complex is not paved to comply with the Indian traditions. The Landians are firm followers of traditions and rituals, as you probably have observed."

"To the Landians, the dead, be of whatever origin, should be rigorously reverenced. Landians are, in general, opposed to conventional burial under the ground. They consider important some degree of body preservation. All the actions of Landians are permeated by rituals, as Yuri told me many times" (and I knew from experience).

The next day, we waited for Mayra to call us for breakfast since we had planned to explore the left arm of the cave. However, the time was 6:15, and Mayra didn't call us. I knocked at her door with no answer. Soon after, Mayra came into the dome, panting and sweating profusely.

"Sorry, sorry, I went to jog and got lost in the trail."

However, Mayra looked tired, but not the typical tiredness of healthy physical exercise. She looked worn out, like someone who didn't sleep well or had done some tiresome manual job. Following our policy of trust, we asked nothing of her.

But, despite being tired, she kept to our plan and refused to postpone it. We helped her with preparing the breakfast and we had a nice breakfast.

Our backpacks were loaded with survival equipment, carefully selected by Mayra, according to her Girl Scout Survival Manual, Level 3. Some examples: ropes, guidelines, candles, matches, lanterns and batteries, solid food, liquid food and paste food. Cell phones, first care kit, etc, etc, etc.

We got to the Dome 2 by car and assembled everything there. We decided to follow the route from the lab's external door, passing through the cemetery. That way, we didn't need to go outdoors.

We left Dome 2 and descended to the radioactive hall (where Isobel and Fabiana were found dead). From there to the great hall then, through the laboratory and, then, to the cemetery. At all doors we prevented their accidental closure using pieces of wood thrown at the jamb.

Beginning at the external laboratory door, going to the cemetery, we hooked our guideline, just as an additional precaution, since Mayra knew this part well. Then, as we were walking, we extended the guideline. Passing the cemetery section, we came to the paved segment of the corridor. After about 100 meters, there was the entrance of a natural tunnel at almost 90 degrees to the left. We had come to the left arm of the cave.

Now, from here, began unknown territory for all the 3 of us.

"None of the arms I know since my way was limited to the main corridor, between the laboratory and the main cave hall," Mayra told us.

At the crossroads, we attached the guideline to a stone and went down to the left arm. This corridor was paved, being also part of the cave system. It was about 4 meters wide and 4 meters high. The walls were natural rock throughout. About 50 meters away, the corridor began to enlarge, both in width and height. Then, it ended at a big artificial wall. The wall blocked all the transversal sections of the cave, and had about 15 meters in width by 10 meters in height. Close to its center there was a large door 2 meters wide by 3.5 meters high. We found that this size was excessive for such a door, especially its height.

The door was closed and was held by enormous hinges, 4 in total. The hinges were to our right. At the left side a big sliding bolt went to a hole drilled into the steel jamb. No keyed locking mechanism. To open the door, the bolt was to be moved to the right after unlocking it by rotating it on its guiding rail. After sliding it open, we locked it to the open position. According to my brother, the bolt itself was a masterpiece. Engineers...

The door opened to the inside and was very heavy. *Landians had a compulsion for doors*, I thought. And, I felt some fear. We were before an immense hall. On the floor, many pieces of wood and some rails were scattered, which we used to block the eventual closure of the door. This was a quite necessary measure since it had no opening mechanism from the inside.

On the wall there was a light switch that I turned on. The illumination was weak but revealed an enormous natural hall, certainly part of the cave complex. Here, it had expanded.

Slowly, we got to understand the complexity of the place. For some reason, the main lighting was confined to the center of the hall, where the roof formed a dome about 15 meters high. The remaining of the hall was thrown to an almost obscurity.

At that central region, a huge metallic tube was attached to the highest point of the dome and descended, vertically, up to 3 meters from the floor. We came to a position below the tube. Its wall was approximately 2 cm thick, and its internal diameter was about 90 cm. The tube was perfectly incrusted into the rocky roof above. It was possible to see, throwing our flashlights upward, that the tube extended well above the rocky roof, I would say about 20 meters more. The tube was very smooth on the inside and outside surfaces. Its construction revealed a very sophisticated technology, by the precision of the cuts. At the lower portion of the tube, there was a shorter tube, about 3 meters in length, concentric and internal to the main tube. This tube had retractile rungs that fitted into niches. While within their niches, the rungs were invisible from below. I took one rung out from its niche and holding it, I could pull down the entire short tube to about 1 meter above the floor. What I found curious about the retractile rungs was that they had only 2 stable positions. Either fully recessed or fully opened. Not intermediary. A sort of spring made this an ON-OFF contraption. Then, I perceived that the retractile rungs extended all the way up the main tube.

I asked my brother to illuminate the tube and began climbing up. Each rung could be flipped easily off its niche. But, being all rungs collapsed into its niches the tube's internal surface became absolutely smooth. I went up to the top and got to a domed hatch with a bolt that fitted firmly to the jamb. I opened it and put my torso out into a sunny day.

My brother and I began to theorize about the whole contraption while Mayra decided to explore the surroundings of the tube region.

Our first idea was of an escape route. Well, an escape route is something to be used in a hurry. But why retract the rungs into its niches only to need to pull them out in a hurry?

"Come here, you two, come here to see this!" shouted Mayra, as she came running to us.

Mayra, then, directed us to a darker part of the hall. Initially, we saw nothing but, as our eyes adapted, we saw it.

Concentrically arranged around the central tube and near the wall, there were hollow cylinders with thick and transparent walls. Each cylinder measured about 170 cm in height and 70 cm in diameter. They were floating above weights resting on the floor and were attached to the weights by means of chains. Then, we saw what was keeping the transparent cylinders afloat. Each cylinder was linked, by a chain, to those same gray cylinders that we knew so well: the negative masses.

But, what we didn't know "so well" was the content of the transparent cylinders.

Each cylinder contained a human body. They wore beautiful, colorful gowns. Each one had a large golden medal hanging from the neck and displayed on the chest. The medals had inscriptions and were studded with small precious stones. Around the head, they had bands made of a brilliant fabric. Right in the middle forehead, the bands pressed medallions against the skin.

The hands were attached to each other at the front by means of golden chains. There were 18 men and 2 women. The gowns were gorgeous and scintillated to the light of our lanterns. Their colors were crisp and alive: blue, red, green. Some colors had metallic tinges.

We approached the bodies.

They were immersed in a clear liquid, and their expressions were serene. They fitted just inside the cylinders; some were slightly pressed to fit. Considering the aspect, the liquid seemed to be glycerin.

Their blond hairs floated above their heads. The women had their nails painted shiny red and wore rings. Also, they wore bracelets adorned with small diamonds, shiny against our lights. The men wore white gloves up to the arm. Their bracelets were worn over the gloves and were plain.

The counterweights keeping the system from going up were different from body to body. Each counterweight had a base from which a rod was fixed. The weights were formed by adding 20 kg or 50 kg units like those used in barbells and made in Brazil, as I could read.

I pulled up a complete set, and the combined weight was about 8 kg. The chain fastening to the counterweights had a locking system slightly different from the rudimentary one we had used in our previous launchings.

We concluded that the hall we were in was a launching platform. The dead were Landians who had died either during the long trips Landa to Earth or from their colonies on Earth. Probably, they were heroes of sorts.

Also, it became clear to us that the launchings were done through the big tube. For that reason, the tube's interior needed to have a smooth internal surface while launching, but it also had to allow climbing through it, which explained the retractile rungs system.

"This all means that we were right to have done the launchings of Isobel and Fabiana, Frederico, the "bomb," and the embryos," my brother commented.

"And, now, it's up to us to launch the remaining bodies!" I said.

Then, I remembered Greg's letter saying that I had a mission. This might be part of my mission. I also began to understand why they had chosen me and tested me so carefully. I hadn't been chosen by my intelligence and scientific or medical knowledge. Probably, they chose me by my character, my ingenuity, my courage and the trust I had in them, having jumped from the cliff.

And, why had they the trouble of explaining so many things to me, to letting me know their mother-ship and the disc? Why had they allowed me to know Antonina and to experiment with her love? Was that to make me certify myself they were capable of love and gratitude? Yes, I thought. *They were capable of love and gratitude!*

And, then, at that moment, inside that cave, with its strange launch pad and before the serene faces of their dead heroes, I suddenly became proud of myself. I began to find a logical connection between all those strange things I was confronted with and my extraterrestrial friends. And, I felt I was missing them.

After some more exploration of the hall, we decided to go to our dome, rest, and come back in the evening in order to launch a few bodies into space.

We went back to our dome, had lunch, and rested all afternoon. After dinner, we went back to the launching platform. I climbed up the tube and opened the hatch. The night was warm, and a breeze blew from the south.

We picked one of the bodies and placed the set well below the tube.

My brother went up to search for planes and I climbed once more in order to put the rungs back into their niches. In the morning, I had taken detailed photos of the mechanism of releasing the cylinders from the counterweights. It was way simpler and safer than our method of screw-pulling. The system, here, was a very ingenious lever that could be rotated in order to lose a pin.

I pulled the mobile tube down to less than 1 meter from the floor, leaving out of the tube only the counterweight and the releasing lever.

"Can I release?" I shouted to my brother.

"Yes" he shouted back.

I rotated the lever counterclockwise; the cylinder was released and went up along the tube. It had been easy.

We decided to launch 4 more bodies this evening since someone might have seen the first launch and begun to pay attention.

Just after the launching of the last body, I thought:

How big it is an honor to be buried in space for those who, willingly, defied the dangers of space travel.

The next evening, we launched 5 more bodies and went to sleep very tired. In the morning, we waited for Mayra to call us to the breakfast. As I said, when my brother and I woke up, the breakfast table was usually already set. Mayra did that for us. And after breakfast was ready, she knocked at our doors every morning.

However, this particular morning, we woke up to an empty table.

I knocked at Mayra's door, and only after many knocks she answered.

"Coming," she shouted without opening the door.

Soon after, she came into the hall with a very tired countenance, bags under her eyes, disheveled hair, and very bad humor.

"Haven't you slept well, Mayra?" I asked her

"I haven't slept a second! And if you allow me, I'll just have a juice and go back to bed. I have a terrible headache!"

Chapter 93

Adorable J-Rod

Some more dark nights and we had launched all remaining bodies. An important part of the mission assigned to me had been accomplished. We were very tired after those days of work and decided to rest and meditate over the recent happenings. We used this period to walk along the so many trails on the farm, many of which were still unknown to us. We used to rise early and, after a nice breakfast, went on to our walks.

However, this routine was sometimes broken. Some mornings, Mayra woke tired and bad-humored. On those mornings, after having breakfast, she excused herself to her room. On these occasions, my brother and I employed the time to do other tasks on the farm.

In one of the mornings when Mayra woke well-disposed and had prepared an excellent breakfast, I suggested that we explored a different part of the farm. For this, we prepared well our "survival" equipment, under the expert orientation of Mayra.

After we had walked for about 40 minutes along a very interesting trail, Mayra suddenly stopped.

"I have a feeling someone needs us desperately!"

"Who is it, and where, Mayra?" I said

"I just don't know, but this is real, I guarantee!" she said.

Then, we continued on along the trail.

"There is the right arm of the cemetery cave! We have never entered there," Luiz suddenly said.

"And, each time we explore a new place we find someone that needs our help!" Luiz went on.

"Yes, Luiz, you are right. That way, we found Mayra!" I said.

Therefore, we decided that an exploration of the right arm was deemed essential.

Mayra, as former Girl Scout, was appointed to organize this expedition. Soon after lunch, she began preparing the gear checklist for our approval.

The next morning, after breakfast, we began our journey to the right arm of the cemetery cave. The route was: Dome 2 > Radioactive hall > Great Hall of the bomb > Laboratory > Indian cemetery > Paved cave > Cave's right arm.

We followed the usual route described above. After passing the exit for the left arm, the cave enlarged in width and height, forming a small hall. From this hall began the right arm. It was an elongated cave with a paved floor. At the crossroads, we lighted a candle and connected our guideline to a stone. The cave corridor went on to the right, level. From the rocky roof hang dozens of stalactites that dripped water down. In some places, on the floor, there were stalagmites, as in a mirror image of the stalactites above. They were formed by the deposition of calcium minerals carried in the dripping water from the stalactites above.

Now, the concrete pavement was slightly downhill, and the water trickled discreetly down.

Finally, we came to an artificial wall identical to the one at the left arm that delimited the launching hall. The door was an exact replica of that in the launching hall with the exception of the bolt system. Here, there were 2 identical bolts, one above the other.

The door was closed and locked, from our side, by the two bolts.

We slid open the bolts and locked them in the open position. The door opened to the inside and, like its twin, was heavy. Like the other, this door couldn't be unlocked from the inside.

We entered after throwing pieces of wood and other debris into the door frame in order to prevent the door from closing "by chance" and locking closed, also "by chance". We knew Isobel and Frederico weren't around anymore, but who knows?

Like the other hall in the left arm, we found a light switch. The difference, here, was the lights were on. Someone coming out forgot to turn off the lights!

We found that this hall was also part of the same cave complex and a bit larger than its twin on the left side.

Here, however, the contents were quite diverse from the twin hall.

The general layout was of a morgue: many big benches, autopsy tables and large sinks with faucets. Placed against a wall, there were many plastic cylindrical reservoirs exact copies of those containing the bodies that we had launched. These, were empty.

In another part of the hall, there were nude bodies on the autopsy tables. The bodies, however, were inside transparent plastic bags partially filled with a clear liquid. On shelves along the wall, there were folded ceremonial gowns, which we could verify by taking one down. They were splendid pieces. On other shelves, there were medals, medallions, socks, and soft sneakers.

It was clear that, in this hall, the bodies were prepared for launching. This idea was reinforced by the presence of small loading carts. The general idea coming to our minds was that the prepared bodies in this room were transported to the left arm of the cave to be launched there.

Mayra had detached from us and was exploring another part of the hall.

"You two, come here, come here!" Mayra suddenly shouted.

We ran to her. Mayra was kneeling on the floor. At her side was what seemed to be a child, partially hidden below a shelf with the legs covered by a piece of dirty tarpaulin.

The "child" was breathing. Mayra raised her head. Immediately, large eyes opened, and a small and delicate mouth exhaled a feeble moan.

Mayra took the orange juice bottle, filled a small glass and took it to the mouth of the creature. She drank avidly. One more glass was offered and promptly drained.

I took the child from the floor and placed her on an empty and clean bench after lining the surface with some clothes.

Then, we could get a clear view of the creature.

Clearly, the being before us wasn't of terrestrial origin.

And, that was the first time I saw, undeniably, an alien being.

I'll never forget that experience!

The body measured about 110 cm, but the head was larger than ours. The eyes were beautiful, almost glorious, the irises a deep green, and the pupils were way larger than ours. The eyes looked tired and sad.

She had blonde hair, cut short, military style.

She was clothed in a sort of crew uniform, deep blue, displaying symbols that looked like insignia, revealing a sort of military rank. The uniform adjusted to the body and seemed to be elastic in texture. It covered the legs and arms and also the neck, up to the chin.

The footwear consisted of soft and elastic shoes with fine soles.

The arms were covered by the uniform's sleeves, but the hands were uncovered. They deserve a description apart.

The hands were extremely delicate and small, like those of a 10-

year-old. Long fingers: the opposable thumb and only 3 parallel fingers, proportionally longer than ours. No nails.

What caught my attention was the precision of the hand movements.

The legs were shorter than normal for their stature, and they looked fragile.

The face skin was thin and white and, in some regions, let see small veins beneath.

Mayra proffered to her one more glass of orange juice. This time, the child took hold of Mayra's hand and helped Mayra move the glass to her mouth. Then, she closed her eyes for an instant, only to open them, seconds later, with a beautiful smile in her mouth.

"Thank you" she spoke with the voice of a pre-pubescent child.

She then held, delicately, Mayra's hand.

"My name is Jason Rodney, but they call me just J-Rod," he said with a firmer voice.

Mayra had her eyes completely wet. Not able to restrain herself, she then wept plainly.

"I knew you were in need of me, she said to J-Rod. I just knew it!" she kept saying while she wept.

Meanwhile, J-Rod perceived we did not like his smell. He excused himself and went to a shelf, whence he took a heavy suitcase and, from it, a new uniform. Then, he climbed onto a bench and went inside one of the sinks that served him like an ofuro bathtub. Then, he calmly opened the faucet and filled the sink with warm water, regulating the proportion of hot/cold from the faucet. Apparently, he had done this many times here before collapsing from starvation.

He used a sort of shampoo and did not hide his lean body, which was very white. Also, we could see, clearly, that "she" was a male.

Finishing his bath, J-Rod dried himself with a towel from the room and put on his clean uniform.

This one was deep marine green, full of insignia and stripes on the wrists and shoulders, like those of an airliner pilot's uniform.

J-Rod came down from the bench very cute and he smelled like a baby after a bath.

"I am entirely at your service, my rescuers" and, this, he said with some pomp and made a hand gesture of servitude.

Mayra was out of herself with J-Rod. She was simply enchanted.

"Who are you, and how did you end up here?" asked Mayra, excitedly.

"Who am I?" said J-Rod, now putting on some airs.

"I'm one of the pilots of the disc that landed here. Actually, I am a commander, the highest rank of the pilots."

"But, then, what are you doing in this place?" asked Mayra.

"That's a long story. I was selected to help in the embalming of the bodies since I know something about this line."

Seeing that J-Rod looked firmer, we decided to return with him to our dome.

"J-Rod, can you walk with us to our home?" I asked him.

"Of course, I can!" he said, seeming a little offended.

Mayra looked at me in reprimand.

However, as soon as we began to move out, we saw that J-Rod wouldn't be able to follow us. Mayra offered to carry him, and J-Rod rapidly jumped to her back and closed his arms around her neck.

I grabbed J-Rod's suitcase to carry it but, very soon, perceived that summing up the weight of my backpack, I wouldn't be able to. We decided to attach J-Rod's suitcase to a pole and carry it between me and my brother.

I now remember it was a very tiresome return.

The normally tortuous journey up to Dome 2 got much more difficult with J-Rod and his suitcase. Finally, we went up to Dome 2 and rested. We had some food, and Mayra prepared a coffee. With the passing of time J-Rod was becoming more and more extrovert. And he loved Mayra's coffee and the fast foods we had at Dome 2.

Instead of going to Dome 1 and bringing the car to Dome 2, I decided it would be easier if we walked the 800 meters from Dome 2 to Dome 1. It was a bad move.

Then, we began our march to Dome 1.

As soon as his hunger was quenched, J-Rod began to speak. And, speak he did! Since Mayra was getting tired of carrying J-Rod and hearing his voice so close to her ears, she asked for a stop and a change of strategy.

First, J-Rod said he was now "super strong" and could walk. And, since Mayra was free of her burden, we resumed our march toward Dome 1. Soon, however, J-Rod said he was sleepy and wanted to sleep for a few minutes. I, immediately, perceived that it was an excuse.

My brother offered to carry him and Mayra and I took hold of the pole with J-Rod's suitcase.

Finally, we got home, exhausted.

I offered to J-Rod an exclusive container.

His response was immediate; he began to dance, yes, to dance!

Soon, he took up his suitcase and disappeared inside his private quarters. He reappeared some half hour later, having taken another bath and changed his uniform; I think this one was green.

And he began to talk of the most diverse subjects, always giving some hints to his abilities, his courage, his prowess.

Mayra was completely taken.

But, soon he tired off and fell to sleep right before us, not without smiling in his dreams. I carried him to his bed and, with the help of Mayra, covered his little body. Mayra wept. Maternal instinct, I suppose.

Later in the afternoon, J-Rod reappeared, now attired in a resplendent yellow uniform and wearing gloves. He exhaled a delicious herbal scent.

Now, it became evident to us all who was the object of so much exuberance: Mayra.

Not long after this, Mayra announced that dinner was ready.

"And you also live in Landa, J-Rod?" I asked.

"We are nomads. We are called Lesser Landians, and we live in our discs. And, our discs can go anywhere in the solar system!" he said with a proud air.

"But our base is Landa," he concluded while eating non-stop.

"In Landa, we have our main source of food. Our species has about 1 million people distributed in some hundreds of discs, all of them certified to travel anywhere in the solar system."

"In Pluto we obtain the materials to maintain our fleet and to construct new units. In Ganymede, we find important and rare metals. In Europa (another of Jupiter's satellites), we can live long periods of time since there is water plenty that allows us to get oxygen. Also, Europa has many eatable animals and aquatic edible plants.

As we had finished the main course, Mayra brought some desserts.

This was a mistake, as we would soon find out. It appears that J-Rod wasn't cognizant of sweet foods. We had cheesecake and chocolate cake, bought at a nice store in the city.

J-Rod went for the chocolate cake and Mayra placed a slice onto his plate. He took one mouthful. Immediately, he closed his eyes and began slowly moving his head from side to side. Then he finished his slice, which was a small one. He asked for one more slice and I said it would be his last since we didn't know if his digestive system was able to deal with this new food. He agreed after I told him I was a doctor.

"Oh, are you a doctor? That's very good to know since I have a few questions for you."

"OK, J-Rod, let's leave this for our private talk," I said, and he flushed, immediately.

Then, J-Rod asked Mayra, in a low voice, if she could get him just one more slice of chocolate cake. I didn't hear it but shook my head to Mayra without his seeing it.

"No, J-Rod, orders from the doctor. But would you like some brandy?" and, that, I didn't hear her saying.

And I continued to talk about something with my brother. When I looked at Mayra and J-Rod, I saw him just finishing gulping down liquor from a goblet. It was the brandy.

And, it was too late...

J-Rod closed his eyes and, slowly he began to sing a strange but nice song. Then, he stood and looked at us and, especially, at Mayra. And, he began to dance. Soon, he calmed down and asked if he could get just one more dose of brandy. I shook my head again at Mayra.

"No, J-Rod, we still need to see if these new things are OK for you. Doctor's orders."

"But, J-Rod, what do you do when there is no piloting?" Mayra asked.

J-Rod recomposed and went on:

"Our discs are small cities and each citizen has a primary role or function and secondary attributions. As I said, my primary role is as a pilot. But I'm an entertainer also. You see; there are families living in the disc, many children and old people. No one is left unassisted. And, entertainment, we consider an important part of people's lives."

Then, I felt it necessary to ask something to J-Rod.

"J-Rod, that's very nice to know that you are an entertainer. I think we here are in need of some entertainment!"

As Mayra looked at me with very negative eyes, I perceived to have made another mistake. How easy it was to make mistakes with J-Rod around...

Trying to buffer my inquiries, Mayra went on:

"And, J-Rod, entertainment is a very ample business. What's your specialty in that area?"

"Well, my main specialty in this area is as a magician and illusionist since I have some expertise in working with people's minds, you see? But I also sing, dance, and do juggling."

My God, I thought, *not this anymore. Is he going to dominate us?*

"OK, J-Rod, but tell us about the propulsion of the mother-ship."

J-Rod explained that the mother-ship has no proper propulsion systems, only for maneuvering actions. The main propulsion of the ship is the disc itself, he said.

"Larger Landians think they are too intelligent, but all they got was through the knowledge they are receiving from Procyon 2. They are too narrow-minded and have idiotic rules. I couldn't live a single day in one of their colonies."

And J-Rod didn't stop his fire against the Larger Landians.

"They can live here on Earth because they are handsome according to Earthian standards. But, in reality, they are ugly, very ugly at that!"

"Then, J-Rod, you find me ugly too?" asked Mayra with sort of a contrite face.

Now, I wanted to be very far away, perhaps in Alfa Centauri.

We saw that J-Rod perceived he was in a very dangerous predicament. But, after some thought, he managed to come through:

"Beauty is an illusion! By the Earthian standards, you are a very beautiful girl, Mayra! But what matters is the beauty down here!" He said, knocking at his head.

And, this triggered another wave of J-Rod's talk. It was like the many days he stayed "cloistered," he had accumulated a great quantity of words in his mind. And, now, he was letting them off.

"Without our discs and our pilots, the Larger Landians would not be able to get off the ground!"

"It was our scientists who discovered how to defy gravity and not only defy it but use gravity itself to push us into space. The mother-ship is only a steel casket, well designed, it's true, but without our disks, she doesn't move."

And this talk went on and on. And, while talking, J-Rod continued to put in some airs and facial "contortions" expressing contempt for the Larger Landians. And he also threw occasional glances at Mayra, who was enraptured.

But, one thing about J-Rod was very true: he was a good entertainer, sure he was!

I knew I had seen a box of ping-pong balls anywhere. Yes, they were in Frederico's container, a place where I had entered only one time, in a hurry. I went there and came with the box.

"J-Rod, can you show us some juggling tricks?" I asked him, handing him the box full of ping-pong balls.

Mayra looked at me with flaming eyes. Probably, she thought I had put J-Rod into some plight.

J-Rod handed the box to Mayra and asked her to throw him 2 balls, one after the other. But J-Rod didn't take the 2 balls into his hands. He took the first ball with his right hand and threw it up before the 2nd ball had arrived at his hand.

Then he asked Mayra to keep throwing balls to him. I think the box had some 30 ping-pong balls, and J-Rod managed to keep all of them in the air. Then, he asked Mayra to place the empty box on the floor, and he began throwing the balls back into the box, one at a time. All balls landed safely into the box.

Mayra was absolutely enchanted with J-Rod's performance, clapped hands, and ran to embrace him and kiss him. And, we heard J-Rod whisper something to Mayra. She went to the kitchen and brought a generous slice of chocolate cake to him. Things were getting out of control...

J-Rod told us that he would explain the antigravity system, but not now. And I suggested that we keep some days for his recovery.

"Yes, Jota, I still feel very weak. But after returning to normal, you will see that I am strong and very, very brave," and as he said this, he kept looking at Mayra, who gave him a kiss on the face. He blushed immediately but kept his composure.

"Please, would you excuse me now? I will rest a bit at my quarters." And saying this, J-Rod marched to his container.

Immediately, we felt some relief and went to rest ourselves in our rooms.

Later on, we met at the table for tea and some talk.

Soon, J-Rod reappeared. He came attired in a red uniform, black boots, and white gloves. Around his head was a beautiful headband. He also brought his sword, sheathed, at his waist.

"J-Rod! How nice you look! Why did you come armed with a sword? What is it for?" asked Mayra.

My brother and I exchanged some looks...

"This sword I brought just to show you. We all use it to defend our honor, just for that. Otherwise, we use very sophisticated weapons that I may show you later."

Mayra hurried to embrace him.

"J-Rod, I want you to defend me with your sword!"

J-Rod knelt with one knee before Mayra:

"Mayra, I will defend you with my life!"

Now, that was too much to hear before dinner, I thought and gave one more look to my brother, who made a slight movement of his head.

With the plea of Mayra, J-Rod gained energy.

He went on to tell us that he had tackled many dangers in different parts of the solar system.

"We, Lesser Landians and, especially me, don't know fear. In our job, the danger is routine," he said while looking at Mayra, who was "melting."

But, the unforeseen happened:

As J-Rod got taken by his own rhetoric and stood showing off, another being, oblivious of the risk, came to the scene.

A beautiful, white, and fluffy female pussycat slowly entered the hall.

At seeing the cat, J-Rod gave out a shout, jumped onto the table, and, at the same time, drew out his sword.

Princess, that was her name, jumped also ... onto Mayra's lap and hid her head beneath Mayra's shirt.

"What animal is that?!" J-Rod cried.

"J-Rod, come down please and sheathe your sword. This is Princess, my pussycat. Let me introduce her to you."

Now, my brother and I were hiding our faces because avoiding laughter was impossible.

Hesitatingly, J-Rod came down to the floor. Under the command of Mayra, Princess also went to the floor and began, cautiously, to sniff J-Rod.

"J-Rod, take off your gloves so that Princess can sniff at your hand. That's the way cats get to know people."

J-Rod looked at us all, in search of some encouragement, what we all gave him by nodding.

He took off his gloves and extended his hand to Princess. She, apparently, approved of his smell since she began to purr and licked J-Rod's fingers.

"She wants to eat me, he cried desperately. She roared and tasted my hand!"

And, saying these brave words, he jumped onto the table again.

We were all in trouble now and more so since J-Rod was armed!

How to calm down J-Rod? He was shaking with fear and flushed with shame!

My brother came up with the solution: a slice of chocolate cake and a goblet of brandy.

Well, all remedies have their side effects.

J-Rod chose to gulp the brandy first. He changed immediately.

First, he began laughing, then dancing and chanting. Soon he ate the chocolate and began to talk and excuse himself for the performance.

The danger was over.

And, such was the proof of J-Rod's courage.

Mayra was weeping silently. Her hero had vanished in a puff of smoke.

I asked J-Rod why he didn't return to the disc after having helped with the preparation and launching of the bodies.

"Well, Jota, these deaths occurred during the trip, and this time, there were a greater number of deaths. All the Larger Landians dying during the mission are considered heroes and are entitled to honor burial: launching to space."

Clearly, we all perceived that J-Rod didn't answer my question. Later on, we would question him again.

In order to better understand the intentions of J-Rod, without questioning him directly, I asked him if he would like to live with us here on the farm.

Hearing this, J-Rod began to weep and, between sobs, said he would be the happiest creature in the Universe.

Thrilled with my invitation, J-Rod asked if we would care to see his things.

Mayra anticipated:

"We would love to see your things, J-Rod!"

J-Rod marched to his quarters, and 15 minutes later, he reappeared with a different uniform. Now it was sky blue, with boots matching. And we had a surprise: he was bringing his suitcase, all right. But, carrying it with no apparent effort!

J-Rod placed the suitcase, carefully, onto the table. Now, with better lighting and at closer look, the suitcase transpired technology. It was metallic and its surface was smooth but had a look of ground glass in texture. And, it seemed to have some sort of sheen.

Chapter 94

J-Rod's Suitcase

The smooth surface of J-Rod's suitcase certainly had received uncountable hits but didn't present scratches or dents.

The suitcase was absolutely crammed with the most diverse items. Its interior was divided into numerous partitions and had many levels, both in the lower and the top halves. There were, absolutely, no empty spaces. The partitions were thin but resistant and could be taken out.

Considering the variety of uniforms with which J-Rod had impressed Mayra, we suspected that a good portion of the suitcase space would be occupied by them. We were wrong.

"Where are your uniforms, J-Rod? I can see just a yellow one!" asked Mayra.

J-Rod gave a condescending smile and moved a "secret" region in his red uniform. Immediately, it transformed into a fascinating sky blue color. Mayra gasped.

Then, J-Rod moved the same part (we couldn't identify what part was that), and the uniform, instantly, took a metallic green color with stripes and insignia.

And, this was only the beginning of the show!

Then, J-Rod, assuming a formal posture, explained:

"In this suitcase, the most important item is not visible. It's *energy*. Without energy, there is little we can do, but having energy, we can do almost everything."

"Here, I have two sources of energy: the first one, less powerful, is a battery that employs radioactive graphite coupled to energy-storing super capacitors. The other source for heavy uses, so to speak, is cold fusion."

"But, what do I need energy for?" He continued.

Now, J-Rod was revealing a new personality: a teacher, and a good one at that.

"All items I have here are related to survival, in one way or another. And, all are essential. However, most need energy. Remember, we are nomads and we work in the most diverse environments, most of which have no oxygen and much less, an atmosphere."

"On many planets or satellites, there is water, which contains oxygen. So, the first device I will show you is the oxygen generator, which employs electricity to cleave water molecules into oxygen and hydrogen, in a process called *electrolysis*. Electricity is generated by a mini cold fusion reactor, and stored in capacitors."

"We force an electric current across the water, and this breaks the water molecule into oxygen and hydrogen, as I said."

"But, J-Rod, how much oxygen can you get from water? It doesn't seem too much!" I said, but repented soon after.

J-Rod ignored my question and, making a face, went on:

"Each liter of water contains 55.55 moles of H_2 and 27.77 moles of O_2. And, remember that what we breathe is O_2."

Each mol of O_2 has 22.4 liters of O_2. This means that each liter of water generates 22.4 x 27.77 = 622 liters of O_2"

"OK, J-Rod, can you go to the point, please? Mayra is yawning." I suggested.

Mayra threw me a fulminating glance while J-Rod simply ignored my comment.

"My body uses 150 ml of O_2 a minute and not 250 ml like humans, and thus with the oxygen content of 1 liter of water, I can breathe (622/0.150) = 4,146 minutes or 2.9 days."

And, finally, J-Rod sat down and looked firmly at me and then smiled at Mayra:

"Did you understand, Jota? Pretty simple eh?"

Mayra clapped her hands and went to kiss J-Rod, while giving me a contemptuous glance.

To explain this, J-Rod used a sheet of paper he had taken from his suitcase. He explained this sheet was, in fact, a small computer since, as J-Rod was writing the numbers, the sheet made the operations and organized everything into a sort of spreadsheet.

"And, so you see that water has many uses," and saying this, he gestured to his throat as if he were thirsty.

Mayra hurried to the kitchen and brought him a glass of mineral water.

Now, we were beginning to get some glimpse of what J-Rod actually was. The playful, exhibitionist, and whinny had transformed, before our eyes, into a good and patient teacher.

"OK, folks, then we saw that water can provide me with some oxygen. And, of course, we drink it and use it for cleaning. Well, well. And what else does water serve me for?"

My brother and I were caught off guard, while Mayra looked defiantly at us.

"Ahaaa, and how am I going to feed the cold fusion reactor? With hydrogen, of course! And where does that hydrogen come from? From water, of course!" and saying this, J-Rod threw a malignant look at my brother and me, while Mayra was exulting.

"OK, OK, J-Rod, you got us in this one," I said.

"But where does hydrogen come down into the fusion reaction?" asked my brother in the hope of getting J-Rod into a predicament.

"I thought this subject was already in your knowledge," said J-Rod with a bored face. Nuclear fusion or nucleosynthesis is a process in which nuclei from lighter elements fuse, giving rise to heavier elements. But, there is a difference between the initial masses of reagents and the final mass of products, and this difference is energy, according to the equation $E = m \times C^2$ proposed by Einstein, who, despite being an Earthian, had a great intelligence."

"However, in my suitcase, fusion occurs through a process not completely understood by us."

"Here, there is a reactor that transforms hydrogen into deuterium, which is a hydrogen isotope having a proton and a neutron in its nucleus. Also, tritium atoms are formed, which have 1 proton and 2 neutrons. By a process also unknown to us, atoms of deuterium and tritium fuse, generating helium, that has 2 protons and 2 neutrons. And, this is the energy-generating step. We also can't explain why free neutrons aren't formed, what would make this process very dangerous."

"The reactor where the fusion process takes place consists of a mixture of platinum and palladium formed into a very fine porous metal. This catalysis fusion reaction works by forcing the atoms of deuterium and tritium to get very close to one another and fuse. This system converts the fusion energy directly into electricity". I found that this description differed a bit from Antonina's, who said element 115 was also necessary. But, I chose to say nothing.

"Certainly, this is different from the fusion inside the stars, at temperatures of millions of degrees and unimaginable pressures.

But, for us, the result is energy production in great quantity. Our scientists are still trying to unravel the details of this process, and, while they do that, we use our energy," concluded J-Rod, giving a sarcastic laugh.

While J-Rod was giving his "lecture," he looked defiantly at my brother and me, enjoying our astonished expressions. But, after finishing, he looked, proudly, at Mayra.

Then, we had a problem. Mayra was sleeping peacefully, embracing Princess, who also slept with her little mouth wide open and her tongue hanging by a corner.

That was a bit too much for J-Rod. And he was unprepared for this. His reaction was obvious: he began to weep and complain that Mayra disliked him, etc, etc, etc.

Among all the confusion and noise, both Mayra and Princess woke up from their slumber.

Seeing J-Rod in this humiliating condition, Mayra went to embrace him and kiss him while she asked us what had happened. And, she looked defiantly at us in a protective manner toward J-Rod.

Seeing that herself was the cause of J-Rod's suffering, she justified before J-Rod:

"J-Rod, your voice was so secure, so soothing that I couldn't resist."

These consoling words from Mayra complemented by a generous dose of brandy, put J-Rod in working condition again. Also, Princess helped the healing process by climbing up to his lap and purring loudly at him.

As a complement to calming down J-Rod, we had tea with bread and J-Rod was served a special slice of chocolate cake. This was enough to bring J-Rod back to his professor stance. And, he came back with a vengeance.

"Then, we know that the energy produced in the fusion reaction is thousands of times larger than that necessary to electrolyze water into hydrogen and oxygen. However, having oxygen to breathe is not enough if the planet or satellite we are on has no atmospheric pressure. Without an atmosphere, my body would boil and explode. You have seen how astronauts in space or on the moon's surface need a special spacesuit that provides them with oxygen and pressure."

"And, when we are in a celestial body with no atmosphere, we use ... This".

And, with some suspense, J-Rod took from his suitcase a small packet the size of an apple. He opened the pack carefully, revealing a very thin plastic fabric. Then he connected it to his suitcase by means of a hose. It began to fill up, resembling a sleeping bag. But, before completely filling it out, J-Rod opened a sort of zipper and entered the bag. The bag was then filled, with J-Rod inside it. Now, the bag seemed to be under high pressure. J-Rod was smiling and throwing glances at Mayra. From inside the bag, his voice could be heard perfectly.

"If I were in Ganymede, I could remain here for a long period, breathing oxygen and pressurized"

I grabbed the chance to throw some factoids into J-Rod's "lecture".

"This same procedure was used in the Everest climbing to stabilize climbers suffering from HAPE (High Altitude Pulmonary Edema), a dangerous condition caused by a combination of low oxygen and low atmospheric pressure. The device is called "Gamow Bag" since it was invented by Igor Gamow, son of the great Soviet-American physicist, George Gamow."

My comment was not welcome by J-Rod, who saw it as a means to lessen his lecture. He didn't complain, however, and continued, oblivious of my presence.

"Another advantage of this device is protection against low temperature since the inside air can be temperature conditioned. It is good to remember that temperatures on Ganymede can reach easily -120 degrees Celsius. Not only does the body need to stay warm, but the inspired air must also be warmed somewhat. The breathing of too cold air can remove heat from the body at a high rate, and this is not a good idea when you are at Ganymede, for example."

"And, J-Rod, have you ever got lost in such dangerous places, too cold and without oxygen?" asked Mayra.

That was exactly the sort of question J-Rod was waiting for.

"You ask if I got lost in dangerous places. Of course I did, Mayra. And, many times!"; and, as he said this, he came out from his cocoon, changing his uniform color to a fascinating metallic purple. Then, he folded the bag carefully and placed it into a special compartment in his suitcase.

"Yes, Mayra, I have been in such situations. It was in Titan, one of Saturn's satellites that are visible from here, and I may show it to you this evening. Titan has a somewhat poisonous atmosphere, terrible winds, and is very cold. This day, a storm got us unprepared and I had to use many resources from my suitcase and was even able to rescue a companion from a sure death."

Mayra, having been told of the happy end of the J-Rod adventure, got calmer and took a chance at asking another question:

"But, J-Rod, how can you walk being inside that bag?"

My brother threw a hateful look at Mayra, already foretelling the "terrible" consequences of her question.

J-Rod, however, was unfazed. He just took a transparent hood from the suitcase and attached it to his uniform. Then, doing some theatrical gestures, he hooked a hose to his uniform, which he also hooked to the suitcase.

Immediately, J-Rod began to inflate and got very "fat". Then, he grabbed his suitcase and began to parade before Mayra. The Princess got so scared that she jumped to Mayra and hid beneath her coat.

"Now, I am breathing oxygen, pressurized and walking!" J-Rod shouted from a distance.

Mayra ran to him, embraced him, and kissed him.

My brother and I looked at each other and sighed.

After the return to normality, we all sat at the table to have tea, coffee, and toasts. J-Rod was served a slice of chocolate cake.

"But, J-Rod, tell me what do you do with the helium, which is a by-product of the fusion. It is an inert gas, can't be burned, and what?" I asked.

I repented, later, having raised this question to J-Rod. Everything had returned to normality, and we had had a nice tea. The prospects for a nice afternoon were great! But...

"Let's go outside. I was expecting you to have asked that question, Jota. Actually, I need to charge some capacitors, and for this, I will activate the fusion reactor, and you will see," responded J-Rod, energetically.

We went outside into a delicious afternoon, a bit windy though. J-Rod deposited his suitcase onto the ground and turned on the fusion reactor. At the same time, he connected an empty balloon to an outlet that he pulled from the suitcase. Slowly, the balloon began growing larger and upwards.

"That's the helium," said J-Rod, showing us the balloon beginning to take off but restrained to the ground by a small rope and a stake. And the balloon didn't stop growing larger and larger. And, it really was pulling up the rope strongly. J-Rod, meanwhile, was testing the rope tension and the balloon size.

"J-Rod, it's OK, you convinced me and it's all right. We all can see the balloon wanting to rise."

But J-Rod was waiting for something else. When the balloon reached the size of a small room, J-Rod tied the rope around his right wrist and, with his left hand, disconnected the rope from the stake.

We were totally unprepared for that!

In an instant J-Rod shot up into the air. He had miscalculated the helium volume and let the balloon fill too much.

In seconds, J-Rod was higher than the tallest Eucalyptus.

"Let go the gas, we shouted, let go the gas!"

Mayra was desperate since the wind was carrying J-Rod to the Eucalyptus forest. And she began running below the balloon to keep track of J-Rod's position.

Then, apparently, J-Rod let go off the helium and the balloon began descending. But, it was too late, since J-Rod was already above the forest. Finally, he landed safely.

Onto the top of a tall Eucalyptus.

"Hold there, J-Rod!" we all cried loudly as he sat onto a branch, the balloon already empty, hanging down.

While Mayra was talking to J-Rod, from the ground, I went with my brother to get some ropes.

While we did that, J-Rod began to weep.

"I'm going to die, I won't see my family again and why did I do this?"

With the help of my brother, we could climb the tree and attach a rope to the branch where J-Rod was seated.

Then, we all climbed down gripping the rope.

Finally, we were all safe on the ground.

Mayra only wept and blamed me for having challenged J-Rod to explain the use of helium. She was embracing J-Rod, who was still weeping and trembling. And, she was weeping too.

"I love you, J-Rod, don't you ever do that again to me, promise me and promise me," she said among her sobbing.

We went to the dome and each of us took a warm bath and changed into clean clothes.

Later, with everyone clean and calmer, Mayra announced an earlier dinner. But first, J-Rod, our hero, would be served brandy and chocolate cake. He was now a star, having survived a terrifying experience. My brother and I only praised his ability with the balloon.

"J-Rod, you did it right. The problem was that gust of wind. No one could foresee that!"

Mayra arranged an outfit for J-Rod from a pair of her pants and a shirt. And, J-Rod looked very cute in that outfit.

One problem was that one of J-Rod's 2 uniforms had been scratched and torn in many places. Mayra, who had some knowledge of sewing, was assessing the damage. And, she was really concerned.

But not J-Rod...

J-Rod's damaged uniform was rapidly washed in warm water and left on a hanger in Mayra's room to dry. Dirty as it was, there was no question about servicing it, as Mayra commented.

We had an excellent dinner, and J-Rod was now completely recovered, physically and psychologically. He was talkative and took the chance of his accident to tell us some other stories of his misfortunes. Which of those were real? Nobody ventured a guess.

Then, he and Mayra presented us with a little show. Mayra had taught him some Brazilian songs and their lyrics. In this way, they sang one or two songs. Well, not bad.

But, a surprise was waiting for us.

Mayra had to go to her room for something, and we heard her

shouting with joy. She came running to us carrying J-Rod's previously damaged uniform.

Now, it was brand new, a light blue, magnificent.

We all looked at J-Rod, who was smiling.

That was one of the surprises J-Rod had for us. His uniforms were self-healing.

Chapter 95

Holographic Projector

After a nice dinner prepared by Mayra and ... J-Rod, we were having coffee and some liquor. It was then that Mayra asked J-Rod:

"J-Rod, I'm so curious to see something of your family! Don't you have some photos to show us?"

"I believe I have something in my suitcase," said J-Rod with an air of indifference.

J-Rod opened his suitcase and took from it an object resembling a computer mouse. Then, he connected it to the suitcase and asked us to turn off the lights. The room got pitch black.

What J-Rod did forthwith, we couldn't see.

What we all could see was that we weren't in our home anymore. It seemed to us we had been transported elsewhere. Around us was a strange landscape covered by dark snow and big chunks of ice. A gray sky, where a light in the sky was casting phantom shadows.

We were so shocked that no one said anything. We were just trying to understand what had happened to us.

Then, we began to see well. In the scene, there were many "children" and, among them, appeared, clearly, J-Rod. The children seemed to be all around us. The characters were not moving. I got up and approached a beautiful girl.

"That's my younger sister," said J-Rod.

Mayra stood and approached another girl who seemed to be a 10-year-old. She had, however, a well-developed woman's body, well-defined breasts, a narrow waist, and wide hips. The face was childlike.

"This is my older sister," informed J-Rod.

I, then, came round the scene and checked that the children had given me their backs.

"This static scene was taken in Landa. It was warm since we were just beside a magma well."

I, immediately, perceived myself to be "within" a super advanced hologram.

Then, J-Rod switched something in the "mouse" and we were transported to another location. We were, now, inside a craft, as inferred from the general layout of the place. A huge quantity of instruments was blinking and running. A humming sound pervaded all. Soon, two youths of about 17, a man and a woman, appeared. And, they began to sing. Their voices seemed to come from their own mouths. We had the impression of being before living people.

"Those, are my parents, and we were inside our disc. This was in Pluto, I think. We were collecting metals", said J-Rod.

In another scene, static, we were "transported" to Ganymede, a

Jupiter's satellite. It was surreal. The disc craft was seen at a distance and, in the foreground, were J-Rod and other crew members, all using spacesuits of a different design, more like the ones used by human astronauts (the "spacesuit" he had shown us was an emergency one). In the background appeared Jupiter, taking up most of the sky, and other satellites. We were brought inside the scene; such was the realism.

We stayed up to one in the morning watching the holograms of J-Rod, and we all went to bed with our heads turning.

Chapter 96

J-Rod Explains

The next morning, we woke up a bit later. At 8, my brother knocked at my door. Mayra had prepared breakfast and was waiting for us at the table. Also seated at the table was J-Rod wearing a white uniform, so absolutely white that even his super white skin seemed darker. Seeing our inquisitive looks, J-Rod:

"This uniform I use in white regions, such as snowy places, in order to disguise myself from enemies and beasts. Using this attire, we become invisible. In order to prevent J-Rod from beginning another long, extraordinary, and heroic feat, I asked flatly:

"J-Rod, how come you got trapped in the morgue?" My question came at a price: a very vengeful look from Mayra. She was vigilant on anything that might scratch J-Rod's curriculum or, even, irritate him.

"Well, Jota, I was helping in embalming the bodies, and they simply forgot me here. Then, I had to continue working with the Larger Landians. There was no other choice since, due to my superior looks, I couldn't get mixed with Earthians."

"During this terrible period, I slept and lived all the time in the morgue. I received food from the Landians. But then, the Landians left the farm, and I was left behind. I had to keep hiding in the morgue. Since my food supply was finishing, I began exploring the cave. I came, eventually, to the laboratory, and from there, I ended up at a residential dome where three beautiful girls were living."

"I, then, began taking some food from their stocks when they were sleeping. Certain night, one of the girls, a Landian, saw me and ran after me. I ran back, retracing my route and ended up at the morgue, hiding there. Seeing that she would not be able to find me there, she closed the door and trapped me there."

"Always Isobel, always her!" shouted Mayra, enraged.

After many days living with us and being treated like a king by Mayra, J-Rod recovered completely. He was now always well-disposed and talkative. He became friendly with Princess, who followed him everywhere. It seemed that J-Rod had shown us all his powers and, now, what remained of him was that he was a very nice companion. He filled our lives with happiness and good humor. Sure, his encounters with danger continued, at a lesser scale, though.

But, when things seemed to have gotten back to normality (J-Rod's normality, of course), a turn of destiny made J-Rod notice the many chessboards, chess books, and chess things, scattered throughout our dome. The Landians took everything essential in their run and, it seems, chess was not one of them.

Anyhow, J-Rod got curious about chess. And, he asked if I played chess.

"Yes, J-Rod, I can't say I'm a chess player. I know the rules; that's, essentially, all I know."

J-Rod confessed that he also wasn't a prime player but was forced to play due to his coexistence with the Larger Landians. And, saying this, he rolled his eyes and put out his tongue to demonstrate indigestion.

"They think themselves a lot brighter and use to demonstrate this by winning chess matches against us. I don't give a damn about this, because I know I'm a lot brighter than those fluffy Landians" and J-Rod was letting off his entire wrath.

All this information was a preamble to say that one evening, after dinner, J-Rod invited me to a chess match.

We began, and I got the whites. I moved the king's pawn 2 squares. J-Rod began moving the king's knight. As the game proceeded, I got the impression that J-Rod wasn't, actually, a master. But, possibly, better than I was.

However, as the match went on, I began to find strange things on the chessboard. I thought, even, that I might be getting into a confused state of mind. The position of my pieces seemed to have changed; I didn't remember what my last move was. And, I began to feel confused. Also, from J-Rod's side, things were no better off. No one else was watching our match, and then, I was all by myself or ... by J-Rod.

Finally, I told J-Rod that I was not feeling well since I couldn't remember my moves.

"So, Jota, you want to give up, to lay down your king?"

"Yes, J-Rod, you got me, really!"

"Then, I'll do it for you. Pay attention"

I kept my eyes fixed on the chessboard. Then, very slowly, my king began to lean, lean, until it lay down, completely.

J-Rod was laughing loudly, to the point that Mayra and Luiz came to see the reason for such a commotion.

"What's that, J-Rod, how in the hell did you do this??" I shouted.

"Watch again, Jota." As I fixed my eyes on the chessboard, my King began to rise, and the Queen, up to now, immobile, began to move very slowly and entered the square left empty by my pawn.

Now, Mayra and Luiz were mystified.

"This is called *telekinesis,* and I am beginning to learn it. For the time being, only small and very near objects"

And, as J-Rod finished saying this, all pieces lay down at the same time, without making any sound.

Too good, we had finished dinner.

Mayra clapped her hands and embraced and kissed J-Rod while looking defiantly at me.

But, as the initial surprise and fun dissipated, I began to feel fear. I couldn't say I was completely recovered from my episodes of mind conditioning.

However, after we had some coffee, liquors, and chocolate cake for J-Rod, he looked, firmly, at my eyes and said:

"No, Jota, I'm not what you think; I'm not going to interfere with your mind, be assured. I know everything about what the Larger Landians do to Earthians."

"And what other mental powers have you got, J-Rod?" we all asked at about the same instant.

J-Rod became introspective. I perceived that he was thinking about some answer or the ups and downs of some possible answers. It became evident to me that J-Rod was much more than what he appeared to be, considering his frequent pathetic attitudes. And then, I realized that this thought was only a distorted view of mine that extroverts and show-offs are mediocre. There are very circumspect people who are mediocre too. And those last may be the majority.

And, maybe J-Rod was really as brave as he says. And, I began to perceive that behind a loudmouth might be a creature very interesting and deep-minded. And powerful!

"They are not 'powers', but rather, 'characteristics'," he said, suddenly.

"Can you give us an example, J-Rod? Look, I'm not asking for proof because you have given us much more than proof!", I said.

J-Rod looked at me and:

"Jota, bring me a book in English."

That was easy, I had 'Moby Dick' (by Hermann Melville) open, on my bed.

"Jota, open the book to any page and hand it to me."

The book was already open, revealing two pages, side by side. They were the pages I was reading some hours earlier.

Then, J-Rod looked at the two pages for about 10 seconds.

"Now, Jota, take the book away from me, but keep looking at what is written there."

We all went to another sofa; I sat in the middle, with Mayra and my brother on each side. And, we were looking attentively at the written pages.

Then, J-Rod began reciting word by word, the content of the two pages, without making a single mistake.

Mayra was out of herself. As was her costume, he ran to J-Rod and embraced him, and clapped her hands.

"J-Rod, now you deserve a nice slice of chocolate cake and a goblet of brandy", Mayra said loudly to all hear.

And, J-Rod was exultant. He was the center of attention for all of us, especially Mayra.

"But let me tell you this. What I did requires memory, not intelligence, do you agree?" said J-Rod, now that he had captivated the audience.

We all nodded

"To show you my intelligence, I don't see a way right now. Quite frankly, I don't even know if I'm more intelligent than Earthians. But, maybe there appears a chance"

Our dinner this evening was very particularly nice. Secretly, J-Rod and Mayra had worked on that. And the recipe was J-Rod's, yes, sir.

After dinner, we talked about many subjects, but without lectures, shows, etc. Just talk. We were always curious to know what J-Rod's routine in the disc was. And he delighted us with his stories. We were all becoming addicted to J-Rod.

The next morning, I woke up a bit earlier and went to the kitchen to get some juice. Then I heard the key turning in the lock, the door opened, and Mayra and J-Rod entered the dome hurriedly.

"We went for a walk before you woke up, said Mayra. Let's do breakfast," she shouted at J-Rod, who looked suspiciously at me and ran after her.

During breakfast, I noticed that Mayra wore a tired countenance, yawning repeatedly and, even, looked a little dirty. J-Rod was absolutely quiet and looked sideways at Mayra from time to time.

Chapter 97

Return to the Morgue

Since J-Rod had completely recovered, we decided to return to the morgue with two aims: prepare the remaining bodies for launch and explore this hall in more detail.

A few days later, we departed our dome in the morning after a nice breakfast prepared by Mayra and J-Rod. In a curious way, it seemed, to me, that Mayra was dominating J-Rod and, I suppose, not in the same way Antonina dominated me.

This morning, J-Rod was very excited since we were going to a place he (supposedly) knew well. At any rate, he was the center of our attention. He wore a nice uniform; let's say ... yellow, black boots, sunglasses, and his sword (just in case). And, he carried a backpack that seemed full of items. I asked him about the contents of his pack, and he responded that Mayra knew and that was enough. Despite his load, J-Rod seemed to be navigating well through the trail between Dome 1 and Dome 2.

During this open-air part, he was very talkative. Also, he proved agile and strong at the ladder, to the point of carrying Mayra's backpack down the ladder from Dome 2 to the floor below.

We, finally, got to the morgue. There were still 4 bodies to be launched. They were nude and within plastic bags filled with glycerin.

They still had to be placed within the plastic cylinders in order to be launched to space. That part was not difficult.

The most difficult step was to attach the plastic cylinders to the negative mass cylinders. But J-Rod knew about this, as well as calculating the amount of counterweight to each body. Therefore, I decided to spare the reader from this boring operation.

"J-Rod, what's the use of these transparent cylinders? Why not send the bodies wrapped in some tarpaulin, like we did in our previous launchings of Isobel and Fabiana and later with Frederico and other things?"

"Jota, these cylinders are pressurized chambers. Of course, we could use the bags in which the bodies are now. They can also be pressurized. However, due to a question of honor and some protocol, the Landians require the cylinders to be used. It has to do with the ceremony of launching, too."

It's only important to say that the final assembling of the cylinders with the negative masses was done in the hall of the left arm of the cave, where the launching tube is located.

It took us two more visits to the right and left arms of the cave in order to leave everything ready for the launching of the remaining 4 bodies.

Finally, on a very dark night, we could send all the bodies to space, and I had, in part, fulfilled the mission the Landians had left to me.

We went to our dome, thinking that we would never have to return to those two arms of the cave.

Little did I know that it was not to be so.

One evening, after a nice dinner, I asked J-Rod about the negative masses.

"Tell me, J-Rod, I got very curious about those negative masses. How are they used in the disc's propulsion?"

"Jota, those masses are not used in propulsion. How did you get that idea? We use them as a negative counterweight in order to neutralize part of gravity."

"And how did the Landians obtain these negative masses?" I asked.

"Well, in Landa, it was found that some rocks have small quantities of particles of negative mass mixed into the much more abundant normal matter of the rock. This was found by accident when some rocks were pulverized. A very keen operator observed that some part of the powder went up and was kept at the upper part of the reservoir."

"This was an extraordinary discovery that upended physics and made the theoreticians pull out their hair. All physical laws forbid negative mass. Not even antimatter could have negative mass."

"To separate those negative mass particles from the normal ones is easy in principle, but quite laborious in practice. The negative mass particles are concentrated at the upper part and later combined with a low proportion of high-performance cement. One aspect of these negative mass particles is their enormous density of 25 grams/cm^3. They seem to be formed by an unknown element. Happily, they are not the least radioactive."

"OK, J-Rod, now I understand, but then what brings about the discs' propulsion? Are you going to hide that from me?" We were at the table, and someone kicked my shin below the table.

"No, Jota, I'm not hiding anything from you. The disc's propulsion uses gravity waves."

And, J-Rod went on:

"In the dark side of Landa, they found certain rocks capable of repelling objects. Initially, it was supposed they were magnetic. And, the effect was weak. But, then, it was found that the repelling material was extremely diluted in the rocks, something like what had happened with the negative mass particles. After some years, they could purify the repelling material, and they found something extraordinary. The material not only repelled other similar materials, but it also repelled itself."

"Now, J-Rod, that is too much. How come something may repel itself?"

"Jota, look this way. Suppose a chemical rocket fuel. If you burn it in an open place, it produces an enormous expansion of gases. But, since the gases expand equally in all directions, you get no thrust. If, on the other hand, the gases are burnt inside a bell-shaped chamber, they expand in only one direction. And, they move the rocket in the opposite direction."

"The same reasoning our engineers used for the gravitational waves. They found a material that reflects gravitational waves. Using this material, they constructed a bell-shaped chamber.

Then, they observed that, placing the repelling rocks inside such a chamber, the recoil of the gravitational waves pushes the closed portion of the bell with an extraordinary force, and this provides thrust."

"But, how can they keep the repelling material inside the bell?" asked my brother.

"That was the easy part, Luiz. It was solved by just closing the other side of the bell with a material that is non-reflecting for gravitational waves. Just remember this, Luiz: what matters is that you create an asymmetry in the system."

Now, it was my turn to ask questions:

"OK, J-Rod, this is all very nice. But where does the energy of these waves come from? This gravity motor requires astronomical quantities of energy!"

"Our scientists already knew that the vacuum is a repository of energy and, actually, the vacuum is not empty. It has even been demonstrated that vacuum exerts pressure, and this was discovered by an Earthian physicist, Hendrik Casimir, in 1948. It is the *Casimir effect*. In Landa, our scientists, and I mean, Lesser Landian scientists, suggested two theories to explain the origin of energy in the gravitational waves. Some of our scientists found that the repelling material is capable of absorbing the vacuum energy and transforming it into an intense gravitational radiation."

"But, another group didn't accept that theory. This last group proposed that the new material, under adequate conditions (that I will explain later), was breaking the protons into their constituent quarks. They knew that the proton mass is way larger than the sum of the masses of its three constituent quarks. And that mass difference was being converted into energy. And, a huge amount of energy at that."

"They proposed that it was analogous to nuclear fission, with the difference that it wasn't the nucleus but the proton that was suffering fission. And, the energy that keeps the quarks "glued" inside the proton is way, way, way larger than that released in the nuclear fission or even in nuclear fusion."

Then, I had the unhappy idea of asking J-Rod my question.

"OK, J-Rod, very interesting. But, very funny, too! You are telling me that you people are using a motor whose energy source is based on theories?? And, worse still, whose principles you ignore?"

At my comment, J-Rod threw a look at Mayra. But Mayra, this

time, didn't seem to bother with my comment. What I saw was Mayra simply nodding at J-Rod.

"Well, well, Jota, you are quite right here. But, what about seeing this in another way?"

"All living beings breathe, right? And, they have been doing this for millions of years. However, the biochemical mechanisms of respiration were never known to animals, and only recently have they been known to men. Despite that, we all breathe, do you agree? And, we have been breathing since a long time. How does that strike you, tell me? Isn't that funny too?"

This time, J-Rod got me really unprepared. Mayra and even my brother clapped hands at J-Rod, who was elevated to heaven and received a good slice of chocolate cake, a dose of brandy, and many kisses from Mayra.

For myself, I decided to keep my mouth shut for some time. And, it was my brother, as an engineer, who asked J-Rod the next question:

"J-Rod, and how do you control the thrust generated by the gravity motors?"

"Well, Luiz, this was an intelligent question!" said J-Rod, looking at me.

"We use a method that has many things in common with what is used in the fission reactors on Earth. We discovered that if the mass of repelling material is small, the gravitational waves are very feeble. But, increasing the mass, the gravitational waves increase in a much larger proportion, and consequently, the propulsion force"

"And, I give an example: one of the small bells generated a thrust of only 100 kgf. But, bringing together another identical bell, the propulsion force increases 100 times and goes to 10,000 kgf. And we have much larger bells. In this way, we control the disc thrust by changing the distance between the bells.

"And, how do you change thrust direction? How do you tell the disc where to move?" asked Luiz.

"There are two means of changing the disc direction. There are fixed directional bells pointing to many directions. If we want to move to the right, we activate the bells pointing to the left. To move left, we activate the bells pointing to the right. The same holds for upward and downward movements.

The second process is through gimbaled bells, which can point to any desired direction.

But, in reality, computers do that for us. We simply set the direction we want to go and the disc's acceleration or velocity. The computers find the best combination of bell's thrust and direction."

Despite my previous idiotic comment, I felt I needed to ask J-Rod's opinion:

"But, J-Rod, there is something I don't quite understand. You always mention that "our scientists discovered this", "our scientists developed a method for that," and so on. However, I was told that all advances in science were either obtained thanks to the Larger Landians or came from Procyon 2 in the form of a constant inflow of data. This is what Yuri, Greg, and Antonina told me."

J-Rod began to laugh loudly:

"And, you, Jota believe in all they tell you? Do you believe those "transmitters" from Procyon 2 know everything? They know a lot about medicine, so there is no question. Also, Larger Landians became bureaucrats; they don't do research anymore."

"Also, Jota, there are many things they didn't tell you, but if you excuse me, I will finish my answer to your brother's interesting question," he said, putting on airs.

"As I explained, Luiz, the gravity motors/reactors are entirely controlled by computers. But there was a time when this task fell upon the pilots. And many accidents happened, with hundreds of lives being cut short."

"What sort of accidents can happen?" Luiz asked.

"Well, you, Earthians, had the nuclear accident in Chernobyl in 1986. The graphite moderator rods couldn't control the chain reaction, which went out of control. In the case of our gravity reactors, the accidents can get even more dramatic. If too many bells get together, the gravitational forces attain immense values and the disc becomes a projectile out of control."

"And, J-Rod, do you know how to handle the disc controls?" asked Mayra who was, up to now, suspiciously silent.

Luiz and I looked at each other, already waiting for J-Rod's exhibitions.

"Are you asking if I know how to handle the disc controls?" said J-Rod, assuming the stance of a general.

"I am the master of all pilots. It was I who taught them to control the reactors. I hope one day I can show you my expertise!"

Little did we know that this day was not too distant.

Chapter 98

More on J-Rod's Suitcase

This night we all went to sleep a bit late, after having listened to J-Rod's numerous adventures, some real, others not so much. I remember well that at about 5 in the morning, it began to rain heavily. The dome's two coverings absorbed the rain's noise quite well, but despite this, it was clearly possible to hear the violence of the storm. The howling of the wind and the gusts of rain made my sleep lighter than usual. At 6 in the morning, not being able to sleep anymore, I went to the kitchen to get something to drink.

It was, then, that I heard the noise in the lock. Soon, Mayra and J-Rod entered the dome. It was a deplorable scene. They were absolutely soaked and covered in mud and plant leaves. J-Rod's uniform changed colors erratically, probably due to some short circuit in its internal controls. The color parade was incredible, with many of the colors unknown to me. The extraordinary show of colors and lights was in sharp contrast to his predicament.

"We went for a walk, and it began to rain. And, we were too far from the dome!" Mayra was saying, as she wept.

J-Rod was silent and looked down at the floor, not knowing what to say or having been instructed by Mayra not to say a word.

Then they moved quietly to their quarters. My brother and I had breakfast at 8, alone at the table.

It was only at 11 in the morning that Mayra appeared in the hall, well disposed, as if nothing special had happened. Soon after, J-Rod appeared, very quiet, and throwing some inquisitive looks at Mayra. J-Rod wasn't wearing his uniform and was nicely attired in some Mayra's pants and a t-shirt.

"We are going to prepare a nice lunch for you!" Mayra said, grabbing J-Rod's hand and drawing him to the kitchen.

While they were in the kitchen, I commented with my brother about the mysterious absences of Mayra and, more recently, Mayra plus J-Rod.

"Do you think, Luiz, they might be having an affair?"

Hearing this, my brother had a fit of laughter.

After a delicious lunch, we all went for a brief siesta.

Later on, I was in the hall talking with my brother when Mayra and J-Rod appeared suddenly.

"J-Rod, why don't you show us a few more things from your suitcase?" asked Mayra, more as an announcement. They certainly had essayed this.

At this, J-Rod went to his room and promptly brought his suitcase and placed it on the table. Doing a sort of staging, he opened it and took out what appeared to be a big pair of binoculars.

"This is a universal viewer," he announced.

"And what does it serve for?" My brother asked.

"Well, it serves to view things," J-Rod said, putting on an innocent air.

"And, what sort of things can we view using it?" I asked.

"Well, Jota, that's difficult to answer since, with this, you can view almost anything. Come here, Jota, take the binoculars."

And, saying this, J-Rod connected the instrument to his suitcase, adjusted something on it, and lay down on the table.

"Jota, now see me," he said, pointing to his chest.

"Put it against my chest and look," he said to me.

As soon as the instrument touched J-Rod's chest, I began seeing his internal organs. It was like something you see in an ultrasound exam, but a hundred times sharper, and in color and 3D. I could see J-Rod's lungs; there were two of them, one on each side of his chest, and I could see them inflating and deflating. However, where I thought to be the heart, there were 3 pulsating structures.

One heart was bigger than the other two. Arteries, veins, and ducts were seen perfectly.

"How come you have 3 hearts, J-Rod?"

"Yes, Jota; we, Lesser Landians, have 3 hearts. The big one is for the arterial system. It irrigates all organs. The slightly smaller one at my right is a venous heart, and it brings venous blood to my lungs, so that they can uptake oxygen and eliminate CO_2."

"OK, J-Rod, but what about that small heart, well above the big heart. You forgot it?"

"No, Jota, I didn't forget it. This is the brain's heart. It irrigates my brain. Don't you people think my brain deserves an exclusive heart?"

"Yes, J-Rod, your brain deserves much more oxygen than those of some people I know," said Mayra, looking at me and my brother.

"But I see they don't pulse in synchrony," I remarked.

"Sure they don't, Jota. All three hearts have independent control, and they beat in accordance with the needs of their target organs. When I exercise, my big heart beats faster and stronger. The venous heart also beats more. But the brain's heart doesn't change much. But, when I use my brain, as you have seen me using it, the brain's heart beats faster and stronger."

"Take a look, Jota; now, I will close my eyes and relax. See what happens to the brain's heart."

Then, J-Rod closed his eyes and relaxed. Soon, the smaller heart irrigating his brain began beating slower and slower, until it stopped beating at all.

"J-Rod, J-Rod, wake up, your brain heart stopped!" I shouted, shaking him. Mayra was raging at me.

"What have you done to him, Jota!!" cried Mayra, almost getting to my neck.

J-Rod, then, opened his eyes and began laughing loudly.

"I forgot to tell you that the big heart also sends blood to my brain. Actually, the small heart didn't stop completely. It kept beating at only 5 beats per minute," shouted J-Rod, laughing.

Another difference in J-Rod's anatomy, that I saw, was his vertebral column; it wasn't "vertebral" at all. It was formed by a single and strong cartilaginous tube and was very flexible, according to J-Rod.

Well, I couldn't keep examining J-Rod since Mayra and Luiz were on the line to use the binocular on J-Rod. And then, came Mayra's turn to view J-Rod's interior department.

"How beautiful you are, J-Rod, everything is working in concert, like an orchestra!" exclaimed Mayra.

Finally, it came Luiz's turn to observe J-Rod.

"And, what else can we view inside the body, J-Rod?" said my brother, after viewing J-Rod's tour number 1.

J-Rod adjusted the controls in the binoculars and asked my brother to examine his own hand.

"I can see my bones, arteries, muscles, I see everything!"

exclaimed Luiz.

"J-Rod, apart from the human body, what else can we see with this instrument? Can we see things far away?" I asked.

As an answer, J-Rod invited us to the outside. It was a nice afternoon, not too hot.

"Can I see the Sun with your binoculars?" I asked J-Rod.

"Yes, you can see the Sun after I make some adjustments. And, remember you all, that looking at the Sun with any optical instrument is very dangerous. It can make you go blind permanently!

Look at the Sun only with appropriate filters"

After the adjustments, J-Rod handed me the binoculars, and I pointed them at the Sun. What I saw, I had only seen in photographs from big telescopes. I could see enormous sunspots, and, at the limbo, gigantic flames seemed to be leaping from the Sun.

Chapter 99

Changed perceptions

The next morning, as I left my room, I saw that breakfast was already at the table. Mayra and J-Rod were finishing the table, and they did not look tired. On the contrary, they were well-humored and talkative. However, J-Rod repeatedly looked at Mayra as if he were waiting for some instructions. *What if Mayra is dominating J-Rod?* I thought in a sort of humorous vein.

After breakfast, we went out since the morning was glorious.

Mayra was meditative, letting J-Rod do the talking. And, talking, he did, all right.

With the passing of time, I got more and more concerned about Mayra not having asked more of Antonina. It seemed to me that she knew all she wanted to know or all that there was to be known regarding Antonina. And, she forgot to disguise that.

Also, I believed that the first questions she asked about Antonina, when we found her imprisoned in the cave, were mostly to make us think that she was ignorant of Antonina's whereabouts.

In this way, my instinct regarding things not asked and things not said came back to poke my mind.

We had lunch, took a siesta, and talked all afternoon inside, since the sun was too hot.

After dinner, we went out to see the Moon rising. It was a nice evening, with an ideal temperature. The moon had already risen and was glorious. In the moonlight, all things acquired a phantom tinge. J-Rod's uniform had lost most of its color but was now, sort of luminescent.

"J-Rod, what is the advantage of having so many color options on your uniform? Besides aesthetics?"; I asked.

That was one question I shouldn't have asked, but it was too late. Surprisingly, Mayra didn't get upset at my question. I think she was foretelling my predicament.

"Jota, the many color options are not an objective; they are a consequence or byproduct of a sophisticated system of altering perception. Do you think we would be concerned with such futility as colors?" He said, using a voice tone that heralded a counter fire.

"Our uniforms can work at two visibility extremes: invisibility and maximum visibility."

"Can you give us an example, J-Rod?" asked Mayra. She didn't like long explanations and was for immediate results.

"OK, please close your eyes and look away from me." said J-Rod.

We turned away and closed our eyes.

"OK, now you can look at me!"

The night was advanced, and the only light came from the Moon. We were on a stretch of ground covered by very white sand. Our bodies cast long shadows on the white sand. Everything had a surreal tone, like happens when the Moon is the only source of light.

But, there was no sign of J-Rod.

"Where are you, J-Rod?" shouted Mayra loudly, assuming he was distant.

"I'm right here!" There came a voice 15 meters away.

From his voice, we knew that J-Rod was quite near us, but we didn't see him.

"J-Rod, please, where are you!" again shouted Mayra, a bit upset now.

"I'm here, right in front of you!"; J-Rod said in a low tone, indicating he was about us.

Suddenly, appeared in front of us, about 10 meters away, an orange luminous creature, so brilliant it cast our shadows on the white sand. It seemed to be floating about half a meter from the ground.

"Here I am, and those are the extreme modes of visibility of my suit. And, this is achieved by the interplay of ... colors, Jota. Does this answer your question?" said J-Rod, giving the "coup de grace" to my question.

But, soon, J-Rod proved to me he was not upset at my provocative question.

"How did you do that, J-Rod?" Mayra asked as she went to kiss him.

"Don't do that again, J-Rod, you have scared me!" she said.

J-Rod explained that the "invisible" mode of his suit was not actually invisible.

"What happens in the 'invisibility mode' is that the uniform has a computer that analyses the background and adapts to it. It's like a chameleon. And for the head, we use this!" and he took off a hood that was covering all his head, leaving only an aperture for the eyes.

"And, there are other modes," J-Rod said as if casting a bait.

Mayra took the bait.

"And aren't you going to show us the other modes, J-Rod?"

"Since you insist, I think I can show you something else." Now, J-Rod was full of himself and was just waiting for Mayra's question to give his final push.

"There is a special mode in the uniform that serves to confound or scare a threat or an enemy. Be it an animal or even another humanoid."

"And how is this done?" my brother asked J-Rod.

J-Rod placed the hood onto his head and stood about 10 meters in front of us.

What we saw was something really confounding and then scaring.

J-Rod had transformed into an illuminated sign that changed the views, like those signs at Times Square in New York City.

But, soon, the scene changed to horror. J-Rod had transformed into a monster, into a lion, into a zombie. Into gargantuan mouths opening menacingly. And, sounds. Horrific sounds.

"Stop, J-Rod, for God's sake, stop this, please!!" shouted Mayra.

Immediately, J-Rod transformed into ... J-Rod.

"And, what does the invisible mode serve for?" asked my brother.

"Being invisible has many advantages for hunting and for not being hunted," laughed J-Rod.

"OK, J-Rod, but how can you support cold in this uniform so thin?" asked Mayra.

"Oh, yes, I forgot to mention this. Our uniform has *active heating*."

"But, what is this active heating all about?" asked Mayra, a bit upset with the enigmatic definition of J-Rod.

"Can't you go more to the point, J-Rod?" she insisted.

"OK, I'll give an example: when it's cold, we use a blanket to sleep, right? And with more cold we use two blankets. But, the question is: does the blanket warm us?"

"Of course, the blanket does warm us! What a nonsensical

question!"

Something happened that Mayra wasn't defending J-Rod at all costs. Mysteries...

"In fact, the blanket makes us warmer but it does not warm us. The blanket does not provide heat for us," said J-Rod.

"Oh, J-Rod, c'mon. Are you making a fool of me? If the blanket does not provide the heat for me, then who provides, tell me?" asked Mayra now, fuming.

"Mayra, when you cover yourself with a blanket, the heat provider is your own body. The blanket simply prevents your own heat from dissipating. And then, you get warmer."

Mayra was listening in silence. And J-Rod went on:

"But if it is really too cold, then the blanket cannot warm you anymore, since there is a limit on how much heat your own body can provide. And here, enters the electric blanket and, this one, heats you."

"But, I can't see any electric blanket over you, J-Rod," replied Mayra, now not only upset but also bored by the long explanations of J-Rod.

J-Rod sighed and took from his suitcase a little bag which he attached to the back of his uniform, like a small backpack.

"Come here, Mayra, and touch me."

Mayra touched J-Rod's uniform and retrieved his hand, shouting:

"It's too hot, J-Rod."

"This is what we call *active heating,*" said J-Rod.

"OK, J-Rod, what you have shown us is really fantastic! But why do the climbers in the Himalayas not use clothes with active heating instead of wearing heavy clothes? And, even so, they risk having fingers amputated due to intense cold!" I asked, more to give some continuity to the talk.

"Well, Jota, remember when I explained that the *energy* was the most important item in my suitcase? The answer to your question comes exactly from this."

"This suit of mine, in the mode of active heating, was spending 2 kilowatts of electrical power. A conventional battery, having a reasonable weight in order to be carried in a backpack, wouldn't keep my uniform heated for more than half an hour. It is energy, Jota, it all comes to energy!"

Chapter 100
How They Live

J-Rod told us that all of their species live on the discs and are in constant change of location.

"We are *nomads* and *extractivists.*"

"What are nomads and extractivists?" asked Mayra.

"Nomads are those people who have no fixed residence, since they are extractivists," he explained.

This answer left Mayra still more confused and, now, upset. And, this was what J-Rod was aiming at.

"Mayra, extractivists are those people who have no agriculture or raise animals for food. They just hunt and harvest what they find in the forests and fish in the rivers."

"When their food gets scarce they have to move and, as such, they are called *nomads.* Agriculture and animal raising are very recent; they exist only for a few thousand years".

"And a *few thousand years* is recent, J-Rod?" asked Mayra, each time more upset with the enigmatic talks of J-Rod.

"Yes, Mayra, it's quite recent if you consider that humanoids have existed for millions of years."

"The primitive populations were all nomads and extractivists," I remarked.

"In reality, we are not totally extractivists, since we obtain much of our food in Landa," went on J-Rod, oblivious of my remark. Another part of our food comes from the arrangements we have with the Larger Landians. They furnish us food and we provide them with *transport services*, using our discs."

"Our entire life orbits around our disks. They are our home and our transportation. A major part of our activities is related to the discs' maintenance and this has to do with the obtaining of the gravity rocks. Each disc is a small community composed of pilots, mechanics, engineers, medical doctors, dentists and other specialists. And, their entire families. Men and women have identical functions. We reckon the marriage bond; we generate children and raise them very well. We all live together in the discs, but we have our privacy and our private quarters.

"Our discipline is military and we have a hierarchy. We have a sort of "general", commanders and other ranks. Obedience is absolute. However, our rigid costumes have finality: our survival. This is opposed to the Larger Landians, who have useless rules based on beliefs and transmitted from generation to generation by the monks. Our rules are malleable and based on common sense. But, they must be obeyed. For example, if a given couple decides to separate, this is taken to a council and solved rapidly."

"And, J-Rod, tell me: are you married?" asked Mayra.

"I'm not yet married since I'm too young. I'm only 60 Earthian years old. However, as I don't know if I will ever reunite with my people, I'm looking for a wife right here on Earth," he said, putting on an indifferent air.

Mayra blushed immediately. And, everyone laughed.

Chapter 101

J-Rod's Weapons

The next morning, after a breakfast prepared by Mayra and J-Rod, we went for a walk. I don't know why J-Rod decided to bring his suitcase. Fortunately, I found a bag cart among the many items left behind by the family in its run. Certainly, J-Rod's intentions in bringing his suitcase were some sort of showing off.

"J-Rod, not counting your amazing sword, have you got any useful weapons in your suitcase?" I asked during a brief stop in our walk.

J-Rod didn't like, in the least, my satirical question.

"As a matter of fact, I've got something on that line; want to see?" J-Rod answered in an even more provocative way.

Then, he opened the suitcase and, theatrically, extricated from it what seemed to be a metallic rod 40 cm long and about 3 cm wide.

"That's a laser, Jota."

"Yes, I can see it all right. It's those paper-burning lasers, right?"

"In a sense, yes, Jota; it does burn paper, among some other things. Is there some target here where I can test it?"

"There, J-Rod," and I pointed to a dead Eucalyptus tree, some 30 cm in diameter at the base.

"You can try your laser there," I said

Joaquim

J-Rod connected the laser to his suitcase, by means of an electrical cord, made some adjustments in the laser, and handed it to me.

"You are the one to try, Jota. See this red button, it works in two stages. The first stage is just to aim and, pressing all the way down, fires the laser. Try it, Jota, and put on these special glasses."

It was a fast adaptive optics glass and it was already dark due to the day's glare. I did as J-Rod told me and pressed the red button halfway down. A very bright green dot illuminated the Eucalyptus trunk. I aimed the dot at the center of the trunk and, then, pressed the button all the way down.

There was a very high clicking sound coming from the tree and some smoke appeared at the site.

"Is that all, J-Rod? I see it really burns some of the wood."

"Why don't you go nearer, Jota, maybe you'll find something else?"

When I fired the laser, I was about 30 meters away from the tree. As I got close, I could see it. There was a hole the thickness of a pencil going all the way through the trunk. It was so perfectly cylindrical that I believe no drill bit could have done it with better precision.

"You have used it at low energy, Jota. We use this mode to hunt medium-sized animals. With less energy, we can hunt birds, even flying birds. At higher energies, it can pierce armored vehicles."

"Now, J-Rod, suppose you are lost in a desert and your water reserve has finished. How can your suitcase help you?" I asked this, trying to change the subject a bit since I had been really humiliated by my comments on weapons; not counting that J-Rod might have been offended.

"That's a good question, Jota, and I think I have the answer right here". And he tapped his suitcase.

And he said: "Even in a desert with very low humidity in the air, there is still some water in the air. Thus, it is a question of extracting that water from the air."

"Suppose you have 100% humidity at 30 degrees Celsius. Then, you have 30 grams of water per cubic meter of air. In a desert, at 30 Celsius and 10% humidity, you have 10 times less or 3 grams of water per cubic meter of air. So, even in the desert, you have some water in the air; see what I mean?"

"Let's do the experiment right here. We may have some 50% humidity today. And, doing this demonstration is important, since I can check if the equipment is working OK."

From one of the numerous "secret" compartments in his suitcase, J-Rod took a device looking like a hair dryer of sorts. He made some adjustments to it. At the output of the device, J-Rod placed the bottom of a cut soda plastic bottle. Then, he turned on the device. Soon, water began dripping into the bottle and, in some 15 minutes, we had about 100 ml of the purest water. J-Rod explained that the water generator passes the air through a system of frozen coils that condense the water vapor from the air.

"Again, this is a question of energy. To cool the coil, we need electrical energy. This one uses the *Peltier effect*: an electrical current creates a temperature difference across a system. One side gets hot and the other side gets very cool".

And the water was very good!

Chapter 102

J-Rod Goes to the City

I think it was the next day after J-Rod's exhibition of his suitcase. We were relaxing in the hall, after a nice dinner prepared with J-Rod's recipes. Then, out of the blue, J-Rod asked us if we could take him to the city.

"I've never been into a city. I saw the cities from very high above or in photographs and movies. I would like so much to enter a real city. Is it true that there are lots of people close together and they don't know each other?"

Then, we promised him that we would take him to the city the next morning. We also had to do some shopping there since our food stocks were diminishing rapidly. Actually, too rapidly to tell the truth and that coincided with our bringing Mayra to our dome.

The next morning, as we were preparing to go to the nearby city, we came to a question: how to disguise J-Rod into a "normal" boy. He had the right size and was lean. The problem was his big head and his large eyes which made him different from "normal" boys. For the head, a nice cap would do the job. For the eyes, dark glasses would work. But there were other problems. He had too short legs for his stature and he walked in a very curious way. Then, there were his very peculiar hands. The final solution was to clothe J-Rod in Mayra's clothes, make him use gloves, dark glasses and Mayra's boots. Also, we asked J-Rod to strip off his uniform lest it might get temperamental and begin showing lights, you know. In the remote case someone asked about him, we would say that the "boy" had a skin condition. One minor problem, that J-Rod didn't speak Portuguese, was easy. He was American or English.

So, our difficult mission, this morning, was to take J-Rod to the city, disguised as a "normal" boy: easier said than done.

We, finally, got to the city and parked at the supermarket. As soon as J-Rod saw an ice cream parlor at the market complex, he said he wanted an ice cream since he had never tried this sort of food despite having heard "nice things" about it, that it was tasty, delicious, etc.

I bought an ice cream in a cone and, that, was a mistake. As the day was hot, the ice cream began to melt and drip down J-Rod's gloves and, without our seeing it, he took off the gloves. That, was the second mistake. By a sad coincidence, a boy, led by his mother, was passing by and he noticed the peculiar hands of J-Rod.

"Look, Mom, that boy has strange hands!"

We decided to go to a retired space while J-Rod finished his ice cream, which was about ruined with all the ensuing confusion.

Mayra, then, bought a family pot of the same ice cream and we promised J-Rod he would eat at home. In this way, not only J-Rod, but we all would enjoy the ice cream at home.

In order that J-Rod didn't get too upset, Mayra bought him a Coca-Cola, which he drank through a straw. J-Rod loved the Coca-Cola and said it was the most delicious beverage he had ever drunk. That, was a lie, as we would, later, verify.

The remainder of our shopping trip went on normally. On the way home, J-Rod was very talkative, saying he could not understand why so many people could stay so close together without knowing each other. And many other questions in the same line.

We had a rapid lunch at home and, after that, we all retired for a siesta. It should be mentioned that we used to have tea at 5 and, thanks to J-Rod's military discipline, 5 o'clock was really 5 o'clock. He was conditioned by the rigorous timetables in the disc.

That said, we were all seated at the table, tea ready, just waiting for J-Rod. Something was terribly wrong since it was 5:05 and no sign of J-Rod.

Mayra went to J-Rod's container and knocked at the door. No answer. She, then, got inside. The room was empty. The next step was the bathroom; and Mayra knocked at the bathroom door.

Then, she ran to us:

"J-Rod is dying", she cried: "please help!"

We all went to J-Rod's container and I knocked at the bathroom door.

"J-Rod, what happened?"

"I'm sick; I'm going to die!": and he was weeping desperately.

While we all were trying to see what happened, my brother had gone to the kitchen and, soon, he came back holding an empty pot of Vanilla Ice Cream, 500 grams.

Result: we had tea without J-Rod, and no one had ice cream for dessert after dinner.

Chapter 103

J-Rod as a Physician

For some reason, I slept badly this night and woke up with a terrible headache. Mayra and J-Rod had already prepared breakfast. They and my brother were talking at the table, waiting for me.

J-Rod had, completely, recovered from his intestinal problem and had a good disposition. He tried to justify his assault on the ice cream:

"I couldn't resist its flavor and consistency. Never had I savored such a delicious "aliment". I'm so sorry, etc, etc."

I came to the table looking really bad and Mayra got concerned with my strange appearance.

"I woke with a terrible headache, took all possible remedies to no result" I said.

J-Rod listened, silently, to my drama.

"I think, Jota, that we can solve this and without any drug;" he said smiling, sympathetically, at me.

He went to his quarters and brought his suitcase. Opened it and took from it a sort of hood. Then, he covered my head with the hood, adjusting it delicately on me. Then, J-Rod connected the hood to the suitcase by means of a cable.

"Now, Jota, sit comfortably here" he said, indicating the sofa, while he brought the suitcase to my side.

I sat as indicated while Mayra and my brother watched, attentively, the Hippocratic performance of J-Rod.

"Now, Jota, close your eyes and try to relax."

I think that some 2 minutes went by when I heard:

"Now, Jota, you can open your eyes": it was J-Rod talking to me.

Then, J-Rod removed the hood from my head and said:

"Now, Jota, let's have our breakfast."

And, it was only then that I perceived something was missing. My headache!

Our breakfast was a mixture of my recovery, J-Rod's recovery and J-Rod's extraordinary medical feat.

"But, now, I want to apologize to you all because I have lied to you" J-Rod said, out of the blue.

"I have told you that I remained here by mistake. It wasn't by a mistake. I was expelled from the disc for misbehavior."

"What happened, J-Rod, please tell us, I don't believe it" said Mayra in desperation.

"I was expelled because my superiors found me lying on the floor in the passenger's section of the disc, while we were parked at the farm."

"But, J-Rod, what is wrong with that? You may have fainted or have had some other problem. This happens every time!" I said

"No, Jota, it wasn't a health problem: I was drunk!"

"But how come, J-Rod; we know you like liquors and so do we" my brother said, amiably.

"I found a very beautiful bottle left over in the passenger's section and I tasted the contents. The taste was so good, but so good, that I couldn't stop drinking it. Then, I think I lost consciousness. My colleagues looked for me in all parts of the disc and, finally, found me lying on the floor, saying strange things and with a strong breath of alcohol. My superiors told me I was to stay grounded until they decided what to do with me. And that the other option would be prison in the disc. I chose to stay grounded since they told me my case would not be taken to the council."

"But, J-Rod, what kind of beverage was that that you have found so irresistibly good?"

"You ask if I remember the label. I'll never forget that damned label *"Cachaça do Norte, A melhor do Brasil"* that was the label" and it meant: *"Cachaça from North. The best of Brazil"*

Chapter 104

J-Rod on Domination

As the days went on, our life on the farm ran without incidents. The only deviations from normality were the occasional absences of Mayra and J-Rod, always synchronized. But, with the passing of the days, my brother and I began to find some regularity in these "events" since they occurred every three days. As we lived under complete liberty and independence, and having discussed this with my brother, we decided to ignore the events. The dome's door was locked during the night and the three of us had the keys. And, having keys implies responsibility and trust.

One night after dinner, I asked J-Rod about the process of domination occurring between Larger Landians and Earthians. In reality, only Mayra and I had gone through that process, with my brother completely unaware of it. In due time, I would explain to him.

After my question, J-Rod became silent; and we all perceived he was thinking about the best way to answer my question. Then, he sighed deeply:

"Jota, I was expecting this question from you and Mayra. Mayra told me of your relation with Antonina."

"Look, you two, Jota and Mayra. I know everything about this domination process. Remember that we, Lesser Landians, travel together with the Larger Landians between Landa and Earth and vice versa. This means more than 5 years of interaction for each roundtrip. Despite our differences, we discuss our problems openly. And, Jota, I also know of the recent discoveries of Dr. Alten Felder on the neuro-anatomical basis of the domination/submission process and also on the role of pheromones. And, yes, Jota, I know the specifics of your case. However, I don't know the details of Mayra's case."

While J-Rod was saying all this, my brother was very confused and asked if it would be better if he did not participate in the discussion.

"No, Luiz, I think you should stay because it is important that you understand what is going on," said J-Rod.

"The first thing I want to leave very clear from the beginning is that I am totally opposed to this process. I, and all Lesser Landians, know about this and we deplore it. We would never accept the manipulation of another being's mind."

"To summarize, in one phrase, the domination/submission process and also to make it clear to Luiz its significance, I have to say:

"The Earthians that go through the domination/submission process become **pets** of the Larger Landians."

"But, J-Rod, I don't understand. Why do they use Earthians as pets? Why don't they use other animals like we do here on Earth?" said Mayra, indignantly, and caressing Princess, who was sleeping on her lap.

"The reason, Mayra, I tell you the reason. First, there are no animals in Landa except Landians and Earthians. Sure, there are fish. And, the *inferior animals*, there, are the Earthians. And, due to the huge difference in intellectual development, Earthians are, naturally, prone to dominations. It's not something intentional. Just by interacting with the same Landian for an extended period of time, the Earthian gets dominated. He or she submits, spontaneously and naturally, to a given Landian mentor.

It's something like a self-submission, so to speak. It's a law of lesser effort. And, curiously, it's a fantastic arrangement for an Earthian to get dominated and be submitted to a Landian."

"But, J-Rod, what is the benefit for a Landian having an Earthian as a pet?" Mayra asked, even more upset.

"Look, Mayra, it's not a question of 'benefit'. It's a matter of love. Ironically, as it may be, it's all love. It's *domination through love*. In other words, it is a domination/submission occurring by means of love. The Landians love their Earthian pets the same way you love Princess, Mayra. And the Earthian pets love their Landian masters even more. It's love all over. It's absurd, it's wrong, but it's love all over."

"Try to look this way, Mayra: a dominated Earthian, called a Lamb, does no work whatsoever for his or her Landian Shepherd. And the Lamb eats freely, enjoys all comforts, and has liberty to see other Lambs, date them, marry them, and have children with them. And what do they do in exchange? Just love, just love, Mayra. It's like you and Princess: she needs you and you do need her: don't you need her, Mayra? And tell me; what keeps you and Princess together? Just love, Mayra, just love."

"I understand this, J-Rod, but Princess can't talk to me, she can't tell me if she likes me, if she loves me."

"Now, Mayra, now, you have a point. For a Landian Shepherd, his or her Lamb is a much more sophisticated pet than Princess is for you. The Lamb can talk; he can express love in a more complex way than Princess can express her love for you. Despite Earthian language being rudimentary as compared with Landian language, despite that limitation, Mayra, the Lamb can express love to the Shepherd in a much richer context. I must confess that, even being opposite to this practice, I can understand very well the necessity of Landians to have their Lambs."

Now, I was observing J-Rod. Behind the bohemian, loudmouth, Don Juan, showman, there was a super bright and mature being. Honest in principles, comprehensive, and very "humane".

And, J-Rod went on:

"Look this way, Mayra. Do you talk to Princess? Does Princess play chess with you or does she sing to you? Does she caress you (forbidden)? Does Princess tell stories to help you sleep at night?"

"Also, Mayra, I know you have been dominated by Yuri. News travels very fast! And, I have to tell you that you, Mayra, have been, to Yuri, a much more sophisticated pet than Princess is and never will be, for you!"

Mayra listened, silently, to the reasoning of J-Rod. Then, she stood up and ran away from the hall and, weeping profusely, went directly to her container, slamming the door shut. My brother remained quietly confused. I still would tell him all the facts.

After about 15 minutes, we all went to Mayra's room. I brought coffee with brandy and some sweets we had bought in the city. I sat at the border of her bed and held her hand, which was cold and damp. She was trembling and sobbing. J-Rod stood close to her, and my brother sat in a chair.

And, I said to her:

"Mayra, this all now belongs to the past. I also suffered the process and even more intensely than you did. I had crises, Mayra, and want to tell you everything one day. The important thing, now, is that we survived the domination process without permanent effects, of which I will also tell you in due time. We are Earthians, Mayra, and we are on our planet, the Earth, which is a paradise. Our lives will go on, we are materially rich now, Mayra. With only the stones and jewels in Isobel's room, we are rich. And, there is much more here, and it's all ours. Now, Mayra, you are part of our family, like J-Rod."

Then, it was J-Rod's turn:

"Mayra, try to look from this perspective. Don't you love Princess?

Don't you do everything for her? Isn't she happy with you? What would be the fate of the Princess if you abandoned her in the forest? What would happen to her? Don't you know Mayra?"

"Then, I will tell you. Princess would revert to a *feral cat.* Little by little, she would lose her docility and be transformed into a little beast. She would need to hunt to survive: birds, rats, anything that moves. Her life would be short and harsh. She would suffer cold, hunger, predators and, permanently, being challenged. But you, Mayra, you gave her a life and a very nice life at that. You have dominated her. And, you did this in the name of love, just love, Mayra."

"Then, Mayra, it is possible that what Yuri has done to you was the same that you are, right now, doing to Princess."

Then, Mayra calmed down, asked for more brandy, and some sweets.

"J-Rod, then you are saying that now, free from Yuri's domination, I have reverted to a state of wild beast?" asked Mayra.

"That's exactly what I said, Mayra. You have reverted to your original state of wild beast and came back to live in your jungle, which constitutes your own society. Now, free from Yuri's domination, your behavior, your desires, and your emotions and, yes, your problems and conflicts came back and are, now, a part of your original and wild personality."

And, J-Rod went on:

"For each race, and each intelligence degree in the Universe, there are different levels of wilderness; they are all relative concepts. This wilderness is the natural personality of the individual, being he or she, immersed in the corresponding society. Then, each one of us, be Earthians, Landians or whatever, has our natural or wild personalities. But, at being confronted and living with species having intelligences much superior to our own, our wild personality will modify, will adapt, and ... will submit. This occurs naturally between Larger Landians and Earthians, but occurs forcefully among other races, as I know very well, but want to keep it to myself."

"And you, Mayra, having been dominated by Yuri, you found refuge in his mental universe which is, supposedly, more elaborate and sophisticated than your own mental universe. In the same way your own mind is much richer and elaborated than that of the Princess. And, there are in the Universe, races having mental constructions way more complex than mine, for example."

"But, then, J-Rod, what should I do with Princess? Release her into a forest? Have I been wrong in adopting her? Am I ruining her life?"

While saying this, Mayra's eyes went wet with tears, and her features became sad and anguished. My brother and I became static, not knowing what to say. Again, it was J-Rod who answered:

"Mayra, don't worry about Princess. She is happy staying with you and you are happy, too, taking care of her and giving your love to her. You are necessary to each other. I won't judge Yuri. This is past."

"J-Rod, you are a great psychologist and a great friend," I said, and offered him an extra dose of brandy.

Chapter 105
J-Rod's Farewell

A few days after J-Rod's "lecture" on the domination process, we had just finished dinner and went to our rooms to wash. Then, we returned to the hall to talk as we did every evening, mainly after J-Rod began living with us.

However, strangely, J-Rod did not return. We waited and waited and no J-Rod. Then, Mayra went to his container to see what went wrong. Soon, she came back:

"Come, come, J-Rod is lying in bed and weeping."

We all went to J-Rod's container; the door was open. I sat on the only chair, my brother stood, and Mayra sat at J-Rod's bed and held J-Rod's little hand.

"What happened, J-Rod? Why are you crying?"

J-Rod, still facing the pillow and sobbing:

"I was summoned to work. We have a new mission!"

"And do you have to go, J-Rod?" asked Mayra, beginning to weep.

"Yes, I have to go. To refuse is certain death!"

"OK, J-Rod, but, after all, it's your job, isn't it? So, why do you get so sad about it?" I replied.

"Yes, J-Rod, why are you so sad?" Mayra repeated, pressing, lightly, J-Rod's hand.

"You don't know how nice it is living here on Earth! Here is the Paradise!" J-Rod answered, now, having stopped weeping.

J-Rod explained to us that the disc would pick him up here at the farm, 5 days from now. And he showed us his communicator with the countdown in decimal hours: 120.0234455 hours. The last three digits did not stop changing. The third digit after the decimal point decreased by one unit every 3.6 seconds. J-Rod said the countdown could be changed, but it was unlikely.

Two days before the departure, we threw a farewell party for J-Rod. But no one was happy at that party. Mayra was heartbroken and wept for anything. She couldn't imagine separating from his dear friend and counselor. We all were very sad and tried to make up for the time we had lost, not "savoring" J-Rod completely. Now, it was too late. We all knew we would never see J-Rod again. And that thought hurt our hearts.

On the fatal night, we had dinner earlier and reunited at the soccer field where the disc would land. J-Rod explained he had a very powerful signaler, and the disc would land precisely near, with no need to light signaling lights.

I will never forget that gloomy night. No Moon, it was very dark. The sky stared aggressively at us as if it was claiming J-Rod. The scent of the vegetation, of the damp earth and of the Eucalyptus trees permeated all. Everything brought me back to the gone phases of my life. Walking in the bush at night, the meetings in the open, at night, talks of strange creatures, ghost stories. I even remember one night I was alone, lying on the ground, looking at the stars. And, then, a large shadow came in at high velocity. Just a shadow, no sound, passed overhead and was gone.

A few minutes before landing, we were looking at the sky.

J-Rod wore his uniform, set to yellow, with all insignia, white gloves to the mid forearm, and black boots. He had a wide and ornate belt around his waist where his sheathed sword hung. Around his head was a yellow band. His uniform emitted some phosphorescent luminosity. The suitcase was on the ground beside him.

Now, J-Rod was silent, and it was clear to us he was very emotionally taken. I took a look at the countdown in his communicator: 0.324675. Mayra wept uncontrollably, holding my hand.

Then, J-Rod spoke:

"They are coming, look!"

We all looked up and saw a dark circle hiding the stars. But, we had no time to fix our sight because a strong wind began blowing from the soccer field toward us. In no time, the disc had stopped, and soon, we heard a strong boom arriving late, from about 20 km above us.

The disc was hovering at about 4 meters aboveground and, this time, it did not rest on the balloons. It oscillated slowly, like a ship at sea.

It exhaled a hot wind mixed with the smell of electrical machinery and hummed strongly. I could observe that the ground below the disc vibrated and seemed to recede down slightly, as if being pushed by a gigantic force.

J-Rod was static, just looking at the disc.

I could also observe that some parts of the disc became invisible, despite there was no smoke whatsoever. The invisibility alternate regions of the disc and, once, the entire disc got invisible for about 2 seconds. I, then, remembered the reports of Bob Lazar describing the invisibility of alien crafts, under certain angles. He explained that it results from the strong gravitational waves that distort the space.

About two minutes later, a chain was thrown to the ground. Then, there was a surprise for us. Just below the lower border of the disc, a window opened, revealing an illuminated interior. Two crew members appeared and waved at us. A ladder was lowered, touching the ground. But since the disc oscillated, the ladder sometimes detached from the ground.

J-Rod waited no time and, looking back briefly at us, ran and grabbed the ladder, which began being hoisted, carrying him to the disc's interior. Soon, J-Rod appeared at the window, along with 4 crew members, and they all waved at us.

But the window closed, and the disc was dark again.

Mayra wept profusely with her head on my shoulder.

J-Rod had told us about some green warning lights that were lit about 2 minutes before lift-off. We should move away from the disc about 100 meters, not to be sucked by the vacuum of the lift-off.

We moved away and waited.

Some seconds later, a circle of green laser lights around the lower rim of the disc began illuminating the ground so strongly that we had to avert our eyes. Then, the lights blinked three times.

At the last blink, a strong wind pulled us, strongly, toward the disc's position and, as we tried to keep our stance, nothing more was visible on the ground or the sky. Soon after, we heard a loud boom.

But J-Rod had prepared a surprise for us.

As we looked toward the south, there appeared some strong yellow lights that blinked.

What followed I will never forget. The disc had stopped at about 10 km away, to the south, as I calculated by its tiny illuminated silhouette. Then, it came toward us. It was so fast that we couldn't fix our vision on it. And it was flying so low that it appeared as if it was coming directly at us. What we could see was only an incandescent half circle at the front and a big conical cloud at the rear. Soon after it passed over us, we heard two loud booms in sequence. They were the famous "double sonic booms".

Then, there came a strong wind that shook everything; and the tall

Eucalyptus trees bowed to and fro two times.

Some seconds later, a great quantity of leaves, small branches, birds, and bats began falling dead to the ground.

Shame on you, J-Rod. He did not think of that. Then, a fine rain, very cool, began to descend over us. It was the condensed water vapor from the disc's tail.

And, finally, the silence.

J-Rod and his companions were in space. What destiny? We will never know.

We went back home, devastated. The absence of J-Rod created, in us, an immense hollow and this hollow hurt.

When I entered my container to get a bath I found a packet on my bed. Opening it there was J-Rod's super binocular and a short letter.

"My dear Jota, I leave these binoculars to you as proof of our friendship. I want to tell you, Jota, that you, your brother Luiz, and Mayra were the most amazing and dear creatures I have ever met. I hope to see you all someday in some part of the Universe.

Your eternal friend, J-Rod"

Chapter 106
Mayra is Pregnant

The departure of J-Rod left us a bit lost in space and time, so to speak. We sort of lost our ground. He filled our lives so intensely that we all felt a vacuum inside.

Due to J-Rod's departure we also went to bed a little late and, accordingly, raised late also. As I went to the hall I met there my brother and with his help we prepared the breakfast and waited at the table for Mayra showing up. Maybe Mayra went for her mysterious walks and didn't return. So, I decided to check at her room. I knocked at her door and she told me to come in. As I entered I saw that Mayra was at bed, weeping.

"What happened, Mayra? Don't cry, we are all sad about J-Rod's departure. Come have breakfast with us, everything is on the table."

"No, Jota, it hasn't to do with J-Rod. I'm feeling very bad and have something to tell you and Luiz."

I called Luiz, who sat in the chair. I sat at the bedside. Mayra held my hand, still weeping.

"There is no way to hide it anymore, Jota, I'm pregnant."

"How come Yuri did that to you and went away?" I said, indignantly.

"No, Jota, it wasn't Yuri; there is no father. I have received an embryonic implant. Yuri and his team implanted an embryo in me at the request of Antonina".

"And why are you weeping, Mayra? Is this bad news?"

"I accepted receiving the implant to fulfill Antonina's wish, since I was sure it wouldn't work. But, it worked; I just did the test and it is positive. And there are other signs also in my body. Not counting that I vomited the whole night, but I think I can eat something."

We went to the table and all stayed in silence. Then, Mayra drank a cup of coffee and began to talk.

"I didn't tell you, Jota, but I was becoming friends with Antonina. She was my confidant, and I used to tell her all my problems with Yuri and the experiments with the embryos. All nights we talked, either in her room or in mine. Antonina was a wonderful woman in all aspects. Our nocturnal talks were interrupted by the trip of Antonina and you to the mother-ship. But when you two returned, our talks continued and our friendship got even stronger. And, after your trip to the mother-ship, Antonina had many things to tell me; things that deeply tormented her."

Seeing that Mayra was stronger, I served her a coffee with milk and some toast with butter. She ate with gusto.

"I must tell you about the ampoules with the embryos. In fact, not all embryos were sent to space. I brought you only those embryos of the Indian chiefs. There is still a Dewar with some embryos."

"And what embryos are there, Mayra, please don't make such suspense. You want me to have a heart attack?" In fact, I felt my throat tightening, in advance of something terrible.

"We all have our embryos there, Jota: there are embryos of Greg, Marco, Frederico, Yuri, Isobel, Fabiana, Mayra, and Jota."

At this moment, I heard my brother sighing, relieved.

"But, Mayra, you didn't mention Antonina's embryo!"

"Jota, Antonina's embryo is here!" Mayra said, pointing to his abdomen.

"Antonina will be reborn in me!" said Mayra, and she went sobbing and embraced me strongly.

Mayra explained us that a team of Landians, led by Yuri, implanted, in her, Antonina's embryo. She said it is a very complicate process that uses advanced techniques.

After I had been assured that my own embryo had not been implanted in any woman, I lost part of my fear to ask a few things from Mayra.

"But, Mayra, can you tell me what sort of things Antonina told you about me?"

"Antonina told me that you and she were in love with each other. She said you two made love at the mothership. She said it was an impure act on her part because you were considered as vulnerable according to the Landian laws."

"And, there is more, Jota. Antonina left me a letter when she knew her destiny would be death. And I have this letter with me."

My brother looked at me open-eyed, without knowing what to do or to ask.

"Luiz, calm down, I will tell you everything. All is under control now, and you can be assured of that."

The letter of Antonina to Mayra was long and full of regrets and complaints of all sorts. In her letter, Antonina explained to Mayra how the domination process worked in Landa. However, Antonina's explanations were different from those of J-Rod and also different from those of Dr. Alten Felder to me. And, even different from the explanation of Nurse Rita to me.

J-Rod's explanation on the domination-submission process was way more direct, according to Mayra, and that was the reason Mayra got so upset.

It seemed to me that there wasn't a single consistent theory. But, Antonina's letter also had some requests. In her letter, Antonina begged that Mayra married me and we both took care of Antonina II, as if she were our daughter.

The next day, I made an appointment with a doctor in the city, to see Mayra.

Chapter 107

Visiting Antonina

Life on the farm went on and, after the revelation of Mayra's pregnancy, about three months had passed. Our life on the farm had got to a nice routine. We continued to explore the farm's underground, and from the big halls hidden below the surface, we began to organize the hundreds of items. We had found fantastic objects, devices, and things completely unknown to us.

One of our concerns was in relation to the maintenance of the various systems in the farm, in case some service should be necessary that required the coming of external personnel. We were not prepared for that. Fortunately, everything was working adequately. The farm's infrastructure had been well built.

We had a huge trove of precious stones and jewels, scattered among Antonina's tomb, Isobel and Fabiana's quarters and a few more places we found later. These and the occasional sale of some of those items guaranteed our financial independence. Our only excursions out of the farm were to shop in the city.

Mayra was being followed by a gynecologist in the city, and her pregnancy went by, normally. She was now in the 5th month of pregnancy, and the baby was found to be a girl.

Mayra was happier each day in being a future mother, and my

relation with her was getting stronger and stronger, and moving to a mature love.

However, none of us had taken the move to a physical approach. Mayra made it clear that some questions needed to be solved before. I would, soon, find out which questions those were. The mysterious absences of Mayra during some nights continued, though, with regularity. As I have commented, my brother and I have decided to ignore those leaves. I, from my part, trusted Mayra completely.

It's true that J-Rod's departure left us a bit lost in our initiatives. J-Rod had been a powerful link binding us together around his wonderful persona. We had been extremely enriched by his stay. His good humor, his affected petulance, and his intellectual prowess brought a dose of mystery to our lives. No days were equal with J-Rod and each day brought us a delicious surprise and also a few problems. Just to know that there were races in the Universe intellectually and technologically superior to us indicates that we should be humbler. At the same it gave us hope of better days.

Little by little, our depressive mood at the departure of J-Rod was disappearing, and our exploratory vein came back with a vengeance.

Mayra had told us, on many occasions, her desire to visit Antonina's tomb. However, I always delayed, justifying in one or another way. I was sure this visit would depress me and bring me sad remembrances.

It was on a morning, while we had our breakfast, that Mayra expressed her urge to visit Antonina.

"I just feel that I need to see her, that she needs me badly. And I think you two should come with me," she said.

Then, one day, we decided to comply with Mayra's wish and visit the tomb.

From our dome, we descended to the basement, from there to the bunker and the lower hall, whence departed the two tunnels: west and southeast. Our backpacks were filled to the brim with survival gear carefully chosen from Mayra's "professional" checklist.

Our progress through the southeast tunnel went on without incidents. We got to the second gate, the one that had betrayed my brother and me, trapping us below the ground. We also found out why the gate had locked, automatically, behind us on that fateful day. There was a sort of bolt, similar to the ones found in many apartment doors. The expression "locked out" conveys, exactly, what happened to us, with the difference that we had been "locked in".

To prevent a temperamental locking of that gate, we placed numerous pieces of wood at the jamb.

This time, the lighting of the tunnels was working and, soon, we came to the great deposit hall whence departed the tunnel to the tomb and the uphill tunnel which had been our escape route.

At the great hall we rested, drank the delicious water from the faucet, and had coffee and sandwiches.

Thus restored, we proceeded along the tunnel leading to the tomb. Just at the beginning of our walk through this tunnel, we all perceived a light wind coming from the tomb. And, in this wind, I felt, intensely, the scent of Antonina. However, I didn't make any comment on this.

Soon, we got to the fallen tombstone that lay exactly as we had left it many months ago.

And, we entered the tomb.

The big hall was illuminated by the big cylinder of light and many lamps, now functioning. Antonina's scent was, now, very intense and seemed, to me, to have a viscous consistency.

We entered the tomb's hall and, immediately, Antonina's mortuary chamber caught our eyes. Mayra held my hand strongly.

The chamber was empty.

"What happened?! Where's Antonina?" I shouted.

As we came closer to the mortuary chamber, I saw that the lid was open, and a complex mechanism of hinges became visible.

We began, hurriedly, to examine the big hall to see what might possibly have occurred. The scent of Antonina was so intense for my still sensitive olfaction that it seemed something almost solid.

Joaquim

"Come here!" shouted Mayra

Mayra was kneeling on the floor, beside a camping mattress. On the mattress lay Antonina, her eyes closed. She wore the same blue gown and was breathing calmly. Her features were serene, peaceful. She was a bit thinner but, still, so beautiful.

"She is sleeping," said Mayra, drying tears from her face.

Mayra, then, touched Antonina's arm lightly at the same time she held her hand.

"She's warm," Mayra said.

As soon as Mayra said this, Antonina opened her eyes, the same wonderful green eyes that, so much had fascinated me.

As she saw us, her features revealed some hesitation as if she was trying to identify us. I approached my face to her eyes. Antonina smiled shyly and, hesitantly, raised her hand to my face and touched it lightly. Then, she moved to my hair and caressed it. I began to weep and placed my head on her chest. She grabbed my head lightly and began caressing my face and hair. Silently.

"Let's give her some orange juice; she looks thirsty" said Mayra.

Then, Mayra led the bottle to Antonina's lips. Antonina smiled at me and took a sip of juice as she closed her eyes, savoring the juice. As soon as she finished the first gulp, she held Mayra's hand and brought the bottle again to her own lips. And, in doing this, she kissed Mayra's hand.

Mayra, then, went to get a pillow for Antonina's head and adjusted her head to the pillow. Then, she came to us and said in a low tone:

"She has a big depression at the back of her head!"

As we turned our attention to Antonina, she had sat on the mattress and was looking, questioningly, at us.

My brother brought a lawn chair and we helped Antonina to sit down. She smiled at us and we saw that she tried at speaking but with no success.

Mayra, then, decided to speak to her.

"Antonina, do you want some coffee?" Mayra asked while holding her hand.

Antonina nodded and when Mayra came with the coffee she drank it, savoring it between the gulps. And she did all this holding the cup in her own hands.

"Antonina, do you care for a chocolate bar?" I asked.

She smiled at me and nodded. As I brought the bar to her, she held my hand and kissed it long on.

Then, Antonina made a sign to Mayra that she wanted to sleep a bit. Mayra adjusted the pillow and she lay, calmly, on the lawn chair and closed her eyes. Then, Mayra signaled us to move to another part of the hall to let her be alone.

We, then, decided to examine better the general disposition of the "tomb". And, we found out that many things had changed since we had left the place that fateful day. This finding led me to suspect that someone was taking care of the place.

Now, we had better illumination and could see some order surrounding the mortuary chamber. It looked, now, more like a bed in an intensive care unit room: many intravenous (IV) equipment, flasks containing IV fluids, tubes, and needles. Cartons containing drugs, powerful injectable antibiotics still in their packs, some Landian stuff as we saw by the letterings.

Bandaging kits, kits for dressings, disinfectants. Everything was well ordered. The general impression was that Antonina was being cared for by someone with some medical expertise.

The nice clothes we saw on our first visit were still hanging on the walls and looked as if nobody had used them. Apparently, Antonina had used only a few gowns and some pajamas that were collected in a drawer.

Luiz and I began exploring other corners of the big hall while Mayra took care of Antonina, now seated comfortably in the lawn chair.

We located the shelves with the boxes; it seemed that no one had moved anything there. Apparently, Antonina's foodstuffs had been brought from elsewhere.

Some minutes later, Mayra called me saying that Antonina wanted to see me. She was seated in the lawn chair and I knelt on the floor at her side. Her scent invaded me with hundreds of remembrances and I was taken by a profound nostalgia and compassion. But, that was all that Antonina brought me. Gone was the fascination she exerted over me.

Antonina looked intensely at me and caressed my hair and my face. And, she was weeping quietly. Her glance, now, conveyed a plea, as if she was excusing herself for not being the previous Antonina, for not being capable, anymore, of dazzling me with her voice, her intelligence, and her sensuality. I perceived that plea and said, close to her ear:

"My love, I still love you and will love you forever! Nothing will change my love for you!"

She smiled humbly and kissed both my hands. And, as she looked at me, intensely, I understood she was excusing herself for not having been able to love me as she wished. In that look I saw, clearly, her regret for trying to take her life and her shame for not having been able to accomplish it. Also, her glance told me she was deeply sad for having failed in everything. Then, her look changed, ever imperceptibly, and I could see she was asking for my forgiveness.

"Antonina, let's go home!?" I asked her holding her hand.

She shook her head. Then, it was Mayra's turn, who had approached us.

"Antonina, don't you want to go home?"

Antonina shook her head again and pointed to the floor with his forefinger and moving her hand up and down, as if saying: "I want to stay right here!"

"Can you write, Antonina?" asked Mayra.

She nodded, and my brother brought a notebook and a rollerball pen. Then, Mayra handed the items to her.

"Antonina, write down whatever you want," Mayra said.

Antonina took the pen in her hand and began scrawling on the paper. Then, she looked at us as if she were excusing herself for not being able to write.

However, despite all the incredible unfolding of events, my "extra sensorial" perception was still active. Many small things looked amiss and did not fit together. And, that, converged on Mayra's attitudes. Each time, I got more and more the impression that Mayra was staging some acts. What caught my attention most was Mayra's initial reaction upon finding the mortuary chamber empty as we entered the tomb's hall. Her "surprised" reaction didn't seem sincere to me. It was too feeble. However, I chose to wait for more.

Not long after those ideas had passed through my mind, Mayra called me at a corner and asked if I thought it appropriate for her to tell Antonina of her pregnancy.

"Mayra, I think you should tell her; this will make her happier" I said.

Then, we all approached Antonina as Mayra prepared to tell her the news.

"Antonina, I have news to tell you. I'm pregnant!"

And, in saying this, Mayra pointed to Antonina and then to her own belly.

"You are here, Antonina!"

Antonina stood quiet with a thoughtful expression. Then, she held Mayra's hand and pulled her close. She held Mayra's head with her two hands and kissed her long in the face, forehead, and on top of her head as she wept quietly.

"Antonina, show us your home" Mayra said.

Antonina smiled shyly, stood up, and held Mayra's arm, showing her where to go. The two of them went on through the hall, my brother and I following them. We soon came to another room, up to now, unknown to me and Luiz.

Here, there was a complete kitchen with a refrigerator, a big freezer, a kitchen bench with a nice sink and faucet. There were many cabinets with glass doors revealing diverse items. And, through a door from the kitchen, we entered a big and complete bathroom with a bathtub and a shower.

"Now, you two get something to drink because I'm bathing

Antonina" and, saying that, they entered the bathroom and Mayra closed the door.

After Luiz and I had a beer and talked a little, the two girls reappeared with a refreshed look, and both smelling of bathing essences. They both were wearing nice bathrobes and had their hair wet.

Despite Antonina not being able to talk, Luiz and I got the clear impression that she and Mayra were communicating quite well. And, it also became clear to me that the girls had been in periodic contact since the "accident" with Antonina. Things were beginning to take shape, slowly, in my mind.

Also, it was clear that Antonina had an important mental deficit. Since her visible lesion was at the back of the head, I would expect some sort of visual deficit. However, that didn't appear to be the case. Anyhow, Landian's brains were different from ours.

But, what became evident for me was a general decrease in her higher brain functions. The shine in her look that revealed Antonina's geniality had disappeared. Her eyes, despite still being wondrous, had lost the flow of intelligence that fascinated and dominated me.

Antonina's proximity didn't give me anymore of that protective feeling, mental completeness, and security. On the contrary, I felt, now, his protector and I felt pity for her. Antonina wasn't anymore Antonina.

Seeing that Antonina was now well cared for by Mayra, Luiz and

I got back to our dome. We promised to come back later to have dinner with them.

As soon as we got to the dome, my brother and I began to process the mysteries of what we had witnessed in Antonina's tomb/apartment. Considering that she was alive, how could she have survived a fall of 40 meters or more from the cliff and onto rocky ground? I, then, remembered the protection net and I knew I had taken pictures of the cliff the day we explored the southwest tunnel and found Antonina's helmet lying on the rocks.

Another fact was that Antonina's lesions seemed to have been circumscribed to her head, since she was walking and moving normally.

I brought the camera and began analyzing the pictures of the cliff with the help of my brother.

With a small zoom, there was no indication of the protective net. Then, I remembered that the net was almost invisible and, even when I was down onto it, I couldn't see the net threads. But, by increasing the zoom, the fantastic Greg's camera revealed the delicate web of the net. Yes, the net was armed all the time and certainly was there when Antonina jumped to her "death".

But, the photographs revealed more. With the engineering expertise of Luiz, we could estimate that the net extended about 15 meters from the cliff's wall. This guaranteed that, whoever was being subject to the 'proof' would fall on the net, even if the jump extended a bit farther from the cliff wall. In order to surpass the net, the jumper would need some additional horizontal velocity that could only be achieved with a run.

And, Antonina, despite being a physicist, didn't take that into account. Once you are going to take your own life, you don't do much mathematics!

The result of our physical analysis was that Antonina knew she needed some horizontal impulse to clear the net but she may have, somehow, slipped before jumping. Anyway, she almost cleared the net. Almost.

Clearly, she had hit the net before falling to the rocks; otherwise, her death would have been instantaneous. By a combination of factors, her body hit the net border, lost momentum, and went down to the rock. However, most of her body must have fallen into the pool, explaining no damage to the body. But, her head hit the pool's rocky border, explaining that only her head suffered trauma. It seemed that we had solved the first part of the mystery, but there were still other, even more mysterious events.

Somehow, her friends found out that she had fallen from the cliff and came to rescue her, in time. And, certainly, she received medical attention, probably surgical manipulations.

Who could have provided this medical care? The only doctor in the group was Yuri and, probably, he got the help of another doctor from a Landian colony nearby. Antonina was operated on and placed at an ICU room. This, probably, was done at the farm's hospital, an annex at the cave.

But, then, the unexpected: the family had to leave the farm in a hurry. Antonina was now a chronic patient, still recovering from surgery, but unable to be transported.

Solution: Leave Antonina on the farm. But where on the farm could she be under medical care? She needed expert medical care.

Enter Mayra.

For some reason, the farm's hospital, at the cave's annex, could not be used. Probably, all equipment was removed, since the family would need it for a new colony, like they did with all the computers in the bunker.

The present tomb hall and all its facilities must have been constructed to maintain someone in need of medical care for a long period. And, even, for maintaining a dead member of the family during the post-mortem period when they believed the deceased needed some sort of comforts.

The strange design of the mortuary chamber where we found Antonina intrigued me. Also, from the medical point of view, I couldn't see how Antonina could be placed there without constant care from someone else.

Here, came to my mind a few possibilities, two of them based on real resources of Medicine: hyperbaric chamber and semi-intensive care;

or a combination of the two. A third possibility crossed my mind en passant but, due to the advanced status of Landian medicine, I couldn't discard: *hibernation therapy*. That last possibility came to my mind the instant I knew that Antonina wasn't dead. How come we saw her inside that chamber the night we got trapped? She was so serene and didn't seem to be breathing at all.

With our heads full of theories, my brother and I came back to the tomb at the end afternoon, bringing clothes and some food for Mayra and Antonina. Mayra insisted on staying the night with Antonina, taking care of her and, eventually, convincing her to move living with us at our dome.

As soon as we got to the tomb, I went with Luiz to examine the mortuary chamber, carefully. Immediately, it became clear to us that the chamber had other functions than that of keeping a dead body inside. It looked way more appropriate for keeping a living body.

There was some flexible tubing connected to the box, and we heard a low sound of air flow. Placing my hand against the inlets, it was possible to feel a gentle flow of air. I placed my head inside the chamber and the refreshing breeze of 100% oxygen invaded my nose. I saw, also, that on the walls of the chamber there was a system of valves, suggesting some mechanism of pressure regulation.

"Here is part of our puzzle"; I said to Luiz in a low voice.

"This is not a mortuary chamber; it is a life-supporting system" I said to him.

From everything we had found, we decided it was no use exploring more. It was clear that Mayra knew much more than she was trying to demonstrate. Since I trusted Mayra, I began considering that there was some reason for her keeping that entire mystery aura.

There was a battle in my mind regarding what I should do to get the truth from Mayra. I knew that whatever reason she had to keep me and my brother in this partial reality, that reason was valid.

Luiz and I came back to the dome, leaving Antonina under the care of Mayra. I couldn't get the necessary calm to sleep. Many things I had seen didn't make sense to me.

How could Antonina remain alone after a possible delicate neurosurgery? I knew that all members of the group left the farm in a hurry; being exceptions Fabiana, Isobel, and ... Mayra. And, of course, Frederico.

Who could have cared for Antonina during the post-operative period?

Everything pointed to Mayra.

All these questions came to my mind on the day we found that Antonina was alive and, of course, the answer to them would require some time.

As such, it became gradually evident that Mayra had been taking care of Antonina all the time since the accident. Except for the period

Mayra was imprisoned in the cave. And that was just a few days. During the period Mayra was trapped in the cave Antonina was for herself and, maybe, she was in a sort of induced coma or hibernation. Not counting that Antonina might have minimal conditions for self-care.

There was, now, only one thing to be done and that was a serious talk with Mayra.

The next morning, we left the dome early, without breakfast. We went to the tomb; I determined to learn the truth from Mayra.

Arriving at the tomb, we had a surprise as we met the two girls. Antonina looked better and was resting in the lawn chair. Knowing we had left without eating, Mayra called us to the kitchen to serve us some food and coffee.

Then, she began to talk:

"I know, Jota, that you and Luiz are not buying my narrative regarding Antonina anymore. But, before telling you the facts, let me justify. I was complying with Antonina's wishes. She asked me to hide the fact that she was alive and, mainly, that she was half-dead. She didn't want you to see her in that state; she said it was humiliating for her. She asked me to hide everything from you. She had been sincere in her letter to you. She really would kill herself but failed. She failed in dominating you, failed in being true to her oath and failed in killing herself. She wanted to be forgotten by you, Jota, just be forgotten."

And, Mayra went on:

"I helped Yuri on Antonina's surgery, it was at the hospital of the big cave, where are treated and operated the Landians arriving at Earth with problems. As soon as Antonina recovered from surgery we brought her here. She couldn't stay at the hospital since all the equipment had been moved from there."

"I took care of Antonina all this time but during the period I was locked at the cemetery. Even after you found me in the Indian cemetery, I took care of Antonina during the night, while you were sleeping. It was quite tiresome. As you probably have noticed, it wasn't all nights since Antonina was getting better and could take minimal care of herself. I've told everything to J-Rod, who agreed that nothing should be revealed to you. And, after he came to the farm, he went with me to help with Antonina. J-Rod is an extraordinary creature. Sure, he likes to show off and he got a liking to me and a sort of Don Juan sprouted in him. This, however, was solved between us and he "calmed" down. What matters for me is J-Rod's essence; and he is a remarkable being."

"I can communicate quite well with Antonina. She is quite lucid despite not being able to write or speak. Also, she says that her intelligence decreased importantly and is now only a bit superior to Earthians (Mayra laughed). She has lost a big chunk of brain mass."

"Finally, after seeing you yesterday, Antonina agreed that I revealed all the facts. After all, there was no way anymore to hide what happened"; Mayra concluded.

"And, how did you enter this place, Mayra?" I asked

"There is a direct communication with the outside, come see here, Jota."

And Mayra directed us to the bathroom. At a corner, there was a shaft with built-in rungs that ended up at a porthole. We climbed up and, opening the lid, saw a blue sky and a sunny day. We went out into the open. Our dome was visible some 500 meters to the northwest.

"Sometimes, and mainly when it was raining, I came here by way of the tunnels. J-Rod preferred the open route, as he was afraid of closed spaces. He has claustrophobia. Yes, J-Rod had many fears, Jota!"

"But, Mayra, when Luiz and I became locked here and found Antonina inside the chamber we still thought she was dead. Were you imprisoned in the cave at that time?"

"That night and that period, Antonina was put into an induced coma of sorts, however quite distinct from what we have in our Earthian Medicine. It's a combination of coma with hibernation, where a patient gets into a minimal metabolic function. There is no need for an endotracheal tube and it's completely monitored. This state can be maintained for about one month typically."

"As you have probably inferred, Jota, this 'mortuary' chamber is, in fact, a hyperbaric chamber too. It was Greg's idea to transform this hall into a ritual place for waking the dead; to help them into the transition phase and comply with all those beliefs Landians have."

"Now, in response to your question: on the night you and Luiz were trapped here, I was, probably, at the Dome 2 with Fabiana and Isobel."

"And, returning to Antonina. She asks, frequently, to be put inside the box, breathing 100% oxygen. There, she feels better, I don't know why."

"But, Mayra, why was Antonina wearing that blue gown the night we found her inside the mortuary box?"

"Ah, Jota, nice question this one. She told me, repeatedly, that she had to be wearing the gown while she was inside the box. She thought you might, someday, enter the hall and see her. She wanted you to see her in splendor. And, that actually took place!"

While we were talking, Antonina rested on the mattress, covered by a blanket. Now, she wore normal pajamas. Mayra told us that Antonina spent most of the time sleeping and, apparently, in a state of half consciousness.

Later on, already in my bed at the dome, I thought about Antonina's drama. *Her state is now worse than death and will only resolve with death. Antonina has been heroic and noble and she doesn't deserve this end.* I, then, remembered that institution, Dignitas, which euthanizes people on demand. Seeking its services are people who have lost all hope in life, tetraplegics, terminal cancer patients and all those for whom life is a nightmare. This institution was mentioned in the excellent book by Jojo Moyes, 'Me Before You'. For a certain sum, all their problems can be solved by way of death, the universal leveler, the definitive solution. You drink syrup with 15 grams of sodium pentobarbital and that's it.

Chapter 108
Mayra's Delivery

While we cared for Antonina and our chores at the farm, Mayra's pregnancy went on normally. Being a non-human fetus, we weren't quite sure of how long the gestation would take. However, we were following the progression, carefully, with an excellent gynecologist in the city. According to the follow-ups, the gestation was running normally.

During this period, we went every day to visit with Antonina, who was well disposed and, each day, more cheerful.

Seeing me, she smiled shyly and caressed my hair in a hesitant way that seemed to convey the idea that she wasn't sure if I liked it. His gaze was intense but had lost the glare of intelligence and authority that fascinated me. Now, Antonina looked at me with eyes that seemed to implore and tried to ascertain if her caresses in me were being liked.

From my part, as I already commented, I didn't feel, presently, any form of domain, command, protection or superior love coming from her. Those feelings abounded in another era. We looked at each other and our eyes got wet. Even Antonina's scents, which obsessed me and put me at her feet, were, now, no more than a nostalgic remembrance.

As mentioned, Mayra spent all nights with Antonina at the "tomb". And it was in one night that she phoned me, saying her bag had ruptured. We went by car to the shaft door, took Mayra, and went to the hospital. It was 3 in the morning. Antonina II was born at 6, from a normal delivery. She was a healthy and vigorous girl. I, later, registered the child as a father, with Mayra registered as her mother. We gave her the name of Antonina.

During the 2-day stay of Mayra at the hospital, my brother and I remained with Antonina all the time and took turns to bring her meals. She ate and bathed without help. Often, she went to the chamber by herself and switched on the oxygen 100%. This, she did many times during the day. The box lid was very easy to handle, and it could be opened or closed from within or without. And, Antonina was an expert at maneuvering the lid and all controls of the box. Unfortunately, all controls.

On the third day after delivery, Mayra and Antonina II were discharged. We went to our dome, now having a new resident. In the afternoon, we went to visit Antonina.

Now, we went to the "tomb" always by the shaft and used the car to go from the dome to there.

This afternoon would be a great day since Antonina was about to get introduced to her clone.

As we entered the tomb, Antonina was sleeping on the mattress and covered by a light blanket. She breathed suavely and her countenance was serene.

"Let's wait until she wakes up and, then, we'll show her the baby"; Mayra said.

Luiz and I went to the kitchen to make a coffee while Mayra and the baby waited at Antonina's side. Soon, Mayra came to call us:

"She is awake."

"We brought a present for you, Antonina"; Mayra said while caressing her hair.

Then, Mayra showed the sleeping baby to Antonina, who extended her arms, asking to hold the baby. Mayra placed Antonina II in the arms of Antonina I.

Antonina held the baby close to her and kissed the baby's forehead. Her eyes were wet. Following this, she gave the baby to Mayra and opened her arms for me. I embraced her and kissed her forehead. At this, Antonina strengthened her embrace of me, brought me very close to her body and placed her head upon my shoulder. Then, she sobbed and sobbed. Her tears were so abundant she wetted my shoulder. Finally, she lightened her embrace and kept looking at me. Then, she looked at Mayra and the baby, who was sleeping peacefully.

Somehow, I felt this was a farewell.

After this, Antonina asked Mayra to bring her some gowns so that she could choose one. She explained to Mayra, in her sign language, that she would like to be really beautiful when the baby woke up and saw her for the first time.

Mayra brought many beautiful gowns and Antonina chose one,

white satin, brilliant. She asked for white soft shoes and an emerald necklace. Mayra, patiently, dressed her.

Then, Antonina asked that Mayra combed her hair and placed, in her head, a tiara studded with small diamonds that she indicated by pointing to a box full of jewels. Then, Mayra combed delicately Antonina's blonde hair and adjusted the tiara, carefully, with hair clips.

Finally, Antonina asked Mayra to apply lipstick to her. Mayra brought some and she chose one light red. While Mayra was applying the lipstick, Antonina looked at us, as if waiting for approbation.

"Antonina, how beautiful you are!" I said.

Soon, after this, we heard a baby's cry. Antonina II had woken.

"I'll nurse her so she stops crying"; said Mayra. After the baby fed and calmed down, Mayra gave the child to Antonina, who took the baby in her arms and stood looking at her small face. I was observing Antonina's eyes attentively and saw a parade of expressions I thought she would never display again, as she looked at her clone.

Then, Antonina approached the child's face to her lips in order to kiss her but the baby put her small arm in front, as if in defense. Antonina's kiss landed in the sleeve of the small coat the baby wore. And, then, the lipstick impression of Antonina's lips got registered there.

I had a terrible foreboding, as if something was coming to an end. Since the baby began to cry again, Mayra took the child from Antonina's arms.

"Now that you two have met, I hope you get to be great friends!" said Mayra.

Antonina smiled, but her eyes conveyed a deep sorrow and melancholy. Since I had had a more intimate contact with her, I may have perceived something that the others did not or did not show it.

Antonina reclined in the lawn chair and closed her eyes. Soon after, she called Mayra and "said" something to her.

"She wants to sleep in the chamber. Needs 100% oxygen," Mayra told us.

Then, Mayra followed Antonina to the chamber and helped her enter.

"Now, she does everything herself and gets upset if I help her with the adjustments. She insists she knows every detail about this chamber."

"How long does she like to stay there?" my brother asked Mayra.

"Oh, not less than 1 full hour and she gets upset if I call her before."

Seeing that the tube of light was super shiny, I suggested that we all went up to the open air to get some fresh air and some afternoon sun.

My suggestion was applauded. Despite the hall being comfortable, there were some grim tones to it and long periods inside brought depressive thoughts to all of us.

We put the baby into a bag and I suspended her through the shaft. Then we all got out into the open air and a delicious sun. My brother and I had transformed the surroundings of the entrance into a garden with the hopes of bringing Antonina out during the warmer periods of the day, so that she could get some sun. We had brought a few beach chairs and a small table. That was, however, something that Mayra still had to negotiate with her. We stayed outside for about 1 hour, when a cold wind began blowing from the south. For the baby's sake, we decided to come down. And, we were hungry.

We all went to the kitchen where Mayra, with the help of Luiz, prepared a nice coffee with toasts and milk. Then, orange juice and chocolate cake were prepared by Mayra, especially for Antonina.

"I think she wouldn't mind if we had some of her cake," Mayra joked.

As soon as we finished eating, the baby needed to be changed and Mayra went to the bathroom where a nice baby stand had been installed, with baby tub and all facilities. Mayra changed her clothes to a new set, leaving the soiled clothes over the stand to be taken later for washing.

Then, we moved to the hall, waiting for Antonina to appear, like she used to do. She got upset when Mayra went to the chamber to call her.

But Antonina didn't come. About 2 hours had gone by since we had gone up to the open air.

So, Mayra went to see why Antonina was still sleeping.

"My God, come here!" we heard her shout.

As Mayra opened the chamber lid, a strong smell of chloroform invaded our nostrils. Beside Antonina's head and in a plate was a big sponge, soaked in chloroform. We, rapidly, removed the sponge and the three of us moved Antonina out of the chamber and placed her on the floor.

"She's anesthetized! Deep anesthesia and not breathing!" cried Mayra.

Then, Mayra began mouth-to-mouth resuscitation while I auscultated Antonina's heart.

"Not beating, cardiac arrest"; I cried. I, then, began performing chest massage while Mayra continued mouth-to-mouth resuscitation.

"There is an AMBU over there; bring it, Luiz."

Mayra placed the mask against Antonina's face and began pressing the bag.

In the meantime, my brother was examining the chamber.

"Look, he called, the oxygen tube is disconnected and another tube is connected to its inlet."

"Try to see what it is, Luiz, I can't stop massaging here."

It is written CO in the bottle, Jota; this is Carbon Monoxide!" he shouted.

"Close the cylinder, Luiz" I shouted while still massaging Antonina's chest.

"But the cylinder is closed and well closed," shouted Luiz. And Luiz knew how to handle industrial gases.

"Look what I found inside the chamber"; Luiz said, bringing me a 500 ml empty plastic soda bottle.

"Antonina always takes soda to drink while she is inside the chamber," Mayra shouted, while still giving artificial respiration to Antonina, with the AMBU.

"There is no way, Jota, she is quite dead. Her temperature is already too low"; Mayra, finally, said to me.

We gave up reanimating Antonina. No question she was dead. And, worse, she seemed to have died many minutes before. We left Antonina on the floor and went to the kitchen to have some water, make a coffee, and think. My brother offered to make the coffee since Mayra and I were exhausted. Then, he went looking for the coffee cups in the cabinets.

"What's this, Jota? It was behind a tall jar"; he said.

Then, he brought us an empty flask: *Sodium Pentobarbital 15 grams. Not for use in humans. Non-sterile powder.*

I ran to the chamber and took the plastic soda bottle from there. At the bottom was a residue of syrup. It wasn't a soda beverage. It was the

Sodium pentobarbital mixed as syrup, all 15 grams of it.

Of course, Antonina wouldn't risk our lives with an open CO bottle. That was a false clue. Why this false clue? To prevent us from doing a *gastric lavage* and, thus, allowing time for the pentobarbital to act. She probably counted on our thinking that the CO and the chloroform had "done the job".

Then, the whole weight of the tragedy came down onto us. Antonina had outsmarted us all. Sure, she couldn't write, she couldn't speak. But she could think! She planned her death. This time she wouldn't fail!

"But, Jota, what about the chloroform?" asked Mayra, as we all checked that Antonina had, in fact, ingested the sodium pentobarbital.

"Well, Mayra, I'm not sure. I think she decided to use the chloroform to sleep before the effect of the pentobarbital."

"Yes, Jota, but she may have died first from the overdose of chloroform"; said Mayra.

"Sure, Mayra, you have a point, but that would need a postmortem exam, something that we won't do!" I said.

"Mayra, Antonina planned everything. She was just waiting to see her clone. All was ready. Why did she choose to be so well dressed? Anyway, the baby will not remember anything, or will she? We don't know"; I said, finally.

Chapter 109

The Launching of Antonina

I will never forget the image of Antonina lying on the floor, in a disordered state, her lips all blurred with the red lipstick, her hair a mess, the emerald necklace all twisted, and the diamond tiara strewn onto the floor beside her. The beautiful white gown was all soiled with our reviving maneuvers. All that was at a stark contrast with the Antonina we saw entering the chamber not long ago.

"She is at peace now, and will rest at last!"; Mayra said.

Then, I remembered the celebrated phrase:

The King is dead, long live the King!

Antonina is dead, long live Antonina!

Now, we just had to recompose. We went to the kitchen. Mayra didn't stop crying. But, later, she got calmer. We had to think about many things since a new chapter was beginning in our lives.

After the initial shock, there came a problem. What to do with Antonina's body? We three looked at each other. There was nothing to say, since it was obvious Antonina deserved the highest burial a Landian could have, to where Landian heroes were sent: into space.

We kept vigil to Antonina's body this night, after placing her into the chamber, with its lid wide open.

During the night, I went to see Antonina. She had a serene expression, no suggestion of a smile anymore. Now, however, the grave face of death was stamped onto her features. I placed my hand upon her forehead. It was cold.

In the morning, we took her to the right arm of the cave, the morgue.

There, Mayra robed her with a beautiful mortuary gown. We brought the diamond tiara and the emerald necklace. We put on her white shoes and white gloves. These later items were available on the shelves. Then, we placed her inside a transparent bag and filled it with some glycerin as a preservative. Placing her onto a gurney, we moved her to the left arm of the cave: the launching pad. There, we found an empty cylinder, the last one available.

But, how to make the connection of the mortuary cylinder with the negative mass?

J-Rod knew the procedure, but he was not here anymore...

It was my brother who discovered something in the architecture of the hall we had not seen before. There was a corner in the hall where the ceiling was quite lower and, there, we saw some negative masses free from their counterweights and touching the ceiling. Also, nearby, there was an elevator manually controlled, a sort of mini forklift that, instead of the fork, had a flat base.

Joaquim

The Landians have planned all.

We placed Antonina inside the mortuary cylinder. We had brought many of her favorite things, many nice clothes. Also, we added some chocolate and cereal bars. I placed inside a photograph Antonina had taken of me. These items would serve to accompany Antonina during her passing to some other dimension and also serve to pad the cylinder sides so that she could be maintained erect inside.

Then, we screwed the lid onto the cylinder and moved the mortuary cylinder to the elevator, adjusting its height until it could connect with the negative mass above. No chain here, just two iron loops that were interlocked using a screw. Now, the mortuary cylinder was hanging down on the negative mass. We began adding counterweights below the cylinder until it came down and had a final weight of about 5 kg.

My brother did all the calculations for the launch velocity, acceleration, etc.

We moved the complete assembly to just below the launching tube and went home to rest. At this very night, we would launch Antonina.

We spent the rest of the day talking and reviewing the facts.

We had dinner and went calmly and thoughtfully to the launching hall. The mortuary cylinder, with Antonina's body hanging upward, challenged common sense. But we were not there for meditation. At least, not now. We had a task, a noble task, and it had to be done.

Mayra and I went up through the tube, climbing at the retractable rungs and placing them back into the niches as we went up. My brother had been charged with the task of uncoupling the ascending system from the counterweight.

The night was very dark, no moon, no clouds. There was a starry sky that seemed to be waiting for Antonina. As usual, a cold breeze came from the southeast.

Mayra and I looked at the sky in search of planes. We saw nothing.

"OK, Luiz, disengage!" I cried down the tube.

I heard a bang signaling that the ascending section was now free.

And, it came slower than we thought. Passed us and began gaining speed, like an object thrown down from a great height. With the difference, it was going up. I followed it until it disappeared into the night.

Antonina was on her way to infinity.

Mayra began to cry and embraced me.

"Now, it's over, and what of me?" she said.

"Mayra, would you marry me, please? At least, to comply with Antonina's wishes?

Mayra, for the first time, kissed me and said:

"You don't need to ask, Jota. I'll marry you anyway. I love you for a long time and you know it!"

Joaquim

END

About The Author

Author (pen name): Joaquim Procopio

Full name: Joaquim Procopio de Araujo Filho

Nationality: Brazilian

Biography:

Joaquim Procopio is an MD and PhD from Universidade de São Paulo.

He had his Medical Course at Faculdade de Medicina da Universidade de São Paulo.

Has a Post-Doctorate at Cornell University Medical College, New York City, in the area of Membrane Biophysics.

Has published over 60 papers in International Journals, in areas ranging from Membrane Biophysics, Artificial Membranes, Bioelectricity, Theoretical Biophysics, Diabetes, Fatty Acids and Physiology Teaching.

Previous non-fiction books are in Physiology:

1.Entendendo a Gordura (Co-author)

2.Fisiologia Básica, 1st Edition (Co-author and Editor)

3.Fisiologia Básica, 2nd Edition (Co-author and Editor)

4. Joaquim Procopio has also about 10 chapters in other

Physiology books.

Previous fiction publication:

"Meu amigo Greg" author Joaquim Procopio, published in 2022 by Editora Ipê das Letras, from Portugal. ISBN 978-989-37-3720-0

The printed version of the book has 746 pages whereas the e-book varies from 580 to 650 pages.

The present manuscript, **"My friend Greg"**, is an extensively modified translation from the Portuguese Edition. It keeps the original plot and all of the characters from the Portuguese Edition.